HARMONY RUN SERIES

PRISMATIC
Brilliantly colored; iridescent

OPALESCENT
Exhibiting a milky iridescence like that of an opal

CHATOYANT
Having a changeable luster; twinkling

NACREOUS
Exhibiting lustrous or rainbow-like colors

Nacreous

Sarah Elle Emm

Best Wishes!
Sarah Elle Emm

Winter Goose
PUBLISHING
where words take flight

Winter Goose Publishing
2701 Del Paso Road, 130-92
Sacramento, CA 95835

www.wintergoosepublishing.com
Contact Information: info@wintergoosepublishing.com

Nacreous

COPYRIGHT © 2015 by Sarah Elle Emm

First Edition, August 2015

Cover Art by Winter Goose Publishing
Typesetting by Odyssey Books

ISBN: 978-1-941058-33-6

Published in the United States of America

In loving memory of the kindest soul I've ever known, my grandpa

Dr. William Coale Standring
"Doc"
May 28, 1923 - May 15, 2015

May we carry on your legacy of love and laughter

For my daughters, Audrey and Sabrina, my nieces, Kiley and Chloe, my nephews, Lane and Coale, and to all of my cousins, family, and friends making up the prismatic rainbow of this world . . . Keep shining your light, loving, laughing, and making this world a better place.

Contents

"Corrie, if people can be taught to hate, they can be taught to love! We must find the way, you and I, no matter how long it takes."

—Corrie ten Boom, *The Hiding Place*

NACREOUS

Exhibiting lustrous or rainbow-like colors

Chapter 1: Caged

February 2051, Indy Mixed Zone Metro Prison, UZTA

RAIN

I was caged in from all sides. Iron bars separated me from the dank interior hallway of the cellblock, and concrete walls enclosed the remainder of the cold, rectangular prison cell. A rancid odor engulfed the air with body odor, human waste, and the lingering smell of death from another life taken too soon.

When I was younger, before the fall of the United States of America, every year at some point or another I would end up on a field trip to the Indianapolis Zoo. The bars trapping me in reminded me of those times.

But unlike most of the animals at the zoo, I hadn't been born into captivity.

In a not so distant past I had freedom, but that was before Elizabeth Nicks, or Nata as we now knew her to be, had dissolved the USA and formed a new government, the United Zones of The Authority, also known as the UZTA. In this new country, she'd instituted an act called New Segregation and divided people into walled zones based on our various racial backgrounds. The mixed zones were built for multiracial people, and they were the worst of the zones, because Nata hated us more than she hated anyone else.

The truth was, Nata had been born multiracial, just like I had, but only a few people knew her secret, and she'd changed her appearance in a series of surgeries and hidden the truth using her special ability, mind control. I'd been one of the few who had discovered Nata's past, and secret identity. She'd not only suffered horrific abuse at the hands of her biological mother and grandmother, she'd turned her back on her father, Niyol, the one man who tried to save her and the one man who showed her love. While we couldn't be sure why she hated us so much, we suspected she had believed all of the deplorable things her abusers told her about herself, and after her transforming into the pale-skinned, blue eyed, blonde she had become, she was determined to wipe out all multiracial people from the world. Plus, we figured she might suspect that there were others like her with special abilities who could do things that weren't explainable, from controlling others to communicating telepathically. She couldn't let us live, were we to actually exist, because we might be able to stop her. And as some of us had discovered less than a year ago, it was true. Certain multiracial people did have extraordinary abilities. I was one of them, and so was my younger brother Daktari.

Daktari and I had been sent to Indy Mixed Zone, one of twenty mixed zones across the UZTA. Our parents had given up their rights to go to their pre-assigned zones, the Caucasian zone for my mom and the African-American zone for my dad, since Nata had no qualms about punishing the people who'd brought us into the world in the first place. The other zones across the UZTA were known to be more tolerable than the mixed zones, but Mom and Dad had refused to abandon us, and so they'd been tattooed with identification numbers upon their arrival, just like me and Daktari, and had been suffering alongside us ever since. Daktari, who had recently turned sixteen, had been forced to grow up overnight after our relocation. While we could've passed for twins at one point, with our matching olive-toned skin, milk chocolate brown eyes, and soft brown curly hair, he had surpassed my five-foot-seven and towered over me at six-foot-two. Plus, he kept his hair clipped short and mine hung in tiny ringlets, nearly to my hips now.

In many ways, The Authority had stolen Daktari's youth, and mine too for that matter, but honestly that wasn't my concern. Not anymore.

It was true that the mixed zones were in fact large prison cities, where we were forced to do slave labor and denied every basic freedom known to man. We were surrounded by barbed wire walls and kept in line by horrifying android police called Droid Dogs and human officers from the Elizabeth Guard, but up until an hour ago I hadn't been confined to the worst part of Indy Mixed Zone, Metro Prison.

I clenched onto the bars and squinted my eyes trying to see as far as I could in the sparsely lit corridor. To my left there was a doorway leading towards the prison exits—a Droid Dog had hauled me in that way—but I couldn't see it now. My breathing sped up as I imagined the door bursting open and the terrifying man, with his stocky build, black crew cut, and hateful black eyes, barrelling through.

He promised to come back for me.

Officer Wolfe, a member of the Elizabeth Guard, was the same man who had led my interrogation and shoved me into an underground hole on my last arrest, and he was a man who kept promises to people he intended to harm, I was sure. Still, there was no sign of him. And no one had returned for my cellmate either.

Other than the occasional moan and babbling of some poor soul imprisoned in one of the cells around us, we hadn't heard anything in the hour or so since our arrests. I knew firsthand what could happen when Officer Wolfe came for us. Last time he had me here, he'd mercilessly beaten my friend, Amal, and shaved her head with a straight razor, for a crime her husband had committed. The crime he had committed was reading aloud from the Bible, and his punishment had been death. Religious practice of any kind was strictly prohibited in the UZTA. Because Officer Wolfe hadn't liked any of my answers during his questioning, he had left me in a tiny box underground, stuffed in there with hardly any air to breathe. My chest rose and fell faster now as I recalled the claustrophobia. Yes, I was afraid of Officer Wolfe. But even knowing what might happen, I just wanted it to happen already.

The waiting was torturous. Mostly because we hadn't a clue what was going to happen to us, or what, specifically, had led to our arrest. There was something about fear. From the moment we arrived in the walled Indy Mixed Zone, Nata had been using fear as a tactic to control us. For over four years I'd wrestled with fear and done my best to conquer it, but in this moment I was struggling with a new kind of fear. The fear of the unknown. As my hand tightened around the cold metal bars, unyielding to my grip, a chill ran down my back. I had to admit, her tactics worked. Not knowing what was going to happen to myself, my loved ones, or to The Freedom Front, also known as TFF, the resistance group I had joined to try to free the zones, filled my chest with a fright I wasn't sure I could suppress. Fear worked. I was afraid.

Marcello's hand gently pressed against my shoulder. "Take some deep breaths, Rain."

I tilted my head up towards him, petrified that he was in here with me because it likely meant The Freedom Front had been compromised, but grateful at the same time for his presence. He wasn't just a member of TFF, with an incredible ability to knock people unconscious, he had become my friend. His black hair was smoothed off of his face and had grown a couple of inches longer in the last few months, going a little past his chin now. His skin tone was bronze, a blend between his Caucasian mother, Trina, and his Mexican-American father, Cesar. He was tall at six-foot-two and muscular like Jabari.

Of course, Jabari was slightly taller, at six-foot-three. He'd been sentenced to Indy Mixed Zone because his mom, Michelle, was African-American and his dad, Francisco, Mexican-American. Like my parents, Michelle and Francisco had asked to be relocated with their son to our zone. I could picture Jabari clearly with his light brown skin, short black hair, strong, fit torso and limbs, and his dark brown eyes that seemed to speak to me with the slightest glance.

At the thought of Jabari, the leader of TFF and my boyfriend, well, technically my fiancé, my heart ached. Right before my arrest, I'd been thinking about our future. Less than a week ago, I'd accepted his marriage proposal, and now it seemed it had been naïve of me to lose myself in my thoughts. I'd been working at Agri Plant, the assigned factory for many teenagers in our zone, daydreaming about our wedding in a free world, desperate to keep my mind on positive things, when Officer Wolfe had shown up with a Droid Dog, hit me, and taken me into custody. I squeezed my eyes shut and sunk my head to my chest.

Marcello patted my shoulder. "Look at me," he whispered, his voice anxious.

I forced myself to respond. His dark eyes held mine, and though a hint of fear lingered in his expression, he was clearly handling the arrest much better than me. "Take a deep breath," he urged.

I inhaled and exhaled slowly, studying him all the while. "It's taking too long," I said after a moment.

"They're probably trying to scare us by making us wait. Just breathe. We need to stay calm. We're going to survive this."

He pulled me away from the bars, turning me towards him, and took my hands in his own. "We can get through this."

"But what exactly are we trying to survive? We don't even know why they brought us here."

The first half hour of our imprisonment, we'd laid out the details pertaining to our arrests. Marcello had been picked up at work in the Construction and Machinery Plant. Jabari hadn't been working with him at the time, but Cole, Marcello's cousin and TFF's computer expert, had seen his arrest. Just like me, The Authority had simply brought him here and left without explanation.

After swapping stories with Marcello, I had used my telepathy to contact Jabari again and then Daktari. Calming them down had been difficult. Both of them had suggested using their abilities, along with Zi's ability to conceal them under her protective image, to break us out. Zi was my best friend, and also a member of TFF, so I knew she'd go along with their plans, but I'd advised them to wait. I had warned them of the repercussions. If Marcello and I suddenly disappeared from The Authority's custody, there would be consequences for our families. I made them promise not to do anything until they'd spoken with Takara, our trusted advisor and the organizer of TFF, and also until Marcello and I had a better idea of why we'd been brought here in the first place. Ultimately, Jabari and Daktari had promised me they would do as I asked, but I couldn't be sure if they would hold up their end of the bargain. Jabari hadn't sounded very convincing. He had made me promise I would stick by Marcello's side at all times and that I wouldn't play the hero and try to save everyone in the prison. He said I just had to focus on getting myself out alive. I'd promised him I would, but if only he knew the truth.

With each second that passed, the heroic part of me that Jabari loved and hated at the same time, was dissolving under the fear and doubt that were filling me. I wasn't my usual brave or "heroic" self at all. How could I be brave when there was so much uncertainty? No one knew what to do. Not even Takara, at least not yet. I trusted Takara. She was our counselor and had organized TFF, using her ability to sense people's gifts. She'd found us and asked us to come to her secret meetings, where she tutored us in various school subjects. Takara was well connected. She even had an ally in the prison who we'd never met. While talking to Jabari he'd wondered if perhaps Takara's mystery prison ally could help us, and then he'd said maybe Eric, our Elizabeth Guard ally, could figure out how to get us out. That's when it had hit me, that I'd never even tried to communicate with Takara telepathically, and if there was ever a time to do it, it was now. After all, Takara was assigned to work in Town Hall, the building adjoining Metro Prison, and if anyone could figure out why we'd been arrested it was her.

It had been so easy to get to her. Just like Bhavna, our ally from a refugee camp in old Virginia, had been able to communicate with Takara, sure enough I was able to as well. Unfortunately, she'd been pulled into another part of the Town Hall building to work today and hadn't heard or learned anything about our arrest when I'd contacted her. But she'd promised to get back to the main office and eavesdrop and find something out. "*Keep hope alive, Rainchild,*" she had said.

I was supposed to communicate with Takara, Jabari, and Daktari as needed and every thirty minutes or so to give them an update and to see if they'd heard anything about our arrests. But so far, they were still at their work shifts so they had no idea what was happening. And when I'd tried to reach out to Takara the last time, thirty minutes ago, she still hadn't been able to get back to the main office to find out what was happening. And no one had come back for Marcello or me.

Marcello rubbed his thumb over my knuckles. "When they come back, just trust your instincts. Use your telepathy to talk to me. Together, we can try to get out of this, and I promise you I will do whatever I can to get you out. But listen, if they take you alone, and you can figure out how to get out of here, do it. Don't try to save me, understand?" His eyes clouded with concern.

"But you wouldn't leave me," my voice hitched.

Marcello's grip tightened. "Listen. This is important. Do whatever you have to, to get out of here, do you understand? Forget about me."

"But—"

"No, Rain. You have to get out of here. I know you always have to be the hero, but not today. You're the most important to everything. The whole plan, everything depends on you. Your gifts are more important to the cause than mine. Everything can still work without me. But it can't work without you."

"Your gifts are just as important as mine."

"Just promise me you won't try to save me. Get out of here if you can. I'll survive this place."

I searched his eyes. Why did he have to be so stubborn and concerned about me? Maybe it was because Niyol had once said I was the key to the mission. Maybe he knew we weren't getting out of here. Maybe he was desperate for one of us to escape. Maybe he was just afraid and couldn't put it into words. "I promise I'll try, but you promise me that you'll try to get out of here, too. And if one of us gets out, the other one works with everyone else to come up with a plan of escape. Even if it means we take our families and go to Gallagher's or Bhavna's."

Gallagher Brown was our ally outside of the zones, who was leading the resistance, gathering refugees to join him, even as Nata was hunting him night and day. We had met Bhavna a few months back, and traveled more than once to her refugee camp in old West Virginia, but I wouldn't want to endanger her family by hiding there. If we escaped, we'd have to hide in one of Gallagher's underground camps since they were actively building the resistance, but TFF really didn't want to do that unless there was a true emergency. Our plans to go after Nata would be more effective if we had the element of surprise on our side. Right now, Nata had no clue that any members of TFF were within the zones. Gallagher wanted us to be the secret weapon against her on the day of the attack. But if we went missing now, she'd likely discover we were fighting with Gallagher, and we didn't want to risk that.

Marcello exhaled. "Agreed. But if you have the chance to get out of here, take it, Rain."

As I shook my head, my lip began to tremble. No matter how I tried, the fear seemed to be getting the best of me. Marcello looked at me sympathetically and pulled me against him into a bear hug. He stroked the side of my head and whispered, quietly reassuring me. "It's okay. Better things are ahead for you. You're gonna marry our fearless leader and have super babies. Focus on your future, Rain. You're okay. You're going to be okay. And I'm with you right now. I'm right here."

Slowly, my heart rate began to steady. I listened to Marcello's heartbeat against his chest and took refuge in my friend's words and the strength of his embrace. He was here with me. I listened to his assurances and felt my hope returning when a loud metal screeching sound jolted me to full-on awareness. Marcello tensed and drew back. We stared into each other's eyes. Footsteps were rapidly approaching our cell.

He lowered his voice even more, leaned in to me. "We can't act like we know each other, okay?"

I nodded, my jaw tensing.

"Be strong," he added before stepping back, across the cell.

Cold swept over me as the distance between us expanded. As the footsteps stopped in front of the cell, Marcello and I were already on opposite sides. He was right. Regardless of why we had been taken here, if they thought we knew each other it might be worse for us. And until we knew why we were here it was best to play it safe.

The door slid open and our space was invaded, and more confining than I thought possible. Four more prisoners, all men, were pushed into the cell, ranging in ages from around thirty to a man probably around seventy.

The guard who dropped them off was unfamiliar to me and left within seconds of closing the door. Two of the men were visibly injured and sank to the floor, one near the bars, another shuffling to the wall, not far from me. With a brief survey, I determined they weren't a problem for me. Neither was the third man. He spared me, and then Marcello, an emotionless glance, and staggered to the back of the cell, disappearing into the corner. The fourth man was talking incessantly and his eyes were wild, with the look of someone who had lost touch with reality. I'd seen people like him a lot out in the streets of our zone. They couldn't cope with reality, barely hanging on. Marcello made eye contact with me, and though I didn't need to use my telepathy to understand what he was saying, I did. "*Marcello, I—*"

"*Walk over to my side of the cell. I don't like the look of him.*"

The man stopped talking abruptly as he noticed me inch away from the wall. My breathing sped up as he smiled at me. "Well, hello. And here I thought I'd be lonesome in here." His greedy eyes swept over me as I carefully stepped towards Marcello's side of the cell. Halfway there, he grabbed my wrist, halting me.

Before I could react, Marcello stepped over, laying his hand on top of the man's who held mine. "Let go of her. Now."

"Back off, kid."

The hand on my wrist tightened and he tried to pull me towards him, but Marcello wedged his way between us and before I could react, the man had fallen to the ground as if he had lost consciousness, which of course, he had from Marcello's ability. As Marcello pulled my hand I noticed that no one else in the cell seemed interested in the sudden collapse of the man.

Marcello pushed me down beside him on the floor against the wall, scooted right next to me, and put his arm around my shoulder protectively.

I looked up at him with appreciation but worry. "*I thought we weren't going to act like we knew each other,*" I said, using my ability.

Seriousness swept over his features. "*Change of plans. Keeping you safe is the most important thing. I'm more concerned about the guards knowing we know each other. When they come back, we'll put some distance between us, but not too much. Maybe the fact that the other prisoners are strangers to us means TFF hasn't been compromised like we suspected. Either way, I promise I won't let that guy hurt you. And I promise you I'll do whatever it takes to get you out of here.*"

Fear filled me anew. "*Stop making me promises. You can't protect me. We don't know what's going on.*"

He stroked my arm. "*Oh Amiga, have a little faith. Just think, you got locked up with me for a reason. So I can protect you. One of these days I expect you to tell Calista about it and earn me some brownie points,*" he said teasingly, referring to the crush he had on my cousin, Calista, in a desperate attempt to cheer me up, I knew.

I tried to return his teasing but it was hard. "*Well you were pretty heroic already . . .*" My eyes began to fill with tears. I was too afraid. Just like Nata wanted me to be.

Marcello studied me, continuing to hold me close. "*Admit it, I'm a hero. And Jabari is going to be so jealous I was the one to save you he'll throw me on a rooftop or something.*" A small smiled curved his mouth and he patted my arm soothingly. "*Make sure you lay it on thick about how I battled with a group of prisoners three times my size to protect you okay?*"

"I'm scared," I said aloud, whispering. My body began to shake uncontrollably. A couple of hours ago, I'd been daydreaming about getting married to Jabari and now I was stuck in Metro Prison. What if this was it for me? For Marcello? What would happen to my family? And his? What would happen to The Freedom Front? Jabari? We needed a miracle.

As soon as the word crossed my mind, a flicker of hope rose in me. Niyol was a miracle worker, and I hadn't contacted him. My nerves must really have been out of control if I hadn't thought to talk to Niyol. I closed my eyes and focused on the old man, Nata's biological father, a multiracial man with long white hair, descending from the Diné or Navajo people on his father's side and Jamaica on his mother's side. He'd know what to do. "*Niyol, Marcello and I are in trouble.*"

His voice answered, "*Rain, hold on. I'm—*"

But Marcello's voice startled my concentration and as he spoke a warm feeling radiated from his hand sliding up my arm and traveling through my limbs.

"I know you're scared, Rain, I know. Just close your eyes and try not to worry for now. I'm right here with you, I promise," Marcello said.

I tried to tell him to stop. But it was too late. Drowsiness overwhelmed me as comprehension hit me. Marcello was knocking me out with his ability. But I couldn't control or resist his power. As my head fell against his chest I thought of Niyol's words, "Hold on, I'm—"

And everything went black.

Chapter 2: Today

RAIN

I'd been taken from my home and sent to live in the Indy Mixed Zone just last night, and somehow, with each passing hour, the nightmare I was living got worse.

Six months ago if I'd been told I would be riding one of the newest innovative advancements known to man, a green-powered hydrogen hover transporter, I would've laughed, but found the idea intriguing nonetheless. But now that I was in one and I knew what they had been designed for, transporting captive citizens of the Indy Mixed Zone to our new jobs, I wasn't laughing. But my biggest concern six months ago had been whether or not my soccer team was going to take the championship trophy in the spring. And now, just like me, the girls from my team had been relocated to one of many racially segregated zones in the new government, The United Zones of The Authority. What would become of all of my friends?

It turned out, I'd probably never know. As I stared at Daktari, who's hand was clammy in my own and the girl, Zi, we'd met before boarding the hover a few minutes ago, who I had a strange feeling was going to need my help in this dreadful zone just as much as my brother, my heart ached for the life I'd been stolen from. The past twelve hours had confirmed there would be no freedom in this zone. There would be fear, torture, even death, and though I was afraid, the only thing that mattered to me right now was making sure Daktari survived. The only way I figured that was possible was if we managed to stay under the radar and didn't draw attention to ourselves. This morning we had seen what happens when The Authority notices you.

The hover had made three more stops since picking us up on the dark street corner, where we'd parted from our parents and had the most horrifying experience of my life—so far. From the expressions of the teenagers and kids riding the hover with us, I figured they'd had pretty awful mornings, too. Still, I was guessing mine had been worse. Not only had one of The Authority's guards hit my mother for speaking up against an inhumane punishment and torture drill, we'd seen first hand what happens to those who would dare to resist the new government. Torture and death. As I pictured the lifeless body of the young boy who hadn't endured the stamina drill, a chill ran down my spine. They'd shot him dead. A kid, who had to be around my age. Dead. Welcome to the mixed zone. I squeezed Daktari's hand a little tighter now. We had to survive. And if Daktari wasn't strong enough for this place, I had to be strong enough for the two of us.

He shook beside me now, his nerves escalating the further we traveled away from Mom and Dad, making my mind race with questions and doubts. *How am I going to keep him safe?* If The Authority sees him crumbling, they might target him. What if they put him in one of those torture drills like we saw this morning? How long can we survive here? Is every day going to get worse?

As panic filled me anew, Grandma Julia's face popped into my mind. I could hear her gentle voice, softly assuring us. "Therefore do not worry about tomorrow, for tomorrow will worry about itself. Each day has enough trouble of its own. Matthew 6:34. Just take it one day at a time, kids," she'd say. Now, more than ever, I understood the significance of the words she'd spoken so often. My chest constricted at the thought of my grandmother, who I already missed so much it hurt to think about it, but I focused on what she'd told me time and again. *Do not worry about tomorrow. One day at a time.* I just had to get through today.

Today, only.

I had to help my brother survive. And though I knew it wasn't my responsibility, when I glanced at Zi, the petite girl with black hair to her chin, and hazel eyes that were watching me constantly as the hover traveled, I knew she needed me too. She'd told me a moment ago how her parents had begged to be moved to Indy Mixed Zone with her, instead of going to their assigned zones. Zi had said her mother, who I'd briefly caught a glimpse of before boarding the hover, was Taiwanese-American, and her father was Caucasian. I realized Zi and her family were in the same boat as my family and me.

The hover came to an abrupt stop and the door slid open. A robotic voice calling from outside gave us orders. "Exit the hover. Line up."

I stood, nodded encouragingly at Daktari and Zi and, still holding Daktari's hand, led the way, stepping off of the bus into the cold morning air. A glance in either direction showed me there were multiple hovers unloading teenagers and kids, even some as young as five, up and down the block. I wondered what The Authority would do with the kids younger than five. Would they be sent to work with their parents? And what was happening to my own parents right now? There were so many questions in this place.

The sun wasn't shining yet, but over the nearest street lamp I read the sign on an enormous dreary-looking factory, welcoming us to our destination. AGRI PLANT. The sign was new, but the factory was definitively old. I imagined it might have been a manufacturing plant of some sort before New Segregation. And standing below the sign were robots, built to resemble humans, but clearly made of the same metallic materials as the Droid Dogs we'd encountered earlier, the police dogs of the zone.

I counted four of the new droids and noticed each one was labeled on the chest with the inscription O3, MODEL THREE OVERSEER.

I took a calming breath. They didn't seem as scary as the Droid Dogs. Maybe this wouldn't be so bad. But my anxiety returned the next moment as two Droid Dogs walked over to the O3 Droids, as though standing guard. I studied the red eyes of the Droid Dogs and their enormous bodies, and prayed they wouldn't hurt us.

As we filed out of the hovers and formed lines, one of the O3 Droids called out orders. "Proceed forward into the building. Remain in the line."

"Agri Plant. Maybe we're growing food or something, Daktari. We'll be fine," I said reassuringly.

Daktari's eyes were wide, still huge with fear, but he shook his head once. Zi nudged him lightly on the back. "I'm right behind you," she whispered. Our eyes met for a second as I turned forward again. Though her voice had sounded brave, she appeared just as terrified as Daktari and me.

"Everyone scan your tattoo," instructed one of the O3 Droids.

We marched into the enormous warehouse and I told myself to be calm. Each person in front of me was following orders to scan their ankle tattoos in front of a machine that made me think of a time clock near the entrance.

One of the O3 Droids stood beside the time clock, giving instructions to each person who scanned in about which group to join. It was grouping us off in order of arrival in groups of sixteen as far as I could tell. My turn finally came, and I sighed with relief as I realized Daktari and Zi would be assigned to the same group as me. I didn't know what would happen in our group, but I figured staying together was a good thing. I turned my ankle towards the scanner and watched as my number lit up. 1276.

I was literally a piece of property with a number ID tattoo to The Authority now.

Memories of last night flooded my brain. Daktari screaming as they held us down to tattoo us. Mom crying. Dad passed out from being tasered.

"Group five," the O3 Droid ordered, breaking me from my thoughts.

I followed the boy who'd gone before me towards our designated group and glanced over my shoulder as Daktari stepped hesitantly towards the time clock scanner. As it illuminated his ankle tattoo, he paled. The O3 Droid pointed towards my group, the slight gesture making Daktari flinch. He was visibly fragile, and understandably so after the morning he'd had. He'd already seen the body of a kid near our age in the street and Mom hit by one of the guards this morning. As he reached my side, I summoned encouraging words. "At least we're still together, right Daktari?"

His eyes were wide as they met mine, but he sounded brave. "Yeah."

"Don't forget me," Zi whispered, taking a step closer to me. "I may look little but don't underestimate me."

Daktari smirked. "Look little? You might be five feet tall. Maybe."

Zi raised a brow. "You're only five four. Maybe. And anyway I'm five one."

"I'm still growing," Daktari returned. I could see a hint of amusement in his expression, and a bit of relief filled me. Zi had made him smile. If we could keep some level of positivity, we could get through today.

"No talking," the O3 Droid closest to us ordered.

We quieted as it surveyed our group of sixteen. "Follow me. This group will be planting soybeans today."

Daktari and Zi and I exchanged hopeful looks. Planting couldn't be the worst job in this new zone, I was sure. As we trekked, the Droid gave more instructions. "You will scan in and out each day and join this group. I am the O3 Droid responsible for your group. You may call me O3. I will assign you to your work area each day. There is no talking. Keep your head down. No breaks. Lunch break only. Do your work and you will not be punished. You will be punished for disobedience."

When O3 looked away for a moment, I turned to Daktari and Zi.

"We can do this. Whatever happens, just do the work they give you. The three of us are going to get through today. Unharmed. We're going to see our parents at the end of today. Just get through today. Okay?"

"Sounds good to me," Zi said.

Daktari inhaled deeply. "Okay," he mumbled.

I could see him struggling with the fear consuming him, so I smiled. He had to see me being positive. I couldn't show any fear. "We'll be fine. I promise."

He offered me a half smile in return, and then turned back towards O3, who was beginning to explain our new jobs. After being assigned to planting and given basic instructions and a tour of the newly fitted growing rooms for soybeans, our group was put to work. Hours ticked by and every time I thought I might collapse from exhaustion or from dehydration, I'd look up and make eye contact with Daktari and Zi. When O3 wasn't watching, we risked looking at each other and offering assuring glances, even a smile here and there.

When lunch finally arrived my hopes soared. We had to be nearing the end of our shift. They wouldn't work us into the night, would they? We followed O3 to the lunch area, where we each accepted a tiny portion of soup and were directed to long lunch tables with benches on either side. The three of us huddled close together and when none of the O3 Droids were watching, we risked conversation.

"They call this lunch?" Zi whispered.

"It's just broth," Daktari agreed. "It won't even begin to fill us up."

"Remember what Dad said, Daktari. Eat it all. We don't know when or how we'll eat at home," I said.

"There's nothing to eat. It's just liquid. But don't worry, I'll finish every drop. I'm starving. They didn't even let us get a drink of water the whole day."

I grabbed his arm and squeezed it lightly. "Hang in there. We've got some water at the apartment. We just need to get back there."

"My dad recognized one of our old neighbors from back home this morning at the hover stop. He said he'd been moved here a few days before us. So Dad was planning to ask him about food and everything. I'll let you know what he finds out," Zi offered.

I smiled. "Thanks. The officers last night told us Elizabeth Nicks would be letting us know more soon, but how can we believe anything she says after everything that's happened?"

Zi sighed. "I know. My parents even voted for her. They are so angry with themselves for buying it all. It was just a trick. And a good one. I heard that people are calling her 'Tricky Nicky.'"

"She fooled our parents, too," Daktari offered.

A resounding beeping noise blared through the room, drawing our attention as a screen descended from the ceiling on one end. And there was our president, Elizabeth Nicks, standing behind a podium, gazing intently at the camera. My heart lurched to a faster than normal pace.

"Attention. I am speaking to each of the mixed zones, all twenty of you, across the United Zones of The Authority. First, welcome to your new zones. As you were informed upon arrival, you will be expected to board your hovers for transport to work at five twenty each morning, Monday through Friday. Some of you will be required to work Saturdays and Sundays, and your commanding O3 Droid will inform you of your selection for this schedule. I want to remind you that any attempts to escape the zones will be punished accordingly. Do not try to defy me. Do not try to escape. Keep your head down. Do your job. No questions asked, and I'll allow *your kind* to live."

She paused, a smile pulled at the corner of her mouth, as goose bumps covered my arms. The way she had said *your kind* filled me with despair. The rumors had been true. Every one of them. She hated people who were multiracial for some reason. She believed she was superior to us because her skin was white and her hair was blonde and her eyes were blue. How had this happened? Weren't we living in the twenty-first century?

"Of course, your kind isn't the smartest. As was proven to me this morning in Indy Mixed Zone particularly. Let this be a warning to those who might defy me."

Her face disappeared as the screen was filled with video clips. There was a recap of the torture drill outside of my apartment playing on the screen; only it showed everything that happened before I left my apartment this morning. I couldn't believe she would record it but understood why. She wanted to keep using fear against us. She wanted to scare us. And it worked. Daktari's hand shook and he dropped his spoon as the boy fell to the ground in front of the guards. All of the people who had tried to escape were required to stand up with their hands above their heads. They hadn't been allowed to sit down. It was an impossible request to make. The boy had fallen twice and when he couldn't get up the last time, he'd been shot.

The president's words rang over and over in my head as the TV screens withdrew into the ceiling. *No questions asked and I'll allow your kind to live.*

A tear slid down Daktari's cheek, as I struggled to contain my own. Before I could say anything an older woman who had been eating quietly beside us spoke up. "Don't think about it. We must keep hope alive if we're going to survive in here. You can do it, young ones," she spoke smoothly.

I studied her now. She had white hair pulled into a knot at her neck. She was little, smaller than Zi. Her wrinkled face framed the greenest eyes I'd ever seen. Her features suggested Asian ancestry, though I knew she had to be multiracial to be in here with us.

"We're going to survive this. All three of us," I reassured her, my voice strong, if nothing else to try to make myself believe the words.

She gazed back at me. "I believe you will. What's your name?"

"Rain. This is my brother, Daktari. And our new friend, Zi."

"I'm Takara. It's good to meet you."

"Which group did you get assigned to?" asked Zi.

"They think I'm too old and weak to handle manual labor, so they put me with some of the other older people to watch over the little kids, too young to work yet, but I'm told they're coming for me soon. I heard one of the droids say they need an old person to help in the office at the Town Hall building."

"Well, that's too bad," Daktari muttered. "I already liked you."

Takara chuckled. "I like you kids, too. But I'm sure I'll see you around. After all, you three are going to survive in here, right?"

The way she asked the question was almost like she was challenging us. She was telling us to be strong. I couldn't explain it, but I could feel the weight of her words. I nodded back at her. "Yes. All of us."

Screaming erupted at the entrance to the break room, and we strained to watch as a girl tried to get around one of the O3 Droids. "Let me out of here," she sobbed.

My stomach dropped. What was she doing?

"Let me out of here," she repeated, hitting the droid, but it blocked her easily, pointing to the table. Evidently, the O3 Droids were very strong, like the Droid Dogs.

"Sit back down or you'll be punished," it said easily.

"No!" She hit and screamed and out of nowhere a Droid Dog appeared and pinned her to the ground with one foot. Her head must have hit the floor because she was motionless now. All eyes were glued to the front of the room now. You could hear a pin drop it was so eerily quiet.

The Droid Dog scanned the room. "Keep your head down and follow the rules," it growled. I hadn't know the Droid Dogs could speak and its voice was so menacing it sent waves of goose bumps over my body. It bent down, grabbed the girl by her ankle and dragged her out of the room, her body still in its wake.

After a moment, Daktari, Zi, and I made eye contact, shock on all of our faces. Takara interrupted the silence. "Like I said, young ones. Keep hope alive."

A human officer rounded the corner and stopped beside one of the O3 Droids. The next moment the O3 Droid called out. "Number two-thirty, Takara Jones, come forward."

I darted my eyes to Takara's. Her whisper was urgent and distinct. "Keep hope alive. We'll meet again."

She stood up and ambled towards the front of the room and I watched as she left in the custody of the human officer to go to her new job at Town Hall. She had been the most encouraging person I'd met all day, and somehow though we'd only spoken briefly, I felt strongly drawn to the older woman. Maybe something about her reminded me of Grandma Julia. Whatever it was, I hoped she was right about seeing us again.

A small cough drew my attention, and I noticed Zi patting Daktari's hand gently, even as tears filled her own eyes. He wiped another tear away and I grabbed both of their hands in mine, squeezing them tightly. "Okay, guys, remember what Takara said. Keep hope alive. We just have to get through the rest of today."

They both managed to nod in reply as the O3 Droids began calling each group back to work. I wondered what would happen to the girl they had dragged out of here but knew I couldn't help her.

I was no longer a thirteen-year-old girl with the usual problems like winning soccer trophies and getting good grades. I had a new job entirely. I had to help Daktari. I had to help Zi. We had to be survivors. We didn't have the luxury of time on our side to turn into survivors. We had to be them now. In this moment. And we had to get through today.

Chapter 3: Fear

February 2051, Indy Mixed Zone Metro Prison, UZTA

RAIN

"Rain, wake up."

My eyelids felt groggy, but the voice was urgent and familiar.

"Rain, wake up."

Marcello's voice.

My eyelids shot open. Metro Prison. I surveyed my surroundings, quickly discovering I was still perched in the crook of Marcello's arm. Then I remembered what he had done. "Don't ever do that to me again," I said harshly.

He looked sheepish. "I'm sorry. You were freaking out. I just wanted to calm you down. I shouldn't have done it, okay?"

"You shouldn't have done it *because* I was talking to Niyol right when it happened. And right when he was beginning to tell me something, you knocked me out," I whispered accusingly.

"Oh," Marcello groaned softly. "I'm so sorry. I panicked."

As much as I wanted to stay mad at him, I understood why he'd put me out. I'd been on the verge of losing control. He'd only wanted to help. I sighed. "It's fine."

"Experience has taught me that when a girl says it's fine, it's not." A charming smile lit up his face, and I felt relieved he could still find the ability to tease me. It meant he was hanging in there, in the midst of the obscure prison cell, doing better than me. I knew I could use some of his strength.

I did my best to sound upbeat. "So, *no*, I don't give you permission to use your ability on me again, but I understand why you did it. I was falling apart, but just so you know, if you do it again, I'll hurt you."

He squeezed my shoulder lightly. "There's the Rain I know. Forgiving me and threatening me in the same sentence."

I gave him the slightest smile before letting my eyes sweep the cell again. The man who had threatened me was starting to come around. I leaned closer to Marcello instinctively.

"Don't worry," he whispered, sensing my fear.

Before I could rattle off the endless list of legitimate reasons I had for worrying, I was interrupted by the sound of footsteps echoing down the corridor, and my pulse quickened.

Marcello lifted his arm from around me and put three feet between us. We couldn't let the guards know we were friends. At least until we found out why we'd been arrested. If we'd been brought in because someone had reported we were a couple or because of any implication regarding a relationship between us, we had to convince them otherwise.

With the distance between us, and the man on the ground batting his eyes open, Marcello gave me one last look, mouthing the words *It's okay*.

The next moment, Officer Wolfe arrived in front of the cell, along with an officer I'd never seen before, who was maybe around thirty and had light brown hair. Right behind them was a Droid Dog. Though Wolfe's eyes scanned the cell, they landed on me. "On your feet. Time for the party," his voice had a teasing, yet deadly, tone to it that made me shiver.

Once the door slid open he motioned for the two men closest to the door to exit, and one at a time, the other officer fastened their hands behind their backs in restraints, while the Droid Dog stood guard. The two older men went first, and as Marcello and I edged closer to the doorway the man on the floor got to his feet, mumbling under his breath. I could feel his eyes darting between Marcello and me, but I tried to avoid eye contact.

He jabbed a finger at Marcello's chest. "What did you do to me, kid? You're dead if you touch me again."

Officer Wolfe narrowed his eyes. "I ask the questions around here. No talking unless asked to," he barked.

"What are you gonna do, torture me again, Wolfe?" He let out a hysterical howl and burst into laughter, seemingly unconcerned about Wolfe's reaction.

My eyes widened as I waited for Officer Wolfe to order the Droid Dog to attack the crazy man. No one talked to him like that without consequences, I was sure.

Wolfe's mouth curved in an evil smile. "I told you not to talk. Good thing I came prepared. Parker, the tape," he ordered, motioning towards the other officer.

Officer Parker reached to his waist and handed a large roll of tape to Wolfe, making my heart sink further. Parker pulled the crazy man's hand into restraints, and Wolfe put heavy tape over the man's mouth and shoved him in line. One by one, Wolfe taped the mouths of every prisoner as Parker continued with the cuffs.

As they approached me, I started to panic. I'd been interrogated before but never with the cuffs and tape. I couldn't help myself. "Please, why are we here?"

Wolfe pressed the tape across my mouth then grabbed my neck hard. "ID check," he ordered, never taking his eyes off me.

Of course, he remembered me. I could tell by the way he looked at me. Not even two hours ago, he'd been so pleased to inform me that the president had ordered we only be addressed by our numbers going forward. I'd bravely told him my name was Rain, and he'd informed me my name had been deleted.

The Droid Dog approached, and Wolfe shoved me towards the ground. "Show him your tattoo."

With his hand still clenched around my neck I pulled my pant leg up so the Droid Dog could scan my number. The red illumination reflected off of the Droid Dog's eyes, and Wolfe jerked me upright again.

He spun me around to look at him, clenching his nails into the skin on my neck. "Like I was saying, One-two-seven-six, no talking. Understand?"

In my peripheral vision, Marcello was inching closer. I glanced at him, noting his eyes were wide. I locked eyes with Wolfe and nodded my head adamantly.

Wolfe scowled. "Good."

He released me and proceeded to tape the mouth of the last prisoner. Once we were all secure, he gestured to the front of the line. "Follow the leader."

I peered into each cell we passed. They were overcrowded even more than they'd been the last time I'd been there. It had to mean more people were being sent to our prison for resisting The Authority in other zones, and also that more people had been arrested in the wake of the last power outages, even though it'd been a few weeks since then. When the power was out for so long, like it'd recently been, people couldn't feed themselves or stay warm, and many got arrested for anything from trying to steal food to causing public disturbances. Though my eyes searched each dark cell, I couldn't find anyone I knew. The inhabitants were either too far in the back of the cells, or in some cases lying on the ground, curled up. I wasn't sure if my friend, Maha, who'd been thrown in prison for getting pregnant, another violation of The Authority rules, or Jabari's dad, Francisco, who'd been arrested on false charges of meeting in secret, were in this cellblock, and just as I considered using my telepathy to contact Francisco, a man abruptly stepped out from the shadows and collided with me. I crashed to the floor with him, along with a large container he had been carrying.

Fortunately, my head had narrowly missed the floor, and as I rolled into a seated position, I studied him. He was an old man, probably in his eighties, like Takara, and dressed in street clothes, so he couldn't be a prisoner.

"Rain," he whispered urgently. My heart lurched to a faster pace as our eyes met. Maybe he was the friend Takara had spoken of who worked inside the prison. I noticed the large container he'd dropped and the cup that went with it, as well. I'd heard about someone delivering drinks of water to the prisoners throughout the day.

He fumbled for the cup as Officer Wolfe yelled from behind the line, "Out of the way, old man."

I grabbed the cup and offered it to him as Wolfe yelled to hurry up. He tapped my hand anxiously, and leaned in as I was getting to my knees. "I'm Tony. Takara said to warn you the Big Bad Wolf is on her way here."

The Big Bad Wolf. Our code name for Nata. Elizabeth Nicks was coming here? What was I supposed to do?

My mind raced as I wished I could yank the tape off my mouth and blurt out questions to him. Before I could react, Officer Wolfe yanked my hands upwards and I stood up, watching in horror as he kicked the old guy in the stomach and he fell to the floor again, clutching his torso and moaning.

I strained my head, glancing over my shoulder as we continued the path down the hall, away from the man. Tony. I hoped he'd be okay. He'd thrown himself in harm's way to warn me about Nata, and now I had no idea what to do with the information.

And then it occurred to me . . . Since waking up in the prison cell, I hadn't tried to contact anyone again with my telepathy. They had to know about Nata, but what was the plan? Did Takara want me to do something or was I supposed to sit and wait for our rescue? And why was Nata on her way? I needed to warn Marcello.

"Marcello?"

"Are you okay? That old guy came out of nowhere." His voice was full of concern.

"He knocked me over on purpose. He's Tony, a friend of Takara. He had a message."

"What was it?"

"He said the Big Bad Wolf is coming here. What are we going to do?"

"Oh no. Let me think. I don't know."

"Should we try to run? If she gets ahold of me or you, you know she'll find out the truth."

"You're right. We can't let her question either of us. We'll have to find the right moment. I'll use my ability. We'll have to get out before she arrives, Rain. Stay in contact with me though. We'll work together when I say to, okay?"

"Okay, but wait, Marcello. Let me try to message Takara again. Maybe she can tell us something helpful."

"Hurry, Rain."

As we continued through the door at the end of the hall and down another dark corridor, I called to Takara, who answered immediately.

"Rain, you got my message from Tony?"

"Yes, and we don't know what to do. We're going to try to run, we think. We can't let Nata question us."

"Rainchild, have patience. Help is on the way."

"What do you mean? Who?"

My mind ran over the possibilities. Even if my friends were on the way, how could they save us from Nata?

"I can't tell you in case she questions you and makes you talk before it happens. Just try to fight her like you did the last time. And keep hope alive. Everyone is working together to help you."

"Okay. Thanks, Takara."

"Peace be with you, Rainchild."

"And with you."

As soon as Takara was gone, I realized her concern about telling me the details was valid. And it meant I shouldn't try to contact Jabari or

Niyol or anyone who might know the plan. It could get me in trouble if Nata got here before the rescue plan happened. I filled Marcello in our Takara's advice and he seemed relieved and said we needed to trust her. She'd have told us if we needed to run.

For the rest of the walk I tried not to let fear creep over me, but the more I thought about Nata coming, the harder it was. Still, Takara had said we'd be okay. Help was on the way. I just had to believe.

We were led down a series of hallways and through somewhat familiar doors until finally we were pushed into a fairly large interrogation room. I recognized the set-up from my last trip here. But this room was larger. There were chairs lined up in a long row, twice as many chairs as there were people and a bright solar light illuminated the chairs in an otherwise dark, concrete room. My eyes instinctively searched the ground, checking for holes or iron bars like the last room I'd been questioned in. Either there weren't any holes to lock people in here or I couldn't find them. Part of me knew they'd be located in the dark corners, away from the light and though it should have made me more afraid, the hole was beginning to concern me less as I thought about the impending arrival of Nata.

Hands pushed me forward, and I was shoved into a metal chair. Glancing in either direction, I noticed that Marcello was right next to me on one side, and the crazy man was right beside him on the other side. But there were still six more empty chairs to my right.

Before I could wonder about the empty chairs any longer, the door opened and tension filled me anew. Was it Nata? She was here?

Surprise and relief replaced my tension as a tall man with light brown hair, Officer Eric Collins, our secret ally from the Elizabeth Guard, spared me a quick glance as he entered the room. Maybe Takara had sent him here. I closed my eyes. *"Marcello, maybe Eric is our help. He'll help us get out of here,"* I said excitedly.

"I'm not sure about that," Marcello replied.

I opened my eyes and glanced towards Marcello, noting his alarmed expression. I snapped my head back to the door, expecting to see Nata. Why else would Marcello's eyes have seemed so fearful?

But as my eyes settled on the doorway it wasn't our evil dictator who was entering the room. It was a group of more prisoners, six to be exact, staggering into the room with another Droid Dog behind them. Their mouths weren't covered with tape like our own, but their hands were cuffed.

The second prisoner in line stopped dead in her tracks as our eyes met. A drumming sound filled my ears. *No.* This couldn't be happening. It wasn't Nata, but it was worse.

The Authority had arrested my mom.

Chapter 4: Stronger

February 2051, Indy Mixed Zone,
Construction and Machinery Plant, UZTA

JABARI

"Jabari, I'm in trouble," she'd said. Everything she had said was racing over and over in my head. *"I'm in Metro Prison. Behind bars."*

The past three hours had crawled by, each moment full of terror, as my imagination overran with chaos and what-ifs. Only one thing was certain: The Authority had arrested Rain and Marcello, and I had no idea why.

Though part of me knew it could be something minor, like crossing the street the wrong way, since The Authority really didn't need a reason to arrest one of us, part of me knew it could be the worst case scenario. Someone could have discovered any of the crimes against The Authority Rain or Marcello had personally been involved in since this past August. Rain had used her ability to attack Officer Darryl with brown recluse spiders to stop him from hurting her friend Maha, she'd helped Amal, a prisoner, escape, both she and Marcello had helped capture Officer Dean when he was torturing Rain's mother, and finally, they were both members of the resistance, The Freedom Front. If they had been linked to any of those acts, they'd be sentenced to life in Metro Prison. Just like my dad.

Four days ago, I'd asked Rain to marry me. I had told her we could still dream of our freedom and our future together, and we could make it a reality. And now they'd been arrested. But as far as I knew, no one else from The Freedom Front had been, and though I knew nothing about the reason for their arrests, I knew I had to get them out.

Cole ran a hand through his messy, chin-length blond hair and glanced anxiously at me as the clock-out line progressed forward. We were finally getting off of work. "Have you heard from Rain again?"

"Not since the second time. She said she was fine, but she sounded bad. I can tell she's really scared. I told her not to play hero and to stick by Marcello, but . . ." I paused, thinking of Rain's habit of helping everyone but herself.

"Yeah, I get it. I know how she is, too." Cole patted me on the back lightly. "But look at it this way: She's a survivor, Jabari. She can handle whatever happens."

"But even if something bad happens, and she, or Marcello for that matter, need to use their abilities, they don't want to get caught. Rain told me she's not planning to use her abilities because of the cameras. And until we can get you to the hideout, you can't hack into Metro to cut the cameras."

"We're almost out of here."

"She shouldn't even be there. Neither should Marcello," I snapped. "This is my fault. I have to fix this."

Cole raised an eyebrow. "We need to plan this right," he cautioned. "We need to fix this together. Talk to Takara first."

"We will. Listen, go find Daktari and Zi. You guys meet me at the hideout. I have a feeling I need to head over there. I want to check it out to make sure it's safe. And if it is, I want to message Gallagher right away. If we have to escape, we might need his help."

Cole eyed me suspiciously. "You already have a plan? You're thinking of escape as an option? I thought we were going to talk this out with everyone."

"We will. I just want to run the idea by Gallagher. And we'll talk to Takara about it before we do anything. You're going to need to hack into Metro Prison's camera system and shut it down for us to get them out."

"Sure, no problem, but why do you think this is your fault? You don't even know why they were arrested."

"It's just that Rain wanted to run a few months back. Take all of our families and as many people as we could and go to Gallagher's. I talked her out of it. Besides, I'm the one who got her and Marcello involved in TFF to begin with. What if they've been arrested because of that? And if they're sentenced to life in Metro . . . like my dad," I swallowed a knot forming in my throat.

Cole shook his head. "Enough said. I know it's hard with your dad being locked up."

As we approached the time clock to scan our tattoos, I felt a surge of guilt. Cole always had my back, no matter what, and I shouldn't have said anything about my dad. After all, Nata had murdered his parents. He'd had to deal with more pain than any of us. "Sorry, Cole. I shouldn't have said that. You lost both of your parents to her."

"It's fine. I don't want either one of them locked up in there either. It sucks. Look, I'll meet you at the hideout with Daktari and Zi, and we'll figure out what to do. Be careful. I know your ability leads you, but make sure it's not a trap or anything, whatever it is that's tugging at you."

"Thanks. I'll be careful."

Cole smiled up at me. "We're gonna get them back, you know. They're our family."

"I know."

Once out on the street I took off running, my mind on Rain and her wondrous ability to run like the wind. I had long legs and was tall, reaching six three, but I couldn't run like her. No one could. If only I could run through the prison and break them all out. If I were Niyol, I'd burst through the prison in a gust of wind and free them. But my abilities were different. I didn't have speed, telepathy, or the power to turn into a funnel cloud or morph into an owl, but I had plenty of gifts.

My ability to sense trouble or situations I needed to help with was reliable. I knew I had to head to the hideout now, but I wasn't sure what I'd find. I also had a new ability that I hadn't spoken to anyone about. I just couldn't. If they knew what I could do, they'd be afraid I might use it on them. To have that kind of power could be dangerous. For now, I'd just keep it to myself and hope I never had to use it in front of them. But today, given the dire circumstances we were in, I knew I'd do anything to free Rain and Marcello. Anything, including the use of my new ability.

Like Cole had said, we were all like family to each other now. And whether or not our plans as The Freedom Front were successful, I had to take care of them. And even more important than that . . . Rain was my present and my future. Without her, I couldn't function.

I refused to live in a world with no Rain Hawkins.

As I turned another corner, running at a steady pace now, I thought of the first time I'd seen Rain.

I'd been asleep.

It started with one dream. But it was a dream like I'd never had before. She was sprinting down one of the streets of our zone. I remember the awe I felt when I first saw her. It wasn't just her looks or the long curly brown hair and matching eyes. She was the most beautiful girl I'd ever seen, that was true, but there was a determination in her expression that intrigued me. She was strong, yet sensitive somehow. I knew that she cared deeply about something. Though I didn't know what it was exactly, it didn't matter. After I awoke from that first dream, I had the most bizarre feeling that she was real. And I needed to find this mysterious girl from my dream.

But I couldn't find her.

Day after day, I searched the streets, but though she returned to my dreams on a nightly basis, I couldn't find her in real life. Until one hot summer night in August, when I sensed someone was in trouble. I followed my instincts and then there she was. Just like she'd been in my dreams.

She stood with her curly brown hair cascading down her back, her brown eyes fixed on me, studying me with the slightest bit of curiosity in her expression. It felt like she was about to cross the street to me. And I wanted her to. There was a magnet pulling me towards her, the oddest feeling. But it wasn't the right time. The danger I had sensed had been real, and Droid Dogs had detained her.

I followed her home from a distance, watching with fascination as she stubbornly defended herself to the Droid Dogs and refused to show them even an inkling of fear. Once they left her and I knew she was safe, I sat down on the curb and smiled. I'd found her. My world had crumbled around me more and more each day since arriving to the mixed zone as living conditions had deteriorated and then my dad had been sent to Metro Prison. But at last I'd found the girl from my dreams, and I felt hope. I felt alive.

As the high school came into my view now, I focused on the facts. Rain and Marcello were in trouble, and even if it meant we had to take our families and escape, and endanger the lives of the people we'd leave behind, I had to rescue them. We had around eight weeks left until our resistance planned to go after Nata, but I'd risk it all if it meant rescuing them.

I slowed down to a jog and then a walk as I surveyed the surrounding streets, looking for stray onlookers, anyone Droid or human, who might observe me sneaking into our hideout. I wondered what exactly had been pulling me here, but figured I'd head to the hideout and message Gallagher in the meantime. Once I knew the coast was clear, I made my way to the back of the abandoned, locked up high school. I was about to remove the secret storm hatch to crawl down, when a distinct hooting sounded directly above me. My eyes darted up to see the great horned owl perched on the rooftop. Niyol. It had to be him. That must have been what I'd sensed.

I stood back up, held out my hands as if to ask what he wanted, and he hooted again. "You want me to come up there?" I said aloud.

It hooted once more, and I knew what I had to do.

Fortunately, my abilities had been getting stronger in the past few weeks. I glanced at the side of the building and studied it quickly. The drain pipe ran the first six feet off of the ground, and then a boarded up window with a sill about six inches in width jutted out to the right. To the left of it, a few feet higher, was another window ledge I could use.

Adrenaline shot through me, and I jumped halfway up the drain-pipe. Strength was the easiest and most dependable ability I had. And though my friends knew I was strong, they had no idea how strong I'd become lately. Something was happening to me. I was getting stronger and my abilities were getting easier to use. They were better than before. Within ten seconds, I'd climbed up the entire gymnasium wall and was standing on the rooftop.

The owl hooted once more and then he flew up in the air, fading into a funnel cloud. The next moment, Niyol stepped out of the funnel in his human form and stepped over to me. He was multiracial, like most of the people in our zone, his mother had been Jamaican and his father one of the last of the Navajo Indians, only he didn't live in the zone with us. He'd never been captured, and his daughter didn't even know he was still alive. Without him, TFF wouldn't have made it as far as we had. From healing Daktari's fatal wounds from a mountain lion attack to repairing our wrecked hover, somehow, he was always there when we needed him. He was dressed in jeans, moccasins, a dark coat, and his silver-white hair hung straight to his waist. "Jabari, you're getting stronger."

"Yeah, but I don't understand how."

Niyol tilted his head. "You also have a new ability you haven't told anyone about, don't you?"

I narrowed my eyes. "How do you always know everything?"

"My abilities have been strengthening for decades."

"Is that why I'm getting stronger? With time, I can do more?"

"That's how it is for some of us. As long as you have good intentions."

I couldn't waste time asking him what that meant exactly. Rain and Marcello needed my help. "Are you going to help us get Rain and Marcello out? You know about that right?"

"Yes, I know. I am working on something to help them. But I came here because I realized I needed to caution you. You're planning to break them out, aren't you?"

Guilt swept through me. Sure, I'd told Cole we could talk about it, but I'd pretty much made up my mind. We had no choice as far as I could see. We had to break them out. How did Niyol know everything? How many abilities did he actually have? "I just came here to message Gallagher to ask if there's no other option and we have to break them out, if we can bring all of our families to live at his camp. It's not set in stone or anything," I said defensively.

"I understand you're afraid. But that's why I came here. Be patient. I found out why they were arrested. It's too soon to tell what will happen, but I'm on my way to help Gallagher now. He's already creating a diversion to get Nata away from your zone. Once the attention is off of Rain, Marcello, and the rest of the prisoners, they should probably be released. If you can just be patient . . ."

"Did you say Nata? She's here?" My heart slammed to my throat and my pulse sped out of control. She might kill them or torture them at the very least. Why were we standing here talking?

"She's on her way."

I started walking towards the ledge. I had to do something. Now.

"Stop, Jabari," he said harshly.

I'd never heard Niyol get that tone, and I automatically obeyed, turning back to him. "But Nata might kill them."

"She won't. She's coming because she's still looking for her missing EEG guard, Officer Dean."

"Then why Rain and Marcello? Did someone turn them in? And how did they get discovered and the rest of us didn't?"

"Listen, from what I've gathered, Nata ordered a general round up. I don't think it has anything to do with TFF. She wanted anyone brought in for questioning who has been a threat to her system lately. She's not just looking for suspects regarding the missing officer. Someone supposedly saw Rain and Marcello together and reported it in exchange for food. I expect Nata wants to make the most out of her visit. This zone has been bothering her lately. Too much has happened here that she can't explain."

"You mean, like how we helped Amal escape?"

"Yes. Fortunately, for you and TFF, Jonah escaped from the New Texas Mixed Zone, so this isn't the only zone on her radar at the moment."

Jonah had used his ability to cut electricity to escape from his zone, and I figured he was considerably safer than we were at the moment, living with Gallagher the way he was. Jonah never would have found Gallagher if it hadn't been for Rain helping him. And even though I knew Niyol was trying to comfort me with his news about Nata being unhappy about other zones, I still felt miserable. "So what do we do? I can't just sit here and be patient while you and Gallagher try to lure Nata away. What if it doesn't work? And how are you going to do that anyway?"

"Gallagher is going to prove to Nata that he has Officer Dean. It should help get rid of her at the very least. She's determined to arrest Gallagher so she'll go after him. But listen, I have to go because he needs my help to pull this off. And then we can figure out how to help Rain and the others once Nata isn't here."

My shoulders sagged a little. That could work. Nata wanted Gallagher Brown more than anything. He was the most wanted fugitive in the UZTA.

"I get the feeling you aren't telling me everything," I said.

Niyol tensed, but then shook his head. "There's one more thing. Nata is planning to take some prisoners away from here with her. I'm not certain what she's doing with them. But she needs what she considers the weakest prisoners for whatever she's up to."

"What are you saying?"

"Rain and Marcello are both strong. They won't come across as weak to Nata. But she's arrested more than the two of them."

"Who else do they have?"

"Nata requested the list of people who were on Officer Dean's torture list. Or 'lessons,' as she calls it. I discovered it while investigating at their training facility. She had the list of people who Dean targeted before his disappearance sent to the officers here . . . to bring them in for questioning about his disappearance."

"They've got Rain's mom," I blurted.

"Yes."

"And that means Rain won't be thinking clearly. She'll do anything to save her mother. She'll be a hero. Even if that means using her abilities and getting busted in the process." My heart sank. How was I supposed to save her now?

"Perhaps, but listen to me. I know Rain will contact you again. Tell her to stay strong, and that Nata is looking for weak people. And I know you want to break them out. But promise me you'll wait until Nata is gone before you do anything. And promise you'll trust your abilities. I know you have a new ability. I know you could burst into the prison and use it on everyone and free them. But you won't be able to get away with that while Nata is still here. Unfortunately, she's stronger than you are . . . for the moment."

"Then why do I have this ability if I can't use it?"

"You'll grow stronger over time, just like you have been. You'll know when and how to use it. Now, I have to go, but just give Gallagher some time to get Nata away before you do anything."

"Time? Are you crazy? Your daughter is on her way here to torture people I love, and you want time?"

"I understand you're angry. I'm not asking you to sit back and do nothing. I'm only asking that you trust your instincts and that you wait until Nata is gone before you do anything. You are very strong. You're getting stronger. You're going to keep using your abilities, all of them, to do the right thing." He placed a hand on my shoulder, a fatherly look coming over his face. "Jabari, you don't have it in you. You can't become like Nata."

"How did you know I was having doubts?"

"I was once like you. We all struggle with our abilities. Even though they're unexplainable and awesome, we still have a choice to make about how we will use them. I watched my own daughter choose the path of evil. She never considered using her gifts to help people."

I wanted to talk to him about my new ability and how I was afraid I'd misuse it or make a wrong choice, but there wasn't time. "I understand."

"Trust your instincts, Jabari. And remember to warn Rain . . . It's important that Rain and Marcello and Grace appear strong."

He waved his hand and then started to jog away across the rooftop. A funnel cloud appeared and then a second later a great horned owl sprung from its interior and Niyol flew away.

I jumped to the side of the building, checked to make sure no one was around and then shimmied down the brick wall, jumping from sill to ledge to drain pipe until my feet hit the ground. I slid the storm hatch off of our secret hideout entrance and hurried underground. I would heed Niyol's advice and trust my instincts. I'd even let him use Gallagher as a diversion to get Nata away. I'd make sure Rain got the message to stay strong. But I had to do more than that. My instincts told me I had a role to play in their rescue. Rain and Marcello, and even Grace, needed my abilities.

And I was going to help them.

Chapter 5: Accusations

RAIN

As my mother stood frozen with her terrified eyes locked on my own, I sent up prayers like I'd never done before. If there was ever a time for Mom to play a role, it was now. She couldn't let them know I was her daughter.

I shook my head to the right, pleading with her to keep quiet, praying she would understand my silent message. If she hadn't handled everything she'd learned about my friends and I so terribly last month when we'd rescued her, I would have used my telepathy on her. But she wasn't stable. And she'd made us promise we'd never speak of our gifts to her. I tilted my head towards the empty chair and her jaw clenched, emotions flickering across her face as she debated. Officer Parker nudged her on the back. "Keep moving," he instructed.

Mom's frail form stumbled forward and plopped down in the chair as instructed. She tilted her head so her brown hair, just past her chin, fell off her face and she stared at me. Her blue eyes searched mine, but she didn't say a word. It would be so easy to use my telepathy on her, but as my chest constrained I knew I couldn't. It would push her already nervous state beyond her limits.

"You've been brought here for various reasons," began Officer Wolfe, drawing our attention forward.

He scanned the group of prisoners, his eyes lingering on me for a moment, as he took the time to smile. My stomach flipped. Was he going to interrogate us before Nata even arrived? How could I get Mom out of here? Was that even possible? Where was Takara's help? Wasn't

Eric supposed to save us? Sweat trickled down my back despite the cold room.

Wolfe cleared his throat. "But one common reason ties each of you together." I leaned forward in my chair slightly. This was the moment of truth. The reason we'd been arrested. What was the common reason that tied us together? A reason so condemning it meant Nata was coming for us?

"You're here because you have all betrayed The Authority."

My shoulders sagged a little. He was toying with us. This was a game to Officer Wolfe. I hated games. But mostly I hated not knowing why my mother and I were sitting in the same room for defying The Authority. What did they have on us? If it weren't for the tape restraining my mouth, I would have asked.

Mom snapped her head up in a defiant gesture I hadn't seen for years. "What did we do?"

Officer Wolfe's head jerked towards my mom. Why couldn't she just sit still and be quiet? Guilt replaced my fear. Hadn't I just admitted I would ask Wolfe why we were here if it weren't for the tape? Was it so surprising that I took after my mother a little?

He took two steps so he was standing in front of my mother. "Scan her tattoo."

The Droid Dog closest to Mom approached her and scanned her ankle. "One-two-seven-five," it recited.

"Show me the list," Wolfe barked at Eric.

Eric offered a clipboard tablet over to Wolfe, who glanced over it quickly. "Well, it says here, you're wanted for questioning regarding the disappearance of one of the Elizabeth Guards."

He smirked, scrutinizing my mother with a stare, and my mouth dried up. Officer Dean was missing, and that's why we'd been brought in. Of course. And Mom had been one of his victims. That's why Nata was coming. She wanted to know what happened to her precious EEG guard. And Mom, though she didn't know what we'd done with Officer Dean, still knew too much. If she were questioned by Nata, we were going down for sure.

Wolfe scowled. "As if she could do anything to one of our men. She's so weak I doubt she'll last the winter." He inched closer to Mom, darkness filling his eyes. "So, how did a weakling like you get involved in the disappearance of an officer?"

Mom peered up at him. "I don't know what you're talking about."

"I'll beat the truth out of you if I have to, and I'll enjoy it, trust me. But the thing is, it'll probably kill you. So why don't you just tell me what you've done to end up here?"

"I haven't done anything," Mom whispered.

He lifted his hand, and Mom winced, preparing for the impact. Protective instincts rushed through me along with annoyance. They'd done this to my mother after all. Men like Officer Wolfe had made my mother weak. I started screaming against the tape. Wolfe's eyes darted to me and he crossed over. He ripped the tape from my mouth, causing me to cry out in pain. "Have something to say?"

I didn't waste a moment. "I didn't do anything either. You said it yourself, some of us are too weak to fight one of the guards. Why don't you let us go? The weak ones, that is. Pick on someone who can handle it."

His hand connected with my cheek, knocking me backwards, along with my chair, onto the ground. As ringing filled my ears, adrenaline and blood coursed through my body. I opened my eyes as Wolfe's black military boots stepped in front of my face, inches away. I peered up at him, preparing for more.

"I think you can handle it. Now, listen up. Do not speak unless spoken to. Got it?"

I ran my tongue over the sore part of my mouth, wincing from the pain. "Got it," I said softly.

"Now back in your chair."

He picked up my chair and slammed it against the floor in front of me. I struggled to my knees and climbed into it, noting the alarm on both Mom and Marcello's faces. *"It's okay, Marcello. I just wanted to get his attention off of my mom."*

"Well, next time, a little warning would be nice, Loca. And I don't think your mom took it well."

I noted his use of my old nickname. He'd finally stopped calling me crazy about a month ago, but understandably he was upset with me about the stunt I'd pulled. *"I'm sorry, Marcello."*

I glanced at Mom. Her eyes were huge, but I shook my head at her again, a reminder to keep quiet. She sank back in her chair, seeming to accept what I needed her to. *"We just can't let them hurt my mom,"* I said to Marcello.

"But we also need to be patient and stay alive and unharmed until Takara's help comes," he argued.

"What if Eric was the help and now he can't save us for some reason?"

"Just hang in there. I'll come up with something, Amiga."

Wolfe grabbed the list and spoke in urgent whispers with Eric. What was happening? Normally, Officer Wolfe had more purpose and sense of command. But it definitely seemed as if he didn't know what he was supposed to do with us. After a moment, Officer Wolfe shot a look towards the Droid Dogs. "ID scan all of them and recite their numbers for me."

One by one the Droid Dogs went down the line, reading our numbers. Officer Wolfe hovered over the tablet list before him, Eric refusing to look in my direction. Officer Parker stood along the wall, a nervous expression intact. I wondered if he was new at the prison. He didn't seem comfortable at all, and I had the feeling it had everything to do with Wolfe and his interrogation tactics.

"Humph," Wolfe huffed, still perusing the list. Somehow, our numbers had told him something valuable, and he approached Marcello with new purpose. He bent forward, ripping the tape from his mouth in one swift movement. "You're here because an informant reported seeing you meet in secret, a clear violation of The Authority laws. Care to tell me what you're doing holding secret meetings?"

"I don't know what you're talking about," Marcello answered easily.

I winced as Officer Wolfe's hand came down on Marcello's mouth. I knew he'd punch him, but seeing it was worse than I'd imagined.

"Marcello, oh, I'm sorry."

"He's fishing, Rain. He said secret meetings, but what if they don't have anything else? They just want to catch us saying something incriminating. And I won't talk."

"But he's just going to keep hurting you."

"Like I said earlier. Don't worry about me. If Nata shows up to question us, you have my permission to worry, Amiga."

"This is not the time for jokes."

"I wasn't joking."

"According to this report, someone saw you meeting in secret in your home with someone else in this very room."

Comprehension hit me like a ton of bricks. The day I'd gone into Marcello's apartment with him. It'd been so long ago.

"They saw us together, Marcello."

"We didn't do anything illegal. They can't prove anything. Don't admit to anything."

"I don't meet in secret. I've never held meetings. I'm just a teenager doing my job and nothing else."

"We'll see. I have ways of making people talk. Some of you know about that." His voice trailed off as he looked at me again. He took a step closer to me and narrowed his eyes. "So, this is your boyfriend? Is that it? Or are the two of you plotting against The Authority? Maybe a trip to the hole will jog your memory again?"

"What are you talking about?" I feigned innocence, just like Marcello had told me.

"The report states that number one-two-seven-six was reported going to a secret meeting with this number," he said gesturing to Marcello.

"Its' a lie. I don't even know her," Marcello insisted.

Wolfe's hand collided with Marcello's jaw again, making me jump in my seat.

"He's telling the truth, I don't know him. Put me in the hole if you want. It's true."

"That's a pretty bold statement considering your history in this place."

The crazy man beside me started yelling under his tape, shooting looks at Marcello and me.

"Don't worry, you'll get your turn," Wolfe promised.

After a moment he turned to Eric and Parker. "Take off all of the tape. I want to question them all. The president wants us to get answers to report back to her, whatever means necessary. She wants to know who here is a threat."

Eric and Parker proceeded down the line, removing tape from each prisoner's mouth, as Officer Wolfe scanned the list, and my mind raced over what Wolfe had just said: "To report back to her." Maybe Nata wasn't coming here and Officer Wolfe, alone, intended to interrogate us about our disobedience to The Authority. Maybe something had happened since Takara sent the message to me. Maybe Gallagher or Niyol was doing something to prevent Nata from making it here to question us. Yes that had to be it. As Eric removed the tape from the crazy man beside me, I tried to ignore the uneasy feeling he gave me and focused on hope. Help was on the way. Wolfe didn't have the ability to control us like Nata. We could lie about everything and still, somehow walk out of here in one piece. Assuming they would let us go.

But as soon as the tape was gone from his mouth, he reacted. "They're lying to you."

Wolfe cut him off. "Someone reported that you've stolen food from The Authority. Are you saying someone lied to us?"

"How can I steal food from a government that doesn't even feed us? There's nothing to steal. And I wasn't talking about that. *They* are lying," he said gesturing towards Marcello and then me.

Officer Wolfe shrugged. "Oh yeah? About what?"

"They're hiding something from you. I saw it earlier. He protects her. They know each other. He did something to me. I swear, he—"

But before he could finish his sentence Marcello sprung from his chair, his hands still cuffed behind him, but it didn't stop him. He pummeled his body against the crazy man. "Liar!" Marcello yelled as their bodies slammed into the concrete. Eric and Parker jumped into action with Wolfe right beside them, pulling Marcello off of the man.

"He's not moving. He must have hit his head on the floor," Wolfe said quietly, eyeing Marcello now. I stared, wide eyed as they nudged the man and he didn't move. His chest rose up and down slightly, but he was unconscious. Somehow, Marcello managed to get his hands on him during the struggle. And Eric, Marcello, and I were the only ones who knew the truth. Even Mom didn't know about Marcello's ability to knock people out. We'd kept her in the dark about everything we could.

I glanced at Mom to survey her reaction, and she gawked at us with terror written all over her face. I wanted to tell her everything would be fine. But I couldn't risk letting Wolfe make the connection between us.

Wolfe stepped in front of me and jabbed a finger at my shoulder. "Maybe we'll put your boyfriend in the hole first."

"He's not my boyfriend," I shot back.

"We'll see about that." Wolfe paused, studying the list. He seemed aggravated. "Let's move further down the list. I want to know about the missing officer. Whoever comes forward, willingly, with information about his disappearance, I promise I'll go easy on you."

He paused glancing up and down the row. "No takers? Well, okay, but let me assure you I will be getting answers sooner or later. Now, I've got nothing but time. I sure do get bored in here though. Now, what could I possibly do to pass the time?" He voice was thick with sarcasm and somehow I knew he'd fix his eyes on me again.

"One-two-seven-six, can you think of any good ways to help pass the time? Why don't you tell the other numbers in here about the hole? I've got one in here, too, you know. Just your size."

I closed my eyes. I really didn't want to go into the hole again.

"Collins, help me out." My throat constricted as I fought off memories from the hole and being stuffed down in it and left for what felt like hours in the tiny dark box underground with hardly any room to breathe.

I shot my head back and pleaded with him as he approached me. "No. I mean, let's talk."

Wolfe was already at my side. He grabbed my arm and pulled me to my feet. "Too late for talking. You had your chance. Come on, Collins, move."

Eric had been standing to the side, his expression blank but his eyes were searching back and forth like he was desperate for a solution. He was supposed to be our ally now, and months ago he'd apologized for his involvement in my last interrogation. Would he help me now?

He set his jaw and started towards me. And as he grabbed my other arm, my hope slipped away.

I was going back to that hole.

As they dragged me across the room, I panicked. Sure, I'd told them to put me in the hole if they had to, but now that it was happening, I felt like I couldn't breathe. I kicked and fought. I couldn't let them suffocate me again without at least trying to flee. Screams sounded behind me. I heard Marcello yelling, but mostly I heard Mom. "Stop it, let her go!" she screamed. I wanted to tell her to stop screaming, but the words lodged in my throat. As I struggled against them, Mom screamed louder.

Finally Wolfe hesitated and turned back to face her, still holding my arm so I could see Mom's face now. "Shut up," he commanded.

But Mom wouldn't. She jumped from her chair and ran to us, ramming into Eric with her body, but they wouldn't release me.

"Parker, restrain her," Wolfe demanded. Parker's eyes were huge, as if he weren't sure what to do. He stood gawking from the side of the room.

Mom kept screaming. "Let her go! Let her go!"

I was about to stop her. I had to tell her to stop yelling. But the door opened and it was too late.

Two men I recognized as the bodyguards of Elizabeth Nicks waltzed through the door. And right on their heels, was the president herself.

Chapter 6: The President

RAIN

Mom was still screaming, unaware of the president's arrival. Before I could warn her, Wolfe released me and slapped my mother's cheek. She fell back, instantly quiet, and as she noticed the president standing in the room now, the little color left in her face drained.

My own heart seemed to lodge in my throat, choking me. Nata was clad in white from her long wool coat to her gloves. Her blonde hair was swept into a knot at her nape, gold jewelry decorated her neck and ears, and her bright blue eyes, full of hate, took in every detail of the interrogation room. I'd forgotten how tall she was, at least a head taller than me. She took a step in front of her guards, and tilted her head towards my mother. "What do we have here?"

From the corner of my eye, I could see Officer Wolfe's shocked expression. Apparently, he hadn't known Nata was on her way. I wondered how Takara had discovered the information. The only logical explanation had to be Niyol. Somehow, he'd known. What were we going to do now?

I looked at Marcello. "*No one came to save us like Takara said.*"

"*It's not too late. Don't think like that.*"

"*But she's here.*"

"*But they obviously are just fishing. They can't link us to the missing officer. No one can prove we were together. Stick to the plan. We don't know each other. Help could still be on the way. And besides, even if we get thrown into a cell again, we know for a fact that TFF can come for us under Zi's image. Focus on staying alive.*"

"Okay . . . And Marcello, try not to look her in the eyes."

"Got it."

Wolfe cleared his throat. "Madam President. How good of you to visit us. I was just questioning the prisoners as requested about the missing officer and following up on the other reports about their disobedience. This one," he paused, nodded at my mother, "just wants to scream and deny her crime. And this one," he pointed at me now, "won't talk either. I figured I'd give it time to think about it in the hole."

Nata's expression remained hard as she waved her hand dismissively. "I am running out of patience. I knew I needed to come here myself. I can get answers out of everyone. Put them back in their chairs," she snapped.

Officer Wolfe's face flushed red. "Yes, Madame President," he replied, barely concealing his embarrassment. "Collins," he barked at Eric.

As they dragged me across the floor and pushed me back in the chair, I stole glances at Nata. Did she remember me from when she tasered me and Takara at the fountain? Out of the thousands of people across the mixed zones, surely she had interrogated too many to remember us all.

"Tell me about this number. It seems familiar. Why was it arrested?"

She was pointing at me and my heart beat faster. Sook's warning from our last trip to their camp filled my head. Sook lived with our allies, Bhavna and her family, and he had the gift of seeing people wherever they were in the world, as if they were standing right before him, if he closed his eyes and concentrated on them. He said he had seen my cousin, Calista, looking at photographs of her extended family with Nata, and that she had sworn to hurt us. I knew Calista was only pretending to hate us. She didn't have a choice since she'd been selected to be part of Nata's new pure zone, and Calista was truly on our side. But what if Nata recognized Mom and me from the photographs? Would she let Calista fulfill her oath to hurt us herself, or would she just go ahead and do it now? Either way, this was not good. She couldn't interrogate me. I couldn't resist her mind control ability. I'd tell her anything she asked me. I'd tell her the truth. And even if Nata recalled my face from a photo, she had no idea about my connection to TFF. And I needed to keep it that way.

Officer Wolfe pointed at the list in his hands. "We rounded up prisoners based on incident reports as requested. Plus, we brought in the special list of prisoners you asked us to. These two are here because someone reported seeing them meet in secret. Both of them deny it."

Nata's focus shifted from me to Marcello and back to me again. I instantly put my head down, avoiding her eyes. After a few seconds, she stepped further down the line. "And why is this chair empty? What happened to him?"

She must not have figured out how she recognized me yet, which should have comforted me, but I knew she was pointing towards the crazy man lying on the floor behind Marcello. What if he woke up and told her about what he'd seen Marcello do? Desperation filled me. Takara had told me to be patient and that help was on the way, but what if something had changed? "*Niyol, we need help.*"

He replied, "*Rain, hang in there.*"

"*But Nata is here to interrogate us. They have my mom, too.*"

"*Did Jabari warn you to stay strong?*"

"*No, I mean, I haven't spoken to him again. But what do you mean? Is someone going to help us get out of here? What if Nata questions me?*"

"*Rain, this is important. Stay strong.*"

"*But does she recognize me from the photos she and Calista looked at? Or from the last time she was here and she interrogated me and Takara?*"

"*No, Rain. She hasn't put it together. Yet. She's looking for the weakest prisoners. You must be strong.*"

"*But she's looking for whoever took Dean.*"

"*That's not all she wants, Rainchild. Listen to me carefully. Be strong. Show her you haven't given up.*"

"*Who's coming to help us?*"

But Niyol didn't respond. I tried again, "*Niyol?*"

Officer Wolfe's agitated voice interrupted my thoughts. "This one knocked the other prisoner out during the interrogation. Said it was lying," Officer Wolfe answered Nata.

Nata's unfriendly gaze swept the group of us. "I'll get answers. But first things first. Officer Collins," she began slowly. I risked a glance in her direction. She was reading Eric's nametag.

"Yes, Madame President," Eric replied.

"Which one of these prisoners, in your opinion, is the weakest?"

The weakest? That's what Niyol had said. Why was she looking for weak prisoners?

He answered smoothly, as though in a trance, and I knew she was using her ability on him. "The prisoner on this end is the weakest."

Nata walked slowly towards the old man who'd been imprisoned with Marcello and me. He didn't look up at Nata or even seem to be concerned about her presence. "Officer Collins," Nata commanded.

"Yes, Madame President."

"Make him look up at me."

Eric moved over and tilted the old man's head up, so he could face Nata. A vacant, emptiness was in his expression as though he didn't care about anything anymore. Perhaps he was too sick to care. He looked like a skeleton almost; he was so frail.

She peered into his eyes. "Why have you been brought here?"

"I don't know. And I don't care."

Nata snapped her finger at Wolfe. "What does the list say?"

Wolfe scanned the tablet and answered, "Its number was on the special list you sent."

Nata sneered at the old man. "Makes sense. Tell me, were you involved in the disappearance of one of my Elite Elizabeth Guard officers? He's been missing for a month now. Evidence suggests something befell him outside of this zone, but since this zone in particular has a history of defiance, I decided to dig a little deeper. Were you involved, old man? Was he about to finish you off, so you plotted with someone else to hide him?"

"No. I would never betray The Authority."

"Good. Why wouldn't you betray me?" Nata pressed, staring in to his eyes.

"Officer Dean taught me my lessons. I understand my place."

"So, I see you do." She turned to one of her own bodyguards for the first time. "This one will do. Load it up."

My mouth fell open a little as one of Nata's guards marched to the old man, blindfolded him, and pulled him up and out of the room.

Nata turned to Officer Wolfe. "Who is the second weakest in here?"

"It's hard to say. One of these two. They were both on the list you sent me."

My heart lurched to full speed, pumping hard in my chest. He'd pointed at one of the prisoners who'd come in with my mom's group, and then he'd pointed at my mom. They were side by side. *No. They can't take Mom away.*

Mom's face was wide with terror as Nata strode towards her.

"So, another one of Officer Dean's worthless *numbers*. Tell me, do you know where he is now?"

For once, I was beginning to see the bright side of us being labeled with numbers. Nata didn't see us as humans. We were simply numbers that labored for her and numbers to be taught lessons to suffer because of her determination to make the world suffer for what had been done to her as a child. It was deplorable, but it also meant that Nata truly didn't recognize Mom's face from the photos she'd been looking at with Calista. We weren't important enough for her to recall. And maybe it would save us now.

"No," Mom replied automatically.

"Did you plot to do something to my officer because he was teaching you my lessons?"

Her casual tone as she spoke of the lessons, which were really torture methods used to instill fear and terror in people like my mother, filled my chest with rage. I told myself to be calm. Mom was still here. She was okay. Mom looked at Nata and answered easily. "No, I did not."

She turned to the man beside Mom and asked the same questions. Of course, he didn't know what had happened. Marcello and I exchanged anxious looks. We were the only two in the room who knew the truth about Officer Dean.

Nata turned to Wolfe. "Is this the best you can do? I ask for potential suspects and delinquents to be brought here and this is it?"

"I apologize, Madame President. No one is talking in the streets. I can bring more people here . . ." he offered nervously.

"You will find me someone who knows what happened to my EEG officer. But first let me finish with these prisoners." She turned back to the line and started questioning the prisoners on the other side of Mom.

Nata towered before each of them. "Did you do something to Officer Dean?" Each time, the answer was no. Frustration was filling her. No one had the answers she was looking for. Finally she glanced at me and then strutted to Marcello. "And you're here for defying The Authority. I asked Officer Wolfe to bring in numbers that have been reported as causing problems in my zone."

"I didn't do anything wrong."

She pointed at me. "And this number is involved?"

Marcello swallowed as Nata stared into his eyes and her ability began to overpower him. "That's what Officer Wolfe says."

The unconscious man began to cough, and sat up on the floor. "She's his girlfriend."

Nata leaned in closer to Marcello. "Is it?"

"No she's not," Marcello insisted.

The man began laughing hysterically like before and all eyes shot to him. "Tricky Nicky. Tricky Nicky. You can't fool Tricky Nicky, kid."

Nata flinched, obviously annoyed by the use of the country's nickname for her. "Well, welcome back. Why is this one here?"

"Stealing food," Officer Wolfe replied.

"Don't think I feed you enough?" she asked, stepping towards him.

"You don't feed us anything. It's a joke. Just like you, Tricky Nicky." He burst into laughter again, and I felt sorry for him. He'd become insane because of her, after all. It happened too often in our zone.

Nata gestured to Officer Parker, who was practically cowering along the wall. "Make yourself useful. Take him to one of the cells in isolation. No food for three days. Then, release him."

As Parker's face flushed red, he nodded his head obediently. "Yes, Madame President," he stammered.

While Parker escorted the man across the room, Officer Wolfe wrinkled his brow together. "Excuse me, Madame President. But why do you want to release him? We could just leave him in the isolation cell like we do the others."

"You shouldn't question me, Officer, but remember this: I need the strongest numbers in this zone to keep working. There is much more to be accomplished."

The crazy man began screaming in protest as Parker led him towards the doorway. "They're lying. Why don't you punish them? He protected her back in the cell!"

My mind raced. She needed the strong ones alive, and some of the weak ones she was taking somewhere. But where? Why? I had to warn Marcello.

"Marcello, stay strong. Niyol said she wants weak ones for something and we have to be strong. He said help is coming."

"Okay, but how can we protect your mom?"

"I don't know. I'm working on it."

Nata gave the prisoner a brief look as he disappeared from the room and then turned to Marcello again. "Did you protect that number earlier?"

Marcello hesitated as he fought to resist Nata. But she was too strong. "Yes."

"Why?"

"That lunatic you just had taken away tried to hurt her. It was the right thing to do."

"The right thing to do," she said in mock tone. "You're all weak, regardless of how you ended up in this zone. Some of you are just weaker than the rest," she finished as her eyes settled on Mom. My mom had given up her rights to stay in the Indy White Zone so she could keep her family together. But to Nata, anyone in here, regardless of his or her appearance, was inferior to her.

As she studied my mom, she reached her hand out towards her body-guard. "My taser," she said.

Once the taser was in her hand, her expression darkened. "In the last few months, there have been two disappearances associated with this zone. I can't let that go unpunished. And I need another weakling for a very special project. Let's see who the weakest link is, shall we?"

Her armed raised towards my mom. My breathing sped up as every-thing around me seemed to slow down. The taser shot a jolt at Mom and I lunged across the room, attempting to block the taser, but I was too late. The guards grabbed me, pulling me back as Mom flailed on the ground, shaking from the taser.

Officer Wolfe slammed me to the floor and I screamed as his black military-style boot was careening its way into my side, where he rammed it over and over, relentlessly. I stopped screaming, as I couldn't breathe. I was choking. "Stupid mixed breed girl," he yelled.

A moment later he stopped and Eric was leaning over me, grabbing at my arms. "I'll throw it in isolation so you can continue your interro-gation, Madame President," he said sharply.

As much as I didn't want to leave my mom, I knew Eric was only trying to save me. And separating me from this room was probably the only thing he could come up with.

"No. I'm not finished with it yet," Nata commanded. My body sagged to the floor as Eric still held my arms up. Nata scowled at me. "Why do you care what I do to this number?" She gestured towards Mom, who was moaning softly on the floor right in front of me as she woke up.

I avoided her eyes, closing my own tightly. "You don't have to hurt her. She's not weak. She's just smaller than some of the people here."

"Then prove it to me," Nata said.

She stepped closer to Mom, but for some reason she turned her head away, not looking Mom in the eyes to control her. With her head angled away, she spoke. "Stand up if you're not weak."

Mom glanced at me and I bobbed my head, encouragingly. She had to be strong so they wouldn't take her away. By some miracle, Mom struggled to her feet.

Nata snapped her fingers at me. "Get to your feet."

I stood up as instructed, and Eric released his grip on me. Even though he was right beside me, I knew he couldn't help me.

"Take their cuffs off. Both of them," Nata instructed.

Eric obeyed right away, and within moments, Mom and I both had our hands free. As I prepared for the taser to hit me, I told myself to be brave. Nata raised the taser in my direction, but then paused and walked to Mom, still not looking in Mom's eyes. "You do it," she said, holding out the taser for Mom to grab.

Mom's expression was understandably confused. "But—"

"Prove to me you aren't weak!" she screamed. I'd never heard her scream. She was always in control; she always spoke in a calm voice, even when she was being sadistic.

"Taser the girl!"

For some reason, as if testing her, she wasn't using her ability to control people. She was giving Mom a choice to obey her.

Mom shook her head and took a step backwards, refusing to grab the taser. "No," she replied firmly.

Nata smacked Mom, and as she fell I dove to catch her. I barely caught her and cradled her head in my lap as we pummeled to the floor. Mom scooted to her knees beside me, visibly shaking now, but staring defiantly at Nata.

The next moment Nata was peering into my eyes, and her voice was deadly calm. I could feel her ability working through me. My limbs were tingling all over. "Why won't she do it? I told you she's weak."

The tingling circulated throughout my limbs as Nata's ability worked through me. "Answer me."

I had no choice. Her ability was too strong. Just like the last time. "She's my mom."

Comprehension swept Nata's face, and she stood back up. "Now I understand. Maybe I'm looking at this the wrong way. Your mother was being taught lessons by my missing EEG officer. You knew about it," she accused. "Didn't you, mixed breed?"

She leaned forward again, clutching my chin, and her power was so overwhelming I couldn't focus on anything but telling her the truth.

"Yes, I knew."

"You did something to my officer, didn't you?"

As I fought to resist her, words raced through my mind. I tried to form a prayer or to call out to Niyol, but everything was getting duller and hazier as she held my face, her fingers were digging into my skin.

Just when I knew I couldn't resist her any longer and I had to answer her, the door swung open. The bodyguard, who had taken the weak prisoner away earlier, had the most horrified expression on his face. "Madame President. Something's happened."

Nata released me and I collapsed forwards, fighting off the tingling with all of my might. I watched as they spoke in hushed whispers, and then Nata got the most bloodthirsty look on her face I'd ever seen. She glanced at Officer Wolfe. "Release them. Send them all back to work," she snapped.

"But what about the list and the reports we gathered? Shouldn't we detain them longer? And this one might know something about Officer Dean." Wolfe's face was dumbfounded as he gestured to me.

"I just received news about Officer Dean's real location. Send them back to work. These mixed breed weaklings will work for me until they *die*." She pointed a finger at Wolfe as she shrieked.

The reminder of our death sentence made my face flush with heat. "*You're just like us, Nata.*"

She turned on her heel and her hostile eyes swept the room.

I focused on the ground. I couldn't believe myself. I'd used my telepathy on her. What if she didn't leave now? Had she heard me? What if she figured it out? *Please, God. Don't let her realize what just happened.*

I risked a glance up. A distant look came over her face as if she were being pulled into deep thoughts. Abruptly she shook her head and refocused. She pointed at the man who'd been sitting beside Mom. "Load that one up, too," she barked.

Her bodyguard hurried over to him, blindfolded him as he had the other prisoner, and pulled him to his feet, heading towards the door.

And with one fleeting glance in my direction, Nata, the most terrifying and evil woman I'd ever known, exited the room.

Our help must have come through.

Chapter 7: Romeo and Juliet

RAIN

I should've felt relieved. I'd only just told myself moments ago that as long as Nata weren't here, I could handle whatever Officer Wolfe had in store for me. But though her entourage had left and her orders had been clear, "Release them. Send them all back to work," the way Officer Wolfe was surveying me now was making me uneasy. He'd been embarrassed in front of us because of the way the president had yelled at him, and I had a sinking feeling someone would have to pay for his mood.

Still, Nata was gone. She'd been in the same room as me, inches before me, she'd even clutched my face, peered into my eyes and worked her wicked spell on me, and I'd still managed to get away unscathed. Plus, she hadn't found what she was looking for. Of course, she had taken two "weak" people away for some unknown reason. But she hadn't done anything to me or Marcello or my mom. And as far as I knew no one had discovered TFF. So I tried to think positive. Niyol or Gallagher or some wonderful person had done something to get Nata away from us. They'd protected us. So I should've felt safe.

But I didn't.

"Marcello."

"We're almost out of here, hang in there."

"I have a bad feeling. Do you see how Wolfe is looking at me?"

"Yeah, it'd be hard not to notice. But you heard Nata. She gave him orders to release us."

"But—"

"No buts. Listen, she's gone. I'm not letting anything, and I mean anything, happen to you, got it?"

"There you go with promises you shouldn't make again."

"I promise, I'm getting you out of here."

Eric went to the front of the line, started giving orders to Parker, who had just returned to the room. "The president said to release them. Let's take their cuffs off and walk them out of the main entrance."

As they started on the front of the line, I stood up from the floor, pulling Mom to her feet beside me since we were the only two without cuffs, thanks to Nata's stunt. Mom clung to my arm briefly as we stared at each other, fear was still in her expression. I smiled quickly at her, hoping it would soothe her nerves. She nodded in response and let go as she turned towards the front of the line.

Eric was busy unfastening handcuffs and avoided my gaze as he passed me in line. I tried to shake off the feeling of dread Wolfe was giving me. I was so close to getting out, yet still, this was Metro Prison, the place of nightmares. I pushed the thought away and made myself concentrate on Jabari. As soon as I got out, I'd find him and wrap my arms around him. I'd come too close to losing him again. If anything, today had been a reminder of how much danger we were in and that we needed to be more careful. Someone had turned Marcello and me in just for seeing us go into his apartment, and that wasn't even illegal. We'd been arrested on suspicion alone. There was no way to guarantee safety in this zone, but we'd have to be more careful nonetheless. So many people were depending on us even if they didn't know it.

I scanned the group, noting we'd all been freed, and took a deep breath.

"Droid Dogs, escort the front half of the group to the exit," ordered Wolfe.

Mom gave me one last look as she was led from the room, and I offered her an encouraging smile. I'd see her as soon as I got home.

Once they were gone, Eric motioned for the rest of us to come forward. "Let's get moving," he ordered.

I joined in step. I was almost to the door, when Wolfe stepped in front of me. He grabbed my arm, pulled me out of line. "Wait, what are you doing?" I blurted.

"You're not done here. Not yet." He squeezed my wrists together behind my back and cuffed me. Then he grabbed hold of my arm securely.

"But, please," I yelled louder than necessary, knowing Eric would hear me. He was my only chance, I just knew it.

Sure enough, Eric turned his attention back towards us and shot his eyebrows up at Wolfe. "What are you doing?"

"I'm going to keep Romeo and Juliet overnight. Parker, grab him," he finished, pointing at Marcello.

My stomach dropped. "No," I blurted instinctively.

Wolfe laughed, then tightened his grip on my arm. "And I thought you two didn't know each other."

"We don't," Marcello said calmly, his eyes darting to Eric.

As Parker approached Marcello he didn't fight him, which I'd half expected. Parker slipped cuffs on him and he didn't react at all.

"Marcello, what are we going to do?"

"Eric might help us. Maybe I can knock him out once we aren't in front of so many witnesses."

"There are cameras," I reminded him.

"Contact Jabari. Tell him what's happening in case they can help, too. Eric will help us, Rain." The officer led Marcello over to Wolfe and me.

Wolfe leaned down, his mouth inches from my face. "Don't look so nervous. You were telling me the truth earlier, right?"

"Yes, we were. But just keep me. Let the girl go," Marcello interjected.

"Now, where's the fun in that?"

As his words sank in, heaviness settled in my chest. I knew it'd been too good to be true. Eric's words sounded muffled, as my heartbeat got louder. "President's orders were to send them back to work," he protested.

"These two can't go back to work anyway. Their shifts ended already. No harm in keeping them here," Officer Wolfe said calmly.

Eric's stare remained blank, but his voice was hard. "Where are you taking them?"

"Stay out of it, Collins," Wolfe snapped. "Parker, you're coming with us," he growled. Parker's eyes were alarmed, but he followed orders. Wolfe led us to the right, down the corridor away from the group.

I strained my head over my shoulder to see Eric. Surely, he wouldn't just let us be taken away. His eyes met mine briefly, but his expression was unreadable. I had to believe he was coming back. But part of me knew he might be too late to help us.

Wolfe pushed me to the left, down another hallway, and Marcello turned towards me.

"*This is bad, Marcello. I know what he's capable of. And he has it out for me.*"

"*We'll make it out. And—*"

Wolfe stopped abruptly and spun me around towards him. "Oh, I forgot," he said with a cruel grin. The next moment my head was covered with some type of cloth sack. He rammed me against the wall. "Hold her," Wolfe ordered. I felt Parker's hands on my shoulders, pressing me against the wall as panic rolled through me.

"*Marcello, he blindfolded me!*"

"*Me too. It's okay. I'll—*"

An electric sound zapped, and I heard Marcello moan. "*Marcello?*" But he didn't respond.

"What's happening?" I shouted.

I listened as a door screeched open, and I was pushed forward. I couldn't recognize the sounds around me other than feet shuffling.

"*Marcello? Are you okay?*" I tried again.

But there was no response.

"Tell me what you're doing," I demanded.

Hands slipped around my throat and shoved me against something hard. "The beautiful thing about blindfolds is that you never know when the pain is coming. It fills your mind with so much fear, you go mad, One-two-seven-six," Wolfe said tauntingly.

"I'm not—"

A fist pounded into my stomach, instantly knocking the air out of me, and I fell hard to the ground. I heard Wolfe's laugh as I tried to breathe, but no air would reach my lungs, and the bag over my head was helping to suffocate me even more. As I choked for air I silently called for help.

"*Jabari, please, help me.*"

He answered right away, his voice strong and steady. "*Where are you?*"

"*I'm not sure yet. Nata was going to release us, but Wolfe took Marcello and me someplace. He did something to Marcello. He's not answering me. And he blindfolded me.*"

"*Rain, I'm coming for you. I promise. Hold on.*"

"*Marcello tried to promise me something like that. But I think they knocked him out with a taser.*"

"*I'm coming for you.*"

A sob formed in my throat. Tears started rolling down my cheeks. Hands pulled me up again and as soon as I heard the metal click freeing one hand, I swung out, blindly attacking my captor. He rounded my hands up the next moment and my body slammed against an unyielding surface.

My hands were raised above me, against the surface, and I heard the metal click again. The next moment my legs were pinned against the surface, but I kept struggling against them. "This is going to be fun. The last mixed breed number I had in here didn't fight me at all. It just bled out on my table without a fight," Wolfe informed me.

"Let me go!" I screamed, trying to free myself from my restraints.

The hood was yanked from my head. I squinted my eyes, desperately searching the room. A single solar lamp lit up the space, which I recognized. It was the same room I'd been in during Wolfe's last interrogation. It had the same eerie feeling as the last time I'd been in it. I found the cage top entrance to the hole. The metal chairs were sitting off to the side this time. The only thing different about the room was the contraption I was tied to presently. I followed my hands upwards and saw they were cuffed to a hook. I glanced at my legs and noted that I was spread-eagle against some sort of board. To the left of me, Marcello was confined to the same type of board, and Wolfe had removed his blindfold as well, only he was still unconscious from the taser. Parker was pacing the side of the room, obviously uncomfortable with whatever Wolfe had in mind.

Wolfe yanked my hair and pulled my head forward roughly. I sucked in a huge breath, clenching my teeth through the pain. "Relax, One-two-seven-six. No need for tears. This isn't the part that hurts," he said.

The little hope I'd been naively clinging to was beginning to fade.

"*Jabari?*"

"*I'm on my way, Rain. We're entering the building now.*"

"*Please hurry. We're in the same room as my last interrogation. The one Eric and Wolfe had me in with the hole. If you can't find it—*"

"*I'll find it.*"

Wolfe released my hair and my head fell forward. I took deep breaths, trying to believe we'd be okay. Help was on the way. If only I could do something to help. But what good were my abilities now? Then it hit me: there weren't any cameras in this room, at least, I didn't see any. I *could* use my abilities.

I could run faster than normal humans. I could make animals obey me. I could get inside people's minds to talk and send messages. But I couldn't control people like Nata. Just animals. And there weren't any animals in Metro, were there? What about the spiders? That had worked before. Of course.

Wolfe picked up some sort of baton from the corner of the room and pressed a button, making the end light up like fire. I was running out of time. Maybe spiders would work again. He closed the distance between us and held the red-hot baton up in my face. It reminded me of a fire poker from our old fireplace in Zionsville.

"This is one of the latest gifts of torture from the president, One-two-seven-six. You and Romeo can be my little lab rats."

Rats. It hit me like a two-ton truck. *Rats.* Takara had mentioned them to me before. They had a hard time keeping them out of the prison, and the guards didn't put much effort into exterminating them for obvious reasons.

Parker stepped forward all of a sudden, with panic in his expression. "Officer Wolfe, are you sure this is necessary? The president said to release them, you know. Is there a point to this, I mean?" his voice shook as he questioned his superior officer. I knew he wouldn't be able to help us, but I felt gratitude for the fact he had dared to speak up.

Wolfe's expression darkened and he pointed to the door. "Get out of here, Parker, before I use this on you, too."

Parker paused, looking between Marcello and me. "Please," I whispered, as more tears fell. I imagined him debating how far he could go to help us. But he had to know Wolfe would make sure he got into trouble if he tried to intervene again. Still, I could see him debating. I wondered how many men were like him, torn between right and wrong, saving one of us or turning a blind eye so their own families could survive.

"Out!" Wolfe repeated. Parker reluctantly broke eye contact and fled, the door slamming shut behind him.

Wolfe leaned in, a scowl crossing his features. "I asked you a question. You ready to be my little lab rat?"

He held the gleaming red stick up in front of my face. I could feel the heat radiating from it as it closed in on me. He paused. "Or maybe I'll wake Romeo up and start with him."

"No," I cried out. I wanted to stop crying, but couldn't.

He stomped over to Marcello's unconscious form, yanked his shirt up to expose his stomach, and lowered the stick, turning to spare me a smile. "Don't worry, you're next. And now that we're officially alone, I can let you in on my plans. This is only the warm-up. I've got a dozen tools I can't wait to play with. But ultimately, you and Romeo are leaving this room in a body bag. Next stop, the crematorium, One-two-seven-six."

I tilted my chin up, enunciating each syllable. "My name is Rain Hawkins."

Then I closed my eyes, prayed for strength, and concentrated on my ability like I'd never done before. As Marcello's screaming filled the room around me, I summoned the rats.

Chapter 8: Team

JABARI

Concealed under Zi's camouflage image, just outside Metro Prison, we watched Nata take off in the long black hover labeled THE UNITED ZONES OF THE AUTHORITY PRESIDENTIAL HOVER. My mind raced. Niyol had promised they'd get rid of Nata, and he'd told me to trust my instincts. I'd waited for Nata to leave, just like Niyol had asked, and now it was time to act. Waiting for Nata to walk out of Metro Prison and leave had been agonizing. My gut told me Rain needed me, but I had waited. And now that Nata was gone, we could go in. And just a moment ago, Rain had contacted me again, confirming my fears. I'd been right. She was in trouble. Wolfe had her and Marcello, and I needed to help them.

We hesitated midway up the steps to the prison entrance as Rain's mom exited the building. She seemed shaken, yet holding it together somehow, after what I could only imagine she'd just been through. She glanced over her shoulder, and I noticed her swollen cheek. Daktari reached his hand out instinctively.

"If you want to go home and heal her face . . ." I began.

He shook his head. "No, it can wait. She looks okay for the most part. And if she knew that Rain and Marcello are in trouble, she'd want me to help them first. There is no way she'd get on that hover if she knew Rain wasn't being released. Come on, let's hurry," Daktari decided, his voice firm.

I hesitated, prompting Daktari and Zi to look at me. "Look, Cole's taking out the cameras on my signal. Why don't I just go in alone? If you two get caught with me—"

"That's my best friend in there. And Marcello. If you think we're letting you do this alone . . ." Zi began, her eyes hostile, even as she held the camouflage image around us so we could blend in to the sidewalk.

Daktari frowned. "We work as a team. Come on."

I shrugged. "I was just making sure. Let's go."

As we continued up the steps, I messaged Cole on the Pinkie device. He would cut the security cameras throughout the prison just in case anything happened with Zi's image. We couldn't leave any trace of our break-in. Hopefully everything would go smoothly and no one would have to get hurt, but I was prepared to do anything to get them out. Which was part of the reason I'd asked Daktari and Zi if they were certain they wanted to do this. If I was forced to use my new ability, I was afraid of what they'd think. How could I share my ability with the others when it made me paranoid myself? I knew Niyol was right, I wasn't like his daughter, but I knew that having more power could mess with the lives of those around me. Besides, even though my power wasn't strong yet, it might grow. Furthermore, if I was forced to use the ability they knew about, my strength, it might scare them as well. They didn't know how strong I'd become. But I could kill Officer Wolfe with my bare hands if I wanted to. No, I didn't want to kill anyone. I'd been trying to come up with ways to rescue Rain and Marcello without resorting to that for that past few hours. But the truth was, Officer Wolfe had been a problem for months, and I had avoided dealing with him.

I pointed to a guard about to enter the building ahead of us. "Let's sneak through the doors right behind him."

We moved in sync, staying close behind him so we could get into the prison.

My thoughts ran on as we entered the small waiting room area in front of the main desk. Officer Wolfe had to be stopped. I should have done something about him after the last time he'd hurt Rain, but I'd been too stubborn, hoping that somehow he wouldn't hurt her again. And then Rain had talked to my dad and told me how bad Wolfe was torturing him and the other prisoners.

It had been making me have nightmares ever since. I'd hoped that Dad could somehow survive his imprisonment, knowing we would free him eventually, but knowing how he was suffering more than everyone else, all to protect the other prisoners, just made my regret worse. I should have done something about Wolfe months ago. And now he had one of my closest friends and my future wife.

Besides, if he stayed in the zone, he'd continue to be a problem for TFF and my dad. The irony wasn't lost on me. At one point, I'd been trying to get Rain to see reason and to solve our problems without killing, which we'd managed to do so far, but today I wasn't sure if there was another solution. I had to kill him to protect the ones I loved.

As we breezed past the main desk in Town Hall and followed a guard through the prison doors, my determination increased and acceptance sank in. Even though it went against everything I believed in, good and evil, right and wrong, I couldn't see another solution.

I tapped Daktari's sleeve, pulling them to a stop once we reached the corridor where the visitation room was. I hadn't been there for a month. The last time we'd been permitted to visit Dad, I'd let Mom go. She needed to see him more than me. Though she wouldn't admit it, I knew she struggled to stay sane and positive most days and missed Dad so much. To the right of us, the visitation room sat empty and dark, and ahead was a door leading to the prison cells and interrogation rooms. I typed in the Pinkie again, waiting on Cole to type back from the matching one, where he was stationed in our hideout at the school.

Daktari raised his brow. "Cole shutting down all of the cameras in here or just this one?"

I waited on Cole's response. He'd said he'd let me know how many cameras he could shut down once he tried. After another thirty seconds, the Pinkie illuminated, and I let out a breath. "He shut them all down. We've got fifteen minutes."

"Let's go," Daktari whispered.

Knowing the cameras were down, we opened the door, and traveled through under Zi's image. If anyone had been watching, which they couldn't because of Cole, they'd have thought they were losing their minds watching a door open and close on its own. We'd agreed to stay under Zi's image the entire time we were here, in case we ran into anyone. If I'd come alone I would have had to deal with anyone I'd encountered alone. The thought made my heart speed up. How far was I willing to go to save Rain? I knew I'd do anything to save her, and the thought scared me. I needed to be able to think rationally and make the right decisions for the good of TFF, that's why I was the leader. And here and now, I knew I'd disregard my own advice if it meant saving Rain and Marcello.

Once inside the cellblock we were overloaded with smells and moaning from all around. I moved to the front to lead.

"Where do we find her?" Zi whispered.

"She's not in here," Daktari said. "These are just cells. Last time she said he took her to an interrogation room."

"I'll ask my dad if he knows where they are. He should be able to hear us with his ability if we can get closer to his cell. You two remember where he is?"

"I know exactly where he is," Daktari said confidently.

He took off, leading the way through a series of doors and prison blocks. No one was around. I imagined the guards were all reeling after the president's visit. They'd probably be gathered in a break room talking. All of them except Wolfe.

Finally, Daktari opened another door. "He's up ahead on the right."

"Drop the image, Zi," I instructed. The image faded and I led the way now, calling to Dad in whispers, knowing he could hear me. "Dad, I need your help." Dad was multiracial also. His mother had been Caucasian and his father had been first generation Mexican-American. He had the ability to hear things from far off. I was about to repeat myself when I heard him.

"Jabari," a raspy voice called out from ahead in the dark.

I rushed down the hall, stopping when I saw his hands reaching out of the cell for me. His left eye was swollen shut, but he had the biggest smile on his face. "Jabari. Daktari, Zi."

I reached through the bars, letting him hug me as best he could with the gate between us. A knot formed in my stomach as I surveyed his recently beaten and bruised face and his eye. "Did Wolfe do this to you?"

Dad sighed. "Yes, but don't worry about me, son. What are you doing here? You shouldn't have risked coming here. But I've missed you. Your mom said you're okay. What's happening?"

"Oh, Mr. Ramirez, your face looks awful. You must be in terrible pain," Zi remarked worriedly.

Daktari grabbed Dad's hand. "Let me heal you, Francisco."

Dad flinched. "It's just that if Wolfe sees my face is better he might ask questions. Maybe you could just get my ribs? I'm pretty sure he cracked a couple of them."

I felt rage filling me at the thought of Wolfe beating my dad. Daktari reached through the bars and placed his hands on Dad's side. He winced at first, then sighed with relief as Daktari's healing powers worked. After a few seconds, Dad gestured over his shoulder.

"What about Ian? Can you fix him like you did last time, Daktari?"

I glanced behind Dad, noting the man passed out on the floor. I remembered Rain telling me how the guy we'd seen arrested at Grandma Julia's had been brought here and shared a cell with my dad. "What happened to him?"

Dad's face sobered. "Wolfe. He's relentless these days. He comes through here to hurt us once a day. Sometimes he takes us to another room where he has tools . . ." he stared off to the side as his words trailed off.

"Pull him over and I'll fix him," Daktari urged.

Dad pulled Ian over, and Daktari bent down and healed him. He opened his eyes, confusion filling them. Dad bent down. "It's okay, Ian. These are my friends. They just fixed your injuries. Okay?"

Ian nodded, unconcerned about who we were or what we were doing. His face was blank. "Thank you," he finally said, then crawled back to the side of the cell. I clutched the bars and motioned for Dad to come closer.

"Listen, Dad, Wolfe has Rain and Marcello in an interrogation room. Do you know where he might take them? I've only got a few minutes to find them."

"It's on this floor. Once you leave here, go through the first door on your right. It's the second door in the hallway. There's a voltage symbol on the door. That's where he takes me sometimes. But Jabari, be careful. If he catches you—"

As worry clouded his face, I cut him off. "I'll be fine, Dad." I turned towards Daktari. "Fix his eye, Daktari."

"But I don't want Wolfe to notice," Dad protested.

"Dad, listen to me. Wolfe won't be coming back for you after today."

Dad paled. "Jabari . . . I know you have to make a lot of tough decisions—"

"I have to make tough decisions out here everyday, Dad. And one of my best friends and the girl who I'm going to marry need my help. And you need my help, too. So listen when I tell you, Wolfe isn't going to hurt you anymore. Daktari, fix his eye. Fast. We have to go. Rain contacted me ten minutes ago. She might be running out of time."

Daktari placed a hand on Dad's face and instantly healed his eye. Once it was smooth and unmarred again, I leaned in, hugged him quickly, "Stay alive, Dad. This is all going to be over soon enough."

He held on to my arm, emotions flickering across his features. "I was only going to say that I'm proud of you, Jabari. You're making tough decisions. I'm not there for you anymore. And I'm proud of you. When Takara asked me to help her, I thought I could do it. But I messed it up. Got thrown in here before I could even get things going. But you're doing it. Things I only dreamed of."

"I'm just finishing what you started. Anyhow, you're playing a role too. Don't discount that for one second. What you're doing to help people in here matters, Dad."

"I love you, Jabari."

"I love you too."

"Go save your friends."

I turned to Zi and Daktari. "Let's go get 'em."

Chapter 9: Officer Wolfe

JABARI

As I led the way, racing down the somber corridors of Metro Prison, Daktari and Zi struggled to keep up. I wasn't exactly concerned about staying under Zi's image. I just needed to get to Rain and Marcello. Daktari and Zi were concerned about our plan, namely that we didn't exactly have one. Well, they didn't have one, but I was beginning to form one, more or less. Still, I hadn't enlightened them about it as I had the growing sense that I would really have to kill Wolfe. And if there were any other guards in the room, I knew I'd have to use my newest ability, which I hadn't even warned anyone about, but I'd have to deal with that if it happened. There couldn't be any witnesses who might report that we'd been in the room.

Daktari and Zi were trying to decide the best way to get into the interrogation room, assuming it was unlocked. Daktari wanted to barge into the room. Zi thought we should try to sneak in under her image. The one thing I told them might be a problem was a lock on the door, and I had suggested that we make a noise out in the hallway, so someone would be forced to leave the room and investigate. And that would be our chance to go in, image or no image. I didn't care if Wolfe saw us. I knew what I had to do.

I swallowed a knot forming at the thought. What would we find in the room?

By my estimation, it had been about ten minutes since Rain contacted me. A lot could happen in ten minutes. If he put her in the hole again, I wasn't sure how she'd hold up. She was still having nightmares about being locked underground in the hole. Her dreams frequently entered mine. But the hole would be better than the alternative. What if he was hurting her? Using his torture tools on her? Bile rose in my throat and I sped up.

"The door we need to take should be just up ahead according to Dad." My voice was strained.

"What exactly did you mean, by the way, when you told him Wolfe wouldn't be a problem after today?" Zi inquired from close behind me.

Daktari responded before I could. "He's gonna kill him."

I jerked to a stop, putting my hand in front of them. "You have a better idea?"

Daktari shook his head. "No. I'm with you on this. We can't let Wolfe walk out of here. He'll not only target Rain and Marcello, he'll target anyone associated with them. And he'll keep on hurting your dad and the other prisoners. It ends today."

Zi raised an eyebrow, her expression stoic. "I agree with Daktari. There's no other way. But how are we going to do it?"

I let some of the air out of my chest. I hadn't realized how tense I was until I heard them say the words out loud. They understood why I had to kill a man. "Come on, we have to hurry. I'll figure out how to do it."

We turned down another hall. I could feel the adrenaline pumping through my body the closer we got. Daktari caught up to me, and in the corner of my eye, I saw him glancing at me. "She's tough," Daktari began. "So is Marcello. But Rain will think of something to survive. She always does," he finished, his voice steady.

"Yeah, she's strong," I blurted, but silently, the panic started again. What if we were too late? How much could Rain handle? And what was happening to her?

The door ahead was the one Dad had instructed us to take and I barreled through, unconcerned about what might be on the other side, only knowing that it would lead us to the interrogation hallway.

Zi gasped beside me as Daktari grabbed my shoulder, pulling me to a stop. "What in the world?" Zi stammered. I was momentarily stunned, thrown off. My mouth fell open as I took in the scene.

"Rain did this," Daktari finally spoke.

Lining the hallway we'd stumbled into, scurrying down the side of the corridor, in perfect unison, were *hundreds* of rats. They were going the same direction, undeterred or distracted by us. Like they were under a spell. I swallowed. Rain's spell. A muffled-sounding voice ahead was shouting words I couldn't understand. Was it Wolfe?

I started forward. "Hurry."

We ran down the corridor, where the door to an interrogation room was standing ajar, and the rats were shuffling through. I hesitated in the doorway, Daktari and Zi on either side of me, and as Zi dropped her cover image, we took in the scene. The rats were swarming over a mound in the corner I couldn't recognize but knew without a doubt was Wolfe's body. To the immediate left of the doorway, Eric's body lay still. Daktari knelt quickly and felt for a pulse. "He's alive. Just unconscious," he said.

My eyes darted to two boards in the middle of the room, where Rain and Marcello were tied, propped upright. Rain's body was slumped forward and her eyes were closed.

Marcello was still shouting, and hadn't seemed to notice us. "It's enough, Rain. We need to figure out how to escape. Stop, Rain, stop!"

For a second I panicked, as I wondered if she were still alive. But then I noticed the slightest rise and fall in her chest, and relief swept through me. We stepped cautiously forward. Rain was either ignoring Marcello or she was so focused on the kill, she couldn't even hear him.

Marcello's shouting stopped abruptly as he noticed us. "Thank God you're here. I can't make her stop. And I couldn't save her like I promised." His head fell forward and he began to sob.

My gut twisted the moment I laid eyes on Marcello's face and chest. Huge burn marks covered his body, exposing bits of flesh all over. He'd been through hell in the ten minutes alone with Wolfe. Zi and Daktari reached out to him, and my jaw clenched as I turned to Rain. Anger rushed through me from head to toe, and I fully comprehended why she was still attacking Wolfe. Just like Marcello, she was covered in burn marks, on her face, neck, and arms, where he'd pushed her shirt sleeves up.

Guilt consumed me. I hadn't made it in time to spare her pain. And not only that, she had killed again. I had wanted to spare her from that. I'd wanted to carry the burden. She'd been through it once before, when she had accidently killed Darryl with the brown recluse spiders, and it was something she'd never be able to forget.

"Thank God you're here," came a voice behind us. I glanced over as Eric was getting to his feet. His face washed over with horror as he noticed Rain and Marcello. "I was too late. I tried to save them. Wolfe knocked me out with one of his tools as soon as I entered the room."

"I think Rain handled it okay," Daktari said softly as he began to heal Marcello.

I stepped closer to her and placed my hands gently under her chin, careful not to touch any of her burns. "Rain, you can stop now. It's over."

I wasn't sure she heard me, but then her head jolted up and her brown eyes, consumed with rage, met mine.

Recognition flickered in them, and her anger dissolved. "You came," she mumbled, her voice weak. Her head drooped again, and she burst into tears.

"Daktari, heal her, quickly," I urged.

He moved his hands off of Marcello, whose face was now unmarred, and reached for Rain. Her tears continued to fall, but her wounds miraculously healed before our eyes.

"Eric, their handcuffs," Zi said.

He fumbled with Marcello's wrists first and after a moment, turned to me. "Jabari, you'll have to break them off. Wolfe must have used a special type of restraint. My key isn't working."

A surge of strength burst through me and I snapped off Marcello's restraints to his hands and legs, and Daktari helped him off of the board. I turned to Rain and freed her as well. Her arms fell and she leaned against me and cried as I pulled her into a hug. Beside us, I noticed Marcello wiping his eyes as Zi and Daktari comforted him. I didn't know what to say. Even though their wounds were healed, they looked miserable. "I'm sorry it took so long," I said mournfully.

"At least you're here now," Eric said. "I don't know where Wolfe has his key to these restraints. They might've been stuck here a lot longer if it weren't for you, Jabari."

I didn't say anything. All I could think about was how I'd been prepared to kill Wolfe myself and then Rain had been forced to do it instead. If only I'd gotten here sooner.

"Is he dead?" She choked out the question as she looked up at me.

I surveyed the line of retreating rats and noted the extent of the flesh wounds. The rats, whether Rain had told them to or not, had targeted his wrists and throat. It was a horrific sight, and I turned just enough to shield her from it. Eric stood up from surveying Wolfe's body and nodded at me. "He's gone."

Rain started crying harder, hearing the words. "I'm sorry I killed him, but . . . he said after he killed us he was going to kill our families. And—" She wiped a tear away. "I believed him."

Marcello pulled her away from me and into his embrace. "I believed him, too. You saved us, Rain. Thank you. I'm sorry I couldn't protect you like I promised. You never should have been burned like that, Amiga. I'm so sorry."

Rain shook her head. "Neither one of us could've seen that coming. He knocked you out before we even made it here. It's not your fault. Besides, he burned you just as much."

Zi pushed her way in between them and hugged Rain. "He can't hurt you or anyone. Ever again. Don't you dare forget that."

"I'll try not to." Her eyes were blank as she studied his lifeless form.

"But what are we going to do about him now? The officer, Parker, who left earlier might come back. He tried to help us, but Wolfe kicked him out. What do we do if he comes back?" Rain's voice heightened with alarm. With each moment that passed, she seemed more fragile than before. She was bordering on shock.

"I'll take it from here. Parker was assigned here from one of the other zones recently. He is terrified of Wolfe. He won't say a word after I explain the rat problem this prison has always had," Eric said with a shrug. He placed a hand on Rain's shoulder. "You did the right thing. And a lot of prisoners are going to be better off. He can't hurt them now."

"I didn't know what else to do," she said, her face sorrowful, her hands beginning to shake.

"Come on, let's get out of here. I'll walk you and Marcello to the front and release you. Zi, use the image to get Daktari and Jabari out. I'll make sure Officer Parker and everyone else knows the rats attacked him. They'll think it was a freak accident. Don't worry," Eric said reassuringly.

"Thank you, Eric," I said, patting his back.

He surveyed Rain admiringly. "I'm sorry about what happened to you and Marcello. I really am. But try to concentrate on the fact that a lot of people are going to sleep better tonight because of you."

Rain slumped her shoulders, her eyes growing wider each moment as she studied Wolfe's unmoving body, the blood pouring out around his neck from the fatal wounds. The guilt was killing me. If I'd only been sooner I could have killed him myself and spared her this pain.

She shook her head. "But I—"

"You survived," I blurted, cutting her off, taking her hands in mine.

Her eyes were haunted, dark. "*I couldn't stop. I lost control,*" she spoke to me silently.

"*You did what you had to do. I only wish I could've done it for you.*"

I wanted to comfort her, to tell her everything she needed to hear. Even more, I wanted to run away from the zone this minute, taking Rain and our friends and families with us, never looking back.

Eric cleared his throat. "We need to get going."

She dug her nails into my skin. "*I just killed a man. Again.*"

My heart sped up as I saw her strength fading. "*Everything is going to be fine. Meet me at the school. I'll follow you back under Zi's image. Promise me you'll meet me there.*" I bent down and kissed her firmly and stood back up.

Rain let out a shaky breath, stepping towards Eric and Marcello, doubt in her every move.

"Promise me, Rain," I said aloud.

She held my gaze for a moment. "Promise."

As she moved away, each step creating more distance between us, my chest tightened. Daktari and I huddled beside Zi as she put her image over us, and with one last glance at Wolfe's lifeless form, we left the room. The worries of the past four hours raced over and over in my mind. Maybe I'd been wrong about leading The Freedom Front from within the zone. Maybe we needed to join Gallagher on the outside.

Chapter 10: Shaking

RAIN

My hands wouldn't stop shaking.

In the small space of our basement hideout entrance, I was pacing back and forth, waiting and thinking. Cole had asked me a dozen questions when I'd climbed down the ladder, and somehow I'd calmly explained everything that had happened while he'd hacked into and shut down Metro Prison's camera system. It had been comforting to see his friendly face, complete with his crooked, though charming, grin, his kind blue eyes, and disheveled chin-length blond hair. He'd hugged me close and said the kindest words and then pleaded with me to sit down.

But I couldn't.

Marcello had snuck in through the storm hatch right afterwards, and fortunately, he understood that I needed to pace. Marcello had chosen to sit down with his cousin, and though Cole had agreed to leave me to my private thoughts, I could feel him looking at me now and then, checking on me from the entrance to the room where TFF met. But I kept pacing the dark dusty space below the storm hatch. Part of my brain anxiously trained on Jabari's imminent arrival. Part of my brain just replaying what I'd done.

If I kept moving, maybe no one would notice how badly my hands were vibrating back and forth. Cole was already worried about me, but he really had no idea how much he should be worried. I was worried myself. But I couldn't come up with a cure for my shaking hands.

I shoved them in my jean pockets and I could still feel them shaking. The rational part of my brain was listing reasons my hands should be shaking. Four hours ago, I'd been arrested. I'd been locked up in a cell for an hour and a half, unsure of why I'd been arrested or what was going to happen. I'd almost been shoved into the hole again. My mom had been arrested, hit, and interrogated. Nata had controlled me. I'd almost revealed the truth to her. My mom had almost tasered me. For some reason, Nata was taking the weakest among us away, and that was a mystery I knew I needed to solve. I'd been dragged to Wolfe's sadistic interrogation room only to be burned repeatedly all over my skin. I'd witnessed one of my closest friends undergo the same torture. Even now, the smell of flesh burning haunted my senses. It was understandable that I was a mess.

Especially when I considered the last thing that had happened. I used my ability to summon hordes of rats, and I'd ordered them to kill Officer Wolfe. The rats hadn't come in time to stop the torture. Wolfe had burned Marcello and me both badly before they'd arrived. He'd promised to kill our families after he was finished with us. But he never got the chance. The rats had finally responded to me. And when they'd arrived, I had controlled them so easily. I sent them after Wolfe. He'd tried to run but only made it a few feet from me by the time they were climbing over him.

And I had made them go for the kill.

I'd never felt my power as strongly as I had in that room. Even after I'd known he had to be dead, I hadn't called off the rats. In some sort of wild way, I'd lost part of myself to my power. I hadn't been able to stop. Or maybe I'd been afraid to stop in case he wasn't really dead. It wasn't like when I'd attacked Darryl with brown recluse spiders and he'd ended up dying in a hospital bed. This was different. I'd concentrated on my goal. I'd been determined to kill him. It had been the only solution I'd been able to come up with at the time.

But what didn't make sense in all of this was the reason I knew my hands were shaking so violently. The truth. I was relieved Wolfe was dead. I was glad I'd killed him. And that had to mean something was wrong with me. My hands should've been shaking because I was overcome with shame and guilt for killing a man in cold blood.

But my hands were shaking because I was glad I'd killed him.

What would my friends say if they knew that? How could they even look at me if I told them the truth? I shuddered at the thought. I just had to keep it to myself.

"Rain, are you okay?"

Bhavna's worried voice interrupted my thoughts. I stopped abruptly and sighed with relief. I envisioned her long black hair she got from her Indian mother, Anshula, and the small gap between her teeth. She was always checking in on me with her telepathic ability, and I trusted her completely. She'd become someone I could talk to about anything. *"I'm fine."*

"Sook found me. He said you were in trouble. He saw you and Marcello being burned by one of the guards. What happened? Are you okay?"

"I'm fine. We made it out alive and Daktari healed us."

I couldn't help the train of thoughts that followed. We had made it out alive, but Officer Wolfe hadn't.

Even if I hadn't known Bhavna was reading my every thought, her tone would've given it away. *"Oh, Rain. I'm so sorry that happened to you. You shouldn't have been put in that position. I don't know what to say."*

"There's really nothing to say, I guess. I'm a killer. Again."

"You did what you had to do."

"That's what everyone keeps saying."

"It's true. I wish I could help you. If only you guys could just come here."

"It's not really safe there, is it? You said yourself the UZTA patrols are more frequent now that Nata's searching for Gallagher."

"Yeah, but we're handling it. We protect the camp. My dad has increased our security patrols."

William, Bhavna's Australian born father, had designed the tree houses at their camp that blended into the trees. It was a brilliant place to hide, and I knew he would keep us safe if we joined them, but none of that mattered. We couldn't.

"We can't. It would put you in too much danger."

"Danger? At least we don't have evil guards torturing us in here. You'd be safe, Rain. All of you would be better here, and you know it."

"The thing is, I can't bail on the people in this zone. We have to finish what we started. If we disappear, Nata will unleash real torture on this zone, or worse."

"How did you get picked up by Wolfe in the first place?"

"I guess it was a random search and pickup. They responded to tips from people looking for handouts. Someone said they saw me and Marcello meeting in secret. But we just met alone once, which technically isn't illegal. But The Authority doesn't need a reason to arrest anyone here. I think Nata just wanted any suspicious behavior investigated because two people have gone missing from this zone in the past six months. First Amal, then one of her guards, Officer Dean."

"You can get arrested for anything there. Another reason you'd be safer with us."

"I know. But you know we can't leave. Listen, Nata was here today, and—"

"Nata was there? You saw her?"

"It's fine, she left. Gallagher did something to pull her away from us. But when she was here she took two people with her. They were in pretty bad shape and she said she wanted them because they were so weak. I'm not sure what she's up to, but I think we need to figure out where she's taking them and what she's doing with them. So, could you ask Sook to try to look into it when he can? Maybe he'll see where she's taking them or something. I don't know if we can help them, but it's worth investigating."

"Okay." Her voice was full of anxiety and I could imagine her forehead wrinkling in concern.

"Are you okay? Has something happened at your camp?"

"I'm fine. I'm worried about you, Rain."

"You're a good friend. But don't worry about me. You should worry about the people who get in my way."

"Rain, like I said, you did what you needed to do."

"Yeah, but I lost it a little back there. It was like I didn't want to stop hurting him. I've never wanted to kill someone like that. What kind of person am I? What would Jabari say if he knew? Or Daktari? Zi?"

"They'd say you are strong and you are a survivor."

"My hands won't stop shaking ever since it happened."

"Understandably, Rain. Are you kidding me? Of course, they are shaking."

"You don't understand. They aren't shaking because I'm ashamed of what I did or because I feel so guilty like last time. It's because I have this adrenaline still rushing through me. I wanted him dead, and I just did it. I killed him, Bhavna. Like it was nothing. And afterwards? I felt relieved. I was glad I did it. My hands are shaking because I'm just beginning to understand how terrible I am. I shouldn't feel glad he's dead. But I do. And I can't tell anyone else."

"Of course you can tell them. They'd understand, Rain. I understand. He was burning your skin. He tortured you once before. This is the same guard who hurts people all the time. Why wouldn't you want him dead?"

"Wanting him dead and killing him are two different things."

"But what were you supposed to do? I'm glad you killed him, Rain. I don't know what I'd do without you. If it weren't for you, Daktari never would've healed Nipa. I wouldn't have a sister. So listen to me, you do what you have to do to survive and let go of the rest. Kiss that hot boyfriend of yours or something. Just be happy you're alive still. I'd kiss Jabari if it were me. And you can take your pick. If you were here, Blakely would kiss you. You're strong, you're a survivor, and guys just fall at your feet. Seriously, you should feel pretty good about yourself right now."

"Thanks for trying to cheer me up."

"Trying? You mean it didn't work?" she teased.

I glanced at my hands, still shaking, and tried to smile but couldn't. *"It worked a little."*

Light spilled in above me, and I tilted my head up as Daktari, Zi, and Jabari were entering the hatch under Zi's image. Daktari hurried down the ladder first and picked me up so my feet were dangling, hugging me tightly. He didn't utter a word; just hugged me close. He must have been terrified that I wouldn't escape from Wolfe.

Bhavna entered my mind one last time. *"Be careful, friend. And don't forget, you're always welcome here if you change your mind."*

"Okay, Bhavna, thanks. Tell everyone I said hi."

"I'll check in with you soon."

A hand pulled at my waist. "Put her down already. I want to hug her too," Zi ordered.

Daktari set me down and gently grabbed my shoulders. "I didn't want to say anything back there in the prison, Rain, because I just wanted us all to get out of there safely. But the entire time you were in there, well . . . I've *never* been so scared. Even when they moved us to this hellhole. Thanks for being a fighter. You saved yourself before we could even get to you."

"Who knows what would have happened if you hadn't shown up. Thanks for coming for us," I said sincerely.

Daktari kissed my forehead. "I'm sorry about what he did to you guys."

Zi pushed her way into my arms and squeezed me. "Me too, Rain. I'm sorry. I hate it that this kind of thing always happens to you. I wish it had been me."

"I'm glad it wasn't you," I whispered, hugging her and closing my eyes. When I opened them, Jabari was standing behind Zi, gazing at me worriedly. I let go of Zi as he approached, vaguely aware of Daktari and Zi continuing on towards the meeting room.

I held up my hands; they were still shaking. In the dim tunnel, he looked from my hands to my eyes, understanding dawning. He might not have known why I was really shaking so badly, but it didn't matter. He knew what I needed.

He closed the distance between us and pulled me into an embrace. After a few seconds, he pushed me back a little and took my trembling hands in his own. He covered one on top of the other, stroking the tops of my hands with his thumbs.

We watched one another in the obscure space, unspoken messages passing between us. Slowly but surely, sparks ignited in my stomach and I withdrew my hands from his and pressed them against his solid chest. He bent down, found my lips, and kissed me softly, over and over.

After a few moments, he leaned back and trailed a finger along my jawline. "There's so much I want to say after everything that just happened. But the most important thing I need right now is to know how to help you. Are you okay?"

I pulled my hands from his chest and examined them briefly. I offered him a small smile. "My hands aren't shaking anymore."

Relief washed over his face and he nodded, taking my hands in his again. Just like always, he'd fixed me.

Chapter 11: Warnings

RAIN

Two days had passed since my release from Metro Prison. I'd been on pins and needles, looking over my shoulder, anticipating another arrest.

No one else was worried about what I'd done. Eric had told Jabari that Officer Wolfe's death had been blamed on the rat infestation alone, so we were free and clear of being brought in as suspects. According to Eric, there were no witnesses, thanks to Cole. He had caused a fifteen-minute blackout of the cameras after Nata had left the building, and during those fifteen minutes everything had gone down. The prison had brought in a special extermination team to kill the rats. They hadn't had a choice. They couldn't risk letting another officer get attacked, or so they thought. They had no idea that a seventeen-year-old girl was the real culprit. I really hoped Eric was right. I just couldn't get arrested again. I felt certain I had a role to play in the weeks ahead and that it wasn't within the confines of a prison cell.

As more time passed, I began to relax a little, but I was still a bit paranoid, even imagining that Nata herself might show up at any moment and arrest me for killing one of her officers. Daktari told me it was probably natural that I felt so on edge, and I had agreed with him. But I still hadn't let him know the truth. That I didn't feel upset about what had happened to Wolfe.

I'd gradually accepted the truth myself. I was glad that Wolfe couldn't torment prisoners anymore. But I felt guilty at the same time. I'd killed a man and wasn't feeling remorse. I was more worried about getting caught than about what I'd done.

I had other things on my mind as well. What was Nata planning to do with the two prisoners she had taken because she considered them weak? Also, my abilities were getting stronger somehow. Not only had I witnessed it with the rats, I could feel it when I ran. I was clearly more powerful than before.

Meanwhile, Jabari and the rest of TFF were anxious to know what Gallagher had done to draw Nata away from our zone the other day. Gallagher had been vague during our Pinkie conversations ever since, and had only assured us that Nata was looking for him more now than ever. According to him, he'd made her so angry she would only be focused on finding him for the moment, concentrating all of her resources on the hunt for UZTA's most wanted fugitive.

I'd used my telepathy to talk to Niyol once since my arrest, and he'd told me he was proud of me for being so strong. He probably knew how I felt about Wolfe. He'd told me I had done what was necessary to survive and told me my skills would serve me well in the weeks ahead. As usual, he'd been vague and hadn't elaborated about the weeks ahead or my role in them. Before ending our conversation he'd told me to trust my instincts, just like he always did.

But my instincts were telling me something was lurking around the corner. Maybe it had to do with Nata taking the prisoners. Maybe it had to do with the way she'd looked around the room when I had accidently used my telepathy and said her real name. Or maybe it was simply the fact that Nata had interrogated my mother and me.

On the bright side, Mom, though still fragile in so many ways, was somehow improving. I'd gone to Mom and Dad's bedroom about half an hour ago and kissed them goodnight. Mom had hugged me close and told me how much she loved me. Slowly but surely, Mom was coming around and resembling the mom I once knew. She was still very quiet, and rarely spoke, but when she did, she wasn't as hopeless as before. I drew strength from it, knowing that if Mom could start to show signs of hope after everything she'd been through, I had to stay positive.

Because of the fresh layer of ice lining the streets and our apartment windows, Daktari and I still had our twin beds pushed together and were sleeping back to back in an attempt to stay a little warmer while we slept. He'd fallen asleep a while ago. I could tell when his breathing had finally steadied.

Gradually, my racing mind began to slow, and I finally drifted off. I succumbed to sleep and entered a beautiful dream. It was winter time, but for once I wasn't cold. I was standing in the interior of my grand-mother's kitchen, and though I could see snow outside her windows, the heat was making her house nice and cozy.

Maha strolled across the kitchen floor. It filled me with joy to see her out of prison and looking so healthy and happy. She smiled at me and held up something in her arms. "Come closer, Rain. See what you did? You saved her. You saved us. You did this."

I peeked over the blanket, at the baby swaddled in her arms. Her baby girl peered up at me, with brown eyes like Maha's, and some-how reminding me of Anthony, her father. I looked at Maha tenderly. I started to tell her that it wasn't all me, and I couldn't take the credit, when a hand dug into my shoulder.

I screamed out in pain and was abruptly spun around. Nata was peer-ing into my eyes; her hands were digging into my shoulders like they were claws. Blood was pouring down my arms. As the blood gushed everywhere I envisioned Wolfe's body as he died. I tried to step away from Nata and tell Maha to run, but I was frozen in place. Nata's mur-derous eyes held my gaze. "You did this, One-two-seven-six. This is all your fault."

Instantly, the temperature around me dropped, and I was freezing. A moment later, Nata disappeared. I turned around, searching for Maha and her baby, but they were gone. The room had changed. I was stand-ing in some sort of prison again, similar to Metro Prison, but different.

There were bars, revealing prison cells lining one wall. Strangely enough, all of the cells were empty. But there were guards in the center of a huge room that reminded me of an interrogation room. Only they weren't just any guards. Their uniforms and the soulless look in their eyes told me they were EEG officers.

I took a small step backwards, and one of them pointed at me. "Get her!" he shouted.

I turned to run towards an open door but only got a few feet before prisoners started filing through the doorway, blocking my escape. In front was Maha, her belly swollen with her pregnancy.

Her eyes met mine. "Rain, please, you promised you would save me. Please, Rain, help!"

Slowly, the room began to darken. I tried to move towards her but couldn't. Something was holding my ankles in place, but I couldn't see what it was in the sudden darkness. One of the guards grabbed Maha and pulled her towards the prison cells. She screamed over her shoulder, "Rain, please! Save us!"

"Rain?" A voice I'd recognize anywhere spoke softly from the doorway, just a few feet from me.

My stomach dropped as I realized she'd been captured. Our eyes locked and I searched for words. But the only thing I could do was say her name. "Grandma Julia."

She smiled at me as tears ran down my face. "It's going to be fine, Rain. Stay strong."

The guards took hold of Grandma and pushed her, along with the others, into a prison cell. Rage filled me, and I kicked at whatever was holding my feet captive. "No! Let me go!" I yelled at the top of my lungs.

I bent down and reached for whatever was holding my ankles. Light spilled into the space, illuminating heavy chains, shackling my ankles to a heavy object. A wave of fear swooshed through my body. The cold dead eyes of Officer Wolfe stared up at me. He wasn't gnawed apart and bloody, like when I'd left him at Metro Prison, but he was dead. Somehow, I'd been chained to his body.

"Help!" I screamed.

Nata's laughter echoed through the room, as if she was all around me, but I couldn't see her.

"No!" I yelled louder, kicking the chains to no avail. I was stuck, trapped, chained to the man I'd murdered.

"You did this," Nata's voice called out from somewhere.

And then, like he'd done so often in reality, the great horned owl flew around me, appearing out of a funnel cloud. He swooped in front of me and effortlessly freed me from my chains. Behind him, Jabari, Daktari, everyone from TFF, Gallagher, and Lieutenant Moretti were releasing the prisoners and capturing the EEG officers.

I took off through the doorway running after them as they emptied the room. The owl flew circles around me, then transformed into Niyol.

He hurried to my side. "You have to stop this," he insisted.

He took my hand and placed an object in it. I turned it over in my hands and looked at it carefully. A pack of matches. The next moment I was running from the building behind me with Niyol flying overhead again in the shape of the owl, and the matchbook was gone. But behind me, the building, one I'd never seen before but knew I'd just been inside of, was burning to the ground.

I'd started a fire.

Maha hugged me as close as she could with her protruding belly, and tears streaked her face. "You did it, Rain. You saved me."

A moment later a scream rang out from the burning building behind us. A chill ran down my back. I'd saved Maha but someone had been trapped and left behind in the burning building. And it was a woman. What had I done? I tried to search the faces around me to make sure Grandma had made it out alive, but everything blurred as smoke filled my nostrils. The air around me became toxic, so cloudy I couldn't see anything. The scream sounded again and this time I joined in, screaming at the top of my lungs until I was choking on the fumes. What had I done?

"Rain, wake up." Daktari shook me lightly, but his voice was frantic.

I opened my eyes. Through the dim light from his solar flashlight I noted his concerned expression. I wiped at the tears streaking my face.

"What happened in your dream?" he asked, his face so serious I knew I couldn't lie to him.

I forced myself to sit up. "I think Maha's in trouble. And maybe Grandma Julia."

Daktari tensed, and then bobbed his head once as if telling himself it was just a dream. He picked up a cup of water he'd stashed near the bed and made me take a drink. I sipped at the water feeling a little better.

Daktari set the glass back down and took my hand in his. "Now tell me everything that happened."

Chapter 12: Interpreting Dreams

RAIN

The air was so cold it hurt my face. But I was nearly to my destination, and though it wasn't heated, it would be slightly warmer than the outside temperature. As I approached Zachary's Market, I took cautious steps across the icy sidewalk. Daktari and Zi had gone ahead of me and through the back entrance today. I was taking the front.

With all of TFF entering the market within a ten-minute period for our secret meeting in the basement with Takara, we'd grown accustomed to sneaking in the back and the front, trying to go unnoticed as much as possible by any random onlookers. But no one was really paying attention. Since it was late afternoon, most of the adults in our zone, with the exception of the elderly, would still be at work. The blinds had been pulled up three quarters of the way, indicating our meeting was still on. I climbed the steps carefully and once inside the market, was instantly grateful for the small increase in temperature.

Zachary looked up from behind the counter and gave me a friendly smile. "Hi Rain."

"Hi Zachary."

"I was worried when I heard about—" He paused, glancing around. We had no evidence of The Authority recording our conversations, but we still had a level of paranoia about discussing anything in public. "I'm glad you guys are okay," he finished softly.

Even before TFF had formed, Zachary had allowed Takara to meet with us and teach us school lessons in the basement of his market, which was technically property of The Authority. Every time he let us meet in his basement for over four years now, he'd risked imprisonment. Takara said it was Zachary's way of getting back at The Authority. They'd taken his wife from him during New Segregation. I wished I could tell him that she might still be alive and if we pulled off our plan, he could even be reunited with her eventually. But I didn't.

"Thanks, Zachary."

He nodded, and turned back to the counter he was wiping down with a cloth, acting completely oblivious to the fact I was walking right past him to head to a secret meeting in his basement. Maybe he wasn't part of the plan to capture Nata and take her out of power, but what he was doing was extremely courageous. I really hoped the day would come when he would be free again, too.

I turned towards the basement steps and nearly collided with a figure breezing past me. One glance at her shoulder-length wavy black hair and olive-tone skin and I recognized my former foe. "Hi," I said cheerfully.

She kept moving as though she hadn't seen me, and I pushed my way in front, gently stopping her with my hands. "Hi Aleela," I said warmly.

I couldn't believe how much our relationship had changed since I'd taught her a few things about cooking and Takara had set her up with a job off the books at Zachary's Market. He let her help him out in exchange for food to feed her and her Mom. Aleela stared at me blankly, and I became worried.

"Are you okay?" I asked.

She kept staring, like she was in a daze or something. "I'm fine," she finally said, and turned away. I peered into the market and watched her heading to the exit.

"Don't forget your groceries, Aleela," Zachary called to her, handing her a small bag as she passed him.

She shook her head absently, as though she was disoriented or something and exited the market. Zachary and I exchanged looks, and he shrugged. As I made my way down the basement steps, her odd behavior had me concerned.

Jabari greeted me as soon as I stepped into the room. "Hey," he said, pulling me into a quick hug. "Are you all right? I've been worried about you ever since last night."

This morning, I'd decided to use my telepathy on him to let him know about my nightmare, but I hadn't needed to. Like had happened so many times before, I had somehow pulled Jabari into my dream and he'd seen the entire thing. This morning, he'd been so relieved to hear my voice in his head. He'd been worried about me ever since my nightmare had gotten to him.

I pulled back and narrowed my eyes. "You're always worried about me, what are you talking about?" I said teasingly.

He smiled. "True. But still. It was so vivid. You sure you're okay?" He raised a brow at me. "Maybe you need help forgetting about your problems?" he teased, running a finger over my bottom lip playfully.

I wanted to push Aleela's behavior out of my mind and concentrate on the present, my hot fiancé smiling at me, but I couldn't let it go. "Before you go distracting me . . . Did you see Aleela?"

Jabari frowned; he started to say something but then didn't.

"She was acting really weird," I blurted. As suspicions started running through my mind, my worries took off. She had after all been a paid spy for The Authority before we'd turned her to our side. What if she was going back to her old ways?

"Jabari, what if she's changed her mind?"

He shook his head, and bent lower, inches from my ear, and whispered, "That's not it. I promise. I have something to talk to you about. Can it wait until we run tonight?"

Takara took her place on a box top, propped her walking cane beside her, preparing to start the meeting. I really didn't have a choice. I leaned back and stared at him. Clearly, he had something important to tell me.

"Okay, if you're sure she's not turning us in right now . . ."

"I'm sure," he said definitely. He pulled my hand and guided me to the circle, where I sat down beside him and Marcello.

"How's it going, Superwoman?" Marcello teased as I sat down.

"Glad to be out of Metro. You?"

"My thoughts exactly, Amiga." He leaned closer. "In case I haven't said it enough, thanks again for saving my butt. I can't believe I let them knock me out like that. We would've been screwed if it weren't for you."

I grabbed his hand. I'd tried to tell him this already. I knew he was struggling with guilt. He felt bad about what happened, but it wasn't his fault. "Marcello, like I said before, you didn't know that would happen. And if it weren't for you, I'd have been in trouble back in the cell with that man. You saved me, remember?"

He sighed. "If you say so."

"I do." I forced a smile. I needed him to be normal. If my dream was giving us facts again, we had a battle ahead we hadn't planned for, and everyone needed to be on top of their game.

"I still say I owe you. Maybe I can pay you back eventually. Jabari filled Cole and me in on your nightmare from last night. Guess we have stormy weather ahead, huh?"

I sighed. As appreciative as I was of the fact that no one doubted my ability to receive clues in my strange dreams anymore, it was still unsettling. We never knew how much of the dream was actually real. "Looks like it."

Takara called the meeting to order. She looked around our circle, and her gentle green eyes settled on me. "I guess you all know about Rain's nightmare from last night."

Everyone nodded. I'd told Zi in person. Jabari had told Marcello and Cole, and I'd used my telepathy on Takara, too. I knew she'd be able to ask Eric about Maha or snoop around a little at work.

Takara continued. "Rainchild. I asked Eric to check on Maha for me like you suggested, and this morning, according to him, she was fine and he hadn't heard anything about her being transported anywhere. Was Sook able to see anything?"

I hadn't needed to contact Bhavna. She'd reached out to me on my morning commute because Sook hadn't been able to discover anything about the weak prisoners who Nata had taken from Metro Prison the other day. I'd informed her about my suspicions from my dream, and she'd promised to have Sook look in on my grandma and Maha. "I haven't heard back from Bhavna yet."

"Okay, well listen, children. We'll ask around, keep our eyes and ears open, and make sure we follow this through. If Maha is in trouble, or Grandma Julia, we'll do what we can to help."

"If Eric hears anything, he'll tell us," Jabari added.

"True. He's one hundred percent on our side," Takara agreed.

"The thing that's bothering me is I feel there's a connection between my nightmare and the prisoners who were taken the other day. But then how does Maha fit in? She's pretty strong, considering everything, right? She's not the weakest prisoner. I don't know. Maybe I'm wrong. Grandma was in the nightmare, too. And she isn't even near this place. And in the dream, they were in a strange building, like a prison, with an interrogation room and all, but the guards were all EEG guards. How would that relate to Grandma and Maha?"

"And you say that we rescued them with Gallagher and Moretti in your nightmare?" asked Cole.

"Yeah, we got them out of there and Niyol was there and somehow we burned down the building. But someone was still in there. And—" my voice wavered. "And I don't know who got left behind."

"Don't go jumping to conclusions, sis. Your dreams and nightmares are accurate and have told us many things ahead of time, but they have never happened precisely the way they do in your dreams. They are just similar," Daktari reminded me.

"I know. I just have a weird feeling, that's all. Maha seemed so real. She was in danger and she was depending on me. If something happens to her, I'll never forgive myself. I promised her we'd get her out of that prison before something else terrible could happen to her."

"What if we're looking at this the wrong way?" began Marcello. "What if this is a warning that we need to rescue Maha ourselves directly from Metro Prison?"

Jabari tilted his head. "I thought about that, too. It could be our chance to move her now, before something happens to her." He looked at Takara. "What do you think, Takara?"

Takara closed her eyes briefly, inhaled and exhaled, before looking at us again. "That might be the case. But until we feel very sure that is the course of action for you, I want to wait. The one thing I have a feeling about is that you all need to continue to work together. I've really been sensing lately that your togetherness is key to your success." Her eyes settled on me, then Jabari. "I've also been getting the feeling that some of you are strengthening . . . tremendously with your abilities."

"Rain definitely is," Marcello blurted. "You should have seen her in Metro with the rats."

I blushed, recalling the relief I'd felt after killing Wolfe.

"Don't be shy, Superwoman. Admit it, you're getting stronger," said Cole.

"I've noticed it. It's true. I'm running faster, too. I just hope it can help us somehow. Is anyone else stronger?" I glanced around the room. Zi was staring off to the side, deep in thought, which made me wonder if she was strengthening, but then the expression on Jabari's face drew all of my curiosity. Takara was staring at him as well.

"Jabari?" I asked.

He shrugged, obviously not interested in talking about it. "Yeah, I didn't want to mention it, but I've gotten stronger. My strength has doubled lately. I scaled the side of the high school and got to the roof in ten seconds the other day."

"What?" Zi's mouth dropped open a little.

Jabari shrugged again. "I saw Niyol as the owl on top of the building. The day Rain and Marcello were arrested. He wanted to warn me to wait until Nata was gone before I went into the prison. He said he was worried I was going to barge in before she left. He said that even though I'm getting stronger, I'm not strong enough . . . yet . . . to take on Nata."

Jabari had already told me about Niyol's visit, but I'd forgotten to mention it to Zi. But he hadn't mentioned his strength. Maybe that was what he was planning to talk to me about later.

"My abilities seem the same, I think," Daktari said.

"Well, you just never know," Takara threw in.

"Yeah, besides, there's something else I've noticed. Sometimes, my abilities seem strong and other times weak. Like my telepathy. It's strange. Sometimes, I can really hear the other person, and other times, they sound so distant," I offered.

"I have a feeling you're all somehow stronger when you're working *together*. Just keep that in mind, children. Another thing I'm wondering about. We still don't know what Gallagher did to draw Nata away from here. But whenever you talk to him again, it might be wise to warn him to look out for the repercussions. Surely, Nata will somehow retaliate or react to whatever he did. And also, before we leave, I wanted to mention Niyol again, Rain. Maybe you could talk to him about the prisoners Nata took with her. Maybe he can discover something."

"I already mentioned it to him. But I haven't been able to reach him for a few days. I guess he can't hear me or maybe he's busy."

Feet jogging down the steps drew our attention. My thoughts went to the worst place, and I thought of Aleela and wondered if she'd turned us in. But to my relief, as I peered over my shoulder, I saw the feet belonged to Kelly, who we'd recently allowed into our circle of trust. Her brother, Anthony, had been assigned to work overtime when his girlfriend, Maha, had been thrown into prison. We were practically the only family Kelly had. Since helping her get her violin to our basement hideout, we'd allowed her to come there to practice, since music wasn't allowed in our zone. Before New Segregation, she'd been preparing for music school.

Kelly scrambled over and collapsed on her knees, her wavy light-brown hair fell forward with the motion. She took a deep breath then tilted her head back and scooted in between Marcello and me. She was breathing fast, as if she'd run the whole way to the market, and she looked like she might burst into tears at any moment.

"What is it, Kelly?" Takara asked.

"I just came from Metro Prison. I tried to visit Maha, like you suggested, Takara, but they wouldn't let me see her. Then Eric pulled me aside when I was leaving. He said I had to find you to tell you—" She swallowed, and her lip began to quiver.

"What is it?" I asked, now on full alert.

"They've taken Maha and some other prisoners to a holding cell. Tomorrow morning at ten, they are taking them away to EEG headquarters."

"Why?" demanded Zi.

The tears Kelly had been trying to contain began to fall. "I don't know, but I know about what the EEG officer did to Rain and Daktari's mom. Do you think they plan to torture Maha? She's pregnant. What about her baby? How could they select her?"

I cringed as realization hit me. Everything Officer Dean had told me about EEG training came rushing back. "That's where Nata must have taken the other weak prisoners. She uses them to train the EEG candidates. She doesn't take anyone who can still work. Like she said the other day, if we are strong enough to do labor for her, she needs us. But the weakest among us she can spare. That's what my dream meant," I said. I stroked Kelly's hair. "But don't worry, Kelly. We'll rescue Maha before the EEG officers can hurt her."

Kelly looked up at me hopefully. "Could you really save her?"

"Well, we have to," I said in a rush.

"I agree with Rain. But how does Grandma fit into it?" Daktari asked.

"I don't know. Maybe she does. Hopefully, she doesn't. You said a minute ago, my dreams aren't precise. And it isn't just that I promised Maha we would keep her safe and rescue her before her baby was born. I believe this dream was telling me the time has come. My gut tells me either way, regardless of whether or not Grandma Julia is involved, we need to save Maha. Tomorrow."

"Where will you take Maha? And the other prisoners?" Kelly asked.

"I'll ask Gallagher if he can take them. I'm sure he will," Jabari said, reassuringly.

"She'll be much safer with Gallagher," Cole offered.

"Even if he's UZTA's most wanted fugitive, he's got the perfect hide-out," Marcello added.

"But what about tonight? Why don't we just bust her out of Metro Prison?" asked Zi.

Even as I started to answer Jabari was shaking his head. "I saw Rain's nightmare. I think we need to rescue them from the EEG headquarters."

"Why? Oh . . . because Nata would come here looking for answers if prisoners disappeared again?" Zi asked.

"It's not just that, Zi. We need to see where they're being taken because we're supposed to capture the guards," I said decisively.

Marcello grinned. "Looks like we'd better get to work."

"You'll need to contact Gallagher this afternoon. You'll have to work out a plan with him. It will be dangerous, going on a last minute mission like this. But I think you are up for it," Takara said optimistically.

"We'll be careful," Jabari said.

"I know. You'd better get going. Peace be with you, children." Takara ended our meeting in her usual farewell.

"And with you," we replied.

As we stood up, Zi furrowed her brow. "One more question. How do we know Nata won't just recruit new men to train for EEG positions right away?"

"Well, she might. But she won't have a place to train them at first," Jabari said, eyeing me.

"And why not, Rain?" Zi prompted.

"Well, I know my dreams aren't precise, but do you remember what I told you about my dream and what Niyol handed me in it?"

Zi paled as she remembered the matches and the fire. "Oh, right. As long as you're sure there won't be a woman left behind screaming like in your dream."

Kelly, the only one who hadn't heard about my nightmare yet, seemed understandably confused. "What are you guys talking about? Why won't there be a place for them to train new recruits?"

"We're going to burn down the building," I replied. As I spoke the words, adrenaline sped through my veins.

I couldn't wait to burn down Nata's EEG training center.

Chapter 13: Confessions

RAIN

The ice had made running a challenge, to say the least, but Jabari had kept up with me, and neither one of us had fallen down. Though at one point, we'd both slid across a patch of ice and run into a streetlight post. And eventually, we ended up at the isolated stretch of concrete where Daktari, Zi, and I had spent many afternoons kicking a soccer ball around during the first few years of our arrival to the Indy Mixed Zone.

The temperature was so low, I sat with my back pressed against Jabari's stomach, and he had his long legs perched up on either side of mine with his arms around me. We couldn't stay out long in these temperatures, even though we wore stocking caps and gloves, and the run had warmed us up some. We'd have to head back home soon in order to beat curfew.

But though neither one of us were saying it, we were both a little on edge. I assumed Jabari was thinking about tomorrow's rescue mission. I was too, but I was mostly concerned about Grandma Julia. I couldn't figure out how she was connected to my dream and tomorrow's mission. Maybe she had just randomly been in my dream. Or maybe it had been a warning. Plus, the woman screaming at the end of my dream had me worried. Had it been Grandma, and was she somehow involved?

I didn't necessarily want to voice my concerns. Either way, we were going on a mission in the morning. I'd watched from our basement hideout as Jabari and Marcello had used the Pinkie messengers to plot with Gallagher after meeting with Takara. I didn't know every detail on

Gallagher's end, but Jabari assured me everything was set. I just hoped that my grandma was safe.

Jabari ran his gloved hand over one of mine. "What's bothering you the most?"

I couldn't help the small laugh that escaped. "You think something's bothering me?"

He bent his face lower, kissing my cheek lightly. "Well, I know you're ready for tomorrow, but still. I can sense your worry, Rain. Talk to me."

"It *is* one of your abilities . . . sensing trouble."

He tensed, and that made me wonder about what he'd wanted to talk to me about earlier. He still hadn't brought it up. Was it just that his strength was more powerful or did he have something else to tell me?

"It is."

Apparently, I needed to talk first. "Okay, so I'm worried about Grandma Julia. She's never in my nightmares like she was last night."

"Do you think we should make a trip to see her? It's the only way we can check in on her unless, of course, you want to try your telepathy on her. I understand why you don't want to use it on Calista. It could compromise her cover and the role she's playing with Nata. But Grandma Julia is alone."

"I know, but what if she really is in trouble, and I use my telepathy on her and it gets her into more trouble?" I scooted around so I could face him. "I didn't want to say this in front of the others, but I was thinking about what Sook said. You know, when he said Calista had sworn an oath to Nata and that she vowed to hurt her ex-family in the mixed zone. Well, he said he also saw photographs of Grandma Julia, Uncle Michael, and Aunt Alyssa on the table during that conversation. Obviously, when Nata was here either she didn't realize that she had two of Calista's relatives in custody since we are only numbers to her *or* she didn't care about it because like Sook said, Calista promised she would hurt us . . . eventually. But the thing I'm wondering is, how does

Nata feel about Grandma Julia? They know she used to e-mail Daktari and me before they took that privilege away from us. So they know Grandma loves us. To Nata, that would be considered traitorous. What if Nata wants Calista to do something to Grandma to prove her loyalty to the new pure race? I mean, I know Calista couldn't hurt Grandma, but Nata could."

I studied Jabari for his reaction, but his face remained blank. "Am I just too paranoid?"

"No. You could be right. There's no telling how far Nata will go to hurt people and we really have no idea what she's making Calista do. All we know is what Sook saw. He really felt strongly about how Calista would betray her family. I know she wouldn't betray you. But what if Nata could somehow be using the families of her new pure zone citizens against them to control them somehow? I think maybe we should go see Grandma Julia after tomorrow."

"That would make me feel better. Seeing her in person. Maybe then I could talk to her about my telepathy and try it out if I think she's safe. I don't know. None of this dream interpreting stuff is easy. For months I thought I was going to betray TFF, and then Sook said it was Calista who would betray us, and then look what happened . . . Marcello and I got arrested because one of his random neighbors saw us together and accused us of being a couple. I wish my dreams were easier to interpret. And I wish I didn't drag you into them so much. You know how bizarre and twisted they can be."

"Some of your dreams are really nice," he pointed out with a sly grin.

"Well, at least you don't only see the bad stuff."

"Your dreams, the good and the bad, are part of the gift you've been given. It's pretty amazing actually." He brought the top of my hand to his lips, kissing it once. "*You* are amazing."

"There you go being all charming again. Don't distract me. You wanted to tell me something earlier, right?"

"Yeah. I mean, kind of," he began. "But that can wait a minute. Let's talk about you and Marcello being a couple, first. Has he tried anything since your date?" he asked with a teasing grin.

I kept a blank expression. "And if he did?"

Jabari scowled. "Not the answer I was looking for."

My mouth curved upward. "Of course he hasn't tried anything. And he was just trying to get under Zi's skin, as you should recall, when he said we'd been on a date. And, as you know, he is in love with my cousin, plus, he knows I'm madly in love with my *fiancé*."

Jabari grinned. "Better."

"I could think of something even better than that."

In response, he leaned down an inch, meeting my mouth with his own. His kiss caused butterflies in my stomach and had me leaning in closer, trying to rid the small gap between us. He lifted me up and onto his leg, so there was no space between us, and he wrapped his arms around my back. He kissed me urgently, making me forget my worries. Everything felt right when we were together. Nothing else mattered.

"*Rain?*"

I flinched automatically, sighing loudly. "Bhavna," I said aloud. I tried, but failed, not to sound disappointed.

Bhavna laughed. "*Bad time, I guess?*"

Jabari raised a brow, but nodded once, understanding what was happening.

"*Never a bad time for you.*"

"*Um, the thoughts I was reading a moment ago would suggest otherwise.*"

"*Bhavna,*" I warned.

"*I'd kiss him too if I were you. You only live once, right?*"

"*Uh-huh. Did you talk to Sook?*"

"*Yes. And I wanted to let you know . . .*" Her words, clearly strained, trailed off.

"*What did he see?*" I prompted.

"He said he saw Maha in a prison cell, and that she's crying. She's nervous and doesn't know why they moved her. Sook said it looks like they put her in a new cell and that's all he saw."

"Yeah, we heard that much. They're moving her out of the zone tomorrow to EEG headquarters. Eric found out. She's probably a mess because she has no idea what's happening to her. I didn't want to contact her though just in case Nata were to show up and question her before our plans to rescue her."

"What do you guys have in mind?" I filled her in quickly so she could be up to date with our plans.

"Wow, well be careful."

"We will. What about my grandma? Did Sook see anything?"

"Yeah, well he finally got an image of her, but he said she seems fine."

Relief filled my chest. I couldn't handle Grandma being in trouble. "Good."

"Yeah, he said she was cooking a big meal in her kitchen. She looked fine to him."

"Okay, thanks, Bhavna."

"I'll check in with you tomorrow, but be careful, okay?"

"We will."

When she was gone, I let Jabari know what she'd said. "Well at least Grandma Julia looks okay, right?" he asked.

"Yeah," I said indecisively. Something was still bugging me.

"What is it?"

"It's just that Bhavna said she was cooking a big meal. Kind of weird, right? She lives alone."

"Maybe she was cooking for some friends or neighbors? You know how she likes to help others out. And speaking from experience, her cooking is amazing."

"True. Oh well, at least she was okay. That's the most important thing, I guess. And I hate that Maha is so scared and I can't offer her any comfort. I really hope Gallagher comes through with his support tomorrow."

"Don't worry, we'll be okay either way."

"That's kind of why I hope he shows up. I get it now. I understand what I can do, and that I can do some terrible stuff with my growing abilities. But I don't want to have to cross the line like that again."

Jabari searched my eyes. "It's okay . . . what you did to Officer Wolfe. You didn't have a choice. I wanted to save you from that. But I didn't get there in time. I know it haunts you."

"Afterwards, my hands were shaking so violently."

"I remember. They were still shaking when I met you in the hideout. Perfectly normal response, I would imagine."

"Not because I was upset about what I'd done."

At Jabari's confused expression I hesitated. Should I tell him the truth? Would he love me less? When I didn't go on, he prompted me. "Why were they shaking then?"

"I probably shouldn't tell you this. You're so good . . . but I feel like I never want to keep anything from you."

"Rain, you can tell me anything."

"Well . . . my hands were shaking because I was glad I killed him."

I waited for Jabari to react. To jump to his feet or shake his head or tell me it wasn't true. But he just studied me somberly.

After a few seconds, I sunk my head. "I know. I'm awful. I was so glad he died. I just kept thinking how he couldn't hurt anyone anymore. He couldn't threaten my family and friends. He couldn't do anything. Because I had killed him. The worst part is, I'm starting to think I'm like Nata. She's the kind of person who would be happy she killed someone. And now, I'm like her."

Jabari squeezed my hand. "No, you're not. He hurt you. He burned you. He threatened everyone you love. And I didn't make it in time to save you. You didn't have a choice and it doesn't matter how you felt afterwards. Of course you were glad he was gone."

"This is the second time I have been responsible for taking a man's life. The first time, I felt so guilty I could hardly look at myself. This time, I felt guilty for a different reason. Because I was happy about what I did. What kind of person have I become?"

"You've always been strong and brave. And now you've just evolved to the point that you know what you have to do to survive. Everything you do, you do for our freedom and the freedom of so many others. Don't forget that."

"So you don't think less of me?"

He shook his head side to side. "Are you kidding? Of course not. If you hadn't done what you did, you guys might not have made it out of there. I couldn't save you. I wasn't fast enough. I never would have forgiven myself. It's embarrassing, yes, that I couldn't rescue you in your time of need, but it's also amazing that my fiancée is so powerful she can handle herself against any obstacle."

"Okay, don't make me sound so great."

"I think what I have to tell you now might make you feel better."

"I doubt that."

"I discovered something recently, and I didn't want to tell you, and I haven't told anyone, but I think Takara suspects it. Niyol knows. That's one of the reasons he came to talk to me the other day. He said not to worry about it, but it's hard."

"What is it?"

"You know how Aleela was acting a little out of it earlier?"

"Yeah, it was like she didn't even recognize me. Like she'd been stunned . . . kind of like how Nata pushes people with her ability." My jaw fell open slightly as comprehension hit me. Could Jabari have the same power?

Guilt swept his face. "Exactly."

"You can do that?" I couldn't help the awe that crept into my tone. He didn't miss it.

"It's not a good thing," he cautioned.

"Of course it is. It will make our mission easier. If you have that kind of ability, we have a better chance at winning, Jabari."

"Wait a second. It's not the same as what Nata does. But it's similar."

"How did you find out? Tell me everything."

"One of the guards at work got in my face a couple of weeks ago, and before I knew it, I was using my ability to encourage him to do the right thing . . . or so I thought."

"That's been your ability for a while. But how was it different?"

"Well, I guess he really got to me. He was taunting me about my dad being in prison, and I told him to stop bothering me. But I ordered him to leave me alone permanently, and it was too late to take it back. I thought he was going to arrest me or punish me, but he got this blank look on his face and said okay. Then he walked away."

"Wow, so you pushed him, like Nata does."

"Only it gets weirder. It's like he never remembered it happening. He never mentioned it again. I can push someone to do something or command them, and I daze them and it makes their memory go blank from the incident. The same thing happened with Aleela. I got worried when I saw she was still working the other day. I know we've helped her out now so she doesn't have to spy, but still, I don't want her to see too much and be tempted at any point. So I tried it out on her. I told her to go home. I didn't want her to see everyone sneaking into the basement."

"That's why she was out of it. She couldn't remember what you told her."

"Yeah," he sounded defeated.

"Why is this upsetting you? This is a good thing."

"Is it? I don't know. It's so similar to Nata's ability, and if I can force people to obey me, doesn't that make me like her?"

"Only if you try to mass murder people," I blurted.

"Rain, I'm serious."

"So am I. You just finished telling me that I shouldn't be hard on myself for feeling happy I killed a man because I'm fighting for our freedom. So you can't be mad about an ability you have to help our cause. And besides, you're Jabari. You're not evil and you wouldn't be tempted to use this ability to do bad things ever. It's not in your DNA. That's what really bothers you about this, isn't it?"

"Yeah. What if I think I'm making a good decision and using my ability for our cause, but I hurt someone? Should anyone have this kind of power?"

"No, not just anyone, but you should. That's why it was given to you. You can be trusted with this ability."

"Then how do you explain Nata? Why does she have this ability?"

"Niyol told me before that we all have a choice to make . . . we decide if we're going to use our gifts to do good or bad. Everyone has a choice to make, Jabari, what kind of people we're going to be. And you always choose to do what's right. So don't let this scare you. Embrace it. You're the leader of a group of teenagers who are going to free our country. You've been given this ability because you're meant to lead us to freedom. Besides, like you said earlier, Niyol said not to worry about it," I finished.

Jabari watched me for a few minutes, then let out a sigh. "You're really good at pep talks."

I grinned. "I know. You should ask Daktari and Zi. I've been giving them since day one in this walled zone."

"I don't know what I'd do without you."

"I don't know what I'd do without you either. When I was arrested, I was . . . afraid," I admitted.

He took my face in his hands and brushed his lips to mine. When he parted, he looked so serious. "I know you feel bad about some of the things you've had to do, but do me a favor and keep fighting like you do."

"Promise me you'll do the same."

"I promise, Rain Ramirez."

"Hey—" I started to tease him that it hadn't happened yet. We had to survive this battle before I could become Rain Ramirez. But he didn't give me the chance. He started kissing me again, and as warmth filled my cold limbs, I lost my train of thought.

Chapter 14: Journey

RAIN

Cole piloted our hover at pulse speed, closely following the UZTA hover transporting Maha and the other prisoners who'd been selected to go to EEG headquarters. Just as Eric had told us, the prison transport left Indy Mixed Zone around ten a.m., and since it was Saturday and we weren't required to work, we'd been idling just outside the zone, prepared to follow. Zi held an image over us as we traveled, concealing us from the enemy and anyone else.

Though quickly thrown together, everyone seemed optimistic with the plan. They agreed that it would be a pleasant change to actually work together with our allies on a mission instead of going in just the six of us as usual. I was slightly on edge, but I did my best to block out the voices of doubt and what ifs. After all, if it all worked out, today we would free Maha from The Authority, once and for all.

According to Cole, we would arrive in Lansing within five minutes, where supposedly Gallagher's men were on the lookout for the UZTA hover and had a plan to make it land just outside of EEG headquarters. It wasn't the old city of Lansing we were traveling to, but the large hub of Lansing, one of the twenty zones across UZTA. The new Lansing comprised of parts of the former states of Indiana, Michigan, and Ohio. Lansing, like the other central zones, was divided up into various racial zones, which were labeled according to Nata's cruel segregation system, just like Indy. There was Lansing Mixed Zone, Lansing Asian Zone, Lansing Middle-Eastern Zone, Lansing African-American Zone, and so forth. But unlike the other central zones of the UZTA, Lansing had another area that few knew about. Just when you crossed the border into Lansing, in an old industry area, was the EEG headquarters. And we'd never have found it without the aid of Niyol.

Gallagher had known all about the EEG headquarters, as he told Jabari last night, because ever since we'd taken EEG Officer Dean to his camp, who had been torturing my mom and many others for years, Niyol had been researching the place. Niyol had discovered its exact location in Lansing, and said that though there weren't walls protecting it, there were security cameras surrounding the property.

Jabari and Gallagher had worked out all the details from cutting security cameras to freeing the prisoners. I'd listened to the plan, with the exception of how Gallagher planned to ground the UZTA hover. Apparently, Gallagher hadn't told Jabari that part. Jabari told me that we needed to trust that Gallagher and Niyol would take care of it. Jabari had also told me to stop being so worried and to just focus on my instincts. But it was difficult. Plus, my nightmare was weighing heavily on my mind.

"You're nervous," Marcello said in a quiet voice, prompting me to look at him in the passenger seat beside me. As usual, the two of us were seated in the back row.

"No," I retorted in a whisper, raising an eyebrow at him.

"You haven't stopped fidgeting since we took off fifteen minutes ago."

He didn't miss a thing. "I'm not nervous. I just don't like not knowing the entire plan. Like how in the world Gallagher is planning to make the UZTA hover land before we get there. How can he do it without alarming the guards inside? What if they alert Nata? Or hurt one of the prisoners before we can even help them?"

"Relax, Amiga. For the first time ever, we are working alongside Gallagher Brown, the other resistance members, and Niyol. On top of that, I know your fiancé wouldn't be going along with a plan he didn't have one hundred percent faith in."

"*He* doesn't even know how Gallagher's going to make them land," I pointed out.

"Yeah, but Gallagher has landed more than a few UZTA hovers in the past year. Not only has he tricked them into landing, he has stolen hovers and other equipment, captured Authority guards, and then convinced them to join his cause. The man's got skills. Cole was right from the beginning. Gallagher Brown was the only one who could have joined our cause and led the battle from outside the zones. It's a miracle we found him like we did."

"Which brings up another concern. That's part of the reason I'm worried. Nata is hunting for him. Landon told us about the camouflage Droid Dogs searching for him and the men she's planting undercover outside the zones. And you know she must be beyond enraged right now after whatever he did to get her away from our zone during our arrest. The Authority hovers, including the one we are following, are on the lookout for Gallagher. What if they know the sort of tricks he plays and don't fall for it?"

"That reminds me, we need to thank Gallagher again, in person that is, for whatever stunt he pulled to get her away from our zone."

"So you're not worried at all?"

"Nope. Besides, like I said, Niyol is involved, too. We'll be fine."

I couldn't refute that. He had a point. I hadn't even needed to contact Niyol to ask for his help. Supposedly, he had shown up at Gallagher's camp right before we contacted him, saying he was going to help us. Niyol's abilities were more powerful than any of ours. So Marcello was probably right. I shouldn't have been so on edge and worked up about one little detail. And truth be told, my biggest concern was still Grandma Julia and how she fit into my most recent nightmare, but I didn't feel like mentioning any of this to Marcello right now.

If he was optimistic, then I needed to let him be. I didn't need to let my fears or doubts get my team sidetracked. I was the one who'd suggested we rescue Maha and go to EEG headquarters in the first place. I'd told them we should listen to my dream. They all knew about the voice yelling and how someone had been trapped in my dream, and they still thought we should go on this mission. I guess that's why I hadn't contacted Niyol myself since having the nightmare. If he had shown up at Gallagher's and was willing to help us, surely he thought it was a good plan. Maybe I needed to have a little more faith in my abilities and instincts, like everyone kept telling me.

I figured I should say something to lighten the mood and let Marcello know I agreed with him, everything would be fine, but a frenzied expression crossed his face. I turned to the front of the hover as Jabari and Cole were mumbling about something. A funnel cloud, almost like a tornado, was overtaking the UZTA hover in front of us.

Daktari grabbed the seat in front of him. "What is it? They might crash."

The hover began to dip and weave, trying to veer out of the path of the storm, but it couldn't. For some reason, the wind wasn't bothering our own hover. The wind spun around the hover again, blocking its path in front and making it sag, and I got a glimpse of something dark brown in the midst of the funnel cloud. Understanding flooded over me. "It's Niyol," I blurted.

"He's gonna make them crash," Marcello's eyes were wide with alarm.

"No, he's making them land," Jabari said evenly. "Cole, put us down a little ways back from wherever they stop," he finished.

"I guess this was the plan Gallagher was talking about," Daktari added.

Sure enough, the UZTA hover slowed down and dropped altitude, landing to the side of an abandoned road with broken pavement. But Niyol didn't let up. The funnel cloud engulfed the hover, and I realized how beautiful the plan was. The guards inside the hover would be frantic, thinking a storm had grounded them, and they'd never see the real threat coming. They wouldn't have time to alert anyone to what the real cause of their emergency landing had been. As long as Gallagher's men acted quickly.

As Cole settled our hover down nearby, a swarm of about twenty people, most with guns trained in front of them, came out of the woods from the side of the road and headed for the UZTA hover, with the towering frame of Lieutenant Moretti among them. From a distance, it was easy to spot the former Navy SEAL, with his long black ponytail and enormous muscled frame. He looked like a hero out of an old time war movie, but in reality he *was* a hero—the real deal. He'd escaped his army base after Nata had taken control and begun killing resistors. He'd found other former military men like him, who wanted to fight back. Eventually, Moretti and his band of ex-military men had met Gallagher Brown and joined TFF. I couldn't pick Gallagher out from the group yet, but I knew he was there.

"We should help them," Marcello said, leaning forward.

"They look like they can handle it to me," Cole mumbled.

"We need to wait a moment. They're planning to make sure there aren't Droid Dogs or anything that might record or take photos aboard the hover before we show ourselves. Gallagher said he wanted to make sure no cameras picked the six of us up and he'd give us a signal when it was all clear," Jabari informed us, his eyes trained on the scene.

It happened fast. The funnel cloud faded away as Moretti and the group closed in. Within seconds, they had opened the hover door and taken the two UZTA guards on board into custody. A couple of the men were carrying a jug of water into the hover, I assumed to offer the startled prisoners a drink. I figured Maha and everyone on board would definitely appreciate drinking water, especially after being in Metro Prison for so long, where water was scarce. As I waited for Gallagher's signal that Zi could drop the image, I searched the group, excitement filling my chest as I recognized my cousin Victoria among the men. She was escorting one of the UZTA guards towards the tree line, where they were securing their hands and searching for GPS watches and UZTA trackers.

Vic had been through so much, losing her father, my Uncle Eli, when they had escaped the Florida African-American zone months back. Uncle Eli had cancer, which The Authority had refused to treat, so he'd helped Vic, sacrificing himself as a decoy so she could escape the oppressive life of her zone. And though I couldn't imagine the pain of not having a mother and then losing your father, I knew she was in the best place she could be, at least for the moment, living with other refugees in Gallagher's hidden camp. Her long black hair was pulled into a ponytail, and she was dressed in combat boots, comfortably holding her weapon and looking strong like the rest of the group. Gallagher had said she was one of their best fighters, which didn't surprise me. Vic had always been tough. She'd managed to hike through a few states, all alone and on the run from The Authority, before Niyol had saved her from an old hunting pit she had fallen into.

A kid with shaggy black hair and medium brown skin tone, who I recognized as Jonah, the boy I'd led to Gallagher by using my telepathy last month, stepped out of the hover. I hadn't even noticed him go inside, but now, I watched as Moretti's men lifted a motionless Droid Dog out and knew Jonah had used his ability. Jonah was multiracial, and had been separated from his Cuban-American father and Danish mother when the first walls had gone up in the zones. He'd been assigned to the New Texas Mixed Zone. But over time he had discovered his ability, and after being assigned to help construct the New Texas Pure Zone, he used his ability to escape as soon as he saw the opportunity. He had the ability to cut power sources, and I felt relieved knowing he must have shut the Droid Dog on board the UZTA hover down before it could record anything for The Authority cameras to pick up.

Adrianne, Gallagher's daughter, was there too. Even if she hadn't been standing beside one of the scruffier looking men, her beauty would have stood out. She had her father's black hair and the same pale blue eyes as her Aunt Mary, and her features captured the memory of her Native-American mother, Kaya, who Nata had murdered on the same day as Cole's parents. Adrianne anxiously scanned the area around her, searching for us, and Cole in particular, I assumed. The two of them had formed a bond upon their first meeting, the day we had found Gallagher's secret camp, and though no one dared say a word in front of Gallagher about it, Adrianne without a doubt had a crush on Cole, and vice versa.

I wondered where Gallagher himself was when the scruffy-looking man beside Adrianne took off his stocking cap and held it up in the air, waving it back and forth. A huge grin spread across his face, but he spun around, waving in different directions, unsure of our exact location. I recognized him as the one and only Gallagher Brown.

Chapter 15: Maha

RAIN

Gallagher's beard and black hair had grown thicker and longer since I'd seen him, and he blended in with the rest of the men, which I realized was part of his plan to avoid arrest. With all of them sporting the same look, it was difficult to imagine the face of a former Senator to Virginia, a clean-shaven and well-groomed man, among them. We'd often teased him about his self-proclaimed "mountain man" look, but now he fit the part even more than ever. He didn't want to make Nata's hunt for him easy.

"Come on guys," Jabari said, opening the hover door. Zi dropped the image and we piled out, smiling as we noticed the startled expressions of the men closest to us. Gallagher hurried over and pulled Cole into a quick hug, patting him on the back. "Cole, good to see you."

Cole gazed warmly up at the man who'd been one of his dad's closest friends. "How did you guys travel north so quickly from your camp?"

Gallagher motioned over his shoulder towards Moretti, who was still over beside the UZTA hover. "We have two hovers now, thanks to Lieutenant Moretti and his men. They took them from The Authority. We just have to be careful and travel only at night so we don't get spotted."

As everyone exchanged greetings and some hugs, Adrianne approached slowly, with her eyes fixed on Cole. As she came into his view, he beamed and hurried to her, hugging her quickly before Gallagher could stop him. She flushed red and smiled back at him as they parted now. Though Gallagher's face was scrutinizing their every action, they kept smiling, seemingly unconcerned about his watchful eyes.

"Adrianne. What are you doing here?" Cole finally asked. "I mean, I am happy to see you, but I wasn't expecting to," he added in a rush, his own cheeks getting red.

Adrianne laughed. "I wanted to see you guys," she said happily, focusing on Cole alone.

Gallagher frowned. "She insisted I bring her for her own safety, she said. Even though I know she would have been perfectly safe back at camp with Amal, Mary, and Chef Yoshi," he paused, raising a brow as he studied Cole. "But I think I'm beginning to understand why she wanted to come along. She threatened to sneak along. And I knew she'd use her ability to do it if I didn't let her."

Adrianne had discovered her own ability a few months ago. She could camouflage herself and whoever she touched, making them invisible to anyone watching, but she couldn't make her image move like Zi's.

Adrianne beamed at her dad, and then at us again. "I'm really glad to see all of you. Oh, and Amal said to tell you hello, Rain," she said as she lifted her arms to hug me. "She's really fitting in well at camp," she added, casting an amused look at her father.

Gallagher raised a brow at his daughter, but then regarded her affectionately. "Troublemaker," he mumbled.

"Well, be sure to give Amal my love," I replied.

I glanced curiously at Gallagher as I spoke. I'd met Amal during her torture, when Officer Wolfe had interrogated me about my involvement in her husband's crime. When Nata had ordered Amal's execution, Daktari, Zi, and I had saved her, and with TFF we'd taken her to Gallagher's camp. From the moment Gallagher had set eyes on the wounded woman, whose head had been shaved and whose husband had been murdered by The Authority, Gallagher had welcomed her with open arms and promised to keep her safe. I wondered if their friendship had become something more since we'd left her at his camp, but the look on Gallagher's face was clear that he didn't want to talk about it.

He cleared his throat. "It's good to see you all even under these circumstances. We'd better get moving. Daktari and Rain, your cousin is unbelievable by the way. And I'm so glad she and Adrianne have become close friends. Not just because she's a great girl. Victoria can fight better than most of the men, and even though Adrianne can hide with her ability, it's nice to know Victoria has her back."

Just then, Vic jogged over to our group and threw her arms around me. "Looking good as usual, cuz," I said.

She squeezed me tightly, then held me back a little, concern creeping into her eyes. "Still too thin. You guys should have some of Chef Yoshi's cooking. I wish you could come back with us."

Gallagher had met Chef Yoshi, a former TV and celebrity chef, when he'd initially gone into hiding, and Yoshi did her best to make the most of the limited food and ingredients they came across. Plus, they were settled near a lake, so fresh fish was usually available. I'd eaten Chef Yoshi's food twice, and I knew how talented she was.

"Chef Yoshi is amazing. Tell her I said hello," I remarked.

"I wish we could come back with you too, Hermosa. But strictly for Chef Yoshi's cooking. My heart belongs to Rain's other cousin, Calista, now. It's official," Marcello teased.

Vic grinned from ear to ear. "Marcello, I missed you. But let me warn you, if you hurt Calista, I'll kick your butt. Even though she's Rain's cousin on her mom's side of the family, I grew up camping with her on our yearly Florida camping trips. Calista is family to me, too," she warned with a laugh, hugging him lightly.

"I have the purest intentions," Marcello said with a wink.

Daktari nudged Marcello out of the way to hug Vic. "I'd be happy to give you a list of reasons Marcello already deserves to have his butt kicked, cuz."

Jonah approached and looked up at me shyly. I smiled. "Hey Jonah, saving the day again, I see." And I bent down to hug him.

"Thanks to you getting inside my head so I could find theses guys, Rain."

Lieutenant Moretti made his way through the small crowd and stopped right in front of Jonah and me. He patted Jonah's back and grinned at me. "Thanks, again, Rain, for finding this kid. The best defense we have against Droid technology. He is amazing."

"Seems like just yesterday you were wondering what such a little guy could do," Jonah teased. Moretti chuckled, and I smiled, recalling the moment when I'd introduced Jonah to Moretti.

"I was definitely off base, kid," Moretti admitted.

"You guys have been waiting for us here since last night?" Zi asked.

"We have safe houses, if you will, everywhere these days thanks to Gallagher," Moretti informed us, giving Gallagher an approving nod. "The people love him."

"I can't take all the credit," Gallagher said humbly, "Niyol pulls all the miraculous stuff off. Like making that hover land just now."

"Where is Niyol anyway?" asked Jabari.

Niyol stepped into my frame, appearing from the edge of the woods, and our eyes locked. "*Hi Niyol.*" I automatically used my telepathy, wanting a private chat with him.

"*Rainchild. How are you?*"

He walked to me directly, and embraced me. I glanced up at him after a moment.

His brow wove together. "*Tell me what's troubling you.*"

"*I know I didn't mention it the other day when we spoke, but I feel awful about what I did in the prison.*"

"*You did well in Metro Prison.*"

"*I killed him.*"

"*You had to.*"

"*I felt happy afterwards. I was glad he was dead.*"

"*That's not strange. He was hurting you and a lot of other innocent people.*"

"*I guess. There's something else though. I had a dream about today, Niyol. Someone got left behind and was screaming in a burning building. And Grandma Julia was in trouble. Do you know something? Is this mission safe?*"

He released me and rested a hand on my shoulder. "*She's fine for now. Come on, we have work to do. Say goodbye to Maha. She needs to hear that she's going to be safe now. And she needs to hear it from you.*"

Marcello eyed us suspiciously. "Hey, you've been using your telepathy on him to have a private conversation, haven't you?"

When neither Niyol nor I denied it, Marcello grunted. "That's so not fair."

"*What do you mean Grandma's fine for now?*"

"*Rainchild, say your goodbyes,*" he replied, nodding towards the hover in front of us.

Marcello shook his head. "Now you're just showing off."

I headed to the hover and ducked inside, vaguely aware that Niyol had asked Daktari to join us. I'd expected to see Maha resting and sipping water, but she was perched in the corner, holding her hands over her ears, with her eyes squeezed shut.

"What's wrong?" I blurted.

One of Moretti's men shrugged his shoulders. "She said to back away. I tried to tell her we are friends, but she's scared of us. I was about to come ask for help. I can't give her too much more time. We need to head out soon," he explained.

"It's fine, I can handle it," I said, waving him away. The three other prisoners were drinking water, and Niyol and Daktari began treating their injuries. Unlike Maha, the other passengers were very old. All of them seemed too weak to stand, but I knew Niyol and Daktari would heal them as much as possible. I stepped over to Maha, gently laying a hand on her shoulder.

She flinched, and her hazel eyes shot open. Her terrified expression faded away as she recognized me. "Rain."

"Maha, it's okay now." I sat down beside her and hugged her as best I could with her protruding belly. Fortunately, even being malnourished, her baby was still growing. Takara had made sure to sneak food back to Maha's prison cell over the past six months.

"Is it really you? I got so scared."

"Yes, it's me. And these men are the good guys, I promise. You're going to be fine now."

"But we were being transported to another prison according to the guards. They said we were going to die there, Rain."

I wiped a tear off of her cheek. "Not anymore. Look around you. See, Daktari is here, and this is our friend, Niyol."

Daktari and Niyol looked back from the seat in front of us, where they were healing another prisoner. "Hi, Maha," Daktari called cheerfully.

"Daktari, wow, this is really happening," Maha said.

"You'll be safe now, Maha," Niyol added.

"But what about the guards?"

I patted her shoulder. "Those guards are gone. Lieutenant Moretti and Gallagher Brown took them into custody. These men are fighting to take Nicks out of power, and they have a safe camp where they're taking you to live until the war is over. I know I couldn't tell you details about it when I visited you in prison, but these are the people who are on our side. They'll take care of you until this whole mess is over. It's not going to be easy. You'll have to be a refugee and hide with them in their outdoor camp, but I promise you'll be safer there than in Metro Prison or the other prison. And my cousin, Victoria, lives at Gallagher's camp. And Gallagher's daughter, Adrianne, is so sweet, too. They'll look out for you, I promise." I glanced over my shoulder, "Hey, Vic, Adrianne, can you come in here?" I called.

They appeared the next moment and climbed inside. Vic eyed Maha's belly. "Oh you poor thing, just wait until Chef Yoshi gets her hands on you. She's gonna cook some delicious food for you and that baby. You'll love it at our camp."

A startled look crossed Maha's face. "You have a chef at your camp?"

Adrianne giggled. "She used to be on TV before New Segregation. She's famous."

I nodded. "It's true. Maha, meet my cousin, Victoria, I call her Vic, and this is Adrianne, Gallagher's daughter. They are fighting from outside the zones to help free everyone."

Maha swallowed, her voice shook a little. "Wow, I'm really going to go live with you now?"

"Yes, you are. We're going to lay low for a day or two and make our way safely back to camp at night. Come out and meet my dad," Adrianne said, invitingly.

Maha let us pull her to her feet and guide her out of the hover. Everyone turned to stare at her belly, and Zi introduced Cole and Marcello, who had never met Maha. Gallagher smiled warmly as he approached.

"Maha, I'm Gallagher. I promise you'll be safe at my camp."

Maha shook his hand and then smiled cautiously. "Thank you for saving me."

"You should thank Rain. She's the reason this rescue mission even happened," Gallagher replied.

Maha threw her arms around my waist and closed her eyes. "Thanks, Rain. You're always there for me."

"I'm sorry it took us so long to get you out of Metro Prison," I offered.

"I can't believe you actually did it. But what about Anthony? Will they hurt him if I'm missing?"

Gallagher shook his head. "No, The Authority is going to assume all of the prisoners are dead after today. It will look like an accident. We've got plans to cover our tracks," Gallagher said, referring to the fire, I was sure.

Jabari hurried over from where he had been talking with Lieutenant Moretti and his men.

He offered his hand to Maha. "I've never met you, Maha, but I've heard all about you. I'm sorry you've been through so much."

"Jabari, I feel like I know you. And if it wasn't for your dad, I never would have survived in prison. I feel so awful about what he had to endure on my behalf." She reached for him to hug her, and he obliged. Francisco had regularly protected Maha from Officer Wolfe. Each time Wolfe had come to torment her, Francisco had taunted him so that he would become the focus of Wolfe's attacks.

After a few seconds, Jabari leaned back. "My dad wouldn't have had it any other way."

"We need to head out," Moretti instructed from nearby.

Daktari and Niyol stepped out of the hover, and Daktari hurried over. "Let me heal you first, before we go."

"That would be great. I've been feeling pretty awful the last few weeks."

Daktari placed one hand on her belly, the other at the back of her neck, then glanced at me. Maha was a bit wobbly on her feet, probably from lack of nutrition and her growing baby. I placed my hands around Maha, too, one on the back of her head, helping Daktari support her weight.

He closed his eyes, and I sucked in my breath. My hand was touching his lightly, and I could feel the warmth spreading from his hand to her entire body, even into mine a little.

After a moment, Maha grinned. "I feel amazing. Thank you, Daktari. That was even better than the last time."

Zi laughed. "He's getting stronger, I know it."

I felt good too and winked at Daktari. "I think you fixed me too. Not sure what was wrong with me, but I feel awesome."

"Did he fix your mental problem?" Marcello teased. "Maybe Niyol should help, too," he added.

"Well he didn't fix my Marcello problem," I retorted.

"I have no problem taking care of that for you, Rain," Jabari said with a warning look in Marcello's direction.

Marcello grinned. "Settle down, settle down. I walked right into that."

Niyol and Gallagher spoke in whispers, and then Gallagher turned to us. "A few of my men will take Maha to our nearby safe house for now. The rest are headed out with us. You'll be safe there until we come back for you later today, Maha. You have my word."

"What about you guys, Rain, Daktari, and Zi?" Maha searched our faces.

"We'll see you again, but not today," Zi said.

"Do you have to go back to the mixed zone?"

"Yeah, we do," Daktari said solemnly.

I took Maha's hands and squeezed them lightly. "But not forever. We're going to end Nata's regime. You're going to hold your baby in a free country."

A tear ran down Maha's face. "If anything happens to me, tell Kelly I'm waiting for her and Anthony, and tell them both I love them."

"You'll see them soon, okay?" Zi said.

"I hate goodbyes." Maha wiped a tear away.

Adrianne stepped closer to Maha and put her arm around her. "As soon as we're finished here, I'll join you at the safe house. Vic too. You'll be safe soon. And we'll take good care of you."

Maha eyed them. "You guys are going on the mission too?"

"We can't let Rain and the crew have all of the fun," Vic said with a small grin.

Moretti signaled to his men and they led Maha and the other freed prisoners away, heading towards the trees. As I watched her retreating form, her words from my nightmare came blaring through my mind. *You did it, Rain, you saved me.*

She paused now on the edge of the trees, and turned back towards me. Goose bumps covered my skin as she gazed at me. "You did it, Rain. You saved me," she called out.

I paled, my stomach feeling weak. Jabari grabbed my hand. I forced myself to nod at Maha and smile before she turned again. Once she was out of sight I let Jabari see my horrified expression. "*That's how it happened in my dream. What if the rest of the dream is the same?*" I said silently, anxiety rolling through me.

He bent down, inches from my face, his expression hard. "It won't be."

Chapter 16: Prisoners

RAIN

I shifted to face the others. If the rest of TFF had any doubts after hearing Maha's words from my dream, they weren't showing it. They were aware, of course, that there was no time for second-guessing.

I glanced between Moretti, Gallagher, and Niyol. "So, what now? I mean, I heard Jabari saying we are going to travel to the EEG building, and go in with you and your men to capture the guards, but how exactly are we getting inside the building?"

Lieutenant Moretti pointed towards the UZTA hover. "We're about five minutes from the compound, taking a hover. One group will take the UZTA hover, and we need some of you to pretend to be the prisoners to replace the real ones."

As Moretti eyed us, prompting us to respond, Gallagher put a hand on my shoulder. "I hate to put you on the spot like this, and this is going to be dangerous. So I understand if you say no, but Rain, Marcello, Jabari, and Daktari, do you think you could pose as the prisoners?"

We nodded our heads, agreeing to the task. "Of course, we will do it if you think that's the way in, and besides we forgot to mention it earlier, but thanks for whatever you did to lure Nata away from our zone when Marcello and I were in custody. We owe you," I said.

"Yeah, thank you, and what did you do? You should've seen her face, Gallagher," Marcello added.

"Well, Lieutenant Moretti helped me. We recorded a video of me talking with my prisoner, Officer Dean, her notorious EEG officer. We wanted to make sure she watched the video, so we put it inside one of the hovers we'd taken from her and programmed it on autopilot to land outside the wall of New Washington."

"So it just landed and they noticed it?" Cole asked.

Gallagher grinned. "Well, we didn't want to take the chance she wouldn't be notified of it, so we made sure the hover would stand out . . . We painted a message in red letters on top of the hover so you could see it from the sky. It said, 'I HAVE OFFICER DEAN,' and we also painted the sides with the letters *TFF* and I even signed my name on the windshield," Gallagher chuckled. "She noticed it all right."

"Thank you again for risking yourself and everyone for us," I said.

"The least I can do. So if you guys are sure you don't mind being the fake prisoners for this mission." Gallagher searched our expressions.

"We're ready," Daktari replied.

Zi frowned. "What about me and Cole?"

Gallagher answered. "We need you two to transport the rest of us in your hover, and Zi, you'll have to hide us under your image so we can get in undetected until the cameras have been cut. We don't want any of the security cameras to pick up a second hover. If The Authority decided to investigate their security feed later on, they might realize that your hover is unfamiliar to them. So far, they know which hovers we have confiscated. I hate to make them suspicious that I'm getting outside help. Plus, we can't let the EEG officers know we are there. We want to sneak up on them to capture them."

"Gallagher, you sure you want to risk going? The officers might put up a bigger fight if they recognize you, you know. You could stay here," Jabari pointed out.

"I want to end her EEG brutality once and for all, just like you. I wouldn't miss this for anything," he replied smoothly.

Moretti cleared his voice. "Now, once we get there, we'll make our move, probably while they are transporting you kids inside. There's a breaker box outside the complex we're going to get Jonah to first. Jonah will cut the power from outside the compound. Then my men will move in to rescue the prisoners and capture the guards. We've scoped the compound already and seen their landing dock. They'll probably take you inside, but don't worry, we'll be in to rescue you as soon as the power is cut."

"What if they figure out something is wrong when the power goes out and hurt them before we can rescue them?" Zi asked nervously.

"Two of my men are wearing the UZTA guard uniforms of the men we already captured."

He glanced behind him, where four men were approaching. They must have been with the UZTA guards until now because I hadn't noticed them before, but I recognized them. They were some of the ex-military men who had joined up with Moretti when they'd been on the run. I'd met them a few times now. There was Officer Samuels, Ross, Jones, and then the fourth, Sergeant Jacks.

Moretti waved them over. "Come on, guys."

Once they were closer and they'd greeted us all, Moretti continued. "Now, Samuels and Ross are in disguise as the guards and will be traveling on the UZTA hover with you. Jones and Jacks, I want you on the other hover. Now, Samuels and Ross won't let anything happen to you. Besides, between all of the powers you have, I think we're more prepared than most people. The six of you, plus Jonah, and even Adrianne . . . Not to mention a Navy SEAL or two, plus our other men, and Victoria. We're headed to EEG headquarters. Let's load up," Moretti instructed.

I looked at Gallagher for confirmation. "You told them about Adrianne's ability?"

Gallagher shrugged seemingly frustrated but torn between pride and frustration. "She insisted on helping. Besides, it's easier to keep her with me so I can keep her out of trouble more than anything."

"I wonder where she gets that from," teased Cole.

"He has a point, Dad," Adrianne agreed.

Gallagher shook his head. "Everyone be careful in there. Oh, and you should take your jackets and hats off. The prisoners just wear their street clothes, but as you have probably noticed, none of them had coats or hats. Adrianne will hold them for you until after this is over with."

We stripped our coats and hats off and handed them to Adrianne. "I'll keep them in the other hover until later. You guys are so brave," she said, nodding encouragingly.

Victoria patted my shoulder. "Be careful, cousin. See you in there."

"You be careful too," I replied.

Jabari grabbed my hand as we loaded into the UZTA hover. "Trust your instincts."

I wanted to ask Niyol to double-check that everything was okay but I didn't see him anywhere.

"Where did Niyol go?" I asked.

"He's running a perimeter check or something according to Moretti. He already headed out," Jabari replied.

Moretti jumped in the hover behind us and tied our hands loosely behind our backs, like Maha's had been, only he made the binds looser so we could break free on our own if needed. "Just so it looks like you're really prisoners," he explained.

I glanced at the others. Daktari, Jabari, and Marcello were bound, just like me, and it made me nervous. "If something happens—"

"I won't let anything happed to you," Jabari cut me off.

Once Officer Samuels and Officer Ross were ready, Moretti closed our door and headed to the other hover.

Samuels piloted the hover and took off smoothly. We had only traveled a few minutes when the hover slowed and Samuels called back to us. "Heads up, we're here. I'm setting us down on the landing spot. It's just outside a set of doors." His voice broke off and I leaned forward to see what had caught his attention.

My heart sped up instinctively, and Jabari tensed beside me.

"What is it?" Marcello asked with a heavy voice.

"Looks like we've got a welcoming committee. Four EEG officers. Stay strong, guys, until Jonah cuts the power," Ross answered.

The EEG officers stood in line against the side of the brick building like trained soldiers, their eyes on our approaching hover. I told myself to calm down. They were just men. But a voice inside reminded me they weren't just any men. They were EEG men, which meant they were either training officers or the newest recruits Officer Dean had told Niyol about who were preparing to enter the mixed zones and torture more people. Either way, these were men bent on fulfilling Nata's evil demand to terrorize the weakest among us.

"Jabari?" I whispered.

"Yeah?"

"Just wanted to hear your voice before those monsters get ahold of us," I confessed, my eyes growing wider as we approached.

"We're going to be okay. Stay with me."

The hover landed with a thud, jolting me forward and onto my knees, as if protesting his words. This wasn't going to be easy.

The door slid open and I tried to be brave as my eyes fell on the EEG officer standing in the frame. He glanced at Moretti's men in the front, and I prayed he wouldn't notice they were new. "You'll need to head inside and sign the transport records before you take off. We were expecting you earlier than this. Go on, right through those double doors."

As Samuels and Ross exited the hover, I felt a momentary bit of relief. So far, our cover hadn't been blown.

The EEG officer focused on us, and I stole a glimpse at his nametag. It read EEG OFFICER HERTZ.

"On your feet. Let's go," he ordered.

Marcello jumped out first, Daktari on his heels. As he started to step down out of the hover, Hertz shoved Daktari in his leg hard and he slammed against the pavement, landing on his face with a moan.

I hurried forward and jumped down from the hover, barely containing a scream, but Jabari whispered urgently behind me. "Don't, Rain."

"On your feet!" a different EEG officer shouted at Daktari. Hertz nodded approvingly at the other officer, and I got the feeling this was part of the recruit training.

Daktari struggled slowly to his feet, and my stomach twisted in knots as I surveyed his face. The right side was bleeding and scratched and already swollen red. I didn't want to react. I knew why Jabari had told me not to. They'd hurt me too if I tried to defend Daktari. But it was Daktari. My brother. How could I not say something?

"Move," Hertz ordered me.

I was stunned and my nerves were rising by the second. Jabari lightly prodded me with his body, and I stumbled forward. Daktari was on the move again, following Marcello, who was being led towards the side of the building, just outside of the doors.

Jabari and I joined in line, following in silence as the EEG officers took us in. "These prisoners are on the verge of death?" one finally said, doubt heavy in his tone.

"Maybe they sent them here as punishment. The last ones were a lot weaker. These look pretty strong. Well, that one doesn't," another said, pointing to me.

"Back up and line up against the wall," Hertz snapped at us. Apparently, he was the EEG Officer in charge.

My eyes searched frantically around, wondering if Cole had landed our hover behind the UZTA hover. Or maybe the breaker that Jonah needed to find was on another side of the building? Would they be able to find us in the enormous-looking compound?

Officer Hertz tilted his head towards Samuels and Ross, who'd been hovering near us. I knew they were torn. They couldn't blow their cover, but they were afraid to leave us alone with the EEG officers. "Get inside and sign those transport records. This compound is reserved for EEG officers and training EEG officers. It is a privilege to be here," he finished, his tone condescending.

Samuels jaw tightened, and Ross seemed to be struggling not to react. But they had to go along with the role if we were going to pull this off. With a concerned look in our direction, they turned and easily opened the double doors in front. A small sigh escaped me as they disappeared inside. The doors weren't locked. At least that wouldn't be an obstacle for Moretti and Gallagher to deal with. Once the power was cut, they could get right into the building to save us.

My heart raced as I glanced at the doors Samuels and Ross had gone through. I just wanted to go in already, even though I was afraid of what might happen. The sooner we got this over with, the better. There were only four EEG officers outside with us now, and I knew there were at least twenty in all stationed at this center according to Niyol, but compared to my experience with Officer Dean, these four didn't seem as cruel. Officer Hertz had been the cruelest, by far. I hoped that whoever he was taking us to inside wouldn't be much worse. And I really hoped Gallagher and Moretti would show up soon to save us. I couldn't imagine what was taking them so long.

Another officer came out of the building and joined the other guards. Now there were five of them, and we were officially outnumbered. As they spoke amongst themselves, my mind went over what-ifs. Was there a Droid Dog around somewhere? Would they scan our tattoos to verify we were the correct prisoners or did they even care who we were? Would it really matter if their intentions were to use us to train the other recruits? And did that mean they planned to torture us *and* kill us?

Sweat trickled down my neck, despite the freezing air, as I searched the sky around us for signs of Moretti or Gallagher. I was about to contact Zi, even though it wasn't part of the plan, just to check in, when Officer Hertz stepped away from us. Jabari edged closer to me, pushing me nearer to Daktari. Flanked between them, I could see Marcello in my peripheral vision standing beside Daktari.

With the tiniest nod of his head, Officer Hertz gave some sort of command, and the other four men ran about twenty feet in front of us and picked up hoses that were protruding from the opposite wall and aimed them at us. How had I not noticed those before?

"One of the goals of the EEG officer is to put the inferior races in their place. These numbers will learn quickly. Turn on the cameras," Officer Hertz shouted.

A red light illuminated at the top of the wall behind them, and for the first time I noticed the security cameras Gallagher had mentioned. Maybe they hadn't recorded our arrival at all. I shuddered as I realized they were going to record this and that if the cameras were still working, Jonah hadn't managed to cut the power yet.

"Begin the drill," he barked at his men.

Before my mind could catch up enough to know what exactly the drill entailed, cold, hard water rushed forward, beating against our bodies, pressing us against the brick wall. I couldn't react. There was no time. Somehow, the noise seemed distorted. I heard screaming, and knew it was my own. My screaming faded as I choked on the water ferociously attacking me. I was shoved to the ground, against the brick wall, and I kept choking as I waited for the attack from whoever had knocked me down. But after a moment, I peeked through my squinted eyes and saw that Jabari, Marcello, and Daktari were shielding me with their bodies. I tried to get up, but Jabari held me down.

"Stay down, Rain," he yelled over his shoulder.

No matter how I fought, I couldn't stand up. They were groaning now and then as the water hit them, and I knew they were in pain. But I couldn't get around the wall they'd formed, and Jabari's hands, though still tied in binds like my own, were holding me down.

"*Get off of me,*" I screamed, using my ability, unsure if any of them had heard me.

The water had soaked me and was still coming down hard, but it wasn't piercing my skin, burning and tearing me apart anymore. But I knew it was doing it to the three of them. *"Stop protecting me, they'll hurt you!"*

Jabari was the first to answer. *"I don't care."*

I guess no one else heard me or if they did, they couldn't or wouldn't answer. As I struggled to come up with a plan, the water stopped. I opened my eyes again, noting clearly now that Daktari, Marcello, and Jabari had all three pinned me down and formed a barrier between the firing squad and me.

"Well, what do we have here? They're trying to protect it." Officer Hertz remarked from the left of us. He'd retaliate for certain.

"Step completely away from it!" Hertz yelled at them.

The guys jumped slightly from his order, and though I could see out from behind them now, none of them moved away as ordered. All three of them were leaning their weight against me to hold me down.

"This should make our training very interesting." He turned towards his men, his tone casual as though he were discussing the weather. "Part of becoming an officer of the EEG means learning how to break them down. Mentally, emotionally, and physically. As you'll see once we continue inside with the training, this process doesn't take very long." He glanced back at us, his gaze fixing on me. "But when there's an instinct to protect like this, I always enjoy it a little more. I assure you, the other numbers will stop protecting it after a little more time. You'll see."

"Jabari, you have to get away from me. They might hurt you guys for protecting me. Marcello and Daktari will follow your lead. Please."

"I don't have a good feeling about this. And Jonah should've have cut the power by now."

"But I can handle this drill, whatever it is, just like you."

"But my gut tells me something's off."

He leaned back a little so we could look at each other. He was afraid. Daktari and Marcello peered down at me, and I could see they, too, were scared.

I shut my eyes and called to Niyol. "*We need help. Now.*"

"*I'm almost there, Rain. Hold on.*"

"Line them up, separate them so we can aim at it alone this time. We want them nice and cleansed before we head in for training. Especially it. You will learn a lot breaking this number down," Hertz ordered.

My stomach dropped again as they focused on me. It. The word rotated around my thoughts, filling my chest with sudden anger. I was not an *it*. As the guards grabbed us, Jabari, Daktari, and Marcello fought with them as best they could with their hands still bound, but Jabari didn't use his super strength. I knew he didn't use his ability because of the cameras recording everything. The three of them were pulled away from me, over to the sides, where the officers held them, and then I was standing alone against the brick wall.

"*Jabari, Niyol said he's almost here,*" I told him urgently.

"*Then where is he?*" he replied angrily.

Hertz stomped over to where the hoses had been dropped and scowled at the remaining officer. "Turn it up this time to full power. The two of us will aim everything we've got at it."

The officer's eyes widened, as he was clearly surprised they were going to attack me with that much force. The force of two of those hoses together on full power, trained on one person my size would be too much. The voices of the boys rang out, yelling at Officer Hertz to pick on them instead, but he ignored them. As the hoses were aimed at me, they stepped closer. Hertz's eyes locked with mine, and he smiled. "You are nothing but a number. Just a number. An *it*," he said venomously.

Adrenaline pumped through my veins and I tossed my head back defiantly. I wasn't thinking clearly, but honestly I didn't care. "I'm not an *it*. I am a girl. I am a human being," I retorted.

Darkness flashed in his eyes. "Not for long."

I squeezed my eyes shut. I didn't want to watch.

Chapter 17: UZTA Traitors

JABARI

I couldn't let them hurt her. I also knew I couldn't let the security cameras pick up any of us using our abilities. If Nata got that kind of information, we were dead. And so was the mission. But I could not sit back and watch them hurt Rain. Something must have delayed Moretti and Gallagher, but I couldn't wait for them. Rain had said Niyol was coming, but I couldn't wait for him either. There wasn't enough time.

I didn't think about a plan. I just reacted. I caught Marcello's eye for a brief moment, and I knew he understood. Daktari was already fighting against the guard who held him, and I knew he'd do what he could to help.

I took a deep breath and concentrated on my strength and flung my arms apart, out of the guard's grasp, and turned around in an instant, pushing him to the ground. I held him firmly by his arms and stared into his eyes, using my newest ability on him as he fought. "Don't move a muscle. Stop hurting us. Stay here."

He froze, as a dazed look covered his face, and I didn't waste any time. I got up and saw that Marcello's guard had already hit the ground.

"Shoot the water!" Hertz's voice boomed at the officer beside him.

"Marcello, help Daktari," I ordered.

In my peripheral vision I saw Hertz drop his hose as the other officer started spraying water at Rain. I vaulted towards Rain, who stood facing forward with her eyes still closed, as Hertz reached for his waist, and I could only imagine what he was retrieving. I didn't have time to try to stop them with my ability. I had to run for Rain and protect her. She thought we needed to wait for help so the cameras didn't see us, but I couldn't wait any longer. Voices were shouting, and I became aware of a brutal wind rushing over us, engulfing the air. I reached for Rain and yanked her to the ground with me, shielding her as the madness around us grew. The cold water assaulted my body, and then over the sound of the roaring wind, a cracking sound blasted, sending fear through me.

I knew the sound. I'd seen it on TV in movies before New Segregation. And I'd heard it ring out in the basement of Health Plex when I'd been searching for Rain and her mother a few months back. A gunshot.

The water stopped beating against me, and I shook Rain lightly. "Are you hit?"

When she didn't move or respond, I rolled her over, facing me. She was blinking her eyes as though she were dizzy, and blood trickled from a fresh lash across her hairline. My eyes skimmed her body, looking for any other injuries as the wind raged on, and I yelled louder. "Rain, can you hear me?" Again, she didn't respond, and her eyelids fell shut.

I glanced around, desperate to find Daktari, but as soon as I looked up, I noted the change in scenery. Moretti, Gallagher, and their team had surrounded us and were taking the five EEG officers into custody. I searched for Daktari and as soon as I spotted him, the wind, now a full-blown funnel cloud, turned towards me, dissipated, and out dashed Niyol.

He knelt down and laid his hands on Rain as she moaned softly. The gash on her head faded away as Niyol healed her. Guilt swept through me. "I must have caused her to hit her head when I tackled her to the ground with me."

"She'll be fine. You did the right thing, Jabari," Niyol murmured.

Commotion continued around us, and I glanced up, noting that Daktari's face was bleeding, but he was more concerned about the other EEG officers inside the building. I could hear him telling Moretti they needed to move in fast.

My eyes shot to the cameras and understanding washed over me. That's why I'd heard a gun shot. They'd shot the camera out while Niyol had blown through as a distraction.

Our hover appeared the next moment, and Zi leapt from it and raced to Daktari. He turned to her and guided her to me and Rain. Niyol released his grip on Rain, and she bolted to a seated position. She clutched onto my forearms as worry consumed her expression. "Daktari's fine," I answered her silent question.

"I'm right here, sis. How are you?" Daktari prompted.

Rain tilted her head to look up at him. "But your face, Daktari."

Niyol patted Rain's cheek. "I'm going to patch his face up now. Are you better?"

Rain nodded fervently. "Yes, thank you, Niyol."

"I'm sorry it took me so long. I had to stop a shipment that was headed here. I spotted it when I was running patrols," Niyol explained.

"But what will happen? How much time before they arrive?" Daktari asked.

"They'll be busy for a while, fixing their mysteriously broken down hover," Niyol explained. His expression sobered. "But I am sorry for what happened while I was gone."

"At least you got here when you did," Zi said.

Niyol sighed, and then reached for Daktari. As he healed his wounds, I studied Rain's panicky face. I pulled her to a standing position.

"Hey, it's fine now. We're going to be okay," I reassured her.

She held herself tight, and finally shook her head once, then fell against me, burying her fingers on my neck, her body trembling in her soaking wet clothes. We were all still drenched from the hoses.

"I heard that gunshot and I freaked out," she admitted.

She'd only been shot a few weeks ago. I didn't figure it was something that she'd ever really get over. "I can't imagine." I stroked her hair, which was sopping from the hoses.

Once Daktari was healed, Zi pulled Rain into a hug. "I'm sorry we didn't get here sooner. We took Jonah to the other side of the complex to cut the power, but the power lines were protected by some sort of fencing. And the lock was jammed, and no one could open it. Everyone started arguing. We knew you guys were unprotected. Gallagher thought we'd have to move in to help you, and Moretti wasn't sure if the cameras were live, directly routing to Nata. He thought maybe if they were and we helped you, she'd notice you guys weren't the real prisoners and get suspicious. Finally Cole, Adrianne, and I told them we were coming to look for you guys. So Moretti left Victoria and another guy with Jonah to work on the jam, and by the time we landed over here, they were spraying you with the hoses and then Niyol showed up, well, in the funnel cloud, and Gallagher said they should shoot the camera out while they had the chance," she explained, her face panic-stricken.

As the rest of the group huddled around us, Marcello gave Moretti a sideways glance. "Took you long enough."

Adrianne's face paled as she surveyed us. "You guys are soaking wet. I'll grab some towels from our supplies in the hover. Be right back." Moretti and Gallagher both frowned. "Sorry kids. Didn't see the lock jamming like that," Gallagher offered.

"I can open it for you," I volunteered.

As soon as I had spoken a crackling sound erupted in the distance and the faint hum that I hadn't paid much attention to until its absence was gone. Clarity spread across our faces.

Adrianne jogged back with towels and handed them to the four of us. "Jonah shut the power off," she said excitedly.

"We need to get inside the building. I'm not sure what's happened to my guys in there, but Cole, can you pick Jonah and them up in the hover and get them over here before we go in? I don't want to get separated from them," Gallagher explained.

"I'll go with you, to cover the transporter, just to be extra cautious,"

Zi volunteered. She put a hand on Rain's shoulder. "Don't go in that building without me."

"I wouldn't dream of it, best friend," Rain said dryly as she worked the towel through her hair.

"Sure you wouldn't," Zi replied, then dashed into the awaiting hover.

As they disappeared, Gallagher continued to organize. He inspected the newest prisoners. "Jacks and Nichols, load them in the UZTA hover. We'll go ahead and add it to our collection. And wait for us out here. Once Jonah and everyone return, we'll head in to round up the remaining EEG officers and release the prisoners. We'll take everyone to the safe house and figure out who is going to which camp once we finish up here."

Adrianne collected our towels as we finished drying off as best we could. Our clothes were still wet, but at least they weren't dripping with water any longer. "I've got your coats and hats in the hover, too. I know you must still be freezing in those clothes."

"This helped a lot, Adrianne. Thank you," Daktari said.

"At least we won't be soaking wet when we go inside now," Rain added.

Gallagher spared the building a glance. "Samuels and Ross might be in trouble in there. I wish we knew what to expect."

Niyol, who'd been hovering near Rain, spoke up. "I can help." He walked over to where Officer Hertz was being detained and we followed. "He can tell us how many more are inside."

"Perfect," said Gallagher.

The men led the other four guards away, as Hertz narrowed his eyes at Gallagher. "I don't know who you are, but you'll all die for this. You're UZTA traitors, and she'll kill every single one of you."

"I'm proud to be a UZTA traitor," Gallagher replied with a smirk.

Hertz didn't reply, but tilted his head towards Rain, his expression deadly.

Anger pitted in my stomach and I clenched my hands tighter around

Rain, keeping her close to me. If I concentrated on her, maybe I could ignore the way he'd begun looking at Rain again.

Niyol placed his hand on Hertz's shoulder. "How many people are inside, officers and prisoners?"

The hatred disappeared from his expression and his tone was monotone as he replied, his eyes vacant. "Six officers. Twenty prisoners."

"Where are they?"

"The prisoner cells are in the basement. That's probably where you'll find the officers. And one is usually in the upstairs office."

Niyol released him and Gallagher glimpsed towards the hover. "So, we'll secure the main level before heading to the basement. Go ahead and put this guy in with the rest of the prisoners."

As Nichols pulled Hertz to his feet, his expression hardened and he pounded his boot into Nichols's shin and lunged for Rain. Though his hands were still tied, it didn't matter; he was careening towards her like a football player tackling an opponent. In a split second I nudged her out of the way, and focused on my strength. He collided into me instead, but I held my stance, and he fell backwards as soon as he hit me, knocking his head against the pavement.

All I could see was red. If he'd tackled Rain, she would've been hurt again, and that was too many times in one day, especially because of the same man. I heard shouting, but blocked it out. My hand found his throat and raised him off the ground. I watched him struggle for his breath as I held him there. People were yelling at me to put him down before he suffocated. I heard Marcello and Daktari among them, too, but I ignored them. Hertz had tried to hurt Rain too many times today, and rage was shooting through me like it never had. Or maybe it was fear. Hertz had said we'd all be killed. Even with us there, taking him away, he didn't seem phased. What kind of peril and evil would we face in the days ahead and could I keep Rain safe? The uncertainty ran though my mind until I thought I'd lose it completely. I shook him, still holding him up with my strength. My power pulsed through my veins making him seem as light as a feather.

"Set him down, Jabari," Rain's voice pleaded with me as she laid her hands on my arms gently.

"You will apologize to her, or I'll kill you." I didn't even realize I'd said the words aloud at first.

"Jabari, please."

I let him drop and heard his moan as he hit the pavement again, but I turned to Rain. She pulled my face towards hers, placing her palms on either side of my face. "I'm okay," she whispered.

I swallowed, concentrated on my breathing. I hadn't meant to react like that. I needed to keep it together. I was the leader of our group. But the stakes felt higher than ever, and losing Rain or any of my loved ones was beginning to feel like something I couldn't risk.

Hertz's voice interrupted my thoughts. "I'm sorry for hurting you," he said quietly to Rain.

Her eyebrow raised and she spoke to me silently. "*You used your ability on him just now, didn't you?*"

"*I couldn't help it. He hurt you too much. Too bad he won't remember apologizing to you.*"

Jacks helped Nichols pull Hertz away and into the hover. Gallagher edged closer and put a hand on my shoulder. "Hey, Jabari, it'll be fine. He'll be held accountable for what he did. We'll lock him up until he can face a trial after all of this, okay?"

I nodded my head once. "Yeah, I know."

A smile spread across his face. "You're really strong, you know that? I mean, what was that?"

"His ability has strengthened," Daktari said.

"Even I don't tease him now," Marcello added.

Moretti sized me up. "You ever want a job, I mean after the war that is, I'll recruit you, son," he added.

As the men laughed around us and talked about my unbelievable strength, Rain gripped my hand, focused her eyes on me. She could tell I was pumping with anger still. "Just take a deep breath," she urged.

A moment later, our hover reappeared, and Zi, Cole, Victoria, and Jonah ran over to us.

Zi and Victoria eyed us suspiciously. "What did we miss?" Victoria asked.

"Oh, not much. We'll tell you later. Hey, nice job with the power, Jonah," Daktari complimented.

"Seriously," Marcello added.

He shrugged. "Sorry if I let you guys down. That box was jammed."

"You didn't," Rain assured him.

"Come on, we're not finished yet," Moretti instructed.

I held Rain's hand in mine as we followed Moretti, Gallagher, and the others towards the doors.

She hesitated and pulled my ear to her mouth. "Remember to breathe. I'm right here with you, and I'm fine," she whispered.

"I would have killed him if you hadn't stopped me. That's how much I need to protect you," I confessed in a low voice.

I felt her tense beside me. "But you didn't. I love you because you protect me."

"I love you because you're the most important part of my life."

She looked worried still, but gave me a small smile. And we shuffled into the dark, powerless interior of EEG headquarters.

Chapter 18: Darkness

RAIN

A single emergency light cast an orange glow up ahead in the pitch-black corridor. Even though Jabari held my hand firmly in his as we trailed Gallagher, I wouldn't have let him go if given the opportunity. The physical connection gave me the false sense of security that I could yank him out of whatever danger lurked in the darkness surrounding us, or that I could calm him down if anything else were to set him off. Zi, Daktari, Cole, Marcello, Adrianne, and Victoria were just ahead of us, with Gallagher and his men in front of them. Normally, we depended on his ability to sense trouble, but he was so wound up right now I was worried he might miss something.

I'd never seen him enraged like that. He'd nearly squeezed the last breath out of Officer Hertz right in front of me. In front of everyone. He'd almost taken a life.

Because of me.

I didn't want to feel guilty, but I did. If he'd gone through with it, he'd be dealing with emotions I knew all too well. What was I doing to him? He never would have done something like that months ago. He was so focused on protecting me, he wasn't being rational. And worse, at the same time the feelings of guilt raced through me, it felt strangely comforting in a way knowing Jabari loved me so much he'd kill to protect me. But I'd go to the grave with that piece of information. Either way, I felt guilty, no matter how I looked at it.

My face brushed into Jabari's shoulder as he stopped abruptly at the sound of whispers from the shadows. A palm solar light clicked on the next moment, illuminating Gallagher's face and the source of the whispering. Officers Samuels and Ross.

"They made us leave the office after signing the transport papers, and we checked out the main level as much as we could," Samuels explained.

"Two men are in the office trying to figure out why their power is down. That emergency light is right outside their door," Ross added.

"Let's get rid of that light, and lure them out," Gallagher decided.

"I can handle the light," Jonah volunteered.

Moretti nodded, and motioned Jonah forward. I watched as they communicated with hand signals and one of the men lifted Jonah off the ground towards the ceiling. Jonah's hands touched the emergency light, and instantly, it was out. Gallagher signaled us to lean against the walls, and then he had the solar light extinguished as well.

A moment later, I heard a strange voice nearby in the darkness. "Why aren't the emergency lights working? The backup power is supposed to stay on when the power goes out."

Huddled beside Jabari, I listened for a response. "I don't know. I'm sure Gregory has sent someone to the breaker room to check it out. I'll head down there too," another man replied.

"That won't be necessary," Gallagher's voice interrupted them as a solar light illuminated the area around the men.

Shocked, they reached for their belts, but Victoria and the men beside her stepped closer, aiming their guns at the EEG officers. "Hands up where we can see them," Moretti ordered.

"Who are you?" the older of the two asked, eyeing Gallagher.

"The Freedom Front," Gallagher replied smoothly.

"That was just a rumor," the younger officer blurted.

"Not at all," Gallagher replied.

The older guard thought about that for a second, then narrowed his eyes at Gallagher. "You're Gallagher Brown, aren't you?"

"Guilty as charged. Let me introduce you to The Freedom Front.

You're being taken into custody until after the fall of Nicks. Normally, we give prisoners a choice to join us instead of imprisonment, but you Elizabeth Elite Guard guys won't have that privilege. You've taken things too far in here."

The other guard glanced doubtfully around. "Even though you've accomplished something with your resistance, you can't beat her."

"We will," Gallagher corrected him.

Once their hands were bound, Niyol stepped closer and laid his hand on the first officer. "Where is everyone?"

"They were downstairs training when the power went out. The basement steps lead straight to a room with large black double doors where you will find the prisoners and guards. But some of the guards might be in the breaker room now."

"Where is the breaker room?"

"Just down the hall from that room is a door marked UTILITY."

Moretti assigned two men to take the guards out to the hovers, and the rest of us followed after him and Gallagher, down the corridor and through a set of doors leading to the basement stairwell. The emergency lights lit the path for us as we descended the steps, along with a few solar palm lights some of us held. After a few minutes we were perched outside the black double doors.

"Here we go," whispered Gallagher. "Ross, Samuels, take Victoria with you and check out the breaker room for any guards. Some of them will probably be with the prisoners, too."

Victoria nudged my arm before following after Officers Samuels and Ross. "Be careful, cuz," she said softly.

"You too, Vic."

Once they'd tiptoed off, Gallagher's eyes settled on us. "Jabari, why don't you all stay behind my men? And keep Adrianne with you. We've got weapons. Let us handle this."

"But we can help fight," Marcello interjected.

"I know, but won't it be nice to let us handle that part for once?" he asked with a wink.

Marcello shrugged, but Jabari tipped his head in agreement. "We'll hang back a little, but we're going in, too."

"Too bad you can't go with us everywhere. It's a lot easier with armed men on our side," Zi said with a small grin.

Niyol, who'd been silent until now, placed a hand on Daktari's shoulder. "Once it is secure, we need to heal the prisoners."

"I'm ready," Daktari answered, rubbing his palms together.

Niyol's eyes wandered to mine. "Everyone be careful," he advised.

Something about his tone concerned me, but there was no time for doubt. Niyol, Lietuenant Moretti, Gallagher, and their men barreled through the doors the next moment with weapons aimed, and I sucked in my breath as tension filled me. Jabari squeezed my hand and pulled me along behind him as shouting erupted in the room ahead of us.

Once inside the room, I froze, forcing Jabari to a halt beside me. Adrianne, Zi, and the others hesitated beside us as well, but Daktari took off towards Niyol. I gasped as I took in the scene. The emergency lights cast just enough light around the room for us to see the results of Nata's evil operation. In the center of the room, a prisoner was tied to a long board, his arms and legs stretched painfully in opposite directions. Dressed in only a thin pair of prison pants, his exposed torso displayed bruises and was so tiny, it reminded me of a skeleton. He'd been beaten, tortured, and starved . . . Could he still be alive?

Daktari and Niyol went to him first, placing their hands on him as Gallagher cut the man free with his knife. The rest of Gallagher's men were moving EEG officers into a cluster on one side of the room, tying their hands and removing their various weapons, of which there were many. I studied some of the metal objects with their razor sharp tips as they were taken and my mind took off thinking of the various ways those weapons had been used to torture people, just because they were on Nata's list. For having the wrong color of skin and the wrong racial makeup.

Jabari's lips moved against my ear. "Stay close to me in case they haven't rounded up all of the officers. Are you sure you want to be in here? I could take you outside to wait if it's too much."

Normally, I might have assured him I was fine, but a feeling of dread was building in me the longer I stood in the room. Maybe it was too much.

Before I could respond, Niyol hurried over to us. His eyes were fierce and his voice urgent. "Go into the cells and check on the prisoners. Let me know the ones who need the most immediate attention," he instructed. Adrianne, Cole, Zi, and Marcello set to work right away, but I stood right where I was.

Gallagher's voice called out across the room. "Move fast, people. We need to evacuate the building ASAP, for the next phase of the plan."

As Niyol began to turn away, he caught my eye, and again, I worried something was wrong. "*What is it?*" I asked him silently.

"*Be extra careful, Rainchild. Use your gifts if you feel compelled to.*"

He took off into a dark prison cell, and Jabari pulled me in the opposite direction. "We'll start on this end," Jabari decided. "You stay right with me, Rain," he repeated his warning.

I wished I felt stronger and more like my usual self. Normally, I might tell him to stop worrying about me and to focus on the safety of the group, but I knew it was pointless. And I figured that after what had just happened outside, he probably needed me beside him as much as I needed him.

"I'll stay right with you," I reassured him as we ducked into an obscure prison cell.

I flashed my solar light around the floor, stopping when I located a girl shivering in the corner. She wasn't as tiny as the man on the board, but too small, presumably from starvation. Her eyes were huge as she took us in. My heart filled with sadness for her, and I took a step towards her.

"Stay back!" she shrieked, pressing her body against the wall.

Jabari's voice was calm and reassuring. "We aren't here to hurt you. We're not with the EEG or Nicks. We're part of the resistance and we want to help get you out of here."

She glanced nervously between Jabari and me. "You're lying," she accused.

"No, we're here to help, like he said," I stated softly. "We have people who can treat your injuries, too. Will you come with us?"

I offered my hand to her, and she stared at it like it might attack her at any moment. All she had known in this prison was torment, and here we were offering her freedom. Plus, we didn't exactly embody the image of health. We were small, though not like her, and we were dressed in old clothes and certainly not the likeliest of *rescuers*. She had to think it was a trap.

She shook her head, adamantly refusing our help, trembling with fear. There was no time to win her trust. There was only one way to get her out. I closed my eyes and called to Jabari silently. *"You'll have to use your ability to get her out of here. We don't have much time."*

"If you think it's the right thing to do."

"I do."

He crouched down so he was eye level with the girl, but not too close to her. His voice was calm when he spoke again. "Trust us. We're here to help you. Now come on out of the cell with us. You'll be safe with our friends." He paused, as if letting the words or his ability sink in, and then offered his hand, palm up. "Okay?" he finished.

She accepted his hand, and her face relaxed as he helped her to her feet. "Okay," she said tranquilly.

We guided her out of the cell and over to Niyol. She let him lay his hands on her head as he began to heal wounds I couldn't see but knew were there.

Once he finished, Victoria jogged into the room. "Samuels and Ross took one EEG officer into custody we found in the breaker room. They should be back here in a minute. Where do you need me now?" she asked Moretti.

"Can you help take these people to our hover?" he asked, gesturing towards a small group of released prisoners, who Daktari and Niyol had healed.

"Sure thing." She approached the girl we'd led out of the cell and smiled. "I'm Victoria. You're going to be safe now, I promise."

The girl nodded and accepted Vic's hand and they walked away, with a few other prisoners and two more of Gallagher's men.

Once they were gone, Moretti turned to Gallagher. "I think we've got everyone. The guard outside must have been off. We don't have twenty, like he said."

Gallagher glanced around. "But all of the cells are empty now. You guys searched the entire building?"

"Yes, sir," Moretti replied.

The last of the EEG officers were being led away, and Niyol held up his hand. "Wait a moment."

Gallagher motioned his men to stop, and Niyol hurried over to them. He placed a hand on one of the EEG guard's shoulders, whose expression softened.

"Are there any more prisoners?" Niyol enquired.

"Yes, in the cage."

"The cage?" I heard myself say in exasperation. Fear started in my stomach and began filling my entire body as I imagined the cage and wondered if it was like the underground hole I'd been locked in at Metro Prison.

Jabari patted my back lightly. "It's okay. I'm right here with you."

"Where is the cage?" Niyol continued.

"The last cell, 16D, has a door inside the back corner that leads to the cage."

Before Niyol could ask anything else my feet were moving. Rage crept up my body, replacing my fear, as I imagined the people locked in a cage, suffocating or enduring something awful.

Jabari called out from behind me, but his voice sounded muted. "Wait up, Rain."

I was vaguely aware that I was using my ability to run faster than anyone, but the thought of whoever was in the cage dominated everything else. I had to find them. I ran into cell 16D and found the door in the corner as promised. I pulled at the handle but it didn't budge. I put all of my force into it, but the door was locked or jammed. As images I couldn't bear filled my head I slammed my body into the door, adrenaline filling me so much I couldn't feel the pain that I should have. I stood back and took a deep breath. I threw my body against the door again, groaning aloud as it didn't budge.

"Move over," Jabari's breathless voice interrupted my defeated and reckless thoughts.

One glance at his face told me he was mad, and I knew it was because I'd run off and not remained by his side as I'd promised earlier, but he didn't mention it. He placed his hands on the door, and with one seemingly effortless nudge, it opened before us. I scrambled in before he could stop me and came to a halt. It was pitch-black. There were no emergency lights here. A small moan, and then another, sounded from somewhere in the darkness.

My hands shook as I flipped my solar light on just as Jabari lit another beside me.

"What in the world?" I asked, my eyes widening in fear.

There was a group of people, all piled together, some of them moaning, the others all lying still.

Jabari knelt down beside one of the men. "Where is the cage?" he asked soothingly.

"You're in it."

"I'm afraid he's correct," a deep voice spoke up, making us flinch.

Jabari shot to his feet as I spun my hand around to shine a light on the man. An EEG officer stood in the doorframe and smiled. "They won't be able to save you in time."

Time seemed to stop as an electric current shot out from an object in his hand. As comprehension settled in, I froze in terror. It happened before I could do anything. Jabari's body fell like a tree towards the floor as the guard disappeared through the doorway. The door closed and clicked as a beep erupted around us. A robotic voice blasted through the room. "Five, four, three . . ."

A countdown? To what? I fell to the floor, bringing Jabari's head into my lap, shaking him, desperate to wake him up.

". . . one. Commence extermination."

My heart hammered against my chest, up to my throat, filling my ears. As the word *extermination* raced through my mind, a thin smoke began to seep into the room through vents above us, I hadn't even noticed until now. The smoke had to be the same poisonous gas she'd used to kill Cole's parents and that she was planning to gas the mixed zones with. It was already burning my nostrils as it reached me. I pulled my shirt up over my mouth, then took Jabari's shirt to do the same to him. We had to get out of here.

I shook him as hard as I could. "Wake up, Jabari. You have to break down the door. Please," I cried.

He didn't respond and with each second that passed, my head felt dizzier than before. I fell over Jabari's chest, clinging to him, squeezing my eyes shut as I called to Niyol. *"We're trapped and gas is pouring in, please—"*

"Welcome to the extermination chamber." Chills shot down my spine at the sound of her voice. She sounded so close, I didn't know how, but it was almost as if she were right inside the cage with us.

"No one will remember you, mixed breeds. No one will ever know you existed."

I sat up and felt my stomach bottom out. Nata was staring at me with her cold blue eyes.

Chapter 19: Choking

RAIN

I stared back at her, confused for a moment, then somehow through the rapidly filling hazy air I saw the edges of the screen. She wasn't in the room with us. She was watching us and talking to us from somewhere else. I wondered if she could see us, too.

"Please, stop this!" I yelled at her. I started coughing again, unable to breathe as the room drowned in the gas.

She didn't react or pause. She continued her rant about the impurity of the mixed races. So she couldn't see us. I leaned forward, shaking Jabari again. "Wake up, please. You're the only one who can break the door down."

He didn't respond. I tried to ignore Nata's words, but couldn't. Panic raced through me, straight to my core. "All of your kind will die like this. Every one of you will be wiped from the face of the earth, and the pure race will thrive."

"It doesn't have to be like this," I shouted at her.

"I'm cleansing the nation. It's beautiful," she continued, ignoring me completely.

"This is the future for those who will serve and obey me. The pure race is our only hope." As her voice trailed off, my eyes found the screen.

She disappeared and new images reeled before me. Images from the pure zone. I'd seen the pure zone children in the video at Gallagher's camp. But there were more of them now. They were blond and blue-eyed and bowing to "Mother" whenever Nata appeared before them. A new image appeared, and a tear slid down my face. Calista was instructing the little ones, pointing to images of people who weren't Caucasian, blond, and blue-eyed, and the children would scream in fear. She pointed at people who looked like them, and they smiled. My poor cousin was in deep. Too deep. But I couldn't do anything to help her if I died in this room.

I tore my eyes from the screen and shook Jabari again. But when he didn't respond, I collapsed on his chest, sobbing and choking. I closed my eyes and clung to him, turning to prayer. I pleaded for our lives so we could continue to fight this battle, so we could free Calista and help the pure kids before it was too late to save them. And then I knew what to do. I had to reach Jabari with my ability. I wasn't asleep, but he was. I'd never tried to reach him like this before, but it seemed like the only thing to do. He was the only one who could free us from this death chamber.

"*Jabari, wake up. You have to break down the door or we'll die. Please wake up. You can save us, Jabari. But I'm out of ideas. We're trapped in a death chamber. The gas will kill us all. But you can save us. Wake up.*"

"*Rain, where are you?*"

"*I'm trapped in the chamber with you. The EEG officer knocked you out with his taser. Just wake up. You have to break the door down.*"

I shook him again, silently pleading with him still. He'd responded to my voice. He was still in there. My hands tightened around him and his eyes batted open. "Jabari!"

He sat up, confusion sweeping his face as the smoky air grew thicker around us. As I fell forward, succumbing to the poison engulfing my lungs I barely got the words out. "The door."

He bolted to his feet as my face hit the floor. As my eyes closed, I heard him shove the door open and the voices of our allies greeting him frantically. I didn't know if I'd live, but I was sure Jabari had made it out.

Hands grabbed me and lifted me. Moments later, I sensed the change in the air. "Rain, hang in there," Daktari ordered.

From the shuffling and shouting around me, I knew they were rescuing everyone from the chamber. Part of me wondered if Nata would send someone for us, or if she could even see into the chamber. Had she watched us escape? But I was so relieved to be out of the room I didn't care much at the moment. Warmth spread through me as hands covered my face and stomach. I opened my eyes to see Niyol and Daktari leaning over me, healing me. Marcello, Cole, Adrianne, Zi, and Jabari all hovered over me as well, their expressions panicky.

"Hi," I said at last.

Zi's relieved cry rang out around us. "Hi? You nearly gave me a heart attack, Rain. And you say hi?" She knelt down between Daktari and Niyol and pulled me up and against her.

"You just rushed ahead on into danger without waiting for us. We got there just as the EEG guard came out and sealed the door. He said it was on lockdown and no one could open the door until the gas had been fully released and everyone inside was dead. Niyol used his ability on the guard, but he said that no one knows how to override the system. Apparently the death chamber has a different backup power supply and runs off a separate power grid then the rest of the building. The door is so thick even Jonah couldn't reach the power source from out here. Gallagher and Moretti tried to use something to blow the door up, Rain, and even that didn't work. We thought you might die," Zi's voice trembled as she spoke, and tears ran down her face.

I rubbed her back gently. "We're fine now, Zi."

"Don't do anything like that again. You hear me?" she whispered, still crushing me in her embrace.

"Won't happen again."

She released me, and I got to my feet.

Jabari grabbed my shoulders. "We would have died if you hadn't used your ability to wake me up."

"But we're fine. You broke the door down."

His voice was strained. "You can't run off like that. If I hadn't followed you as fast as I could, you would've been locked in there without me."

"I know," I answered meekly.

"Stop being a hero," he said so softly, it sounded like a plea. The anger was gone, there was just desperation in his tone. I felt guilt pour through me. He was right. My hero complex was always putting us in danger. I was afraid I might be the downfall of all of us. His grip tightened. "Okay?"

I gulped. "Yeah." And then I remembered Nata. "But what about Nata? Is she going to retaliate now? Have we put our families in danger?" I hadn't thought about anyone else until this moment.

Gallagher approached me now. "She wasn't really watching you or talking to you exactly." He paused, tilting his head towards the EEG officer who'd locked us in the gas chamber. He was standing a few feet away in the custody of Samuels and Ross. "Niyol made him talk when we couldn't open the door, and he told us everything. It's a pre-recorded video that plays when the gas chamber is activated."

I was torn between relief and horror. Gallagher grimaced. "I know. No telling how many people have died in that room . . . her evil words the last thing they heard on earth. We have to stop her. Come on, my men are evacuating the prisoners. We'll get everyone into hiding. Moretti and his men are taking the EEG officers to various temporary prisons we've built until after the battle when they can face the United States justice system," he explained confidently.

The EEG officer snickered. "You will never restore the United States. She's too powerful."

"No one's talking to you," barked Officer Samuels.

Gallagher gave him a sideways glance, but didn't respond.

"She's handling you, Gallagher. She's made sure your so-called Freedom Front can't gain momentum. You can't win," he said smugly.

Officer Ross smacked the back of his head. "Didn't you hear Officer Samuels? No one asked for your opinion."

Niyol had been idling near Daktari and Zi but moved over now, his interest clearly sparked. "You need to tell me more."

The guard flinched as Niyol raised his hand towards him. "I'm not talking to you."

Officer Samuels smiled. "Oh, I think you'll be talking to him," he said with a chuckle.

As the EEG guard cast an irritated glance at Samuels, Niyol grabbed his shoulder, instantly subduing him. "Tell me what you know about The Freedom Front and Gallagher Brown and what the people are saying."

Just like everyone else who'd tried to resist Niyol's power, the officer automatically replied. "When President Nicks forced so many to join the Elizabeth Guard out of the blue, word eventually got out about what she needed them for. People in many of the zones, the ones she had recruited men and women from, heard the rumors about Gallagher Brown and started to protest and resist The Authority. They remembered him."

My friends and I exchanged excited looks. That had to be good news for our cause. If people remembered Gallagher it might give them more incentive to join us and stand up to The Authority when we shut down their Droid machinery and leaked the cyber messages about what Nata was really doing to the mixed zones.

"But she couldn't have that. She decided to create more soldiers to hunt for him. And she's been releasing camouflaged Droid Dogs to hunt for him, too."

Gallagher shrugged, turning to Jabari. "Well we knew that already, didn't we?"

"How has the president responded?" Niyol asked.

"She was worried about uprisings from within the zones, so she took care of it. Now they know better than to talk about Gallagher or the resistance."

This made me twitch. Daktari's eyes met mine. He had to be thinking the same thing. Grandma Julia. I'd had the dream about her. What if she was in danger?

"How has she taken care of it?" Niyol prodded.

"Everyone is being watched and anything suspicious is reported. Punishments for the simplest things are dealt with in the harshest manner. She has even occupied some of the homes with her officers, especially the zones where she has had the most resistance. Between the threat of being taken to the pure zone and the threat of being recruited for the Elizabeth Guard to either hunt for Gallagher or terrorize the zones, the people aren't talking about Gallagher Brown or The Freedom Front anymore. They have no hope. They're terrified."

As he finished, I wondered about what Sook had seen. Maybe Grandma Julia's house was under occupation, too. That would explain why he'd seen her cooking so much food. Of course, he hadn't seen any officers with her. She'd been alone. I decided to wait until later to discuss it with Jabari and everyone else. Gallagher was eyeing his watch.

"All right, you can load him up, guys. I've heard enough," Gallagher said.

As they took him away he motioned us closer. "We've got one more thing to do before we torch this bad boy," he said. He turned to Cole. "Son, I'm gonna need your expert computer skills. If we power the building up again, can you cut the cameras but help me get a message out?"

Cole shrugged. "Sure, that's no problem at all. Where do you want to send a message?"

Gallagher grinned. "I want you to hack into Nata's messaging system she sends to every zone in the UZTA."

"What?" Adrianne asked, dazed.

Gallagher went on. "I want to send a message simultaneously to every zone in the United Zones of The Authority. I want my message to appear on every computer screen, TV screen, and monitor across the land, *including* the ones in New Washington."

Cole wasn't the only one whose jaw fell open a little. But he recovered right away. "Well, we'd better get started . . . 'cause that might be a little tricky."

Chapter 20: Rumors

RAIN

Cole had set Gallagher up in front of a camera in an upstairs office and was preparing to shoot a video, which would stream through every TV monitor in the United Zones of The Authority, including the ones in Elizabeth Mansion. Every single person within the walled zones across the country would see the face of the UZTA's most wanted fugitive and hear his message.

The tension in the room was thick. One glance told me everyone was as nervous as I was, and even Niyol seemed a little uneasy. What Gallagher was about to do was huge. If he were to get caught, well, I couldn't even think about that. Numerous times, Nata had broadcasted messages to all of the mixed zones across the country, but even she had never spoken simultaneously to every single zone before. This was unprecedented. And it was dangerous.

I knew Gallagher had left a message for Nata to find after confiscating one of her hover vehicles and capturing her men, but this time he would be communicating directly with the people. Even though I understood that he wanted to rally their support, I was terrified for him. And I decided he was the bravest man alive for what he was about to do. Either that or the craziest. I never would have thought to send out a message to the zones using Nata's own technology, and I couldn't imagine what her reaction would be.

No one asked him what he'd say. I figured after hearing what the EEG officer had said about how no one had hope or believed the resistance group stood a chance against Nata, he wanted to clarify a few things. If people actually saw for themselves that he wasn't just a rumor, it could mean some of them might join the fight on the day of our attack. Plus, like Gallagher had been doing for weeks, he would continue to keep Nata's focus on him alone, and the six of us could continue to be the secret weapon of TFF. But it would put him and his loved ones in more danger than ever.

"Ready when you are," Cole notified Gallagher.

Gallagher winked at us, where we were hovered behind the camera, right behind Cole. "Let's do this."

Cole counted down and motioned the last two numbers silently as discussed, and a red light signified the camera was recording.

"Hello, captive citizens of the UZTA. My name is Gallagher Brown, and I'm broadcasting live with an important message. I don't have much time. You might not recognize me now. Believe it or not, I was once a Senator from Virginia, and the day I protested with the First Resistance in DC was the day Nicks murdered my wife, Kaya, along with every member of the First Resistance. So many of us have lost loved ones at her hands. Anyhow, pardon the beard. Elizabeth Nicks is hunting for me, as many of you have probably heard. I've had to break into Elizabeth Nicks's camera system with the help of my friends. I'm talking to all of you in every single zone in the country. Many of you may have heard rumors about The Freedom Front. I'd like to set things straight. They aren't rumors. I am leading this resistance group from outside the walls of the zones. The Freedom Front is growing more powerful each and every day. Refugees like myself who have survived in hiding since the walls went up have banded together for the ultimate cause. We're going to take back our country.

"I've heard how Nicks is punishing those of you who have dared to support our cause, and I'm sorry for your suffering. And it's because of the suffering of countless lives that I'm here now asking you for your support. A day will come very soon, you'll know when it is here, when you'll have the choice to make. You'll have a chance to join our cause. I'm not asking you to do anything to risk your lives now. But just know that the day is coming. Don't believe her lies. She uses fear to control you. You might not be aware of the inhumane treatment and suffering of the captive citizens of the mixed zones across the UZTA. They are barely surviving. They are living in concentration camp conditions. The weakest among them are being taken away and being subjected to more torture at the hands of Elizabeth Nicks's EEG officers. Nicks is building the pure zones, and what she isn't telling you is that slowly but surely she is killing off the people across the zones who don't fit into her new pure race. But listen to me carefully. Whatever happens in the days ahead, don't lose hope. We aren't going to let Elizabeth Nicks kill us. We are going to take her out of power. And we are going to restore the United States of America. Stay strong. Be brave. And hang on to every bit of hope. This is Gallagher Brown, the leader of The Freedom Front, signing off . . . for now," he grinned at the camera as he waved goodbye, then motioned for Cole to cut.

Goosebumps covered my skin. We were speechless.

Niyol finally spoke. "What you have done was very brave, Gallagher. You've not only given the people hope, you've helped keep Nata's attention off of everyone here," he said gesturing towards us.

Zi threw her hands up in exasperation. "Yes, but you're going to be in more danger now than ever," she said worriedly, glancing towards Adrianne.

Gallagher patted her shoulder. "Yes, Zi, but it had to be done. And now the people know the resistance is real. I only wish I could have told them about the teenagers who started it all."

"Well, just so you know, assuming we all survive, you've got my vote for president," Zi replied with a small smile.

"Mine, too," Cole agreed as he grinned at Adrianne.

"President?" Gallagher said with a chuckle. "I'd be happy just to have my face off of the most wanted list. You guys are the heart of TFF."

"We wouldn't have made it very far if it weren't for you," Jabari said.

Gallagher shook his head. "We're in this together."

"And you each have a role to play," Niyol added, his eyes landing on me.

"Time to go. I know Cole has skills, but just in case she makes the connection to this location, we'd better move out," Gallagher decided.

"This place will be in ashes before she figures it out," Moretti said.

Jabari held my hand firmly as we moved outside, and I couldn't help but notice the way Niyol was staring at me. But I knew if I asked him directly what he had meant when he said we each have a role to play, he would probably give me a vague response.

Moretti and Gallagher's men had been busy. All of the hovers had been moved back and were loaded up. And a few men were finishing up pouring containers around the property. Vic poured the rest of her container over a stack of boards piled beside an interior doorway I hadn't noticed earlier. I imagined it would be where they lit the fire.

"What is that stuff?" Daktari asked.

"A very powerful accelerant. We brought our own, but this stuff will burn this place down fast. We found it in the basement," Victoria answered.

"Anyone like to do the honors?" asked Gallagher.

Niyol's head titled towards me, and I recalled my dream. He had told me it had to be me for some reason, and he handed me the matches.

I tugged my hand from Jabari's and stepped forward. "I'll do it."

Gallagher raised an eyebrow and grinned. "All right, Rain. Burn it down."

As he placed a pack of matches in my upturned hand, a chill ran down my back. The memory of the woman screaming in my nightmare rushed over me. I turned to Niyol and used my telepathy. "*But in my dream there was a woman screaming.*"

"*The building is empty. Are you prepared to do what it takes to beat her? You, more than anyone, have to be ready to finish it all.*"

"*But what do you mean exactly?*"

"*You'll know when it's time. Let this be your warm-up. Burn her training center down. Defy Nata. She won't be able to hurt people here after this. Use this act of defiance to make you stronger. You'll need strength when you face her in the end, Rainchild.*"

As usual, I figured he knew a lot more than he was telling me, but I knew he wouldn't give me the details. I'd have to let it go.

"Everyone back. As soon as you light it, get into the hover, Rain," Gallagher instructed.

Jabari seemed hesitant to leave me. "Run. As soon as you light it."

I didn't speak, but bobbed my head in agreement.

A moment later, everyone stood back near the hovers, their anxious expressions trained on me.

Niyol stood in front, and our eyes met. "*Are you willing to go the distance?*" he asked.

My mind ran with thoughts and memories of everyone who had suffered and lost, and those who were still suffering because of Nata and her EEG officers, and I knew I was ready for whatever unknown challenge I would face in the days ahead. Niyol wouldn't tell me everything now, but somehow it didn't matter. "*I am willing. And I'm ready.*"

As I crossed to the pile Vic had doused in accelerant, my hands trembled. I lit the match and held my breath as I flicked it onto the pile of boards. I felt the breath release as flames lit up and a feeling of satisfaction slowly crept through me.

"Come on, Rain," Jabari yelled from behind me.

I took off, noting in my peripheral vision how the fire was running away in all directions, following the trail of accelerant.

Jabari pulled me into a quick hug as I reached him. "She can't hurt anyone here anymore. I have to admit, I was worried they might bring my dad here."

"They can't now," Gallagher said.

Daktari approached and tossled my hair. "Wow, sis. You are officially a UZTA criminal," he teased. "I've never been more proud."

As the fire grew more powerful, we watched in silence. One of the officers began yelling from inside the hover with the prisoners. "This won't change anything! She's too powerful!"

Niyol narrowed his eyes. "Let's ask him a couple more questions."

Gallagher shrugged. "Bring him out."

Jacks and Samuels set him on the edge of the hover door. Before Niyol could touch him, he was already talking. "You can't stop what she has already accomplished," he said angrily.

Niyol grabbed his shoulders. "Explain yourself," he ordered.

His voice became soft as he replied. "This is just part of it. The other weak ones have already been sent to a prison holding area for some sort of pure zone training. And I heard she has some sort of initiation ceremony planned for them. I think it is part of the training, too. She was going to take some of the prisoners from this facility, as well. Just because you freed the people here, doesn't mean she won't go after more."

"How is she using them with the pure zone training?"

"She wants to make sure her new pure kids are thoroughly trained in her philosophy." He stared blankly ahead, and I knew he was under Niyol's power. "She's brainwashing them to hurt people who don't look like them. The new pure zone citizens will think like EEG officers, in addition to looking like she wants them to. She wants them to be aggressive and abusive towards others. And she has already sent the pure race teachers to us. Everyone must be conditioned in order to live in the pure zone. Some of them were more resistant than others. But we broke them down eventually."

It felt like a knife had dug into my stomach. "Ask him about Calista," I blurted.

Niyol's brow wove together. "I don't think I should."

"I have to know," I insisted.

"Was there a teenager here for the training, named Calista?"

The guard nodded. "She was one of the hardest ones to break. But we did, eventually."

Tears instantly stung my eyes but I wouldn't let them fall. Daktari grabbed my hand. "She's playing a role, Rain. We know she didn't have a choice."

"I know." I looked him in the eyes as my thoughts ran ahead, saying what I couldn't say aloud. *"But what if they really did break her? What if she's too far gone now?"*

"Then we'll deal with that when the time comes."

"Put him back inside," Gallagher ordered. As the officer was taken away he turned to us. "Listen kids, have faith. We need to head out in case a patrol notices the fire. We'll discuss things with the Pinkie as planned. If it weren't for Calista, we wouldn't have that Pinkie technology on our side. Don't forget what she has risked for our cause. I think she's going to survive this. And who knows, maybe my team and I can do something to help out these prisoners at this initiation ceremony he mentioned. We will keep looking for information about it."

While everyone said quick farewells and piled into the hovers, I reached for Niyol. "Are you going to tell me what you meant when you said I have to finish it? You said that in my dream, too, you know."

"You'll know what to do when it's time," he said, hugging me back. He pushed me back slightly to peer into my eyes. "Remember, no matter what happens in the days ahead, you have to keep fighting."

As he turned to leave, I called out to him. "Niyol, wait. Would you tell me if my grandma is in trouble? And Calista? I'm worried about them both."

He hesitated, seeming to contemplate his response. "Just like everything else, you'll know what to do and when to do it. Keep your chin up."

"Come on, Rain," Daktari called from our hover.

I backed into the hover and sighed as we took off. From the window I watched the burning building fade away with mixed emotions. On the one hand, we'd made sure no one else could be hurt at that training center. We had freed some of Nata's prisoners, including Maha. But I'd learned that Calista had been forced to go through training there, and I couldn't imagine how it had changed her. Niyol had again left me wondering what he knew about the fight ahead and wondering if I had what it took to accomplish my mission, whatever it was exactly.

Daktari leaned over the seat, breaking my train of frenzied thoughts. My jacket and hat were in his hands. "Adrianne brought these back. Put them on. You're still freezing."

As I reached towards my jacket, Daktari grabbed my hand, forcing me to look him in the eye. "Forget about the bad stuff for now. And remember, Calista won't turn on us."

"He's right," Marcello interjected. "And don't forget the best part about today. Gallagher called all out war on Nata. Imagine what the people are thinking right now."

"Guess we'll see how our zone is handling the news of Gallagher soon enough," Cole called from up front. "Next stop, Indy Mixed Zone."

Chapter 21: Family

RAIN

It was early evening by the time we were making our way back to our apartments. I searched the streets as I trekked beside Daktari and Zi, looking for signs of trouble. Surely Nata would react to Gallagher's bold move of speaking to the entire country. But would she retaliate against the zones specifically? Would we be on her list? Jabari felt sure that we would be safe, but that she would increase her efforts to find Gallagher. But still part of me expected to see Droid Dogs out in full force and maybe even a human officer or two enforcing the law or punishing people for no reason.

But there were no signs of trouble. Everything was normal except for one small but significant difference. On the faces of the people in the streets, there was evidence of hope. Zi and Daktari were practically gliding beside me as they whispered excitedly about the subtle yet obvious mood improvement in the mixed zone. If Gallagher Brown could have that effect on the people with a simple video message, maybe when the time came to join him and the cause, the people really would support us.

Despite all of my worries, I couldn't help but feel a little hope myself. It was difficult not to. Still, in the back of my mind I wondered if the Elizabeth Guard was busy tormenting another zone. And I had to worry about Calista and Grandma Julia. Plus, the EEG officer had said Nata would likely need more prisoners, which had me worrying about the prisoners in Indy Mixed Zone, in particular Jabari's dad. We were nearly back to the apartment when I decided to use my telepathy to contact him. Once Daktari and Zi had gone inside, I sat down on the front concrete steps and closed my eyes.

"Francisco, can you hear me?"

He responded right away. *"Rain, are you okay?"*

"Yes, how are you?"

"I'm worried. I was hoping you'd contact me. They took Maha away. I don't know where she is. I heard them come for her, but when she asked them where they were taking her, they wouldn't say. I'm so sorry I couldn't help her. I tried to yell, to get them to take me, but—"

"Wait, it's fine. She's safe, Francisco. That's what I wanted to tell you. We met with our allies outside the zone, and they rescued her. She's in one of the allied camps now. They'll take care of her," I reassured him.

"Wow, you guys work fast. They only took her yesterday. How did you know?"

"Eric tipped us off. And we really didn't do much. It was Gallagher Brown and his supporters."

"I think you're being humble. I know they couldn't have rescued Maha without you all. You kids have been busy. Thanks for letting me know. I've been trying to protect her in here. It's good that she's safe now."

"She said to tell you thank you again for all you did."

"Do you know why they took her?"

I pulled my coat tighter around me. *"That's the other reason I wanted to talk to you. They took a group of prisoners. Nata is targeting the weakest prisoners in all of the prisons. They took them to the Elizabeth Elite Guard headquarters. We think they were planning to use them, at least that's what we discovered, for torture, as part of the training the EEG officers go through to become monsters. We emptied the EEG building and Gallagher took everyone with him. And we even burned the building to the ground, but Nata will retaliate. And this doesn't mean she will stop targeting the weakest prisoners. One of the EEG officers we captured said she will certainly come back for more people. She is planning something awful at some sort of pure zone initiation event coming up. We're trying to find out more about it."*

"You actually burned the training center down? Incredible." I could

hear the amusement in his tone and imagined his mouth lifting into a small smile.

"*Yes, but listen. It is very important that you stay safe and strong.*"

"*Wait, you're worried about me being taken? As one of the weak?*" He sounded amused still.

"*Francisco, I . . . well, of course I am worried about you. I don't think you're the weakest prisoner at all, but I just had to warn you. And I know you look out for your cellmate, Ian, too. You guys have to hang in there. It might get worse now. Nata is angry and she needs more prisoners.*"

"*I'm flattered you're worried about me, but I'm hanging in there. And I won't show any signs of weakness. Don't you worry about me.*"

"*Okay, well, I had to say something. Jabari worries about you, you know.*"

His tone sobered. "*I know he does. But tell him I'm fine. And tell him how proud I am of him, will you?*"

"*Yeah, I will. He's tough, just like you. But I know he hurts. He misses you so much.*"

Francisco's voice was softer now. "*He's lucky to have someone like you, who loves him so much. Don't worry, Rain. I'll take care of myself in here. Thanks for the heads up. And please, take care of yourself. You worry too much about everyone else. Watch your back for me.*"

A minute later I'd said goodbye to Francisco, and I went inside to find Mom sitting at the metal folding table in the kitchen, sipping a cup of hot tea. Daktari was leaning against the counter, his arms folded against his chest. They both smiled at me as I entered the kitchen. Though Mom had been improving more and more each day ever since we had rescued her from Officer Dean, it still seemed strange to see her acting so normal. Months ago, she would have been curled up on the couch, hardly moving, and now she was sitting at the table.

"Rain, sit down and have some hot tea to warm up. Your nose is so red. You must be freezing."

Before I could respond, she jumped to her feet and hugged me tightly. "Oh, your clothes are damp like Daktari's. He told me how the water pipe burst in the street all over you two. How strange."

I figured Daktari had come up with the excuse for our damp clothes and shrugged. "Yeah, it was weird."

She nudged me towards the chair opposite hers. "Sit down, I'll get you some tea."

"You sit back down, Mom. I'll get her tea," Daktari volunteered.

I took my seat and watched as she took another sip. She set the cup down and smiled at me again. I wanted to pinch myself to see if I was awake. Mom had come so far.

"Daktari says you were hanging out with Zi when the message broadcasted earlier. Can you believe it? Gallagher Brown is alive?" Her eyes were huge, and her smile remained intact. She seemed genuinely happy. I wasn't sure how to react.

"You remember him?" I enquired cautiously, as Daktari placed hot tea in front of me.

"Of course I do. Right after that first resistance group disappeared in DC when Nicks took over, his face was all over the news. Supposedly, he was wanted for conspiracy against the government. But who could believe that? He was just trying to tell the rest of us to wake up. If only we'd listened to him. He was one of the most likeable senators. He represented Virginia as I recall. The idea that he's out there and going to stand up to her is honestly a little crazy, but kind of exciting. But what are the chances that he could actually defeat her? But I guess nothing much makes sense anymore. If only we could turn back time . . ." Her voice trailed off as her smile faded away.

"Are you okay, Mom?" Daktari asked.

"I was just thinking about my mother. It sounds terrible, but I try *not* to think about her. It makes me sad."

"I'm sure she's fine," Daktari blurted.

"Even though her e-mails were short and obviously edited, I used to read them when they came. But we haven't heard from her for months."

"I think that's The Authority's way of hurting us, Mom. I know if Grandma Julia could talk to us, she would. You have to know that, Mom," I said.

When Mom looked up again, there was curiosity in her expression. "Have you spoken to her recently?"

"No, I would have told you if the e-mails were working again, Mom," I answered in a hurry, knowing she couldn't possibly be talking about my ability.

On the day she'd discovered that we were a little different, when we'd saved her from Officer Dean, she'd nearly had another break down and said she didn't want to know anything about our powers or what we were up to. She just wanted us to obey The Authority. She specifically had said she didn't want to ever hear a word about our special abilities. She'd been terrified The Authority might hurt us if they knew the truth.

"I'm talking about your ability, Rain."

Daktari and I froze, but our eyes met from across the space. "Um," I began nervously.

"The day you saved me from Dean . . . Takara walked me out of the basement, and she told me everything. I told her I didn't want to hear about it ever again. And then when I confronted you about it later, and I saw how Daktari had healed your gunshot wound, I know I told you not to talk to me about it again."

I proceeded slowly. "You said you *never* wanted to discuss it, Mom. And we respect that."

She sat up a little straighter. "I'm beginning to see things differently, Rain." She turned to Daktari. "I'm so sorry I've been such a terrible mother ever since we came here. There's no excuse for how I abandoned you two. And your father."

"You never abandoned us," I insisted.

"Yeah, and you've been here the whole time," Daktari added.

"I was physically here, but I wasn't here for you at all, and you're just too nice to make me feel bad about it, kids. I know I deserted you."

I reached across the table, gently taking her hand. "Mom, he was torturing you. And you were protecting us from that monster. How could you have been any different?"

Tears filled her eyes. "You guys saved me from him. And if your abilities helped you to do it, I want to know more about how they work. I know I can't expect you to forgive me for how I hurt you. And I can't get the time back that we lost, but . . . I want you to be able to talk to me again. There's so much I regret. It makes my head hurt, literally, just thinking about it." She dropped her head into her hands and shook a little as she cried.

"Stop talking like that, Mom. We forgive you," Daktari said as he crossed the room and laid his hand on her shoulder.

He looked at me and I spoke to him telepathically. "*Go ahead, Daktari. Heal her.*"

"*I will, and you show her how you use your telepathy, Rain. It's time.*"

He placed another hand on her shoulder, and closed his eyes.

After a moment, she sat up again. "Daktari, you did that? My headache is gone. I felt warmth moving from my shoulders throughout my body when you touched me. The day you saved Rain, I was afraid to ask you about it. If anyone knew what you could do, they'd take you away from us. But wow, it is the most amazing feeling." Her voice was thick with awe.

I closed my eyes and spoke to her with my ability. "*Until he actually heals you, it is hard to understand. But it is truly amazing, you're right.*"

Mom's hand shot to her mouth as she gasped. "I heard you. Takara told me you could do it, but . . . how is that possible?"

"*Just close your eyes and respond to me, Mom.*"

"*I can't believe this is happening.*"

"*Don't waste another second feeling bad about the past. You saved us by letting him hurt you instead of us. We love you.*"

Mom let out a nervous laugh and then spoke to both of us out loud. "To think I've been so worried about you two. And you have superpowers. I promise to do better. I want to be a better mom for you both." She waved a finger towards me. "But a little warning first before you use that telepathy on me, okay?" she teased.

I nodded my head. "Deal."

Hope filled her eyes. "You've spoken to Grandma Julia, haven't you?"

"Yeah. She's doing fine. I mean, she's worried about you and all of us, but she's healthy and still hanging in there," I said.

Mom sighed with relief. "Good. I've been so worried about her, especially the past few days. She's been heavy on my mind. I hate not being able to receive messages from her."

As I studied her I decided not to push my luck for today. Mom didn't need to know that we were worried about Grandma Julia too. It might be too much for her, even though she was clearly getting better.

She reached for my hand again. "One more thing, Rain. I'm sorry I've been so hard on you about Jabari."

I gave Daktari a sideways glance. Was he hearing this?

When I didn't reply, Mom went on. "I'm not implying that I want you to risk getting into any trouble with The Authority. Even though your dad tells me every night how one day soon we will be free, I'm not exactly convinced. You have to know that it is hard for me to imagine freedom after everything I've been through. But I don't know what you're involved in, and I don't want to know the details. Your dad tells me Jabari is someone we can trust. I guess what I'm trying to say is I understand that you have feelings for him, and please be careful with your . . . friendship."

"Um, okay," I stammered awkwardly.

I thought back to the months before when she'd repeatedly told me to stay away from him. I understood why she'd done it, and I understood how hard it must have been for her to, in a sense, give me permission to have a friendship with him now. But I didn't know what else to say, so I was grateful when she changed the subject.

"Daktari said he'd get out the cards he keeps stashed in his mattress. Feel up to a game of Crazy Eights?" she asked, smiling at me again.

My mouth fell open a little. Before New Segregation, we'd played cards with Mom and Dad all the time. Mom hadn't touched the deck in years though.

"Of course I feel up to it," I finally managed to say.

The next hour passed in a whirlwind. And even though I knew Dad was working a double shift under horrific conditions, I managed to enjoy the time with Mom and Daktari. It was hard not to feel happy, even with my lingering worries, while Mom laughed and smiled through a game of cards. After the three of us ate a meal of canned beans, Mom decided to curl up on the couch with a book, and Daktari told me to go ahead on my nightly jog since he was going to start rereading *The Chronicles of Narnia*.

As I pulled my ancient sneakers on beside my bed I smiled, grateful for the day and Mom's improvement in spirits and demeanor.

"*Rain, it's me.*"

I collapsed onto the bed at the sound of Bhavna's voice.

"*Bhavna, you nearly scared me to death. What's up?*" I said happily.

"*Hi, Rain, sorry to startle you.*" She sounded worried.

Instantly I knew there was trouble. I could feel it. "*What's wrong, Bhavna?*"

"*Sook has been checking on Grandma Julia like you asked him to.*" As her sentence ended, a sneaker fell from my hand.

I grabbed my temple on either side. "*Tell me she's alive,*" I whispered.

"*She is. She's definitely alive. But there's no easy way to say this.*"

Whatever it was, she didn't want to tell me. "*Spit it out, Bhavna.*"

"*It looks like there are officers from the Elizabeth Guard staying at your grandma's house. Sook says he saw her cooking for them today, and for some* reason he thinks they are actually living with her now. He said he saw an officer rip up a family photo with you guys in it, and she argued with him over it. Rain, I'm sorry to say this, but Sook said the man slugged your grandma. She got up afterwards and was breathing and seems okay now, but we had to tell you. He just saw this happen a little bit ago."

I took deep breaths as my mind raced ahead. My dreams had told me Grandma was in trouble, but I still hadn't done anything to help her. Jabari had said we could go check on her, but what if we were too late?

Bhavna must have read my train of thought. She sounded stressed when she spoke again. "Rain, please don't do anything reckless. I almost didn't tell you because I was afraid you might do something spontaneous. I know you're worried, but—"

"She's my family."

"I know. And I knew you'd react this way. But promise you'll tell me before you do anything and that you'll be careful. Sook will keep an eye on her, I promise."

"Tell him I want him to check in on her every single day, Bhavna."

"He will. And Rain? I know you don't want to hear this, but I have to say it . . . We don't think you should use your telepathy on Grandma Julia just yet to check on her . . . in case this is some sort of trap. What if they've linked Calista to you all and it's a set up? Give us more time to figure out why they're at her house, deal?"

"I won't use my ability on her until I'm sure they aren't using her as a trap."

Once Bhavna was gone, I forced myself to stand. I had to tell Daktari. I had to tell Jabari. Grandma Julia was in trouble, and I wasn't going to leave her stranded.

Chapter 22: Abilities

RAIN

A few minutes later, I was filling Jabari in on everything as we ran down the dark streets of our zone. As planned, he'd been waiting for me to go on our nightly jog. The further away we got from my apartment and the more Jabari and I discussed what to do, the more I realized what had to be done. I needed to talk to Niyol. He could check on Grandma Julia. Jabari agreed that it couldn't hurt, so he led me to our usual spot, the isolated street near our hideout, and we sat down on the frigid curb so I could contact Niyol.

"I know you're scared. And I'm not going to tell you not to be," Jabari said sympathetically as he took my hand in his.

"Thanks for understanding," I replied. I pulled strength from his hand holding mine and closed my eyes.

"*Niyol, I need your help.*"

A moment later he replied. His voice was clear and strong, and some of my tension dissolved. "*Rainchild, what's wrong?*" he enquired.

"*It's my grandma. Sook said he saw an Authority guard hit her and that there are Elizabeth Guards living in her house. Why are they there? Is her house being occupied like the EEG officer was talking about? Why would they choose Grandma's house? Is it connected to Calista? What should I do?*"

"*I'm sorry that happened to her. I know it isn't easy to hear, but I think your grandmother is really strong. She's going to be fine. You have to believe that, Rainchild.*"

As he spoke, I could visualize him flying as the great horned owl, and the air around me somehow managed to drop in temperature. It was almost as if I was flying with him again, like when I contacted him after our hover crashed outside Bhavna's camp. As my mind took in the details of the scene, I realized he really was flying right then. It was dark, but there was a light shining on something below him. After a few seconds, I recognized a group of people, encircled by Elizabeth Guards and Droid Dogs.

"*Where are you, Niyol? What's happening?*"

"*Impressive, Rain. Your ability is strengthening. You can visualize my thoughts and see what I am seeing.*"

I squeezed Jabari's hand a little tighter, a reflex I guess from the surprise. I really was getting stronger.

"*Where are you?*" I repeated.

"*Lieutenant Moretti ran into a patrol on one of his runs to the refugee camps. I'm helping round-up the Elizabeth Guard officers.*"

"*Okay, then. I guess this is a bad time. They need you more than I do. Please let us know if you discover any connection between Grandma and Calista. We want to go see Grandma, but what if it is a trap?*"

"*I've been keeping an eye on Grandma Julia when I can. I think she's going to be fine, though I don't know exactly what is happening in her house. Promise me you'll trust your instincts no matter what you decide to do about her. I'll help you when the time comes, should the need arise.*"

I wanted to demand more. He hadn't exactly told me what to do. But I could picture him landing near the guards now and knew he needed to help our allies.

"*Goodbye for now, Rainchild.*"

"*Goodbye, Niyol.*"

When he was gone and I could no longer picture the dark scene where they were surrounding the Elizabeth Guard patrol, I opened my eyes.

Before I could speak, Jabari shook his head. "Wow, dream girl. Wow."

I met his bewildered expression with my own look of shock. As If understanding my unspoken question, he nodded adamantly. "Yes, I just heard your entire conversation with Niyol and I saw what you saw. He was the owl, flying over a group of people being detained by Elizabeth Guards and Droid Dogs. Just . . . wow."

"But how is that possible? We're awake. I thought you could only get inside my head and see what I see when I'm dreaming. I wasn't even trying to communicate with you. I was focusing my telepathy on Niyol. Alone."

"Like Niyol said, your abilities are obviously getting stronger, Rain. This is amazing."

I shrugged. "It's good that I'm getting stronger I guess."

"You guess?"

"I mean, sure that's good. Maybe it can help us in the days ahead somehow. But that's just the thing. I'm so frustrated. Niyol obviously knows more than he is telling us, as usual. And I know he needs to help Moretti right now, but couldn't he just tell me for once what we're supposed to do? I am so tired of him telling me to trust my instincts. What if I'm making the wrong decisions? I mean, my instincts are telling me that Grandma is in real trouble, and we need to go see her, in person, and check on her and maybe even rescue her. But what if Grandma is being watched or something because of Calista? And is it related to us? And Grandma was hit. And Niyol is talking in riddles, when you know he knows what we need to do." I finished with a groan.

Jabari gathered me closer, draping his arm around my shoulder and taking my hand with his other hand. "Well, he never said your grandma isn't in trouble. He only said he thinks she'll be fine. But he also said to trust your instincts. If you think we need to go see her, just say the words and we'll go. I'm in."

I peered up at him, so grateful for the risks he was willing to take for me and my family, and torn at the same time. It would be riskier than any of our other trips to see Grandma. We'd never gone to see her when her home was occupied. What if the guards tailed her into the woods for her hikes? Could I ask my friends to risk everything just to check on her? There were too many unanswered questions and theories. Still, when I thought about one of the men hitting Grandma, it filled me with anger.

Jabari cleared his throat. "I see the wheels turning up there." He bent down, kissed my temple lightly.

"I know it's risky. But one of them hit Grandma. I just want to check on her. Even if we can't talk to her. I want to see with my own eyes that she is all right."

As soon as I'd spoken the words, I felt better. I knew it was the only choice I could make. Jabari didn't bat an eyelash or seem troubled by my response. "We'll go as soon as possible. We're good on fuel cells. We can map out the details with everyone at our meeting tomorrow."

I sighed and rested against his chest. "Thank you."

He stroked my hair softly. "Thank *you*."

I had to laugh. "For what? Constantly putting us in more danger?"

He pushed back a bit so I could look at his face. "For constantly standing up for everyone. For being you."

His expression sobered. And the way he was looking at me made my heart speed up. "I love you because you always support me, Jabari."

He trailed a finger across my mouth, gazing into my eyes. "I love you because you inspire me to be better."

I didn't say anything else. I didn't need to. He closed the gap between us and kissed me softly. I felt air beneath me unexpectedly as he lifted me across his lap. Nestled in the warmth of his arms, I lost track of time and my worries.

Later on, as I was lying down for sleep, I spun the bracelet and ring Jabari had made for me on my wrist, where I kept them both. A lazy smile remained on my lips as I fell asleep, thinking of our evening.

I succumbed to my drowsiness and a peaceful sleep, and then I heard a voice calling to me in my dreams.

"Rain, you have to help them," the voice said.

A cry escaped her mouth, and then I recognized the voice. It was Calista. The room became clearer, and I could see she was locked in a dark prison cell, huddled in the corner. In her palm, she was staring at the four-leaf clover I had given her when we'd last seen each other.

"Help who, Calista? Is it Grandma?"

"Rain, is it you? Don't get inside my head or she'll find you. Just help them. Please."

"Help who?"

A loud beep sounded, somehow familiar, and I looked behind me as Nata pushed a large red button, triggering what I realized was the extermination gas chamber. I flung myself against the clear wall, and through the hazy air, I could see people locked inside. In the middle, I saw Calista's parents, Uncle Michael and Aunt Alyssa. Beside them, Grandma was trying to hold on to a photograph of all of us at the lake, but a guard yanked it from her.

My stomach dropped. "Grandma . . . Uncle Michael . . . Aunt Alyssa . . . No!"

Nata clenched onto my neck and lifted me in the air. My feet were dangling below me, as I grabbed at her hands. I couldn't scream for help or breathe. Her blue eyes turned red, with flames at their centers. "Listen, mixed breed. They're all going to die with you. Mark my words."

I closed my eyes and called to Niyol. It was the only thing I could think to do. As I desperately called out to him, the gas filled my nostrils. I couldn't scream aloud, so I screamed in my head. Niyol didn't answer, so I called out to everyone else I knew for help.

Daktari's voice broke through the room. "It's okay. It's just a dream. Wake up."

I opened my eyes as my scream faded away.

I was soaking wet from sweat. My body burned from head to toe. Daktari laid his hand across my forehead. "What in the world? You're on fire, Rain. I think you have a fever. Let me heal you. What happened?"

I stared at him with wide eyes. I didn't want to tell him.

After a moment, he pulled me close and patted my back as he healed my fever. "You don't have to talk about it, sis. Don't worry, you're safe. It was just a dream."

Chapter 23: Flags

RAIN

The snow and ice had melted by Tuesday afternoon, and as our hover flew over the entrance to Indy Mixed Zone, protected by Zi's camouflage image, I said a prayer of thanks. It would be easier to try to find Grandma Julia if we didn't need to worry about leaving our footprints behind in the snow. At our last meeting, I'd told everyone about my most recent nightmare and that I would understand if they didn't want to risk the trip to Grandma's. But of course, they all wanted to go. If my dream meant Grandma was in trouble, they wanted to help her.

We were hoping she would be on her afternoon hike in the woods. Of course, no one wanted to say it, but I knew we were all wondering the same thing. Would Grandma have permission to go hiking? What if she was being held as a prisoner?

I promised Bhavna before we left that we'd be careful and report back to her. Sook had spent the past few days watching Grandma for me, but he hadn't seen anything new. But he was positive that her house was occupied by the Elizabeth Guards now, and it worried me terribly.

I looked back, over my shoulder, taking in the crumbling buildings in our zone from our aerial view as the hover sped away. The ice and snow this winter had damaged many more rooftops, and even though a few months ago I wouldn't have believed it possible, the zone appeared even more depressing than ever in its current state.

"Look ahead. Not behind, Amiga."

I turned to Marcello, who was sitting on the back row bench with me, and couldn't help a small smile. "Still trying to rescue me from my demons."

"Well, you had that tortured expression again, and I know how that head of yours works sometimes."

"To think, I used to be celebrated for my optimism and pep talks. At least with Zi and Daktari."

"You still have that side to you. But I think you're distracted a little lately with all of the mystery surrounding Grandma Julia and Calista."

"Of course I—"

Marcello put his hand up to silence me. "I wasn't finished yet. I was going to say you are *understandably* distracted and worried. We are all worried. I was only pointing out that maybe you are a little down, which we all get, but you still need to try to look forward and hope for the best."

My shoulders dropped slightly from my defensive position. He was right. I still needed to think positive. Somehow.

I smirked. "Marcello to the rescue again. I feel positive already."

He beamed back at me and chuckled. "A man's gotta do what a man's gotta do."

"Man?" I asked.

He frowned, and I couldn't resist teasing him. "I was thinking more along the lines of boy. But if you say man . . ."

"Si, Amiga, man. Hombre."

I burst out laughing now, and Marcello smiled, clearly satisfied with himself.

"Well at least I made you smile," he pointed out.

I grinned. "Yes, manly man, you did."

The remainder of the fifteen-minute trip was quiet. And as the Indy White Zone came into view, we all sat up, tensing some. The last trip we'd made here we'd seen so many changes from above. And if we hadn't been warned about the police presence, we would have been even more terrified now. Cole navigated through the hover entryway and began the route to the woods behind Grandma's house.

Everywhere we looked there were new signs, billboards, and flags, with everything from new UZTA rules and laws to warnings about what had happened to the rioters. A huge billboard stood near the center of town, outside the hospital. Gallagher Brown's face was half of the ad, with a huge red *X* marked through it, and the warning: UZTA FUGI-TIVE. Assistance to him, of any kind, punishable by DEATH. Any information leading to his arrest must be reported to your nearest Elizabeth Guard officer.

"Wow," Zi mumbled, still holding her image around us as she stared out the window.

"They must have taken that image of him from the video message he sent. Somehow I guess they recorded it when he broadcasted the message," Cole said.

No one else said a word. What could we say? Yes, it was cool that Gallagher's plan was working, and he had clearly struck a chord with the enemy, but it also meant he was in more danger now than ever. And that was frightening on so many levels. If he actually got captured, how would we take down Nata? He was integral to the day of the resistance attack. I swallowed, trying to force the thought away, and took a deep breath. I searched the town below us, absorbing every detail of Zionsville, the place I once called home.

Stationed on every other block were Elizabeth Guard patrol hover vehicles. And from certain buildings and homes, we could see huge UZTA flags waving from the front entryways. And on some of the front doors to homes were huge red *X*s marked across the doorways. I made a mental note to ask Grandma Julia why the flags were in front of some of the properties and what the huge red *X* marks meant. Daktari spoke up. "What if the flags represent places the Elizabeth Guard officers have occupied?"

"Good theory," Jabari called from the front seat.

"I guess we'll know that's the case if Grandma Julia has a flag in front of her house," Daktari said somberly. "But what do the *X*s mean, I wonder?"

Seconds later, Daktari sucked in his breath sharply, and I turned my head towards the other window he was staring out of. There was another enormous billboard. My stomach dropped, and Marcello clutched onto my hand as I let out a horrified gasp, echoing Daktari's.

Calista was the center of the ad, dressed in white from head to toe, and smiling beautifully. The words above her read: "It was an honor and a privilege to be selected for the Pure Zone of the United Zones of The Authority. Thank you, President Nicks."

My heart seemed to stop. I heard Jabari from the front saying something I was sure was directed towards me, but it sounded muted. Calista appeared so healthy, happy, and loyal to Nata, and even though I knew it was part of the role she was playing, I hated that she had been forced to go there. What was she going through? And what if they'd already made her marry the guy they'd chosen for her? What if we were too late? What if she was already being forced to reproduce for the pure zone and Nata's pure race? There were too many what-ifs, and I felt so helpless as I studied her face on the billboard.

Marcello shook me lightly. "Hey, Rain. Can you hear me? You're scaring me." His voice sounded strained.

I tore my eyes from the billboard. Eyes were looking at me from all around. I nodded at Jabari first. "I'm sorry. I'm fine. I just had a . . . moment."

"Hang in there. We're almost there," Jabari urged.

"Need another pep talk?" Marcello asked.

"Sure."

"Calista had to pose for that sign. She's on our side. No doubt about it. Your cousin is amazing . . . in addition to being beautiful," he added with a wink.

I gave him a small smile. "I feel better already."

As we approached the clearing we always met Grandma Julia in, Cole called out from the front. "Well at least it doesn't look like there are any Elizabeth Guards all the way out here. Looks like the place has been untouched from the recent changes."

"That's what we were hoping," Jabari agreed, his tone positive.

Before leaving the mixed zone, we'd briefly discussed what to do if there were officers in the woods. But we'd taken a leap of faith and hoped for the best. And for once, that seemed to be in our favor. Cole was right. There was no one around.

As soon as the hover was settled under the refuge of clusters of tall evergreen and pine trees, Jabari opened the door and motioned us forward to begin the search for Grandma. Typically, she would hike during this time of day, so we figured it wouldn't take long, assuming we were right about her still having permission to hike.

I accepted Jabari's hand as he helped me out of the hover. He bent down and whispered against my ear. "You all right?"

He pulled back a little and studied me. "Yeah, Marcello gave me a pep talk," I teased.

Jabari raised a brow at Marcello, who tossed his arms up. "I'm here to help."

Jabari spared me a smile and turned to face everyone else. Daktari had his arm draped around Zi, who still covered us with an image. I wondered if he was healing her even as he stood there or if she ever got the headaches she used to get when she used her ability for a long duration.

"We have to leave the hover in the open while we look for her. But the good news is, at least it appears from our landing that no one comes out here still. So it should be fine," Jabari began.

"It's a risk we have to take," Daktari said. "So can Zi drop the image yet?"

"Yes, please do," Jabari agreed.

Zi's hands fell to her sides, and she closed her eyes for a moment. Daktari moved his hands to her temple and neck.

After a moment, she smiled. "Thanks, Daktari."

"Was your head hurting you?" Jabari asked, worriedly.

"Not much. It's not like it used to be. But it feels great now. I think it hurt more today from worrying so much about what we saw as we arrived in the zone. I'll feel better once we talk to Grandma Julia."

"Let's start searching. And we stay together, understand?" Jabari asked.

Without looking, I knew that everyone was going to be staring at me to answer Jabari's question, which was clearly intended for me after our last trip here when I broke free of them and ran to my old house. I looked sheepishly at Jabari. "Understand."

He pulled my hand to his lips and kissed it lightly. "Good. Let's go find her."

We scoured the woods, and with each minute that passed with no sign of Grandma, my hopes dwindled. She wasn't out in the woods today, and that meant we would have to resort to plan B, which really no one had agreed upon.

After ten minutes, I cleared my throat and planted my feet, preparing to argue my case. "We have to go to her house. Zi will have to put the image over us. There's no other choice."

"But how will we get to talk to her? Or are we just going to try to see if we can spy on her through a window or something? Don't you think we have to talk to her, Rain? To make sure she's okay?" Daktari fired off frenzied questions, and I knew he was so worried about Grandma and he'd been holding it in the past few days.

As I stared at his anxious expression, an idea popped into my head. "Don't worry. I've got a plan. Can you guys just trust me on this? Zi, can you cover us?" I peered at her, and she nodded, pulling her hands in front of her chest to project an image to hide us.

"Ready when you are," she replied.

I looked to Jabari for confirmation, and he tilted his head forward. "Lead the way, Rain."

As we crept through the woods, I sped up a little; careful to make sure Zi's image was enveloping us. And I called out to the bird of prey I knew could help us. I didn't know what we'd discover at Grandma's house. But one way or another, we were going to talk to her.

Chapter 24: Help

RAIN

We were almost through the woods, and I could see we were coming up behind Grandma's house, when I heard the light screech of the red-shouldered hawk. As I recalled, it was one of Grandma Julia's favorite birds. It wasn't her very favorite, the kingfisher, but it would do the trick. Assuming it would follow my commands.

As it swooped down in front of us I called to it. "*Land close to me. I need your help, please.*"

It landed on a low evergreen branch to my right, and the group stopped abruptly, watching with fascination on their faces. It had a brown head and a reddish chest with white narrow bars on its tail. It sat expectantly, as if waiting on my instructions. Daktari nudged my shoulder lightly. "I can see Grandma's house through the trees from here."

"Yeah, I thought we'd stop here for a moment. So here's the plan . . ." I began. "We'll need to cross over to the huge evergreen tree in the corner of Grandma's backyard, the one with the really wide base. And when she comes outside, I'll step out from the image and huddle behind the tree and call to her. Hopefully, she'll hear my voice and come over to investigate. You guys stay under Zi's image, and I'll talk to her. If it's safe, Daktari, you can talk to her, after me though, okay?"

"But if anyone is watching and sees you . . ." Zi began.

"I'll stay behind the tree. No one looking from the house should see me. Her backyard is private."

"It's okay with me. Let's just be on the lookout for trouble," Jabari warned.

"But how are you going to get her out of the house?" asked Cole.

"The hawk will do it," I said confidently.

"How can it even see you under this image?" Marcello asked.

"I don't know, but it is responding to me, so here goes nothing."

I led the group, and they stayed close beside me as we ventured out into open space behind Grandma's ranch-style brick house. Even though Zi's image protected us, I felt exposed, being out in the open and so close to Grandma's house. As we neared the tree, something bright red caught my eye in the distance. I tensed as I realized it was one of the same UZTA flags we'd seen on our trip in, and it was flying very high on the front side of Grandma's house. I tried not to dwell on it, and I made myself think positive.

Once we were safely behind the tree, I remained under the image, and closed my eyes. I prayed the hawk would lure Grandma alone out of the house and not one of the officers. Then I called to the hawk once more. I asked the hawk to perch on Grandma's kitchen sink window, which I knew was facing the backyard, and tap on it with its talons. My spirits soared as it automatically responded and breezed by us towards the window, following my instructions to the T. Even if Grandma wasn't a bird expert, or at least the closest to one I'd ever met, she would find it strange to have a hawk, of any kind, tapping on her window. And I was hoping and praying her suspicions would lead her outside and directly to me.

"Wow, Rain, seriously. You never stop amazing me," Daktari whispered.

Jabari grinned. "Me either. That's unreal."

"Let's just hope it brings Grandma out, and only Grandma." I replied.

Daktari tensed beside me. "It's Grandma," he whispered.

She stood in the window frame. I could barely see her, but knew it was her. When she disappeared again, I waited for the kitchen door to open and for her to come investigate, but after a minute, still nothing had happened. The hawk was still perched on the sill, but Grandma was gone.

"Where did she go?" Cole muttered.

I didn't answer. How could I? I just squeezed my eyes shut again and pleaded with the hawk. "*Make some noise. Tap again, please.*"

It scraped a talon against the window, and I waited on pins and needles for her to reappear in the window. When another minute passed and she didn't, I started to get nervous. My hand began to shake. I had to see her. That hadn't been close enough to make sure she was unharmed.

My foot had taken one step away from the tree, when Jabari's hand gripped my arm, halting me in place. "She's coming out."

I peered at the house, and sure enough, the doorknob was twisting. A moment later, Grandma Julia stood bundled up in a coat, cautiously glancing around. She knew we were there.

"You guys, take a step or two backwards so I can lean against the tree, out from under Zi's image. But stay close," I ordered.

I pressed my body all the way against the tree, careful to stay hidden behind it as they stepped backwards and faded away from my sight, and I called out to her. "Grandma, behind the big oak, it's me."

I didn't want to risk peeking around the tree, and I wasn't sure if she had heard me, so I called to the hawk for assistance. "*Lead her to me.*"

The hawk landed beside my feet, and a few seconds later, I heard a soft sound of feet crunching against the earth, and snapping a branch as they neared. I leaned forward as Grandma came into view. Her eyes lit up with happiness and then fear. "Rain, you can't be here. I knew that hawk wasn't just tapping on my window for no reason. But . . . if they find you," she paused, her lip trembling. She stepped over to me and hugged me, and I was so thankful the tree was wide enough to shield us at least on this side.

"That's a beautiful red-shouldered hawk," she said, peering at it now.

I turned to the hawk and closed my eyes. "*Thank you for helping me. You can go now.*" As it flew away into the woods, I looked back at Grandma. There was a bruise on her left cheek from where I knew the officer had hit her.

"I was so worried about you, Grandma. I can't believe that man hit you. Your face looks awful. Are you okay?" I buried my face on the top of her head. She was smaller than me, and she'd lost even more weight since the last time I'd seen her. "And you're so little. Are you eating?"

Grandma straightened and looked up at me. "How in the world do you know what happened to my face? And what's this about my weight? I'm fine. You're the one who needs to put on some pounds. Where is everyone? How did you get here?" She glanced around apprehensively.

"First, Grandma, I have to know. This is very important before we talk any further. Are you being questioned or interrogated by any of The Authority? Because if you are, I don't want you to know anything else that might endanger you. Or anything . . ." I didn't finish my sentence, but she had to know I was referring to TFF. If she wasn't being questioned by them, I could probably even use my telepathy on her from time to time. But I had to know if they'd already targeted her.

She shook her head adamantly. "They only questioned me once about my last contact with you kids, but they let it go. I didn't tell them anything, and they never brought it up again. And *she* hasn't been here to use her power on me if that's what you mean."

Grandma knew all about Nata and her ability, and of course, that's what I'd meant. Nata was the only one who could force the truth out of someone, and as long as the guards hadn't used any of their brutal interrogation tactics on Grandma, she was probably safe.

"Okay, well if you want to talk to everyone else . . ."

"I do. But we have to hurry."

"They're right beside us. Do you want to go under Zi's image with me and talk to everyone? I would have stayed under it, too, but if you're standing on the outside of her image, you can't hear anything happening under it. It's sort of like a shield for whoever is underneath it. Strange how her ability works."

"Well, there's only one guard inside, and he fell asleep on the sofa.

Let's be quick about it, and I'll catch you up on everything. And you tell me everything, too."

Grandma jumped back a bit, startled as everyone came into view as Zi's image enveloped us.

"Sorry to scare you, Grandma, but we were listening to everything. If you don't have much time, we need to start talking," Daktari said, hugging her against him.

"Oh, I've been so worried about you." She hugged each of us and then grabbed Daktari and me by our hands.

"First of all, Grandma, our friend saw you in a vision and he said an officer hit you. Your face looks like it hurts. Are you okay? Can I heal it?" Daktari demanded.

Grandma sighed and her voice became soothing. "Now don't you worry about me, Daktari. Everything is fine with me. And no, you can't heal it. They'd get suspicious."

"Grandma, maybe we should get you out of here," Daktari said nervously.

"I'm fine now. I know the rules and what provokes that man."

Daktari's jaw clenched. He and Marcello exchanged looks as Jabari leaned in closer to Grandma. "Is he the one asleep in there right now?" There was a lethal edge to Jabari's tone that made my heart pick up. I was glad he was protective of Grandma, but what could he do that wouldn't draw suspicions from the other officers when they returned?

"No, that's not him. Listen. Is that why you kids came here? You were worried about me?"

At our collective nod, Grandma threw her hands up. "I can't believe it. This place is dangerous now more than ever. You can't come back here again. Promise me. Not until this is all over with. I'm praying for you guys and know you're going to win. You have to." Her voice hitched, rousing my suspicions.

"Tell me more about what is happening, Grandma."

"Well, I've heard the men talk since they began living with me. Gallagher has been a real problem for Nicks. And then about a week ago, something new happened outside the zones involving Gallagher, and Nicks went berserk. She sent more men on the hunt. Meanwhile, people in our zone heard the rumors about him and banded together and rioted again. It was awful. Nicks sent more officers in here right away and occupied businesses and the hospital and even homes, like mine."

"Is that what the flags are for?"

"Yes, they put them up wherever they are stationed."

"Why did they come here?"

"Mostly to spy on everyone I think. And to make sure everyone is afraid to rebel. Whatever Gallagher and you kids have started out there is making Nicks nervous. I know her real name is Nata, but I don't use it. I'd hate to let it slip. They've searched everyone's home. They chose my house for some of the men who were reassigned here because I was living alone and had space. I have to cook for them and do their laundry, and they use my house as a base. They come and go all hours of the day and night. You see, they are searching every house in this zone and doing things to anyone perceived as a threat to send a message to the rest of us not to join Gallagher or act out of line. When he broadcast live to us a few days ago, people got excited and rioted again." She paused, and swallowed, as if recalling something horrific. "I've seen unspeakable things happening to the people who tried to rebel. And it's not just because of Gallagher. People are being taken left and right for either the Elizabeth Guard to hunt for him or to the pure zone, and some are just disappearing who have broken a law. I hate to think about what has happened to them."

"Why are there *Xs* on some of the doors?" asked Cole.

"If you're suspected of disobeying The Authority, they mark your door and that means among other unpleasant Authority Guard visits, your family receives less food. We're living on rations now since "officially" they've taken over our money and the banks and stopped the ruse that we were ever in control or free. I think it's a slow transformation into something more like one of the other zones. But I'm not complaining. Especially considering what you kids go through. And have been through."

Jabari placed a hand on Grandma's shoulder. "It might get worse before it gets better. But I need to know if you are really safe here. And do you think they suspect you of being involved with us or Gallagher or anything like that?"

"No. I don't think they even know about you kids. I don't think they've made the connection. They think this is all Gallagher. Believe me, I've heard all of the rumors from the guards talking. And there haven't been any about help from the mixed zones or from any teenagers. Plus, from the searches outside the zones and in this zone, its safe to assume they think whoever is helping Gallagher is here or there. So I don't think they know about you kids being involved with him. But there's something else . . ."

Daktari's forehead wrinkled. "Grandma, what is it?" he asked worriedly.

"I think Rain and Daktari are in danger for another reason." She lowered her voice even though no one outside our image would hear her. "The day the guard hit me, I was fighting with him over a photograph. They took all of my photos away and burned them." She glanced at me.

"It was from our camping trip, right?"

"How did you know?"

"I saw it in a dream I had."

Grandma rubbed my hand. "Anyway, they said my only grandchild left was Calista. Did you see the billboard with her on your way in?"

"It was hard to miss."

"Well, she's pretty important for the pure race agenda, as I understand. But now she's really under the spotlight, and I think she's in danger. They told me I'm not allowed to mention any of my other family.

And apparently Calista is being tested for her loyalty; at least that's what I heard one of the guards talking about. Nicks has recently decided to find out who is related to the pure zone people like Calista who were recruited at an older age than the younger ones. So she discovered that Calista has an aunt . . ." Her voice shook. "And that Grace chose to go to the mixed zone. So now she wants Calista to prove she's loyal to the pure zone somehow. And they asked me what I knew about you kids and I said nothing other than the e-mails I used to get, which I don't get anymore. And I don't know how, but I think she might force Calista to help her attack your zone, you know . . . on the day you told me about before. But if I'm wrong, she might be forced to do something to you before that." She griped us tighter. "Promise me you'll get away if they come for you before your plan to take her down. I can't lose you. Any of you."

Tears started flowing from her eyes, and we stood silently, patting her, helplessly looking around. Jabari was the first to speak. "I wonder if she knows who you are, Rain. You said she seemed to recognize you when she interrogated you at the prison."

Grandma interrupted. "You were arrested?"

I nodded as I spoke. "Yes, but I'm fine. She didn't know I was related to Calista then. At least she didn't seem to know. I mean, she would have said something if she had made the connection. But what if she puts it together?"

"Well, she really has no reason to look into it. You aren't exactly a threat in The Authority's eyes. You didn't really do anything to break any of her laws. You defended Takara once, and then you were suspected of breaking a law but that was it, and like you said, she didn't seem to put the two things together. I think she would have said something for sure if she had realized you were Calista's cousin," Zi remarked.

"I wonder if she plans to target Rain, Daktari, and Grace using Calista specifically, or if she is just making Calista part of her grand plan to kill us all on Mother's Day," Marcello said.

"Either way, Rain and Daktari will have to be even more cautious from here on out. If anyone comes to arrest them, it might be a case where they have to run and we all get our families and escape. And come for Grandma Julia, and . . ." Jabari's sentence ended, and I could imagine his brain working in overdrive to solve this problem.

My mind ran with ideas, too, but there was no time for that. I had a strange feeling Grandma wasn't telling us everything. "We can discuss more later, but Grandma, have you told us everything?"

She sighed. "Well, no. There's more, but I didn't want to scare you."

"Grandma Julia, we have a death sentence hanging over our heads. You can't scare us any more than we already are," Zi finished with an encouraging grin.

"Michael and Alyssa are gone."

"Gone?" Daktari blurted.

"Up until the Gallagher message, we were still permitted to phone relatives in other white zones once a month. A few weeks ago, I called Michael to check in on him and Alyssa during our regularly scheduled time, and a computer answered their house phone and simply recited a message that they were gone and didn't live there anymore. I tried to ask the officers here about it, but they said they didn't know anything." Her voice quivered, her eyes scanning us. "I'm terrified for all of you. Can't you just take your families and escape now? Hide with one of the camps?"

I glanced around the circle. Everyone was thinking about it, but I knew we couldn't. "Grandma, if we disappear now, they'll come after our extended families for sure. That means that you and Calista will be targeted for questioning, and certainly Uncle Michael and Aunt Alyssa, too, assuming they aren't already in custody," I said.

Jabari cleared his throat. "And we could save you and take you with us, Grandma Julia, but we have no idea where Michael and Alyssa are. Or what would happen to Calista. It's just too dangerous. As much as I want us to run, it might be too late now. I'm sorry. I should have made us do it sooner before they took Calista, but I didn't think it was the right thing to do at the time. Maybe I messed this all up."

"You didn't mess anything up. You always trust your instincts, and besides, we all helped make every decision so far," Daktari said matter-of-factly.

Grandma patted Jabari's hand. "This is not your fault. We will get through this. But I am worried about whatever she has planned for Calista. If Calista has to prove her loyalty by hurting you guys . . . Just promise me you'll go into hiding if it comes to that. Michael and Alyssa are already gone, and what if . . ." She buried her face in her hands, unable to say another word.

I hugged Grandma tightly as she wept. My head was spinning. I had dreamed that Uncle Michael and Aunt Alyssa were in trouble. In my nightmare, Calista had begged me to help them. I hadn't been sure who she was talking about at the time. I had been positive it was Grandma Julia, but now I had to assume the dream was about Uncle Michael and Aunt Alyssa. But I didn't want to depress Grandma and tell her about my dream. And I knew Grandma was worried we were in danger, but there was also the fact that the EEG officer had told us weak people were being taken for the pure zone initiation, so that could be where Calista would be forced to prove her loyalty. I didn't think I should mention either thing to Grandma. Fortunately, no one else seemed eager to tell her either. So I decided to be optimistic.

"It's all right, Grandma. I'm sure they'll be fine. We just need to have hope and faith that everything will work out," I offered.

Grandma stood up, wiped her tears away. "That sounds like something I would say to you," she remarked, and smiled.

"Rain is really good at pep talks," Marcello said slyly. "She must have gotten that from you."

I gave Marcello a sideways glance. "You're pretty good at them, too."

He winked at me in response.

Daktari took Grandma's hand again. "I hate leaving you here. If they are hurting you, you have to tell us."

"That man hit me once. And he hasn't since. I promise. Besides, not all of the officers are bad like him. Some of them seem like they'd even join Gallagher the way they go on about him when they don't think the other officers can hear them. I think they are afraid of Nicks. Everyone is. Fear is the biggest controlling factor Nicks has. I know she uses her mind control ability or whatever it is exactly, but the fear she creates in the people is her biggest weapon. Anyhow, I know how to handle these officers. I can play by the rules."

"Grandma, I'm glad you can handle this, but I'll still be worrying about you here. What do you think about me trying my telepathy on you? I could check in on you from time to time. I only didn't use it before because I wasn't sure if Nata had questioned you or if they were trying to get information from you. But since they're only using your house, and they haven't sent you to Nata . . ."

"Please, Rain. I'd love to hear from you. Do you think your ability would work on me?"

I closed my eyes. "*It can't hurt to try.*"

Grandma's eyes widened. "Wow. What do I do? Can you hear me?"

"*Just close your eyes, relax, and respond to me.*"

"*I'm scared of losing you all. But I love you, I have faith, and I know you can do this.*"

I grinned. "*I knew you'd be open to hearing my voice. I'll check in on you like this from now on.*"

"*I love you.*"

"*I love you, too.*"

I glanced around the group. "It works. She can hear me."

"Rain can check on you now without us having to come here. But please let us know if you are in danger," Jabari instructed.

"Certainly."

"So if you're sure you're safe," he said slowly.

Grandma smiled at him. "I am. Hey, by the way . . . how did it go?" she asked, suddenly very upbeat.

Jabari beamed in response. "It went very well."

As Grandma's eyes fell on me she cupped her mouth to muffle an excited scream, and understanding washed over me.

"He told you?" I blurted.

"He sure did. Last time you were here. You didn't notice, but he asked for my blessing when you weren't looking. Congratulations, honey. I can't wait to see you walk down the aisle. I can't imagine a better match."

Marcello coughed. "Not even if you were imagining me and Calista?" he teased.

Grandma laughed again. "Oh, you tease. You'd better ask her out when this is all over with, young man. She won't wait around for you forever, you know."

Marcello's eyes lit up. "So you think she really likes me? I knew it. Told ya, Zi."

"Oh, great. Here we go again," Zi mumbled.

A moment later, we all said our goodbyes to Grandma Julia. She cupped my face in her hands and told me to be strong and to never forget how she loved me and was proud of me no matter what happened to either one of us. As I watched her disappear back into her Authority-occupied house, I prayed it hadn't been our last goodbye.

Chapter 25: Off

JABARI

Something was off. But I couldn't pinpoint what it was. My head was swarming with theories and thoughts.

Rain and Daktari's grandmother having her house occupied by The Authority was bad. Hearing the news about Michael and Alyssa being gone had been really bad. And the fact that Calista would be forced to prove loyalty to Nata because of her Aunt Grace and Rain and Daktari's family being in our zone really bothered me. Yet, I felt certain that if Nata had really discovered any sort of connection between Rain and Calista, as far as Rain being a threat to her regime or any connection to Gallagher, she would have done something about it by now. Plus, Rain's grandma had a point: The search for Gallagher and TFF was happening outside of our zone, so they obviously hadn't made the connection to us. Which had to mean that so far, Nata's loyalty test with Calista and her hunt for Gallagher Brown were two distinct and separate items on her agenda. But still, Rain and Daktari could be in danger if this supposed test of loyalty was something other than Calista helping kill the mixed zones on Mother's Day. Our plan to free the zones was going to happen long before that, but what if Nata was using Calista in another way to prove her loyalty?

Then there was the nagging question in my brain about what the EEG officer had said about the pure zone initiation. If more people were being taken still for some sort of event, to be hurt and possibly worse by the pure zone initiates, how could we help? Should we help? Was it worth the risk? A month ago I probably would have said yes, we needed to help them, but lately I had a growing feeling that wouldn't go away that I needed to protect Rain from some unforeseen danger. I couldn't shake the feeling. And in this moment, I had the worst feeling that something was about to happen.

And it was definitely related to Rain.

The entire trip back to our zone, the feeling of dread had been building. I wanted it to be related to anything other than Rain. I'd scoured the ground below for signs of battles, refugees, people hiding, soldiers searching, anything, but it had been a quiet trip. And as we'd flown back into our zone, from our hover view, everything had seemed business as usual. But was it?

Once we'd safely hidden the hover transporter back in the school, we hurried, treading carefully through the abandoned gymnasium like burglars, cautiously watching each step. I removed the gymnasium floor hatch to the storm room, climbed down first, and quickly lit a few solar lights for everyone.

One by one they descended the steps, and I waited for Rain. With each ticking second the storm kept brewing. My ability told me something was wrong, something was about to happen, but I didn't know what. As much as the ability was a gift, it left me with a sense of helplessness in times like this. But I had to tell the group. They depended on my ability for safety.

I watched Rain step from the bottom of the ladder. Her brown eyes were full of her silent worries and pain, but as she turned them towards me, something changed a little. She pushed her frantic thoughts to wherever she stored them, and I could see trust and even hope in them now as she took my outstretched hand.

"We made it back safely. That's something to be happy about," she said as I pulled her against me, crushing her with a hug.

She didn't protest the tightness of my embrace. She laid her head against my chest, and I knew she was listening to the pulse beating louder and faster by the second. Her grip tightened around my waist. She knew something was wrong but didn't move a muscle. She just let me hold her. She knew she was my medicine. I wanted to keep her there, safe in my arms. Nothing would hurt her. But the growing feeling of dread was turning to full-on alert. I gently allowed an inch between us, and she tilted her head back, locking eyes with me.

"*Something's wrong, isn't it?*" she said silently, filling my head with her voice so strong and clear.

I wondered how no one else could hear her. It seemed like she was loud enough for them all to hear, but a glance around the room confirmed they hadn't.

"*I feel like it, yes. But I don't know what. I have to warn everyone.*"

She nodded and turned to the side, but I kept hold of her and wrapped my arm around her waist as I cleared my throat. Standing beside me, connected to me still, meant I could protect her. My mind panicked. But was it her? Was Rain the one in danger? Or was it everyone?

They stared at me, waiting as my thoughts went on. It was five forty-five in our zone, which meant the first shift had ended for many of the adults and the streets would be busy.

Cole and Marcello exchanged nervous looks. "What's up, leader?" Marcello prompted.

Rain squeezed my waist a little. "Just tell them about your feeling."

"Something's off. I started to get a bad feeling the closer we got to our zone. I don't know what it is, and I'm not sure if it is related to Rain or to all of us. And my ability only does this to me before something is about to happen."

"Something bad," interjected Zi, somberly.

I swallowed. "Yeah, that's how it usually works."

"I didn't notice anything out of the ordinary when we were coming into the zone," Cole remarked.

"Me either," added Daktari.

"Maybe it hasn't happened yet," Rain said.

"Are you sure it has something to do with Rain?" Marcello asked.

"Honestly, I'm not sure. But I'm worried about her."

"You're always worried about her though. I mean, with good reason. Trust me, I worry about her, too. But if you're not sure right now, maybe it is something happening in our zone. We should take a look around, don't you think?" Daktari asked.

I couldn't find words. I just stood there staring at them all. I had to pull it together. I'd never felt this strongly that something bad was going to happen. But we couldn't just hide down here. Daktari was right. We needed to investigate. Maybe I could convince Rain to hide though. I looked at her again.

"Are you okay? I've never seen you like this," she spoke into my mind.

"Something bad is going to happen, Rain. I think it might have something to do with you. Would you stay down here until I figure out what it is?"

Her eyes flashed, darker, angry almost, but full of adrenaline. I wished I could read her thoughts, but I didn't have to. One look told me she was daring me to make her stay down here. She was already eyeing the tunnel exit out of our hideout. She would want to check on her mother.

I turned to everyone else. "Listen, I have no idea what it is, but I've never had a feeling quite so strong. Why don't I investigate alone? I'd prefer if you all waited here and—"

"Absolutely not," said Marcello.

"No way," Cole blurted.

"How about we all go check on our families to start with?" Daktari suggested.

Zi nodded her head. "I agree. They'll be home now, well, everyone except Rain and Daktari's dad. If it's bad, we meet back here to discuss? Rain can contact us all using her telepathy."

"Good plan, my short friend. But what if it's worst case scenario?" Marcello asked.

I spoke up. "If it's worst case scenario, we get our families, starting with Zi's. You tell Daktari or Rain, so Rain can talk to us, and bring your parents here. Then we'll organize the rest so you can help move everyone else here, under your image if we need it, okay?"

"Got it. I'd better head out first," Zi replied.

As they started to talk and head to the exit I stopped them. "Be careful. It might not have happened yet, but it will. Something's going down," I warned.

Rain let Zi and Daktari go before her, since we had to sneak out in intervals to get away from the school, but I could tell it had been hard for her. She was anxious, like a horse lined up at the race line, ready to run. I figured she would pass everyone up the moment she got above ground. She'd race using her ability to go faster, to check on her mother, which I understood. But the problem was, I had the strangest feeling all of this had something to do with Rain, not Grace.

If only I could keep her here. I approached her cautiously at first. She was half way down the tunnel, pacing back and forth when I grabbed her, and pinned her gently, but securely, against the wall.

"You can't keep me here," she protested.

"I know," I said lowly.

She tensed, in the dimly lit space her eyes were full of fear. Not of me, but for her family. She was so focused on them she couldn't even accept that she was possibly the one in danger. She always had to rescue others and never thought about her own safety.

"I need to go home and check on Mom," she whispered.

"Watch your back out there," I said evenly.

She relaxed a little, "I will."

I leaned down and her hands laced around my neck. My mouth met hers as I somehow pulled her closer. We kissed for a few moments, then stopped and just stared at each other as emotions passed between us, our breathing faster than ever.

"You be careful, too," she threatened.

"I will."

She withdrew, then turned back and grabbed my face, cupping my cheeks in her hands. She kissed me softly now. "I love you because you worry about me."

"I love you because you're my life, Rain."

She brushed her lips to mine once more and then turned to climb up the ladder. She would head to her home, concerned about everyone except herself. And as soon as I left the shelter, I'd do what my gut told me to do, regardless of the consequences.

Chapter 26: Weakest

RAIN

I trusted Jabari. His ability was never off. But I was worried. He'd been angry when he'd kissed me goodbye back at the hideout. His anger had dissolved into passion for a moment, but he'd been so frustrated that he couldn't convince me to stay underground while he investigated the zone. I understood his concern, but the truth was Daktari had been right. Jabari was *always* worried about me. And sometimes I wondered if his constant focus on me could distract him from everything else. I trusted his ability, but if something was about to happen, I shouldn't hide in the basement and wait until it was over. I just couldn't do that.

As soon as I was sure no one had seen me exit the school and I'd wandered a few blocks in solitude, searching with each step for clues of whatever misfortune was about to descend upon us, I found Daktari and Zi and hurried to catch up with them.

Daktari was searching, just like me, as I joined in step beside them. "I don't see anything off," he remarked, still keeping his faster-than-usual pace.

Zi was struggling to keep up with him. "Me neither. Maybe Jabari's ability was off? Just this once?" she asked hopefully.

"It's not," I said, speeding up. "Did you hear that?" I turned my head back towards them as I sped up.

"Wait, Rain," Daktari called, forcing me to slow back down.

"You heard that, right? A scream?" I asked, my heart racing.

"I did."

"So did I," Zi added.

My eyes locked with Daktari's. He wanted to tell me not to go alone. To be safe. And I understood. "Listen, I just need to check on Mom. I can get there faster than you two. I won't do anything stupid. I'll meet you there," I promised.

We were rounding a corner as he began to answer me, when he quickly pointed ahead. "Rain, look."

I followed his gaze to a row of apartments, similar to ours. The Authority officers were pulling people from their homes, loading them into hovers. As we got closer, we could hear their conversations. One of the officers yelled at another. "Not this one. The orders were to take the weakest ones. *Only* the weakest ones."

The other officer shrugged and released his grip on the young guy. "Go back inside."

The air dissipated from my chest. I stopped and turned to Zi and Daktari, grabbing for both of them. The EEG officer had been right. They needed more weak people. I held tight to their arms as I tried to breathe, but couldn't.

Daktari shook me. "Rain, take a breath. Breathe."

"Come on, Rain, stay strong. Not in front of the officers," Zi pleaded. "They'll think you're weak, and . . ."

Fear rushed through me, making me stand upright. I took a deep breath, as adrenaline returned. "Mom," I said in a whisper.

Daktari shook his head in agreement. "Go, fast, Rain. Get to her. We'll be right behind you."

I turned as his words faded away, and I sprinted. I dodged people, hovers, street-lamp poles, and curbs. I ran as fast as I could, kicking into super speed, an ability I seldom used. I had to get to Mom before The Authority did. They would take her. I knew it. She would be considered weak on their list.

I tried not to notice the hovers stationed in front of housing and the people being dragged into them. I didn't want to think about why so many UZTA officers were in our zone, and taking the weakest people from homes. It had to mean the pure zone initiation would be more horrific than I'd thought possible. I couldn't think about when and where it would be and how we could get there in time to save anyone. I blocked those thoughts.

I had to save my mom. I didn't have a plan. I only knew I had to get to her before they put her on a hover.

I don't know how long it took me, but I was racing up the block towards our apartment, and my stomach bottomed out again. There were Authority hovers on my street, too. How many people were they planning to take? Doors were open with people disputing and being carted away, but I raced past them all. I had to get to our door.

I took all three steps in one giant leap and barreled through the door, pushing it all the way open, and was flung across the room. I landed hard against the floor, bumping my head, injuring my hands, arms, and legs with the fall. I winced, lying still for a moment as I closed my eyes and a soft groan escaped me.

"What's the hurry?" growled a man's voice. I opened my eyes. He stood to the left of the doorway, and from my view I could see his boot was sticking out into the entryway, and it had tripped me.

I was about to respond, when I heard a distinct cry from the shadows. My eyes darted across from the man's boot, where my mother was on her side, clearly in pain. She was holding her side, so I could only assume he'd kicked her in the ribs. "Mom, are you all right?"

"Don't worry about me, sweetie," she whispered.

"Yeah, don't worry about her. She's coming with me," he sneered.

"*Curl up into a ball, protect your ribs so he can't hurt you, Mom.*" I used my telepathy, praying she would hear me as he started towards her.

"*You've got to let him take me, Rain. He's already decided. Says I'm weak.*"

"*Don't be weak. Be a fighter!*" As I spoke the words I lunged for him.

He was reaching down for Mom, and I barreled against him, taking him by surprise, knocking him over. The man had to be two hundred pounds, and I'd body slammed him, which from the expression on his face, had startled him as much as it had me.

But his shock was quickly replaced with rage, and he swung for my face, but I dodged the blow. I wrapped my legs around either side of him, clueless to how I could hold him down, only knowing I had to stall for time and keep him from taking Mom before Daktari arrived. What we would do to him I didn't know, but I couldn't worry about that now. As he reached for me, I wiggled around and concentrated all of my strength through my legs and holding him down. My mind ran wild, trying to figure out what to do, when all of a sudden my scalp burned, like someone was ripping my hair out.

I cried out in pain as he yanked my head towards him, his hand embedded in my locks, and pressed my face to his. "That was a huge mistake, mixed breed. Now, I'll put both of you on the weak bus, just for fun."

"She's not weak. And neither am I."

"Haven't you figured it out yet? You're dead either way. Sooner or later. *You're all dead.*"

His breath was hot on my face, and there was emptiness in his eyes. He wasn't one of the guards who were having doubts about his orders from Nata. He was here to take the weak away, and now he'd take me, too.

"I'm not gonna die in this hellhole," I spat.

He was taken aback for a moment, and I leapt to action. I sunk my teeth into his cheek as hard as I could, and he released my head. But I didn't stop fighting. I jabbed at his eyes with my fingers, poking them as hard as I could, and just like I'd hoped, he cowered away, moaning. I retrieved his taser from his belt and sprang to my feet.

"Rain." Mom's voice beckoned me, but as I turned my feet were swept out from under me, and I landed hard on my back, the air sucked out of me. My head began to spin, but I tried to grasp the taser in my hand. As I flexed my hand, I realized I'd already lost the weapon.

Loud footsteps hammered across the floor and a dark figure descended over me and struck me across the cheek. I moaned again, all too familiar with the taste of blood as it filled my mouth.

"Should've stayed out of it," he barked.

My eyes squeezed shut with the pain, but then Mom's cry sounded, and I had to keep fighting. I propped myself up on my elbows as he went for her. I staggered to my feet and ran for him, glancing around for the taser. Had he picked it up again? I didn't see it but wasn't going to let him take Mom without a fight.

I jumped on his back, but he was ready for me this time. He ran backwards and slammed me against the other wall. Within seconds, he'd reached back with his hand and was choking me as he pinned me to the wall.

I fought for air, and Mom screamed for help. I met her eyes and called to her silently. "*Look for the taser. He dropped it.*"

Her eyes began searching the ground, and then she disappeared into a corner. I dug my nails into his neck, desperate to distract him from Mom as she returned, holding the taser now.

"*Hurry, aim at him and squeeze the button, Mom.*"

Her hand trembled as she raised the taser towards him. He noticed her and stumbled forward. I cried out, "Do it, Mom!"

But we were too late. He flicked the weapon from her hand and slapped her in the same motion, knocking her backwards. And as I took deep breaths, finally able to breath again, he faced me and his dark eyes met mine. I tried to move, but couldn't budge. I braced myself for the pain, but knew it wouldn't help.

Out of the corner of my eye I saw movement, and then the most unexpected thing. Mom threw herself against him, as his hand was moving towards me, preventing his fist from hitting my face. I don't know what she thought she'd accomplish, but she was fighting for me.

My mom was actually fighting back.

He swatted at her like she wasn't anything more than a fly and knocked her backwards again. "Be still," he growled.

As she fell again, I spotted the taser, and forced my feet to move. But I only made it two steps when he struck my head from behind and everything went black.

I liked the darkness. It was easier in the darkness. It was quiet and numb. I wanted to stay there and rest. But then I heard a voice calling to me, and a light began to shine in my perfectly black peacefulness.

Niyol's face came into focus, and he spoke in another language, but he was singing. I couldn't understand his words, but I knew that he was using a native language from his Navajo ancestry. There was smoke billowing around him, but he smiled at me and switched to English. "Finish it, Rainchild. You have to be the one." As he faded away, I tried to call to him, but he didn't hear me. I became aware of a liquid covering my face now, and I imagined it was water. Mom's screaming came blaring back around me, and I opened my eyes, desperate to find Niyol.

But he was nowhere to be seen. I was still in my apartment, but my face was actually wet. I reached for it and winced in pain. I pulled my fingers back. The liquid wasn't water. It was blood running from my head wound.

The guard fastened handcuffs on Mom's wrists and shoved her against the wall. "Stay put this time or she'll pay for it."

Mom cowered under his threat. It hadn't taken him long to figure out I was her weakness. He bent over me and pulled me up, but my knees buckled under me and I fell forward. He slammed me against the wall and pinned me there with one hand around my throat. "I thought you weren't weak?" he taunted me.

I tried to think. What would Niyol do? What had my strange dream meant? Had I just talked to Niyol? Why hadn't I thought to call out to any of my friends for help? Was I too late?

"*Jabari, I need you,*" I called out.

My head was ringing from the pain, but I managed to open my eyes again. I decided I must have lost consciousness again because I could see Jabari running into the room. But why would Jabari be in our apartment? I had only just called to him, and besides he'd never actually risk entering our apartment. That would be too dangerous.

But then he was crossing the room and his voice was full of rage as he yelled at the guard. "Put her down," he demanded as he reached us.

Instantly, I was released, and as I landed in Jabari's outstretched arms, I understood that I wasn't imagining things. He was really in my apartment.

Chapter 27: Bleeding

RAIN

I inhaled deep breaths of air as Jabari's eyes swept over me, assessing my injuries before he guided me behind his back. "Make sure your mom is okay," he said, his voice strained.

Then he turned and grabbed the officer and slammed him against the wall. The officer's face went panicked as he fought against Jabari to no avail. Jabari lifted him higher and higher, till his feet were dangling above the floor and his face was turning red from choking.

"Jabari, put him down," I said.

"Check on your mom," he said, refusing to look at me.

Mom sat staring at us speechless, her eyes huge as she studied the officer. I ran to her and kneeled down. "Mom, are you hurt?"

She shook her head. "No, but you are, Rain. You're bleeding all over the place," she said worriedly.

"It's fine," I cut her off. "Why don't you go back to the bedroom," I whispered.

"I'm not leaving you kids out here alone with him," she paused. "Even though it appears Jabari can handle himself."

"But, Mom—"

"No."

I could tell from the stubborn look on her face, she wasn't going to budge, so I turned around to try to reason with Jabari. We needed a plan. And choking the man wasn't going to help us. If only Daktari and Zi would show up, they could help us sneak the guard away under Zi's image. And where was Daktari anyway? If we snuck the guard away and took him into custody, it would be bad for our zone, of course. But then I remembered Jabari's ability. All he had to do was use it on the guard and we'd be fine.

I hurried to Jabari, who still held the massive guard, easily twice his width and size up and against the wall. "Put him down," I urged him.

"Why should I? He hurt you and your mom."

I placed my hand on his arm. "You know the answer to that."

"Have you seen your face?"

"No, but I can feel it. It hurts."

He turned to me, and the anger faded some. "I'm sorry. I need to help you. I just don't want to let this guy go. He was hurting you."

"We need to figure this out before anyone comes looking for him."

"You're right," he relented. He set the man down. He took huge breaths of air as Jabari leaned in close. "Sit down and stop fighting us. Just sit," Jabari ordered.

He sat down automatically, in a trance of sorts, and a soft creak sounded behind us. I glanced over my shoulder, expecting to see my mom or maybe Daktari, but it was a new guard, aiming a taser at Jabari's back. Mom hadn't seen him come in either.

We both screamed, and as he pushed the taser button I dove in front of Jabari.

I don't know how to describe the pain. It was like fire ripping my chest apart. I'd been shot before, but this was different. It stabbed me almost and filled my body with electricity. The next moment, I was out cold.

I heard Niyol again. "Stay the course, Rainchild," he said.

This time, I could see him flying as the great horned owl. I was riding on his wings. Through the clouds around us, I caught glimpses of the dilapidated mixed zone below. I pulled my eyes from the gloomy scene and looked up. Brightness engulfed me now as air filled my lungs with the sweetest sensation. The wind soothed and cured whatever was wrong. Deep breaths filled my lungs, and I wanted to stay in the air forever.

"What if we can't win this, Niyol? Nata is so powerful."

"Hang in there. The darkest hour is just before the dawn."

Abruptly I was falling through the sky, careening towards the crumbling cityscape when everything faded away and another voice registered. Jabari. He was talking to me. "There you go, Rain. Wake up. Come on, now."

"She's breathing," Mom's voice rang with relief.

My eyelids fluttered open. Mom and Jabari were bent over me. Mom was clutching my hand as she held a towel to my head wound, and Jabari sighed. "Thank God," he said.

I had the strangest feeling the air I'd been breathing had come from him. "Did you give me mouth to mouth?"

He spared Mom an uncomfortable look. "Well, yeah, but only because we didn't know if we had any other choice. He used one of the newest tasers on you. They're more powerful than ever, and you're so tiny, we thought it'd kill you."

Mom nodded. "You were out cold. We didn't know if you were breathing. We couldn't find a pulse. Are you okay now? You look awful. Even your teeth are stained with blood. Rain, he beat you up, and you kept on fighting him. I was terrified."

"He kicked you in the ribs *and* hit you, as I recall. How are you?" I countered.

She held the towel firmly to my forehead. "I'm much better than you, sweetheart."

"Thanks for fighting him, Mom. You really stood up to him."

"Don't thank me. Thank Jabari." She paused and surveyed Jabari. "You two make a pretty good team, you know," she added.

I wasn't sure how to respond to that, so I didn't say a word. Maybe she was in shock. The last time she had been in the same room with me and Jabari together, she'd told him to stay away from me.

"You jumped in front of the taser for me, Rain. That was crazy," Jabari scolded.

"Wait a sec, you came here. Tell me that wasn't crazy," I argued. I glanced at Mom. "For a lot of reasons," I added.

"I couldn't ignore the feeling I had that you were in danger. But you didn't let me finish. I was going to say that was crazy what you did, but thank you for being impulsive. If the taser had hit me, I wouldn't have been able to subdue them."

"What happened? Did you use your ability on both of them?"

"Yeah, they're gone," he reassured me.

"I don't think they'll come back either. They just strolled out of here and left in the hover as if nothing had happened in here by the time Jabari got done with them," Mom added.

"Thanks Jabari," I said with a small moan. My head was aching worse with each minute that passed.

Jabari's forehead wrinkled. "Can you contact your brother? We need him to fix you right away. And your mom is in worse shape than she's letting on," he said worriedly.

"I'll be fine," Mom protested.

"What in the world happened here?" Daktari's voice carried across the room from the doorway he stood in. He rushed over and kneeled down beside us, his eyes wide. "Your face, Rain," he blurted.

"Fix Mom first. Her ribs might be cracked."

He reached for both of us and began healing us simultaneously. I'd never seen him do that before, but apparently it was working because my pain was fading away.

After a moment, we were both healed and Daktari convinced Mom to go sit down at the kitchen table and have a drink of water. I could tell from his expression he had bad news to share and didn't want her to hear. Once she was safely out of earshot, he leaned in close to me and Jabari.

"What happened?" Jabari pressed.

"Is Zi okay?" I asked.

Daktari nodded. "Yeah, Zi is safe at home. But we followed the hover as far as we could. We tried to save her. We couldn't get to her though. I'm so sorry. We couldn't stop them. We tried." His voice shook, and his eyes filled up with tears.

I reached for his arm. "Who did they take, Daktari?"

His Adam's apple bobbed up and down. "It's Kelly. They took her on the hover for the weak. She's gone."

Chapter 28: Down

RAIN

"They took twenty people from our zone. Including Kelly."

I glanced around the storeroom, where we sat beside boxes in Zachary's basement. Everyone was down. Depressed even. I'd never seen them like this. Even Jabari.

When no one responded to her, Takara went on. "I heard the prison guards talking, and they said the same thing that Eric did. The few guards left who are stationed in our zone weren't warned this was going to happen. The hovers arrived out of the blue with Elizabeth Guards from other zones and captured everyone. If Nata had been planning this, she didn't tell them. Otherwise, Eric might have gotten word to us in advance."

Zi wiped a tear away. She was taking Kelly's abduction the hardest. She'd told me later that she'd wanted to save her and would have used her image to hide Kelly and help her, but she and Daktari hadn't been able to catch up with the hover before it had taken off and sped out of the zone. There was nothing more she could have done, and I'd reassured her of that repeatedly, but she felt tremendous guilt.

The thought of what might be happening to Kelly petrified us all. And that was the other thing. We had no clue *what* was happening to her or if she was even alive still. We assumed the latest group of people had been taken for the pure zone initiation the EEG guard had told us about, and we remembered Calista mentioning some sort of pure zone ceremony when we'd last seen her. So we knew it must be the same event, but we had zero clue as to when it was, where it was, or how to get there. Gallagher had mentioned how he would try to find out more about it and maybe even send some of his men there. But should we help him? And even if we knew where the event was, could we save the people, even with Gallagher's help?

Nata would be there for sure.

And though no one had admitted it, I knew that was the biggest fear. Going to an actual event, where Nata herself would be, would be riskier than any operation we'd been part of thus far. Could we chance getting captured by Nata now, when our planned attack, the one we'd been organizing for months with Gallagher, was less than two months away? If we got caught now, everything, our hopes and dreams of freedom, would be lost. But we had to rescue Kelly, didn't we? The more time I spent with the group, the less I was convinced they'd want to rescue her now. They seemed utterly defeated.

Daktari patted Zi gently on the back. "We tried, Zi. We couldn't have caught up with her in time."

"I know, Daktari. Rain said the same thing, and I know it's true. But still. Did you see her face as they carted her away?" Her bottom lip quivered as she recalled the kidnapping. "I'll never forget the expression on her face. And no matter how I try to look at it, I still failed her. I have the ability to hide people with my image, and I couldn't even use it to save her. And now, all I can do is imagine what's happening to her."

"You did your best, Zi. None of us could've caught up with that hover. Maybe Rain, but then what could she have done without your image? It just wasn't meant to be," Cole finished sympathetically.

"He's right," Marcello agreed.

"We need to decide what to do now," Jabari interjected.

Takara raised an inquisitive brow. "What do you think we should do, Jabari?"

He shifted uncomfortably beside me. "I have some concerns."

I tilted my head towards him. He seemed as down as the rest of the group, only I could tell he was planning. Lately, he'd been more concerned with protecting me than anything else, it seemed, and I had a feeling that going after Kelly, even though I was sure he felt terrible for her, wasn't going to be his suggestion. He'd likely choose the most rational path for our group. He'd say we should wait to make our move as planned, regardless of his feelings.

He let out a slow breath and looked up at Takara. "It's obviously getting more dangerous to survive in this zone. Yes, there have never been any guarantees here, and it has always been dangerous, but this is different. Even with the warning from the EEG officer that Nata would need more prisoners, we assumed she'd target actual prisoners if she came back for more people. We never even suspected she'd pull people from the streets. We didn't see this coming. I got a warning at the last minute with my ability that something bad was about to happen, but even that wasn't enough. They took Kelly. And nineteen other people. Directly from their homes. And as relieved as I am that my dad is still safe in Metro, if you can even say it that way, I'm worried. How can we even . . ." his voice trailed off.

"How can we even what?" Marcello pressed.

"How can we even protect each other if we stay here? The safest option at this point, and I know it sounds bad, but it's true . . . would be if we were to take all of our families and go into hiding with Gallagher. We can continue the operation from outside the zones with him."

"You want to bail on everyone in this zone? And you're not even thinking about going after Kelly?" I couldn't help the bitterness and anger in my voice.

Sure, we'd talked about going into hiding, and months ago I'd brought it up myself when I was afraid, but Jabari had been the one to talk me out of it. And I never actually believed that he would consider it. If we left, Nata would punish the people in our zone.

"Rain, I don't want to leave them here. But have you thought about what would happen if Nata were to interrogate Kelly? Kelly knows all about TFF. Everything. She'd lead her right to us. And besides, what if she decides to sweep in here tomorrow and pick up people for no apparent reason again? Even with all of the abilities between us and Niyol and Gallagher on our side, we had no warning that they were coming for us. We're sitting ducks in here."

"But still," I started, and he cut me off.

"We don't know Nata's angle at this point. What if she's planning more? What if this is all some sort of retaliation because of everything Gallagher is doing? She could be looking for more ways to hurt us to make us more afraid just because. And besides, even if we leave, maybe we can come up with a plan from out there to rescue Kelly. And we'd get your grandma, too, and take her with us," he finished.

"But we could just stay here, and go after Kelly and the others before Nata has the chance to interrogate her. And we could stick to the plan," I argued.

Zi reached for my hand. "Rain, please don't take this the wrong way, but you said yourself that you haven't even been able to contact Kelly with your telepathy since she was taken. She might not even . . ." her voice trailed off as she bit her lip. Tears were sliding down her face again.

"You think she's dead?" I glanced around the room. That's why they seemed so defeated. They thought because my telepathy hadn't worked, which it hadn't, that Kelly was already dead. "Believe me, it bothers me too that she hasn't responded to me, but I'm not ready to give up. She's not dead. I'd know if she was."

"But how, Rain?" Daktari enquired gently.

"I don't know. I'd just feel it," I answered hostilely. "What's wrong with you guys? What if she hasn't answered me because she's afraid? Or maybe she's injured. I don't know. There could be any explanation. And besides. The Authority didn't show up here and *kill* twenty people, like they could have. They took them alive. They clearly need them for this pure zone ceremony, whatever it is. We just have to figure out a way to get there."

Jabari's brow wove together as he studied me. "But, Rain, if we take the risk of coming face to face with Nata now," he began.

I held up my hand and waved it at him. "No, don't talk like that. This is The Freedom Front. And you started this, Jabari. If it were any one of us in custody right now . . . If it were me, you'd do everything to get me back. Listen, a few minutes ago Cole said 'It wasn't meant to be.' We weren't meant to save Kelly here. In our zone," I pointed out.

"What do you mean?" Takara asked, her voice inquisitive.

I met her gaze confidently. "I think we are meant to save her at the actual event, and that's why we couldn't stop them from taking her the other day. We're supposed to be there. I know it sounds farfetched, but remember the dream I told you about the other day. We know we're supposed to interpret my dreams. In it, Calista asked me for help, and I thought it was because of her parents and my grandma. But now that I think about it, in my dream, Calista was saying 'You need to help them.' What if she was talking about the prisoners at this upcoming event? And what if Calista needs our help, too? The dream could've meant that Calista is in more danger than usual."

From the doubtful looks on their faces I knew I hadn't convinced them. "Either way, we can't leave the zone now to go into hiding. We'd be signing the death order for everyone we'd leave behind," I added.

"I'm sorry to say this, Rain, but Jabari has some valid points. And we have no proof that Kelly is still alive. And even if they don't come back for us tonight, and if Kelly is okay, they might question her and come for us. They'd go after Grandma Julia, too. If we leave now, we have a better chance of surviving *and* of helping Kelly. From out there," Daktari said, waving his arm in the air. "And I saw you the other day, Rain. The guard beat you, and tore you up. That just happened, and I honestly can't understand how you're standing here now trying to get us to stay here. What happens if they come back for us? How many more beatings can you take anyway? And what if we get separated, and I can't heal you?" he demanded.

My face flushed red as I surveyed them. I understood why Daktari was afraid for me, but everything in me told me it wasn't time for us to give up. Jabari was watching me anxiously. He didn't even seem phased by the way I'd been speaking to him a moment ago. He just looked concerned for me as usual. I groaned as I got to my feet. "But you guys, think about what you're saying. All of you. If we leave and take our families, what will happen to everyone else here?"

No one said a word, they avoided eye contact with me. Everyone except Takara. She stared at me unblinking.

I went on. "You know what will happen. She'll strike back at our zone. She'll kill them all." I paused, noting how they fidgeted uncomfortably as I ranted. "We can't let that happen. It hasn't come to that point yet. We have to stick to the plan. We'll be careful and watch our backs like we always do. But we'll help Kelly, too. Somehow. I'll contact Niyol and see what he can find out. We can also contact Landon and see if he can find out details about the initiation ceremony. Come on, guys. We're not done yet."

I paused as they looked at me with uncertainty, and then I recalled Niyol's words from my vision. They seemed fitting, like they were designed for this moment. "Niyol spoke to me in a vision the other day. He said, 'The darkest hour is just before the dawn.' Well, it's dark now. I can feel it. But the sun is coming up right around the corner, and this is not the part where we tuck our tails and run. We are not defeated," I finished.

It was so quiet. Everyone stared at me, speechless. Finally Daktari spoke. "Well, there's the optimism you've always been famous for, sis." He smiled at me now, even as he shook his head in disbelief.

I couldn't read Jabari's blank expression. I imagined he wasn't happy about my idea, and he'd need more convincing to agree to it.

Zi chuckled as my gaze moved to her. "That was a pep talk for the books, girl."

"Pretty impressive, I agree," Marcello remarked.

"*Rain, can you hear me? Sook saw Nata talking. It's bad.*"

Even as she said the words in my head, I felt the blood draining from my face.

"*Bhavna?*"

"*Oh good, you're there. I have to tell you what Sook saw.*"

"Rain are you okay? You look like you're about to be sick," Cole said.

"What is it?" Jabari asked.

"It's Bhavna, and Sook saw something," I mumbled as I sat down again beside him. I closed my eyes and leaned forward, my head resting between my hands. "*What did Sook see?*"

"*Nata was talking to a blonde girl named Calista. That's your cousin, right? I knew it had to be her.*"

"*Yes, my cousin is Calista.*"

"*Well, Nata told her that she took the weakest people from the different mixed zones and is having fifty of them sent to the pure zone initiation ball where Calista and the others will be expected to 'get rid of them.' Now Sook and I don't know what get rid of them means exactly, but it sounds pretty bad.*"

"*I'd agree with you two. We've been trying to plan something to help. They took twenty people from our zone yesterday.*"

"*I'm sorry to hear that, and I'm sorry to have to tell you this. But seeing as how Calista is involved, Sook wanted me to tell you. He doesn't want to upset you, but Calista appears to be on Nata's side. But I reminded him that Calista is playing a role. Like you said before, she wouldn't have had a choice. She had to agree to anything Nata asked of her.*"

"*Ask Sook if he can find out details about the ball. We don't know when or where it is, but we're talking about going there if we can.*"

"*Do you realize how crazy that sounds? Nata will be there, Rain. She could kill you!*"

"Bhavna, they took one of our friends, Kelly, the other day. We have to help her. We have to at least try."

"I understand. I begged you to come here and save Nipa, and you didn't even hesitate. You can't help who you are. You save people, Rain."

"I'm just trying to trust my instincts."

"Well, then I'll tell you what else Sook knows. He said the ball is this Saturday night in the New Washington pure zone, but he hasn't discovered any more information yet. But I'll tell him to look and we will let you know if we discover any more details. But do you have any other ideas how to find the location?"

"I think I know someone who can help us pinpoint the location."

"Someone you trust?"

"Yeah, Calista left us with an ally before she was relocated."

"Calista? But—"

Bhavna hesitated, and I knew what she was holding back. They still didn't trust my cousin after everything. I understood, but it made me angry.

"Look, if Calista was going to turn on us, like I said when I was at your camp last, she would've already. And she's not going to, Bhavna. She's on our side. She'll die before she betrays us. I'm worried about Kelly, too. But Calista's in danger, also. I've been having strange dreams about it. Anyway, my abilities haven't misled us, and my dreams tell me she's in danger, not that she's a threat to us." I hadn't meant to snap on Bhavna, but I was tired of having to defend Calista to her and her camp.

"I'm sorry, Rain. There's still a level of paranoia regarding her here. But I believe you. If you say she's with us, I really do. I just want you to be careful if you go after Kelly or try to help Calista. Sook's visions are real. Just like your abilities."

"I understand. I'll be in touch. You do the same. Tell me what Sook sees. And Bhavna, you be careful, too. I know we warned you about the camouflage Droid Dogs Nata released and the extra men hunting for Gallagher. I *don't want anything to happen to you either."* My voice was softer now. I genuinely cared about Bhavna and her camp. I didn't want her to think otherwise.

"We're being cautious. Oh, and good news maybe. I think I found a few more people like us who can help somehow. We're just sorting it out."

"What do you mean? Where are they?"

"Well . . ." She paused, and I heard the humor in her voice. *"They are actually in Canada and Mexico."*

"So far away?"

"Well, hear me out. My dad was thinking of ways we could use my ability and Sook's, and he suggested we search for other gifted people outside of the country. What if they can warn their governments or get someone to listen to us? What if the world held Nata accountable or tried to find out more about what she's hiding from them?"

"I never thought about there being other multiracial people like us out there. It's brilliant. You're brilliant."

"No, that was my dad. His idea. We heard that Nata locked down the borders even more. People are being shot by automated weapons if they go anywhere near them. We also heard a rumor that she isn't allowing anyone into the UZTA at all, just some limited imports of technology. Dad thinks that since she's got it completely locked down to a true dictatorship, more than ever, the world will start to demand answers. You never know."

"Takara told us that before the UZTA, there were other countries around the world who had dictatorships, but that no one did anything to effectively save the people. But that we should never give up hope of outside help."

"You just never know."

"You're right."

"Be careful, friend."

"You too."

Once I sat up and opened my eyes again, Takara nodded her head at me. "Tell us what she said, Rainchild."

"Well, Sook confirmed it. The weak prisoners are being taken to the pure zone initiation ceremony, and it's this Saturday in the New Washington Pure Zone. But before I get to that . . . We have to try to save them. And we have to stay in our zone for now. Everyone agree?"

I looked around the room, and though they still appeared nervous, they collectively nodded their heads, even Jabari.

"I'll agree to it. But it doesn't mean we're done discussing the possibility of going into hiding . . . eventually," Jabari relented.

"Fair enough," I said calmly. I rubbed my palms together. "Okay then. First things first. Sook saw Nata telling Calista that they'll have to 'get rid of' the weak prisoners during the pure zone initiation ceremony. And we all know what that means. We'll have to get there before she's forced to do it."

Chapter 29: Project

RAIN

Minutes later, I was standing over the produce table upstairs in Zachary's Market. At least it was where the produce should have been. Today, there was even less than the tiny amount of food to pick from than usual. I pulled a medium sized yam from the small selection as my mind returned to our basement meeting. It would take some effort and a lot of risk on our part, but we were going to go after Kelly and the other prisoners. The others seemed frazzled, to say the least, but they had consented in the end.

Daktari inspected the yam. "Not too bad. We could share that between me, you, Mom, and Dad, and eat it with the rest of the beans you cooked yesterday. I'll get a can of peas with the rest of my money, so we can have something green on our plates," he volunteered.

I raised a brow at him. "Look at you, opting for green vegetables. Mom will be so proud, baby bro."

He grinned and rolled his eyes. "Just give me the sweet potato, and I'll go pay for everything. Zi is waiting outside."

"I'm coming with you," I reminded him.

He glanced over my shoulder. "I think you'd better catch up with us. Looks like someone wants to talk to you."

I tilted my head and caught Aleela staring at me. I smiled at her, and she gave me a small smile back. The last time I'd seen her had been right after Jabari had used his ability on her. She seemed like her usual self today.

"Hi Rain, got a sec?" she called.

Daktari patted my shoulder. "See you at home."

As he strode away, I crossed over to Aleela. She set an empty box down and wrapped her arms around me. Even though we'd come so far since the time when we hardly spoke to one another, it still seemed surreal when she hugged me. I wondered if her mother was still treating her horribly at home but was afraid to bring it up.

"It's good to see you, Rain."

"It's good to see you, too. Working today?" I asked.

She clutched tightly to my shoulders even as I released her. "Yeah, I just got here a minute ago. I'm going to help Zachary clean up today. He doesn't have any new shipments to unload. He's hardly received supplies lately. But he still lets me help out because he wants to help me."

"Well that's a relief. He's a great guy."

"You're great too, Rain. That's one of the things I wanted to talk to you about. I know I said it before, but thank you. The last time I saw you I was feeling out of it, so I forgot to tell you. But from the bottom of my heart, thank you for getting me this job with Zachary. He's the best, and ever since, I've been able to bring food home, and I've even been following your recipes and making the dry food last a long time and, well . . . we're fed, Rain. And you know how important that is in this place. So thanks. If it weren't for you . . ." She looked like she was about to cry.

"Don't say another word, Aleela. You don't need to thank me so much. I'm just happy you aren't starving and you haven't had to do anything unpleasant to get food again."

A funny look crossed her face, which had me questioning that last statement. "Have you?" I asked hesitantly.

"No, well . . . No, but I almost had to," she wrung her hands together and sighed. "I didn't do it. But it was awful."

"What happened?" I lowered my voice to a whisper and leaned in.

"That officer, you know, Wolfe, the one I reported to before you helped me. He found me at work a couple of days after you helped me and said I had to find something. I had to report on anything I'd seen and that I couldn't stop spying for him. I told him I didn't know anything, and he said I'd better find something out or I'd regret it. He said he'd torture me and lock me up. Like he did to that lady and the man preaching, who you helped. Ever since, I've been avoiding him. I changed my route home from work. I'm always looking over my shoulder. I don't know what I'm going to tell him when he finds me again. Every day at work, I just wait for him to come back. But Rain, it's been a couple of weeks now, and he hasn't yet. I'm so afraid. What should I tell him when he comes for me?" She burst into tears. I'd never seen her so terrified, and I understood her fear.

I pulled her into another hug. "It's fine, you're safe. He's not coming back, Aleela."

She didn't know he was dead, of course, and that right after he'd threatened her again, I'd attacked him with rats. I couldn't tell her the truth, but I could tell her a little.

"What do you mean?"

"I heard a rumor about him. He got taken out of here sick or something. He's not coming back."

Her eyes widened. "Really? Are you sure? I mean he could recover and come back for me, and I have to know what to tell him. What if he locks me up? I can't go to prison, Rain. I won't survive in there." Fear filled her voice again.

"Aleela, I actually heard that he didn't make it. I can't tell you who told me, but I trust them. He's gone. So he can't hurt you or anyone anymore. I promise."

Her body slumped against mine. "I hope it's true. He's awful. I mean, he was. I saw him hurt some people before. What he did to that lady's husband before he brought you into that room . . ." Her sentence ended as she shuddered. "He was a monster. I'm sorry again I dragged you into it."

"You were just trying to survive, Aleela. It's over and don't think about it anymore, okay? I don't care about any of that now."

She wiped her tears away and grinned at me. "I don't deserve your help."

"Yes, you do."

"My mom says I'm a waste. That I don't deserve to eat the food I bring home. I'm a disappointment to her."

"Please, Aleela, don't believe her. Those are lies. I wish I knew what causes some people to say and do such hateful things, but I don't. But I do know that you are a beautiful person who has been through a lot. You are very special. Don't forget that."

"Thanks for your friendship, Rain. Sorry, I know it probably doesn't seem like that to you. I know you have friends already."

"Aleela, I—"

"No, wait, let me finish. I know it's not your typical friendship. I don't exactly have those. Well, there was this neighbor. An old man actually, Joseph, he was always nice to me. And sometimes, when Mom would kick me out, he'd offer me a cup of tea and give me something to eat if he had enough. I don't think he ever had enough, honestly. He just shared what he had. We never really spoke. He knew what Mom was doing, but he didn't say anything. What could he say, you know? Anyhow they took him the other day when they did the round up for the weakest people they could find. He was the closest thing I had to a friend in here, I mean besides you and your friends. And especially you, Rain. I even tried to take Jabari from you. I mean, I didn't have a chance. I see that now. He's completely in love with you. But still, I don't deserve for us to be friends, but I just . . . I just need—"

"Aleela, stop." I cut her off. The poor girl was suffering enough. "Listen to me. I am your friend."

She smiled at me sheepishly. "Thank you."

I pulled her close again. "You're making me hug you a lot today."

I laughed and so did she.

"I needed the hugs. Thank you."

I leaned back a little. "Now remember, we are friends. And if you need anything, I mean anything ever, you find me, okay? You know where I live, right?"

"Yeah, you told me. I think I could find it."

"Just knock on the door. Hey, now that I think about it . . . Daktari, Zi, and I are headed to the laundromat a little earlier than usual this Saturday morning, but if you want to join me, I'll go separately from them, so we don't break The Authority law of no more than three people together. We could hang out while we do laundry, I know it's not exactly your typical idea of fun, but what's typical these days?" I couldn't explain to her that we were going earlier than usual because we were going to fly out of the zone in our hover and try to rescue Kelly Saturday night from the pure zone ceremony, but something told me Aleela could really use some friend time, even if I wasn't exactly close to her. It seemed like I might be all she had.

"Sounds perfect to me."

"Meet me there at nine a.m.?"

"Definitely. Well, I'd better get back to cleaning up. I don't want to take advantage of Zachary."

"Okay, I'll see you Sat—"

An alarm blared around us, and Aleela's face went pale. I spun around as an Elizabeth Guard entered the shop with two Droid Dogs, and one O3 model Droid, with the alarm sounding from the Droid.

I stepped in front of Aleela on instinct, pushing her behind me. We lowered down to watch. Zachary looked up from the register, confusion on his face.

"Number one-zero-nine, we are relocating you to the hover plant, effective immediately," ordered the human officer.

"But who will run the market?"

"Not your concern. You've been reassigned for a special project at the hover plant. Let's go."

Zachary stood frozen as he studied the guard and the Droids.

"Move," barked the officer.

He came out from behind the counter and glanced in my direction. I nodded at him from behind the display as he veered towards the door.

The O3 Droid moved behind the counter, replacing Zachary, and one of the Droid Dogs sat beside him.

Aleela flinched beside me and the Droid Dog jumped to alert as it noticed us. It roamed over to us. "ID check," it growled.

We pulled our pant legs up to expose our ankle tattoos for the scan. My number lit up in its red eyes. "One-two-seven-six."

Aleela's number illuminated also, and the Droid paused for a moment. I assumed it was running our numbers for background checks. I held my breath as I waited for it to respond.

It turned away as it spoke now. "Dismissed. This store is under The Authority surveillance and operation. Leave the premises."

I grabbed Aleela's arm, as she seemed incapable of speech or movement, and I dragged her outside. We walked away from the store, my mind racing all the while. The Authority would record any activity around the store and run it now.

Aleela spoke up finally. "How am I going to feed my mom now? What should I do? Zachary was letting me help out there in secret, Rain."

"It's fine. I'll make sure you get food somehow. My friends will help, okay?"

"But—"

"It's no problem, I promise."

It wasn't a problem. We had extra cans of food stashed in our hideout for emergencies, and Takara would find a way to help Aleela, I was sure. The real problem was that TFF had just lost our secret meeting place with Takara.

Zachary's basement had been the one place that had consistently offered me hope and refuge since this nightmare began years ago and Takara had begun tutoring us in secret. And though I knew we'd be okay and we'd figure out another way to meet with Takara, it still felt a little disheartening. Plus, why would The Authority move Zachary to the hover plant? Was there really a special project or was Nata just looking for faster hover production so she could attack our zone sooner?

Either way, things had gotten worse.

Chapter 30: Safe

RAIN

In less than forty-eight hours, we'd thrown together our riskiest plan yet. Despite our latest setback, losing our secret meeting place with Takara, we hadn't a choice but to move forward. At least that had been my angle. After all, I'd been the driving force behind the decision to go after Kelly, and even though Jabari had agreed to go along and had insisted on planning the rescue down to every last detail, he was still reluctant. Or maybe he was just nervous. Something was going on with him, I could tell. But I had to ignore his concern or whatever it was for the moment and focus on what had to be done. I couldn't see any other option. We had to rescue Kelly, or we might as well give up on everything else. She could not die.

So for the past forty-eight hours, I'd plotted, met in secret, contacted every single one of our allies either via my telepathy or with TFF using our Pinkie devices, and everyone had agreed to help us. And though Jabari clearly had his reservations, we were all in this mission together. And honestly, it seemed like it would be our best mission yet because, thanks to Landon, we had more intel than we'd ever had before.

Marcello picked up the Pinkie to read the latest message from Landon. We'd contacted him Wednesday evening after our meeting with Takara to get the ball rolling, and he had been more help than we could have dreamed. Calista had truly come through for us when she found Landon.

"Landon says he found the perfect place to hide our two hovers once we get inside the walls of the pure zone. It's an actual hover parking lot, located a block from the ceremony. He's sending us the coordinates. We might have to tie up a security guard or two, but Landon and his friends will cut all of the surveillance cameras in and around the ceremony, within a half mile radius."

"The perfect place?" Jabari said doubtfully. "We need to warn Moretti and Gallagher about the potential security guards in case Marcello can't get to both of them."

"But you know I can handle it, boss."

"It's not you I'm worried about, Marcello. We're going in blind to this place. There could be surprises or unexpected . . . dilemmas," he finished.

"We're not exactly blind. Landon has found out everything we need to know about the zone. Gallagher and his men are all going to be there. Niyol will be there. We're picking Blakely up to go along so he can provide extra cover if we need it." Cole was staring at Jabari as he listed reasons we were more protected and prepared than usual, but Jabari was peering at me, his expression pensive.

I was sure he was thinking about the fact that Gallagher had asked if we could arrange for Blakely to join us just for extra protection. Jabari knew I didn't return Blakely's feelings for me, but it still made him uncomfortable. When Marcello had teased him about it earlier, Jabari had claimed he was a little concerned only because Blakely had never been on a mission with us and it was risky to invite someone new along. But Daktari had pointed out how Blakely had proved himself, twice already, when he'd protected us with his shield at Bhavna's camp. Then of course, I'd mentioned that we were actually the ones putting their camp at risk by borrowing Blakely, the camp's protective shield, for the mission. Of course, William, Bhavna's dad, the leader of their camp, had agreed that if Blakely wanted to help us it was for a good cause. William had also agreed to take on and board the prisoners that we rescued. Gallagher was going to transport them to William's property line after the rescue. This was by far the largest and most complicated mission yet, so I knew why Jabari was so concerned. Still, I kept my expression blank as he stared at me. We had to go forward with the plan.

When Jabari still hadn't responded to Cole, he went on. "And Gallagher is letting Adrianne go, too, in case we need her image. Even though we've put this plan together quickly, I think it's solid."

"Me too, but does anyone else think it's pretty wild how Gallagher is going to help us? I mean, we're going there mostly because Kelly is there. Not that we wouldn't risk our lives to rescue a group of strangers. That sounds like something we'd do. But why should Gallagher risk going there? He's Nata's most wanted man, for crying out loud. If she catches him, this whole thing could fail. I mean the entire mission to free the zones and all," Zi said nervously. "And more importantly, why isn't he planning to just kill Nata himself or take her prisoner or something while we are there? Why stick to the plan of sending a few teenagers to capture her in another month or so, when he has the chance now?"

Jabari sat up to reply. "Like I said earlier, Niyol said it's not the time to take Nata down," he offered.

"But why not?" she returned.

"We don't know that part. Only that as soon as Gallagher brought up the subject with Niyol, he said it was the wrong time. We have to trust Niyol. He's never led us astray," Jabari said quietly.

"I just wish he would give us a logical explanation for once. I mean, hello, we're going to have Lieutenant Moretti and his men, former Navy Seals, Gallagher, plus more armed men with us. Oh, and don't forget Niyol, Mr. Superpower himself, will be there too. We could just capture her and end it now," Zi complained.

"Amiga, Jabari's right. As crazy as that old man seems, Niyol has been watching out for all of us for months now. We can't ignore his warning. If he says it isn't safe to attack Nata there, as much as I don't want to miss the opportunity, we have to trust him," Marcello calmly reassured her.

"And to answer your other question about why Gallagher is going along in the first place . . . He thinks that whatever she is planning with the pure zone has to be stopped, and if this helps somehow to throw a wrench in her pure zone plans, he wants in. Plus, he said that he wants to make sure he keeps the attention off of us, and if he can take responsibility for ruining her pure zone ceremony, it will continue to keep us off her radar," Cole explained.

"But what if she decides to retaliate?" Zi asked.

"That's a risk he is willing to take. Gallagher thinks that if Nata strikes back, it will be against him, not the zones. He says they'll be prepared for her. I'm not sure what that means, but I have to trust him. Anyhow, when he heard how Rain rallied our support with her pep talk about rescuing Kelly and the others and staying the course, he said she was right. He said he had our backs, too," Jabari added, turning to look at me again.

"You told him about that?" I asked.

Jabari nodded. "Yeah. I mean, if it weren't for you we might not even be going. I think you should get credit for being heroic."

My cheeks turned red. "Heroic? Don't you mean reckless?"

His mouth curved up just a fraction. "No, I don't. Look, I know I'm a little uneasy about putting us all in this type of danger, but you made the right call. We can't leave Kelly behind or anyone else. And like Cole said, we've got a lot of extra help this time."

Cole bobbed his head. "Yeah, and did I mention that Landon will be taking care of cameras for us—all over the building where the ceremony is? We've never gone into a mission with so much help before."

"We've also never gone on a mission after dark," Jabari returned.

It was true. That was another risk factor we were all worried about but hadn't been able to find a way around. The pure zone ceremony was starting at six p.m., and the sunset was around six fifteen p.m., and every mission we had gone on before this had been during daylight hours.

Also, if we didn't make it back before our nine p.m. curfew for some reason, we'd have to sneak into our homes under Zi's image and hope that no one discovered us being out late.

"Don't worry, we'll make it home before curfew, Jabari," I said optimistically.

He studied me intently. "We have to."

"Oh, come on, are you afraid of the dark or something?" teased Marcello.

"Bad things happen in the dark," Zi said dryly.

Daktari reached for Zi. "Listen, we'll be fine. The plan is good. As long as we stick together, we should be fine. Niyol wouldn't have encouraged us to do this if he thought we couldn't. We will have more protection with us than we've ever had."

Jabari cleared his throat. "That's true. Still, I want each of you to be extra cautious. Nata will be there. We've never gone on any mission where we might encounter her. We can go ahead and wrap this meeting up. Marcello, if you'll just message Gallagher the final details about the hover lot?"

"Sure thing," he agreed.

"And tell Landon thank you, of course."

"On it."

"And Cole, you're going to look into the network again to see if anything jumps out about the ceremony?"

"Yes, sir, I've been searching the network when I can, so far nothing. But I'll keep looking."

"Thanks."

Jabari stood up, reached for my hand. "Come on."

I accepted his hand, and he pulled me to my feet.

Daktari tapped my shoulder as he passed me. "See you at home later, okay? Zi and I are going to head out first."

"Sure. Love you."

"Love you too, sis."

Zi wrapped her arms around me and squeezed as hard as she could. "I love you, too, Rain."

I struggled for breath and finally managed to break free and laugh. "Hello, air? I love you, also, Zi, but why do you keep hugging me like it's the last time you'll ever see me?" I teased.

She giggled. "I just don't want you to forget about me."

"I could never forget about you."

"Neither could I, Zi. Not your talent, your charm, your beauty—" Marcello began.

Daktari waved his hand, "We get it, hot shot."

Cole shook his head. "Poor choice of words, Daktari."

Marcello laughed. "He's right though, isn't he, Zi? I am hot."

Everyone was laughing as Jabari led me away towards the stepladder in the corner. He scaled the few steps and slid the top open and hopped down again beside me.

I planted my feet firmly. "Where are we going?"

He pointed upstairs. "It's up there. What I have to show you."

"But we rarely go up into the main building. You always say it's too dangerous."

"You're willing to trust Landon, Blakely, and everyone else about this crazy night time mission tomorrow, but you won't go up into the abandoned main building with your fiancé?" he challenged.

I smirked. "Point taken. Lead the way."

"Ladies first," he said, gesturing for me to climb up ahead of him.

"Don't have too much fun, kids," Marcello called after us.

As I entered the old gymnasium a cold swept over me. The basement was smaller and easier to stay warm since there were no broken windows or doors down there. My eyes roamed up the length of the walls, noting the broken windows allowing the draft and freezing air into the worn down school.

Jabari quickly joined me and grabbed my hand. He led me carefully through the large gym and through adjoining doors. I'd never actually explored the school too much. Jabari had always made us stay below other than to go in and out of the music room where we kept our hover stored. Sure, the building was abandoned and locked up from the outside, but it felt sort of strange, roaming through it now. But apparently Jabari knew where he was going.

He turned a corner and opened the door to an office. A bit of light trickled in through patches of a boarded up window, and I glanced around the dust-covered room doubtfully.

"It's a little musty in here, huh?"

He grinned. "Yep, come on."

He pulled me through the old teacher offices and opened another door. He lit a solar palm light, and I surveyed the space as we entered. This room wasn't as dusty, though I wasn't sure why. It was smaller in the interior of the building, away from the outside, with no windows, and I knew why we were there.

"There aren't any windows in here, so we have total privacy," I remarked.

He lit a second pocket solar light and placed them both on a tabletop that had clearly been wiped off recently. "Did you clean this room up? What's going on?" I asked suspiciously.

His eyes seemed to twinkle, but he didn't reply. He walked to the corner where he picked up a small device I didn't recognize and placed it on the table beside the lights. He pressed a button and instantly music began playing. And not just any music. I recognized the tune, and the instrument.

"Is that . . . but how? That sounds like Kelly playing . . ."

He stepped closer, reaching for me. He wrapped one hand around my waist and the other held my hand securely beside his chest.

"It is Kelly. She recorded it for me with Cole's help using a device he found in the music room. I wanted to do something special. You know, so we could just be normal people in love . . . and forget the fact we have a country to save for a minute. I had planned to surprise you with this later on, before we went on the mission to Elizabeth Mansion, but now," he paused as he swayed us to the music. "Well, I changed my mind. I don't want to wait any longer to dance with you, Rain."

My thoughts went in a dozen directions, but I laid my head against his chest and listened to his heart beating and the music. It was certainly romantic of him to find someplace where we could listen to music and slow dance, but it was a little insane. He turned us slowly around the room, and I had to voice my concern. "If they hear the music . . ."

"That's why I chose an interior room. No one will hear it. No one can see us."

"Okay, but why did you change your mind about when to do this? Are you afraid we won't make it back from the pure zone? Is that why you've been so worried about this mission? Do your instincts tell you something is off?"

"I didn't really want to talk about all of that, but if it's important to you . . ."

"It is. I want to know what's going on with you lately."

He walked to the music and shut it off. He held out a hand to me as he leaned against the table. He pulled me close so I could meet his eyes as he wrapped his arms around my waist.

"Well, I've had a lot of off feelings lately. I can't explain it. Take you having to convince everyone to go save Kelly. Normally, I would be the one giving the pep talk about leading us into something, but you were the one who talked us all, me included, into it. It all seems too dangerous."

"Everything we've ever done is dangerous," I pointed out.

"But it's more than that. The feelings are constant lately, and I can't see a solution. The *only* thing I see lately is you. You come into my dreams at night. You're on my mind all day. Every second you're there."

"You sound a little like it's bothering you," I teased.

He shook his head. "That's not it. I know it sounds weird, but recently, it feels like part of my purpose is simply to protect you, Rain."

"That's just because of what happened the other day. You saved me from that officer. You tried to warn me that I wasn't safe, and I went ahead anyway to check on my mom. And it turned out your feeling was accurate. You were right. But thankfully, you got there in time to save us. I'm sure that's all it is. On top of that, you promised my dad you'd keep me safe. You never should have made him that promise. And you have to stop worrying about me so much. I'm pretty tough, you know?"

"I know you're tough, and it's not just because of the other day or your dad. I've been feeling like this for a while. I don't know why yet or what it means, but I'm worried about your safety more than ever, Rain. I don't mean to upset you. The days ahead are full of uncertainty. Yet, the closer we get to leaving, the more I feel the need to hide you away. I can't shake the feeling."

"But Jabari, if you're too focused on me, it could put you and all of us in danger. You're supposed to be our leader. You have to trust your instincts and make decisions to protect everyone in The Freedom Front. You can't just obsess about me. And you know I can defend myself for the most part. You're going to have to take a leap of faith. We leave for our big mission to trap Nata in less than eight weeks. It will be here before you know it. And all of this will be behind us. Then, we can dance with the music as loud as we like. It will be safe then," I jabbed him lightly in the chest and grinned, trying to lighten his mood.

His somber expression remained intact. "I don't want to wait until it's safe. It might never be safe. I want to dance with you now."

"You sure you don't know something I don't? It feels almost like you're sure something bad is going to happen. Is it your ability? I'm in real trouble?"

"I don't know what's going to happen, and we'll deal with whatever comes our way, but promise me you'll watch your back when I'm not with you."

"I always do. Just like I watch Daktari's and Zi's."

"That's the thing. You're always looking out for everyone else. It's one of the things I love about you. But it's also one of the things that gets you into trouble."

"I've survived so far, haven't I?"

"Promise me you'll be extra careful. Just say the words, Rain. I need to hear them."

"I promise."

He swallowed and began shaking his head slowly. "Okay then. Will you dance with me now?"

"So you can pretend you don't have a bad feeling about me?" I whispered.

He reached behind him and started the music again. He cupped my face. "So we both can have this moment to hold on to in days ahead during any trials we might face. I want to remember dancing with you, holding you in my arms so I can concentrate on what we're fighting for."

I knew he was sensing trouble and that he didn't know what to do. And though I wouldn't admit it to him, it frightened me, too. But what was the point of saying it? He was right. We should dance. While we could.

"*Kiss me. And tell me everything's going to be fine. And I'll dance with you, Jabari.*"

"*Everything is going to be fine, Rainchild.*" His words echoed loud and clear in my head, sending hope through me.

His lips met mine, and I leaned into him, feeling secure as his hands tightened around my back. Slowly he stood and began to sway to the music, and I leaned my head against his chest again.

"I remember this song. You said your parents used to dance to it," I said softly.

"'Kiss to Build a Dream On.' I always kind of teased them when they danced, you know, because I was younger. And it wasn't until we were moved to this place and I met you that I realized how much I wanted to live in a world where we could be free to dance to an old song. It'd be better under a star lit sky, but since we can't do that this musty abandoned building will have to do." He tilted his head back and smiled down at me. "Not exactly romantic, I know."

"It's perfect. As long as I'm with you, I don't need the stars."

The intensity returned to his dark eyes, and he bent down to kiss me again. He broke the kiss off after a second, and I leaned against his chest.

"*I don't need them either.*" He said the words to himself, but I heard him clearly in my head.

As the sultry sound played around us, he led me around the small space in a slow-moving circle. We clung to each other in silence. There was nothing more to say. He was afraid, though he wouldn't phrase it like that. And I was afraid, too, though I wouldn't admit it to him. Maybe we were both pretending now. Pretending that we were safe and that nothing else mattered. Maybe I'd been pretending from the moment I'd stood up to insist we go after Kelly. Maybe Jabari had been right all along.

Chapter 31: Nightmare

RAIN

Ever since Kelly had been taken, I'd been trying to reach her telepathically, on the hour, every hour, to no avail. Frustration was eating me up. That and the overall guilt I felt about losing Kelly. Sure, I hadn't lost her, but I hadn't protected her. And as much as I'd told everyone else, Zi specifically, that it wasn't their fault either since they couldn't have known The Authority would come for more people so unexpectedly, I felt like I'd let everyone down. My ability to learn things from my dreams should have protected Kelly. But it hadn't.

Per my nightly routine, I'd spent the last thirty minutes attempting, again, to contact Kelly, but so far there was no response. If she could hear me, she couldn't respond. Daktari had told me to give up. He thought it was safer if I didn't contact her considering she was held captive by The Authority and might accidently reveal information to them about us. But I pointed out that she already knew too much about us, and if they were going to question her or have Nata interrogate her, we were goners anyway. What would it matter if I had spoken to her? Besides, the main thing I wanted to do was to tell her that in less than twenty-four hours we were coming for her and to hang in there. Bhavna had reported back that Sook hadn't even been able to find Kelly in his searching. He knew The Authority was preparing for the pure zone ceremony, but he couldn't actually see the prisoners. The more time that passed, the more nervous I became.

Huddled under my covers, I closed my eyes and called out to her over and over. Daktari had fallen asleep a while ago, and I knew I should try to get some sleep, but I just had to keep trying. Finally, my thoughts began to slow, and I slipped into a slumber and entered a dream.

I tiptoed down an obscure corridor, straining to hear voices somewhere nearby. A light spilled into the hallway from a door, and I peeked in. Calista was wearing a long white gown, evening attire, but her right cheek was black and blue like she'd been hit.

Nata stood in front of her pointing her finger at Calista and glaring at her. "Don't be one of the humans who lets me down. All of them let me down. They're no use to me. Why do you think I had to get rid of so many?" She gestured behind her as standing on either side were O3 Droids, and the human bodyguards who usually were beside her were nowhere to be seen. Nata didn't wait for a response from Calista. She leaned closer, staring her down. "Are you going to fail me, too?"

Despite her wounded face, which I somehow knew Nata was responsible for, Calista confidently responded. "Of course not, Madame President. I won't fail you."

Nata turned slightly so I could see her face. She smiled. "Good. Now, you know what needs to be done. You have to get rid of them all."

Just then another O3 Model Droid opened a door behind them and dragged a petite girl in who I recognized. My heart sank. "Kelly!" I called out.

Calista's eyes shot to mine, and she narrowed them. "Impure mixed breed. You'll die for this."

Nata laughed, as she turned to me. "Oh, you thought she'd stay loyal to you, did you?" she taunted me.

"Nata, it doesn't have to be this way. I'm sorry about what they did to you, but you can end this. You can stop hurting people."

"I don't want to," she replied icily. She dismissed me with a slight wave of her hand and pointed to Kelly. "Get rid of this one first."

Calista took a step towards Kelly, and I yelled for her to stop, but it didn't matter. The walls of the room began to close in and smoke filled my lungs, just like it had in the gas chamber at the EEG building.

"Help!" My voice croaked as the gas invaded my body.

"Rain, help me!" Kelly called out, but I couldn't see through the smoke.

I pulled my shirt around my face. "Kelly, I'm coming for you."

"Please Rain, hurry!"

This time it sounded like Calista, but I couldn't be sure. "Calista?"

"Yes, Rain, hurry I need your help."

"Calista, I'm coming." But as soon as I'd said the words, I fell to my knees in the hazy chamber.

"Hurry, Rain." This time it sounded like Grandma Julia. Confused, I strained my eyes in the smoke, desperate to find my grandmother. "Grandma Julia, is that you?"

"Yes, Rain . . . Hurry, she's going to—"

But she never finished her sentence. I struggled to my feet and reached in front of me. The smoke parted, and I could see Kelly up ahead. She was trapped, surrounded by smoke, with her legs and arms restrained. She was screaming for help, but she couldn't see me. Niyol swooped down as the great horned owl and picked me up.

Perched on his wings I pleaded with him. "Help, Niyol. I don't know what to do."

"You have to finish it, Rain."

Before I could ask what he meant, I was falling, and I landed right beside Kelly. Through the smoky air, I caught a glimpse of something behind us. A pristine pool of water, built from shining white marble, was only a short distance away. I threw Kelly's arm around my shoulder and wrapped my arm around her waist.

"Rain, she's going to kill us," Kelly said dejectedly.

"Hang on Kelly, we're going to make it," I said, as I pulled her towards the water.

The gas became thicker, and I choked with each step, but then we were by the edge of the pool, and I jumped, pulling Kelly with me. The cold water devoured us and everything became peaceful. Kelly was looking at me under water, smiling like she could breathe just fine. "I don't remember much. They gave me something to make me sleep. I couldn't hear you. But now I can. Are you going to make it in time?" she said into my mind.

"Of course, I am," I replied.

As soon as I had said the words, an O3 Droid appeared and yanked her from the water and away from me. I tried to go after her, but my feet were anchored to the bottom of the pool. Even as she disappeared completely out of my sight, I could still hear her screams for help.

"Kelly, come back," I shouted. "I'm sorry, Kelly."

Niyol pulled me from the icy water. He grabbed hold of my shoulders and shook me lightly. "Get ready, Rain." As I stared at him, speechless, trying to form a question, he spun into a funnel cloud and vanished.

The room was quiet now and dark. I was in a prison cell again. Someone was crying not far from me. "Kelly?"

"Rain, you're not going to make it in time," a voice whispered.

Tears streamed down my face. "Kelly? Calista? I'm so sorry. I'm trying."

Hands grabbed hold of me in the darkness, but they didn't hurt. With their gentle touch came a familiar and comforting voice. "Rain. Baby, wake up. It's only a dream."

"Dad?"

The next moment I was smashed against his steel chest and wrapped in his strong arms. "Yeah, it was only a dream, sweetheart."

"More like a nightmare, I'd say," added Daktari.

I sat back a little and noted Daktari sitting on the foot of my bed. He had lit a small solar light.

"Didn't mean to wake you up, baby bro."

He actually laughed. "Well, I think you woke everyone up on the block."

Dad tucked the hair out of my face. "Can I do something to help you? Do you want to talk about it?"

As much as I longed for someone to help me, I didn't see the point of stressing Dad out. He had enough to worry about, and what was he going to do about my bad dreams?

I shrugged my shoulders. "I have bad dreams sometimes, Dad. A hug is all I need."

"That I can do, but I wish I could do more." He pulled me against him once more and stroked my hair like he did when I was younger.

I closed my eyes and let him comfort me. I suspected it was as much of a comfort to him as it was to me. He was going through so much each day and night at the hover manufacturing plant, working double shifts under grueling conditions.

After a moment, he leaned back a little and glanced between Daktari and me. "I know you guys are being careful, but I worry about you both."

"We're fine, Dad." I tried to sound convincing.

Daktari scooted closer. "We worry about you at the plant, Dad."

"Don't worry about me. Everything is normal there. Unless you count the increase in workers they've transferred over, like Zachary."

"How is he handling the change?" I asked.

"I wish I knew. He works in another area. It's closed off from the part of the factory I'm in. I assume he's building hover parts like I am, but I don't know for sure. Do you think she's just in a hurry to build more hovers before she plans to attack our zone? Not that we need to worry about that. You guys and Jabari are going to stop her," he said firmly.

"Jabari thinks it is a possibility. He said that Nata might be trying to get maximum hover production out of our zone and maybe even planning to move the date up to attack us. We think the growing threat of Gallagher Brown has her paranoid. But we really don't know what she's up to," Daktari said nervously.

"If you suspect anything or see anything strange, Dad, let us know. But above all, watch your back. We have no idea what she might do," I added.

"I'm not worried about myself. Anyway, you guys are going to free the zones. You're amazing. Look what you did for your mom. Slowly but surely, she's coming back. I mean, she'll never be the same as she was before. But she'll be okay, and that's all that matters. You guys did that. If I never said it before, hear me now. Thank you for doing what I couldn't do. I've never felt so helpless. But she's going to survive because of what you did."

"We had help, Dad. And if you hadn't been there holding her and getting her through each night all this time, she'd never have survived. You can't give us all the credit," I said.

"I can give you all the credit I want," he said with a smile.

"Dad, we don't always win. We lost Kelly."

"You did everything you could. And you're going to rescue her. I believe in you," he said matter-of-factly.

As much as his vote of confidence felt good, the memory of Jabari promising Dad he would keep Daktari and me safe resurfaced, and it unsettled me. "Aren't you ever afraid, Dad? What if we fail?"

"Don't talk like that," urged Daktari.

"I'm sorry, Daktari, but sometimes I wish Jabari had never told Dad he'd keep us safe. He never should've made that promise."

Dad picked up my hand. "Honey, it doesn't matter what Jabari said. I'm not naïve. I know I should be afraid, but I can't be afraid, Rain. I have no choice in this. Neither do you. As much as I want to hold on to you, and tell you not to go on dangerous missions, to keep you safe here, you're not safe here. None of us are. If you don't follow your hearts and try to save Kelly and try to save us all, who will? You guys really are the only hope for freeing the zones. I understand why you have nightmares. I can't make them stop. But I believe in you kids. And I believe you're going to win this fight. I can't believe anything else. Every time you start to doubt yourself, just remember how far you've come and what you've accomplished so far. And just think what you've done for your mother. No matter what happens, I'll always be proud of you both. I love you so much."

He reached for Daktari and pulled us into a hug.

"We love you too," Daktari said.

"Yeah, Dad. I love you."

"Try to get some rest, kids. And remember what I always say . . . Keep the fire alive."

When he was gone, Daktari lowered his voice. "You were screaming Kelly's name. Did you discover anything in your dream?"

"Yeah, I think she's been drugged or something. Like she's been asleep this whole time."

"That would explain why your telepathy hasn't been working."

I wanted to tell him more from my dream, like the fact Nata had been protected by O3 Droids instead of humans, but my eyes were becoming heavy. "I'll tell you the rest in the morning, Daktari, sound good?"

"No worries. It can wait. Just think, this will all be over with by this time tomorrow night. We're going to rescue Kelly. Like Dad said."

"I know. Like he said, we don't have any other choice."

Chapter 32: Worry

RAIN

Everything was going according to plan. If Jabari still clung to any reservations, he hadn't let on. He'd led us out of the zone, talked us through every speck of the plan, from the moment we'd lifted off in our hover to this very moment.

As Cole carefully lowered our hover in the woods outside Bhavna's camp, Jabari continued to dictate orders. "Right over there will be perfect, Cole. Just like we planned. You're doing great." His voice had a calm, yet structured tone to it today, as if he was reassuring us all that we'd be fine and this was just an ordinary trip out of the mixed zone for us.

But we all knew it wasn't.

Jabari had recapped my latest dream to me the moment I'd seen him this afternoon. He'd seen it all quite vividly and suspected the dream had been sending me important messages. But like me, he wasn't sure how exactly to interpret them. We agreed that Kelly was probably being drugged, which explained why I hadn't been able to communicate with her. Though beyond that, we hadn't been sure what to make of the dream. We agreed that Calista was being forced to say hateful things so she could survive the pure zone and that there was zero chance she would betray any of us. Even so, it had been scary to hear her say the words in my dream, especially since Sook was worried about her loyalty. In the end, we agreed that my dreams were never concrete, so we decided to proceed with the plan.

And now, just as we'd planned, I let Bhavna know we were here since Zi's image was concealing our hover. *"We've landed, Bhavna."*

"*Good, I can't wait to see you again, Rain. I need to make sure you're still in one piece. You've been through so much, emotionally and physically, since the last time you were here. I mean, I know Daktari is a miracle healer, but I need to see you with my own eyes,*" she teased.

"*In that case, I need to see if there is still a tiny gap between your front teeth. The one that gives you that extra charm Nipa teases you about so much,*" I replied, chuckling. Marcello raised a brow, but didn't say a word as he was used to my silent conversations with Bhavna.

"*It's still there, and I'm as charming as ever. Just ask Nipa,*" she replied happily. A second later, she stepped out from behind a tree, smiling and waving as she searched for us. Her long black hair hung straight to her waist, and I was close enough to see the small gap between her front teeth. She had light brown skin, a blend of her Caucasian father's and her Indian mother's. She had the same brown eyes and tiny frame as her mom, Anshula.

"Drop the image, Zi," Jabari instructed smoothly.

Bhavna jumped back an inch or two as we appeared right before her, and smiled even bigger. I hopped from the backseat and slid the hover door open and ran to greet her.

She welcomed me with open arms and squeezed me in a tight hug. "Wow, you give hugs like Zi, you know?"

She laughed. "I knew I liked her."

I studied Bhavna's face, noting a worried look in her eyes, despite her smile. "You sure it's okay if we borrow Blakely?"

"Of course. I just worry about you, you know?"

"Join the club. You sound like everyone I know," I said with a half smile.

"Why aren't they getting out of the hover?"

"Jabari wants to stick to the schedule. We're in a hurry."

"I understand, but Blakely isn't here yet. He's on his way." She peeked around me. "Can't I at least get a hug before you go?"

Jabari gave the okay and everyone jumped out. Bhavna chatted happily with everyone as she hugged them each in turn.

"Where is everyone else?" Jabari asked after giving her a quick hug.

"They should be right—"

"Here we are," cried Sook enthusiastically.

Sook, Blakely, Dylan, William, and Nipa tromped into the small clearing, followed by a few others from the camp I recognized, including Bhavna's mom, Anshula.

Blakely's midnight-black eyes met mine, but I broke eye contact. There had been a brief moment months ago when Jabari wasn't speaking to me because of a threat to TFF, when I'd been drawn to Blakely. He had broad shoulders and his black hair was long and curly like my own. He wasn't as tall as Jabari, but was still tall at six-foot-two. But the way he'd stared at me from the moment we'd first met had always been difficult to ignore. He'd done his best to lay his heart out there for me, but other than the one time I'd danced with him at Sook's campfire party, I'd turned him down repeatedly. The truth was I only had eyes for Jabari, and I knew my moment of weakness had been because I'd wanted to get back at Jabari for hurting me.

Sook hurried over and threw his scrawny arms around me, pulling me from my memories. He was a little taller than Zi and had short black hair. But no one was fooled by his size. One time, he'd even picked Marcello up off his feet to make his point that there was more to him than meets the eye. "Rain, girl, what's up, beautiful? Have any spooky dreams lately?"

Bhavna gently punched his arm. "Sook, not funny."

"It's fine," I said. "It was kind of funny," I assured Sook, who was grinning from ear to ear. Humor was how he coped with everything, and I had to respect him for it. Whatever worked. During their attempted escape as the walls went up during New Segregation, his parents had been captured. His Korean mother was sent to the Boston Asian Zone, and his dad was sent to Boston Middle-Eastern Zone because he was from the United Arab Emirates. Using his ability, Sook said he could still see his parents and knew they were still alive. I really hoped he'd be reunited with them one day.

Dylan, the multiracial eleven-year-old, with wavy honey-blond hair to his shoulders and blue eyes, who could wield water with his ability, grinned up at me, but didn't say a word. According to Bhavna, he'd rarely spoken since The Authority had murdered his parents years ago.

"Hi Dylan," I said, opening my arms to hug him.

"Hi Rain," he replied as I gave him a quick hug.

Jabari grinned at him and shook his hand next. "Have you saved anyone lately? I'll always be indebted to you for saving Rain. That was really amazing, Dylan."

Dylan's cheeks flushed red. "Um, thanks, Jabari," he said softly.

Blakely patted Dylan's back. "Dylan is the man around here. He helps us with our water filtration system so we can purify the water from the river. He forces the water out and into our containers. It's incredible."

"I'll bet it is," I said.

Anshula hugged me next as her husband, the blond Australian leader of the camp, William, shook hands with Jabari. "Be careful today, Rain," Anshula whispered against my ear.

I gave her a curious look but smiled. "Don't worry about me."

William hugged me. "We always worry about the girl who risked her life to save our daughter, Rain."

"I never would have done it if it hadn't been for Bhavna convincing me to come here," I reminded him.

Nipa tugged me away from her father to squeeze me in her embrace. She had long black hair like her mother and sister, but she was a head taller than Bhavna and didn't have the gap in her teeth. "Bhavna can be a pest, but I guess sometimes it's her greatest characteristic," she said, winking at her little sister. "Thanks for listening to her voice in your head," she added.

"I couldn't ignore it, and believe me, I tried," I teased.

"I'm so underappreciated," Bhavna said with a giggle.

"I know the feeling," Marcello said sympathetically, even as he grinned.

Blakely took a step closer to me, and Jabari eyed him skeptically. "All set? You don't have to go with us if you aren't sure."

Blakely grinned. "Of course I'm going with you. Sorry about the delay. Everyone was acting like they'd never see me again back at the camp. I told them not to worry. I trust you guys." He tilted his head towards me. "You guys trust me?"

"I think so," Jabari said dryly.

My mouth curved upwards. "Yes, we trust you. But I need to try something before we leave."

I looked up at Jabari. "*I want to be sure my telepathy works on him in case we need to use it during the trip.*"

"*As long as he doesn't begin to flirt with you in private, I'm fine with that.*" He said it with a straight face, though his jaw tightened. I couldn't tell if he was joking or not, so I just smiled bigger.

Blakely glanced curiously from me to Jabari, and back to me again. "I'd sure like to know what that conversation was about. Though I suspect I know."

Instead of responding to him out loud, I shut my eyes to concentrate on my telepathy. "*Blakely, I need to know if I can talk to you with telepathy. Can you hear me? If you can, say something in your head back to me.*"

"*You're still the most beautiful girl I've ever met.*"

My face flushed, and I coughed. "It works on him," I said, keeping my voice flat.

Jabari's brow wrinkled together. "I knew it was a bad idea."

Blakely burst out laughing. Bhavna touched his sleeve. "Blakely," she warned with a tiny smile.

He sighed, the grin smug on his face. "Are we ready to go?" he asked happily.

"Everyone in the hover," ordered Jabari.

Then he stepped to William and shook his hand. "We'll see you soon, Will. Thanks for doing this for us. I know it probably wasn't an easy decision to make . . . agreeing to let Blakely help us out and also agreeing to let us bring the prisoners we free back to your camp."

"No problem, Jabari. We're part of the resistance now. However we can help The Freedom Front, we will."

Bhavna hugged me once more and glanced at my friends as they piled into the hover with Blakely. "Don't let Blakely distract you. Trust your instincts and get Kelly and everyone out safe. But *you* stay safe, too, Rain."

"I will. You do the same. And I'll see you when this is all over with."

"We'll have a dance party, with Sook providing the entertainment."

"You're speaking my language now, ladies," he interjected.

I tapped Sook's arm. "Thanks again for checking in on my grandma and Calista so much lately. Let Bhavna know if you see anything else I should know about."

"Will do. Don't worry about us, Nipa's watching the camp, and we have like fifty extra people on patrol. Remember what Bhavna said, *be careful*, Rain."

I boarded the hover and waved goodbye once more before we vanished under Zi's image and took off. Blakely was sitting beside Daktari in the middle row, and I scooted towards the window on the seat behind him. After we were on our way, he turned around in his seat. I could feel his eyes on me and shifted uncomfortably.

Marcello chuckled, and I looked over at him. "Thanks for agreeing to help us, Blakely. With all of this extra help, this should be our best mission ever," Marcello remarked.

"No problem. I'm excited to do something different for a change. You guys always get to have all of the fun," Blakely teased.

"It's not all fun and games," I warned him silently. I didn't know why I'd said it, but I had.

"I know that, Rain. Why do you think I agreed to come along? I was worried about you. I want to help keep you safe. I'm not convinced Jabari knows what he's doing."

"Just concentrate on protecting yourself and everyone else. I can handle myself."

"One of the things I love about you. You're so confidant."

"Blakely, just promise you'll be careful when we get there. Bhavna and so many people are relying on you to make it back to them."

"I guess you can relate. A lot of people worry about you, and a lot of people rely on you, too."

Daktari began asking Blakely questions about where the new people would stay at Blakely's camp when they returned and how much room there was in the hidden tree houses William had built at their camp, so I abandoned the conversation with him.

As we traveled towards the old Washington, DC area, I searched the ground below for activity, but as on every other trip we'd made since finding our hover, I didn't see much. Mile after mile was covered with abandoned buildings and homes, deteriorating roads, and overgrown landscapes. Since the snow had all melted, it appeared brown and duller than usual. I knew signs of spring would appear soon, and hoped it would stir more life into the scenery below.

Within fifteen minutes of traveling at pulse speed, Cole slowed us to moderate speed. Lieutenant Moretti and Gallagher had chosen where we should meet them, and promised that Niyol would lead us to the exact location. I wondered if I should use my ability to reach out to him, but as soon as I had the thought, a great horned owl flew just ahead of the hover.

"This guy is good," remarked Cole from the pilot seat.

"Seriously," added Marcello.

Cole switched the hover from moderate to slow speed and followed Niyol right to the rendezvous location, an overgrown and forgotten road from the days before New Segregation. I wondered if after we won, the new government would reintroduce regular vehicles that traveled by road or if they'd want to continue using the hovers Nata had helped develop. I figured there would be many changes after her downfall but instead of worrying about the many what-ifs and problems that would need to be solved, I decided to just feel relieved that at this point in our journey, with so many obstacles ahead, I could still imagine a future with freedom from Nata and the UZTA. It had to be a good indication that things were going to work out fine. And anyway I figured that thinking positive would help me get through the night. Someone needed to be positive. Jabari wasn't the only one with a worried expression plastered to his face these days.

He glanced back at me now, locking eyes with me.

"*Everything okay?*" I asked him silently.

"*So far, so good. Watch your back,*" he reminded me.

I refrained from telling him I'd gotten his message loud and clear. Everyone was worried about me, and it was seriously starting to get on my nerves. I opted for positivity, or the closest I could get to it. "*You too, Jabari.*"

Chapter 33: Regroup

RAIN

Once Cole spotted Gallagher and Moretti standing beside a hover much newer than our own, Zi dropped the image, and we landed. We piled out of the hover, and Jabari quickly introduced Blakely to everyone.

Adrianne walked right to Cole and hugged him. "Hey Cole."

"Hi, Adrianne," he said with a blush.

Gallagher raised a brow, his skeptical look intact as he surveyed Adrianne and Cole interacting. But then he motioned for Cole to come closer. "I see your dad in you more and more, each time we meet." He gave him a hug and then pushed back. "He'd be so proud of you, Cole."

"I hope so," Cole said, his voice tight with emotion.

Victoria made her way to me and lifted me off the ground in her embrace. "Ready to kick some Authority behind, cousins?" she asked, looking at Daktari as she set me down. Over her shoulder I noticed Niyol, Jabari, and Jonah speaking privately but fought the urge to go over to them. Victoria was staring at me intently, waiting on my response.

"Ready as we're gonna be. How's Maha doing? Is Chef Yoshi taking good care of her?" I replied.

"She's loving the camp and Yoshi's cooking. Mary, Adrianne, and I keep her company and try to make her as comfortable as possible. Oh and she sends her love."

"She must be so nervous since you've left to go on this mission with us."

"Well, she's all right actually. You know Gallagher's closest men, Houston and Davis? They're in charge whenever Gallagher leaves, and they will keep her safe, and she knows it. Those two creeps who tried to hurt you that one time at Gallagher's, you know Mitchell and Timothy?"

"How could I forget," I mumbled, recalling how they'd held a knife to my throat and then been thrown into Gallagher's hole as punishment. Gallagher hadn't been able to let them go because it would have endangered his camp, so he'd made sure they would adapt to his camp rules. He let them experience the hole as a warning, and apparently it had worked. But hearing their names again made me nervous, even though they'd apologized to me the last time I'd been there. "Did they do something else?" I blurted, now nervous for the women at the camp.

"No, not at all, they are genuinely scared of breaking the rules now, but the one time they glanced at Maha and one of them mumbled something about her pregnant body, Houston and Davis got into a fist fight with them," she chuckled, recalling the memory. "Needless to say, they don't even look at any of us girls anymore. And Maha feels quite safe having them around for protection. So you don't need to worry about her, I promise."

"I wondered where Houston and Davis were when we went to the EEG headquarters," Daktari remarked. "Now I understand why Gallagher left them at the camp. Can't say I blame him."

"Well, in any case, thanks for helping her, Vic," I said.

"No thanks necessary. She's one of us now. She's family. Speaking of . . . Watch your back for me out there today. Okay?" Victoria leaned closer to me, concern in her voice.

Suspicion swept through me. "That's what everyone keeps telling me. You know something I don't?"

Vic shrugged. "I heard Gallagher's plan. I won't be with your group, that's all. So I can't protect you with my insane fighting skills," she added with a grin.

Blakely walked over and shook hands with Victoria. "I didn't meet you yet. I'm Blakely," he said.

Vic smiled back at him. "Keep an eye on my cousin for me, will you? I heard you're in her group."

"No worries," he said with a nod.

"Which group am I in? And what exactly is the plan?" I asked as I got nervous. Jabari hadn't mentioned anything about groups to me.

Jabari and Gallagher exchanged apprehensive looks as they circled closer around us. "Gallagher and I planned everything as much as possible, but the reality is we don't know where the prisoners are being held and where Nata will be once we get inside. So we thought we should split into small groups," Jabari explained. I decided not to ask him in front of everyone why he hadn't told me that part of the plan until now.

Niyol had been keeping his distance, but approached me now, Jonah trailing close behind him.

"Hi Rain," Jonah said warmly.

"Hey Jonah," my eyes roamed to Niyol. He seemed to hear my doubts loud and clear.

"You'll be fine, Rainchild," he said smoothly, opening his arms.

I wrapped my arms around him and peered up at his wrinkled face, framed by his long, straight white hair. "*You've been talking to me in my dreams a lot lately,*" I said silently.

"*Listen to the warnings,*" he replied.

Lieutenant Moretti nudged his way into the circle with his usual company of Officers Samuels, Ross, Jones, and Sergeant Jacks. I reluctantly backed away from Niyol. There were so many unanswered questions racing through my mind, but I knew he wouldn't answer them here.

Sergeant Jacks crossed his arms. "Could someone please remind me why we aren't just going to shoot Nata while we're there? We could end everything today."

Niyol's face darkened, and Gallagher sighed. "Like I said before, Niyol has proven his abilities to us many times, and his ability suggests that she will be protected today, in ways we won't necessarily know about, and if we risk taking her down and fail, it could ruin the entire rescue mission," Gallagher said, a harsh tone to his voice.

Apparently, they'd had this conversation a lot, not that I could blame them. Why not end it today? But I knew Niyol wouldn't steer us wrong. If he said it was too dangerous to attack her tonight, then we had to trust him.

"He's her father, isn't he? Why would he want us to kill her?" Officer Jones added.

"Enough," Gallagher said firmly. "Like I said before, no one goes after Nata unless you are given *specific orders from me* to do so. Niyol will help me make that decision once we get inside and analyze the situation. Understood?"

Jacks sighed, aggravated. "Understood."

Gallagher turned to Moretti. "Your crew understands this right? We can't risk the safety of everyone here if we have a loose cannon."

Moretti grimaced. "Everyone understands, right fellas?" He sent a warning look to his four most trusted men, and they collectively nodded.

"Good. Now back to the plan. I know Rain can use her telepathy to communicate with some of you, but I brought some old school technology, too. A couple of people in each group will have an earpiece. We'll stay in touch that way. Also, I'm giving each of you night vision eyewear."

"But it's not that dark out. There's still a little daylight left. And even after sunset, won't there be light inside?" Zi enquired.

Officer Samuels passed out the eyewear as Gallagher spoke. "That's true, Zi, but for our plan to work, we'll need them. Landon is cutting the security cameras, but we plan to have Jonah, on my cue, cut the power to the building, causing a blackout. After we've located the prisoners, that is. And we can only assume Nata will be close to them, so we'll need to act quickly. On my signal, when the power is cut, we'll begin sneaking the prisoners out. So, you'll need the eyewear to see what you're doing in the dark. And we'll need to move fast. Men will be stationed around the building, subduing any guards or security threats. Lieutenant Moretti is on that."

"Gotcha covered. We'll take any threats out," Moretti said coolly.

"When I give you the signal that Jonah is cutting the power, put your eyewear on so you can make it safely to the exits, understand?" Gallagher repeated.

"Yes, sir," Daktari replied, examining his new goggles curiously.

"What's with the groups?" I spoke up. I was beginning to get frustrated they still hadn't explained which group I was in.

Gallagher put a hand on my shoulder. "Well, we'll go in together, all of us, under Zi's image. And your friend Landon is communicating with us via the Pinkie, and he is cutting the cameras for us before we go in. But if all of the prisoners aren't together, we might need to split up. That's where Niyol comes in."

"I'll let you know what I see. But I have a feeling she won't have everyone together," Niyol explained.

I couldn't imagine why the prisoners wouldn't all be together, but rather than ask why he had that feeling or how his strange abilities worked so well, I remained silent.

"And if the prisoners aren't together, we'll need to split up to search for them," Gallagher went on.

"That's how Blakely is really going to help," Jabari added. "He's in our group, Rain. He can use his image to cover us up, like Zi does. Only since his image doesn't move like hers, we want Zi with Gallagher. They'll need a moving image to transport the prisoners under. We'll be at a higher risk. But there won't be any cameras recording us, at least. And our group is smaller, so we can hide more easily than the other."

"Okay," I said slowly. Why was I now having a bad feeling about this?

Jabari cleared his throat. "And I know you won't like this, Rain, but Gallagher wants Daktari to stay with Zi in his group, in case she needs him. And he wants me and you in another."

"Oh." My response was delayed as I let the words sink in.

I'd never considered going on a mission where I couldn't keep an eye on Daktari. Not that I could do much to protect him. It was just my older sibling instinct, I guess. But they were right . . . I didn't like it.

Daktari patted my shoulder. "Don't worry, sis, I'll be fine. It's you I'm worried about. Be careful in there."

I couldn't take it anymore. Even Daktari was warning me to be careful?

"Why are you all treating me like I'm in danger? More danger than you? Everyone keeps telling *me* to be careful. But we're all walking into the lions den, aren't we?"

No one replied. Some stared at their feet, some looked at me worriedly, and then a thought occurred to me.

"Wait a sec, you guys don't trust *me*, do you? You think I'm going to go on some crazy solo rescue mission? Don't worry, those days are behind me."

Gallagher smiled. "We trust you, Rain. You're just very important to . . . well, everything." His eyes wandered to Niyol, and I wondered if the warnings Niyol was sending me in my dreams were related to their odd behavior. Niyol felt I was important to the overall mission, but he never said anything other than "Get ready," or "Finish it," in my dreams.

As I stared between the two of them uneasily, Gallagher went on. "Besides, Jabari, Blakely, Marcello, Cole, and Adrianne are going to be in your group. We figured Cole might need to disable any unforeseen device your group may encounter with his hacking skills, and Adrianne thought she'd better be with you guys in case you need extra cover. I'm counting on you to help keep my daughter safe, by the way."

Was he telling me the truth? Or were they keeping something from me? Had Jabari warned them that I was a loose cannon? Had Jabari had another bad feeling about me and that was what they were so paranoid about? But Gallagher wouldn't send Adrianne in my group if he were worried.

In any event, I knew we needed to head out, so I shook it off. "Okay, then. Let's go free Kelly."

"And the other prisoners," added Jonah.

"Yeah, everyone," I corrected myself. Maybe that was their concern. I was so worried about my friend being in there I wouldn't be concerned about the other prisoners. But that wasn't true either. Either way, it didn't seem like anyone was going to offer me an explanation for their overprotective attitudes.

"Where's Jonah going to be? And Niyol?" I asked.

"Jonah is sticking with Lieutenant Moretti, who will help him cut the building power. And I'll be wherever I need to be, Rain. Don't worry," Niyol replied.

"Okay then. If everyone is ready, let's board the hovers. We'll fly right beside you as discussed, so Zi's image will cover us until we land in the hover parking lot Landon found," Gallaher instructed.

"Sounds good," Jabari agreed.

Once we were boarded in the two hovers, Zi pressed her hands together and created the largest image I'd ever seen, concealing the two vehicles. Niyol took off, transforming into the great horned owl again, and disappeared from view. Evidently, he knew where we were going. We took off and traveled in sync towards the coordinates Landon had given us to find the pure zone.

The largest walls I'd ever seen came into view. They were so tall and wide they had to be the biggest most durable walls Nata had ever had designed. No one would be able to penetrate those walls. No one would go in or out of the pure zone without her knowing about it. Unless of course they were traveling under the protection of Zi's image.

My mouth fell open the closer we got. Huge buildings had been constructed in the new zone, and they stood out from a distance, not only for their massiveness, but for their shape and color. They were simply designed, in tall rectangular shapes, about four stories tall, and they were completely white.

Every building and every sign as far as my eyes could see within the zone we were quickly approaching was white. There was absolutely zero color, with the exception of black lettering on white billboards and signs. It reminded me of a military base or even a prison in a way, except everything was pure white and new.

"It's disturbing," Daktari said, breaking the silence.

"There's no color," Zi added in a horrified voice, still holding her image intact.

"It's creepy," Marcello mumbled.

Cole steered the hover over the walls and Jabari dictated the GPS coordinates Landon had given them. After a minute, we spotted the large hover parking lot, and the two security booths on either end. Even the booths were white and the men inside we could see were dressed in all white uniforms.

As Cole set the hover down, Jabari spoke into his earpiece. "Landon just cut security cameras for five blocks around the facility."

I watched as Gallagher's hover opened and Samuels, Ross, Jones, and Jacks slipped out to capture the security guards.

"Welcome to the New Washington Pure Zone," I whispered, gazing at the eerily white environment. Just like in our zone, there weren't even trees, natural landscapes, or flowers.

Blakely jumped out of the hover before me, and Jabari stepped beside him to offer me his hand. I accepted it and hopped down. He looked like he was about to say something, but I cut him off. "I know. Watch my back," I said, a little more irritated than I'd intended to.

His hand tightened around mine. "I love you, Rain," he said softly.

"I love you, too, Jabari."

We turned to follow the group towards the pure zone initiation ceremony, where we would rescue Kelly and the so-called weakest people from our country, and where I would see once and for all what was happening to Calista.

Chapter 34: Pure Zone

JABARI

We were standing within the walls of one of the new pure zones, closer than we'd ever been with a group of military men, armed and capable of fighting the worst enemy imaginable, and we weren't going to capture Nata.

And while it bothered me more than I'd let on to the core members of The Freedom Front, one thing I was certain of, and that was to always trust my instincts. Not only were they telling me that Niyol was on our side and he was protecting us from something by keeping us focused on the rescue mission, and not on capturing Nata, they were telling me that as insane as it was making me, I needed to focus all of my abilities on protecting Rain.

It would make her so angry were she to know the extent of my concern.

Yes, she'd suspected that I was worried about her, and she'd confronted me about it before we'd left the mixed zone and then tried to ask everyone about it a short while ago, but I hadn't been completely honest with her. The afternoon we had traveled back from Indy White Zone, this feeling had first become so clear, and it had never gone away. Not even after I'd gone to her apartment and found her pinned to the wall by the Elizabeth Guard. The feeling was constant. It was a burning, nagging, unending churning in my stomach and pressure on my chest. Rain needed extra protection.

She was in more danger than normal, and it terrified me. Because of that fear, I'd contacted William and asked if Blakely would consider going along on our mission to provide extra cover. I'd let Rain assume it had been Gallagher's idea, and I hadn't corrected her when she'd mentioned it. If she knew about my heightened senses regarding her safety in the past few days, would that help her or hurt her? In the end, after discussing it privately with Daktari and Gallagher, I'd decided to keep it from her, and entrust everyone else to have her back with me on this one. Niyol had been told everything via Gallagher about my concern and he had pulled me aside and reminded me moments ago that Rain was the key to the final stand with Nata, whether she realized it herself yet or not, and that I needed to continue to focus on my instincts and abilities, and protecting her was my mission right now.

I hated not knowing. I hated that Niyol was so vague when he said things to me like that. He refused to elaborate on how Rain was the key or what her role would be, and I had no choice but to listen to him. And he'd made me feel a little better. He pointed out that my instincts hadn't let me down. He said I'd trusted them on the way back from Rain's grandmother's house, and because of that, I'd gotten to her apartment just in time to help her. So I would continue to follow them.

Zi's image enveloped us all, and since the snow was completely gone now, there would be no footprints or tracks in our wake to rouse suspicions of any lingering security guards. And Moretti's men had knocked out and tied up the guards back at the hover lot. So far, everything was going according to plan. Blakely glanced at me as we walked down the back alley entrance leading to the loading dock area of the enormous white building we were headed to.

"Ready?" he asked softly.

I had a fleeting thought of taking Rain and running away, hiding her from this place. She was a few feet ahead of me now, walking beside Daktari. I figured she'd stick to his side until Gallagher made the call to put us in our groups. But I couldn't drag her away from here if I tried.

I spared Blakely a glance. "Yeah, I'm ready. You?"

"I know what I have to do. I'll keep her safe. Don't worry, boss," he said with a cocky smile.

I knew he just acted that way to get on my nerves. He knew why I'd asked for his help. I'd been specific with William. I was worried about Rain's safety and wanted extra backup. I'd told them how Niyol was certain Rain had a bigger role to play in the final showdown with Nata and how we needed to protect her. I would've loved to have gone on this mission without her, but she'd never have agreed. Besides, in some strange overbearing way, I felt safer having her near me. Like somehow, having her within arm's reach would keep her safe from the monster waiting for us inside the ominous building.

We paused beside a large white container, just outside the entrance, as my pinkie buzzed in my hand with the final message I'd been awaiting for from Landon. "All clear. Twenty-five minutes starting now."

Gallagher looked at me expectantly. "What's the word?"

"He says we've got twenty-five minutes for sure in the clear. Let's go."

With that, Gallagher nodded at Moretti who signaled to Samuels up front. He turned at an angle and was about to kick the door in when I stopped him.

"Wait," I can open the door making less noise." I hurried closer, ignoring the doubtful looks of everyone watching, and I reached for the doorknob.

"What have you got a key?" one of the men asked behind me.

"No key," I said easily, even as I used my strength to pop the handle off the door completely and reached my hand through the hole and unlocked the bolt. I opened the door and grinned at Officer Samuels, who was smiling with his eyebrow raised.

"That works," he mumbled.

Gallagher led the way in, Moretti and his men just behind him with weapons trained in all directions. Zi was still protecting us with her image, and I hoped we wouldn't have to split up. It would make the mission easier if we could stay under her image.

Just like the exterior of the building, the inside was completely white. The room was empty with the exception of a large heating and air system, just as Landon had described. So far, the digital map of the building he'd sent to our Pinkie device was accurate.

"The main room holding the ceremony should be in the center of the building. According to the map we saw, the hallways outside of this room surround the main ceremony room, sort of like a courtyard style. Let's head into the corridors, and remember, until I decide if we split up or not, everyone stay under Zi's image and be prepared to step out of the way of anything that we run into out there," Gallagher instructed.

We followed Gallagher out into the hall, which was quite wide. Niyol, Moretti, Victoria, and everyone managed to huddle close under Zi's image without any problems. I took Rain's hand in mine as we walked, hoping to keep her near. I could feel her palm getting damp the further we walked down the corridor, which had low-lit lamps along the way. Everything in the hall was white as well. It really was unsettling. If this was Nata's vision of a new world, I felt sorry for the people who'd be forced to live in it. It seemed her madness and evil had warped her mind to the point where she literally wanted to strip the world of color. We had to stop her.

Gallagher halted mid stride as a sweet sound made its way to our ears, coming from the direction we were headed.

"It's only music," Daktari said softly from where he stood protectively beside Zi in front of me.

"Sounds like a waltz. Or, you know, some sort of classical music," Cole said.

"You're right," Gallagher replied. "A waltz."

Rain's eyes grew wider, and I wondered if she was recalling the fact that months ago she'd dreamt of Calista being at some sort of party where everyone had been dancing to a waltz. Only Nata had been controlling the dancers, and the rest of the dream had been pretty horrific. "You okay?"

"Never better," she said nonchalantly, as though completely submerged in her own thoughts.

"I love a girl who appreciates good sarcastic timing," chimed in Blakely. I glanced over my shoulder, momentarily having forgotten his presence.

He smiled under my disapproving stare. "I know, I know, focus on the mission, right?"

"Something like that," I replied dryly. I couldn't exactly blame anyone but myself for the annoyance of having a guy along who openly flirted with my fiancée. And anyway, if things worked out the way my gut was telling me they would, Blakely would come in handy before the night was over. And as long as Rain was safe, I couldn't complain about Blakely's commentary.

Rain seemed oblivious to him anyway, which made me even more worried. She was probably plotting her own rescue plan the further we stepped inside the pure zone building. I could see the wheels turning in her head. Though I couldn't have let her know she was right earlier, she'd been spot on. I was concerned she might take off on some rescue without waiting for one of us. She had a habit of acting in the moment and getting herself into trouble. But like Niyol had reminded me, it was my job to protect her now.

The music grew louder, and as we got nearer we could see large arched windows lining the room ahead. Following Gallagher's nod, we lined up along the wall, still protected by Zi's image, so we could peek through the open window arches. The music flowed into the hallway from the room, and as I peered through the archway, words escaped me.

The room itself was enormous. It reminded me of the court of a king or queen from ancient palaces I'd read about in history books, before New Segregation. The ceilings were too high to figure the distance, and the floors were made of white marble. Gigantic columns lined the exterior of the room, creating a rectangular shaped clearing in the middle of the room. On the side closest to us, there was a pristine-looking pool, lined with marble stonework just like the room, and it was identical to the pool from Rain's most recent dream. Every spec of material within the room was white.

Everything seemed to fit in with the room with the exception of one object. On the edge of the room, there was a large, rectangular white container. It was identical to the one we'd passed in the back alley on the way in, and something about it made it seem out of place. I wasn't sure what was inside the container, but couldn't dwell on it too long as the activity in the center of the room was the most alarming aspect of the scene before me.

On the floor, there were dozens of children, ranging in age from three to maybe six years old, all dressed in immaculate white suits and dresses. To anyone watching, it might not seem too upsetting, but to Rain I knew it would. Just like in Rain's nightmare, they were dancing in unison to a waltz as if they'd been trained to make the same repetitive moves over and over. Their expressions were solemn almost, making them seem more like robots than children.

Rain leaned against the window frame beside me, her eyes huge as she watched the pure children dance. "It's like my dream, Jabari. They're dancing like in my dream."

"I remember it."

She tilted her head away from the window, and her eyes searched mine, fear consuming them more and more as each second passed. "What if it's a trap, like in my dream?" she whispered.

I swallowed, forcing fear away, and gave Niyol a sideways glance. He was studying the room with a brooding expression on his face. "Then Niyol will warn us."

She swallowed. "You're right." Her eyes shot back to the children. "Where's Calista?" she wondered aloud.

I searched the room, attempting to take in every detail, and looked for the prisoners. For the first time, I noted the large throne-like chair at the head of the dance floor. I figured it was built for Nata, but it was empty. I wondered why she wasn't watching the dance, but then decided she was probably somewhere near the prisoners, wherever that might be. As the thought ran through my head, my eyes settled on the container again as realization hit me.

"The prisoners are in the container," Niyol said, interrupting my thoughts. "Except one. Kelly isn't in there," he finished.

"How can you be sure?" Officer Ross enquired curiously.

Niyol let out a slow breath. "I just am."

"Where's Nata?" Sergeant Jacks asked.

"I'm not sure," Niyol answered. "But be careful. She's around here somewhere. Gallagher, you know what to do."

"Okay then, let's split up. Jabari, there are a few rooms off of this main one where Kelly might be. Your group can search for her, but you won't have much time. My team will move in close to the container, and Moretti and his men will take Jonah to the control room so he can cut the power on my signal. We have to be out of the building and in our hovers before the twenty-five minutes Landon gave us are up. We're already down to nineteen minutes. You, Marcello, and Adrianne use your earpieces if you need to reach me. Just press the button on your earpiece and you'll be talking to all of us wearing one. I'm going to have Jonah cut the power in ten minutes or less. Do you understand?"

"Yes." I did understand. And we needed to move now.

"What about Calista?" Rain prompted beside me, her gaze fixed on Gallagher.

"If you find her and want to risk talking to her, that's your call, Rain. I trust you." Then his eyes returned to mine, almost like he was saying *Keep your eyes on her.*

I bobbed my head once. "Okay, team, let's get moving."

Gallagher reached for Adrianne as she started towards me. "Stay hidden and do not get separated from the group."

"I'll be fine, Dad. You watch your back. You're UZTA's most wanted criminal, remember?" she said with a grin.

"How could I forget," he replied, kissing her temple before turning away.

Once Cole, Adrianne, Blakely, Marcello, and Rain were gathered around me I reminded them of our plan. "We'll search the three rooms off of the ballroom first, and remember, be quiet and stay close together. If we see anyone, Blakely will hide us under his image. If you are standing near Adrianne and something happens, she will protect you under her image. Between the two of them, we should be able to move about undetected since Landon cut the cameras, too. We've got about ten minutes to find Kelly before Gallagher will free the other prisoners."

Rain turned away, leading us down the hallway, away from Gallagher and Moretti's men. As we approached the first room on the left of the hallway, Rain reached for the door handle but stopped short. "There's a computer lock box on the door, Cole. Can you hack into this to open it?" she asked.

He inched closer. "Sure, I've seen that sort of device before. No problem."

He reached for the lock box, but I stopped him. "Wait," I cautioned.

Rain looked at me hostilely. "We've got to go in, right?"

"Yeah, but if someone is on the other side, I don't want them to see us."

"Then what's your plan? You said yourself, we don't have much time."

"Cole can open the door, and then you guys stand back, and Blakely be prepared to hide everyone. I'll go first and—"

Adrianne put her hand up to stop me. "I'll go in, Jabari. If they see me, I'll use my image to disappear. They'll think they imagined it I'll do it so quickly. I've done it a dozen times out in No Man's Land. It works every time," she said confidently.

I glanced around the circle. Everyone nodded in agreement. I'd been so focused on Rain I hadn't thought about the practical way we could use Adrianne's ability. But still, the risk of endangering Adrianne was very high if she went in first. After a few seconds, I had to make a call.

I couldn't believe I was doing it, but I was agreeing to let Gallagher Brown's daughter risk her own safety for the group. "Okay, then. If you insist."

Adrianne grinned. "You worry too much, Jabari. Everything's going to be fine. Go on, Cole, open it up," she finished.

His fingers ran across the device smoothly as he expertly punched in code, and a green light flashed.

"All set," he whispered to Adrianne.

She stepped in front of him, opened the door, and disappeared into the room.

Chapter 35: Bruises

RAIN

Adrianne stepped out of the room within seconds. Her eyes were huge, and she was nodding at me excitedly. "Rain, I think your cousin is in there."

Before anyone could respond, my feet were moving towards the room, but hands grabbed my waist and halted me. I snapped my head up towards Jabari impatiently.

"Just a sec. Adrianne, is there any one else in the room?" Jabari enquired.

"Yeah, there's another guy in there, arguing with her over something. He's tall and blond, like her. And your cousin is putting on a lot of makeup while they talk. I mean, assuming it's her, Rain. It looks like she was injured or something. Like she's covering up a bruise on her face."

I moved forward once more, but Jabari held me firmly in place. I groaned. "In my dream, Calista was hit in the face by Nata. Come on, it's her, I know it is," I complained.

"We're going in, I promise. Hold on a sec," Jabari said, turning to Marcello. "You knock the guy out so we can talk to Calista, assuming it is her. Move quickly."

"No problem. I wonder if the guy is Calista's soon-to-be husband," he finished, an uncomfortable look crossing his face.

"Just knock him out," Jabari instructed.

"My pleasure," Marcello replied.

Jabari reached for the door and gave me one fleeting glance. "Be careful."

I nodded impatiently again. I didn't have time for speeches. As he opened the door, we rushed in. I ran a few feet into the room and froze. Calista froze too, her mouth fell open, and terror filled her eyes as she saw me.

It really was her.

My heart sprang to a faster pace. Action blurred around me, but I stood still, taking in the scene. Marcello moved towards the guy. The guy was so busy arguing with Calista, who wasn't even paying attention to him now, that he didn't notice Marcello's hands grabbing his shoulders. He instantly succumbed to his power, and Jabari caught him, setting him down on the floor.

I forced my feet to keep going. Even under the heavy makeup I noted her swollen and bruised cheek as I closed in on her.

Calista collapsed against me and a cry escaped her mouth at the same time. "You can't be here, Rain." Her tone was full of agony.

"Nata hit you herself, didn't she?" I demanded, full of rage. I pushed Calista back just enough to study her bruised face.

Confusion filled her eyes. "How did you know?"

"I saw it in a dream. I saw a lot in my dream. Are you in danger? Can you leave with us?"

I knew it wasn't part of the plan, and I figured everyone around me would have something to say about it, but I kept my focus on Calista. Actually seeing the proof on Calista's face that something from my dreams had really happened made me horrified for my cousin's safety, now more than ever. Maybe now would be our only chance to rescue her. What if that's why my dream had led us here? To rescue the prisoners *and* Calista?

When Calista didn't answer me, Marcello reached out to her, and she collapsed in his embrace. "Are you okay?" he asked, his voice heavy with concern. Calista hugged him for another second, then stood back and wiped a single tear away before it could streak her makeup.

She stepped away from all of us just a foot, quickly surveying our small group. I knew she hadn't met Adrianne or Blakely before, but it didn't seem like we had time for introductions. "You guys have to leave. Now," she said sternly.

I stepped towards her again, anger filling me. She was so determined to help our resistance, she didn't care about her own safety. "Are you in danger? Tell me, Calista. Tell me right now."

Doubt, uncertainty, even fear, flickered across her face, but she took a deep breath and pushed her shoulders back slightly. "Not at this exact moment. But you are. And so are the prisoners out there. I'm sure that's why you're here, to help the people who were taken from your zone, but you can't help them. You'll get caught, and she'll kill you. And it's not just that, Rain. She'll torture you first and do unspeakable things. I'm sorry, but you have to get out of here now so you can still take her out of power when it's time. Unless," she paused as she searched our expressions.

"What is it?" Jabari asked.

"Are you here to take her out of power tonight? Did you move the date up? I don't know how you can. She's protected. Even here. No one can get to her."

"You're right. We came tonight because of the prisoners. We were warned not to go after her here," Marcello supplied.

"Good, then don't. Because something happened with her personal guard. One of them turned on her. Between that incident and Gallagher Brown, she doesn't trust anyone now. No one. Not even one single human." She glanced nervously behind her towards another door we hadn't come in through. "I don't have time to explain. But listen, there's some sort of invisible shield she has around her tonight. Latest bulletproof technology. None of us are allowed behind it. And Droids are her guards now. You need to keep that in mind for when you go after her eventually."

Jabari stepped closer. "Can you please tell us before we go, what exactly is happening here tonight?"

Horror covered Calista's face, and she swallowed a lump in her throat. "She's got all of the prisoners in that container out there, except for one. She's having a private session with that prisoner now. The poor girl has been drugged for days. Nata wanted to weaken them because she thinks it's easier for her pure zone kids to help her get rid of them if they appear near death already."

"Kelly," Cole said.

"She's our friend," Marcello added.

"I know you want to help her, but you have to leave," Calista said sympathetically.

"What is she going to do to Kelly?" Blakely prompted.

"She's making me and Benjamin," she paused, motioning to the guy sleeping on the ground. "He's supposed to be the guy I marry next month, by the way."

Marcello raised a brow. "Glad I knocked him out."

"She wants us to be the first to go, so we can be an example to the kids. We're supposed to lead the ceremony. She's having the first prisoner brought out, your friend Kelly, after she finishes demoralizing her in secret I'm sure, you know, to keep her good and scared to the very end." She took a deep breath. "She's having your friend brought out and then she's making me and Benjamin tie her up. Each kid will come forward and say some sort of line from Nata's agenda they've been taught, one of her pure zone lies. They'll say one of the lies to Kelly as they help attach anchors to her harness, and then—" She paused, tears falling now. "It's why we've been arguing. This whole time I figured Benjamin didn't have any backbone, like he was just another puppet of Nata's, and now he says we can't do it. But he can't back out now. She'll kill him, and I have to go through with it anyway. I don't have any choice. If we don't go through with it . . ." her voice trailed off.

"Through with what?" Adrianne asked.

Then it hit me. I remembered the pool of water from my dream. Nausea rolled through me. Now I fully understood why Calista was so scared. "She wants you to drown each prisoner, doesn't she?" I asked.

Shivers shot down my spine as I saw the answer in Calista's eyes. "Yes," she said softly. "But if we don't do it, she'll kill our families. She took my mom and dad prisoner and won't let me see them, and—"

I pulled her against me. "Shh, it's okay. You don't have to talk about it. I'm so sorry, Calista. We're going to fix everything. Somehow. It will all work out."

I didn't know if any of it was true, but I had no choice but to say the words. I had to try to comfort her because she had to pull it together or Nata would want to know what was wrong. We couldn't send her out there to play her role as a true UZTA pure zone supporter if she was sobbing. I understood her urgency to get rid of us more than ever. "If you're sure you won't go with us," I began.

"I can't. She'll kill Mom, Dad, and maybe even Grandma Julia. I have to stay here."

"What about my telepathy? I've been afraid to use it on you in case she's getting inside your head."

Calista shook her head. "Please don't risk it. You were right. She questions me periodically, and I have to stick to the script more than ever if I'm going to survive and more importantly if you guys are going to survive. She questioned me once with photographs of you guys, and made me swear I'd initiate the attack on the day she plans to gas the mixed zones, and I swore I would. But she has no clue who you guys really are. And if she did," she shivered. "Well, you'd be dead already if she knew you were part of The Freedom Front."

Jabari patted her shoulder. "I'm sorry for what is happening to you. And just be careful and stay strong. If I've never said it before, well, thank you, Calista. You are so brave."

She nodded as everyone gave her quick hugs. I heard Jabari explaining quickly who Adrianne and Blakely were, and Calista told them to keep me safe. She was as bad as my friends with her concern for me.

And then she reached for me again, clutching my shoulders. "Please, leave before it's too late. If you don't win, if you don't complete your mission, this is all for nothing. Everything I have had to do . . ." Her lip quivered as she spoke. "Just please."

I hugged her once more as tears stung my cheeks. Anger filled me at the thought of what Calista had gone through for our resistance. I hated leaving her like this. "I love you, Calista."

"I love you, too, Rain."

She began to step away as I heard a subtle noise from behind her. "What are you doing with it?" asked a tiny voice full of shock and fear.

Calista gasped, stepping back even further from me as she surveyed the little boy who was dressed like her in all white and was blond and blue-eyed. He hovered in the doorway with wide eyes. I glanced around, but my friends were nowhere in sight. I knew Blakely had covered them up with his image, but it must have been too late for him to hide Calista and me by the time they noticed the little boy.

Calista's eyes surveyed the room quickly, probably searching for the rest of the group. She cleared her throat. "Just teaching this impure mixed blood a lesson before the ceremony," she spat hostilely. Her words were laced with anger, but her face contorted in pain as she spoke since she'd turned away from the little boy to say them.

They were the words, or at least close enough to the ones she'd spoken in my latest dream. I understood now that Sook really was wrong. Calista really was playing a role. And she wasn't only doing it for her own survival; she was doing it so we could complete our mission to free the zones.

He didn't seem phased by the hateful words she'd said. "Mother says it's time. But why are you alone with the prisoner? Shouldn't it be in the container?" he asked suspiciously.

It.

Nata was teaching them that we weren't even people, identified by gender or name. We were numbers and were to be called *it*. If we didn't win and take her out of power, little boys like him would teach this same propaganda to future generations.

Calista shot me a desperate look, and before I could react, Jabari stepped out of thin air, which I knew was Blakely's image, and was walking toward him, soothing him with his gentle voice. "You haven't seen anything strange. I want you to forget everything about this room. You haven't seen anything out of the ordinary. Go back to the ceremony."

A calm look settled on the little boy's face, and he transformed into an innocent-looking child. As much as I wanted to take him with us and try to teach him the truth and free him from the brainwashing he was experiencing in the pure zone, I knew we had to send him back. We'd never defeat Nata if we messed up now. The day would come when we'd help the children she'd damaged, but it wasn't this day. We had to keep fighting if we were going to win, and as I stared at Calista now, I realized I wasn't fighting hard enough, and I wanted to win more than I ever had before.

The little boy pivoted and walked out of the same door he'd come in through, seemingly in a daze.

"Nice save, Jabari," Marcello whispered as Blakely's image disappeared.

They all gathered close again, and Blakely looked embarrassed. "Sorry about that. I didn't move fast enough to hide you, Rain."

"No worries," I assured him. "No one saw him coming. And he won't remember anything now that Jabari used his ability on him."

Calista pointed towards her sleeping husband-to-be. "Speaking of abilities, Marcello. I have to take him to the ceremony. When will he wake up?"

"He's moving now," Cole said, gesturing toward the guy who was moaning softly.

Calista shoed us towards the door. "Go," she mouthed.

I reached for her once more and kissed her cheek. "We're going to win this, Calista. Stay strong."

"I'm counting on it," she replied. There was so much pain in her voice it felt like it would rip me to pieces.

I hesitated as everyone left, but Jabari pulled me away and into the hallway.

Adrianne and Blakely were looking in either direction, prepared to hide us, and I turned to Jabari, prepared to argue my case. We had to find Kelly. We couldn't leave her behind. "Don't you think for one second I'm leaving Kelly behind," I began.

"We're not leaving anyone behind. Let's go." He pulled me by the hand and guided us down the hallway towards the main ceremony room, where we would conceivably rescue Kelly and a container full of prisoners from their execution.

Chapter 36: Initiation

RAIN

"Welcome to the first annual Pure Zone Initiation Ceremony of the United Zones of The Authority."

Nata's voice.

Even if I hadn't heard it countless times before as it blasted announcements to my zone, and if I hadn't heard her speaking face to face with me on the streets of my zone or in a prison interrogation room, I'd have known it was her. No one else could deliver such evil words with such genuine pleasure in their voice. Only Nata.

I took a deep breath from where I was crouched down below one of the window archways near the pool. According to Jabari, who'd been listening through his earpiece, Gallagher and his team were perched behind one of the side entry doors into the large room and scattered below some of the side window archways, prepared to go after the prisoners when Jonah cut the power.

"Two minutes until they cut the power," Jabari reminded Blakely, who was huddled on the other side of me. Marcello, Cole, and Adrianne huddled a few feet away from us, under the next archway window.

"But what about Kelly?" I asked, exasperated.

"Just pray they bring her out before Jonah cuts the power. Gallagher says if there is still no sign of her, we'll have to just help rescue the other prisoners and head out," Jabari replied.

"That's the plan?" I shot back.

He stared at me, his expression apologetic. "I wish I could do more."

I pointed from where we'd just come, only moments ago. "Back there, you said we wouldn't leave anyone behind," I reminded him.

I suspected he had been trying to pacify me, as if I were a small child. But I hadn't been playing around. I was not leaving without Kelly. Period.

"If they don't bring her out, what are we supposed to do, Rain? Gallagher said it himself . . . We have to be back inside the hovers before time is up. Landon could only kill the security cameras for twenty-five minutes." He sounded exasperated.

"We have special abilities. We don't need the cameras to be cut. We can come up with something, Jabari," I argued.

Blakely placed a hand on my shoulder. "Rain, he's right. We need to follow Gallagher's orders."

My eyebrows went up. "Really? You're taking his side?" I was fuming.

Jabari scowled. "We are all on your side. We all want the same thing, and we want you to—"

I waved a hand. "I know. You want me to be careful. I'm sick of hearing it already."

I hated myself for snapping at him, but I hated feeling this helpless. Maybe he was right. We couldn't do anything for Kelly without getting caught. I made a fist and shut my eyes. *Dear God, please help us get Kelly out of here safely. Help me help her. Please.*

I opened my eyes still praying for her as my mind began to focus on the facts. Calista had said they planned to weigh Kelly down. That would take time. If only they'd bring her out already, we could use our collective abilities to help her. Or maybe we could just grab her with the others when the power went out, like Jabari had said. But if she didn't get out here before that . . . We couldn't just abandon Kelly to be weighted down and drowned. Well, I couldn't at least.

I turned back to the window and snuck a peek. Nata, just like the pure zone children, was dressed in all white. She wore a long evening gown with matching gloves, and her blonde hair was twisted up. She sat perched on her enormous throne and was waving her hands in the air. "My children, are you ready for the purification ceremony?" Her voice carried across the room as though she had a microphone somewhere in her throne.

All eyes were on her as they stood in perfectly lined rows in front of her. "Yes, Mother," they replied sharply, in unison, like an army of trained soldiers.

The room became eerily quiet as Nata signaled to the O3 Model Droid just a few feet from her. If I strained my eyes, I thought I could pick up the slightest outline of a shield around Nata's throne, like Calista had described. She was protected. The Droid opened the doors behind her throne. Instantly, the stillness of the room was replaced by an eruption of noise as the pure zone children howled and shouted hateful words. Some were booing. Everyone was yelling the same words over and over. Their arms were in the air. "Kill it! Kill it! Kill it!"

I couldn't see her yet, but I knew it was her. I inched up a little higher as two Droids came in, and in between them, in their custody, was a very fragile and terrified-looking Kelly, wrapped in some sort of straightjacket.

"There she is." Hope filled my voice as I rose higher, but instantly Blakely and Jabari's hands were on either one of my shoulders, pulling me back down.

I gave them both agitated looks and turned back to the archway, peering at Kelly. She was searching the large room with her eyes, and I knew she was looking for me. How could she imagine we'd leave her to her death? She knew we wouldn't.

The closer she got to the center of the room, the louder they chanted. "Kill it! Kill it! Kill it!"

Goose bumps covered my skin. "Jabari, come on. I'm going after her. You have to help me," I begged him.

His eyes were full of panic. I'd never seen him so distraught. Blakely tapped my hand. "Look, here comes Calista and Benjamin. She must have convinced him to go along with the plan."

We peeked over the window again. Benjamin fidgeted beside her, but Calista held his hand and walked in smoothly, looking so regal and beautiful in her shimmering white gown, despite the bruise she couldn't quite conceal. I knew she was terrified, but no one watching would be able to tell. She was playing the role. And more than that, she was doing what she had to for the survival of her parents and Grandma Julia. She would kill Kelly and everyone in that container just to protect her family.

And I had to help her.

I looked at Jabari, desperation in my tone. "Look, we did this to Calista. She could have run. But she wanted to help The Freedom Front. So she followed their orders, and now she's going to kill Kelly and everyone else because of us, Jabari. We have to get Kelly out of there."

He nodded. "I know." He motioned for the others, and Cole, Adrianne, and Marcello crawled closer to us.

"What's the plan?" Cole asked.

"As soon as the lights go out, me, Rain, Marcello, and Blakely will go after Kelly." He glanced at Cole. "Gallagher would kill me if I risked taking Adrianne in there. You stay with Adrianne. The two of you can wait for Gallagher in the hall and help get the prisoners from the container back to the hovers."

Nata's voice sounded again as the room hushed to her command. "We have a lot of work to do, my children. Help me rid the world of contamination and impurity."

We peered over the archway as Nata waved her hand, and one of the Droids walked away from her and inserted something into the front of the container.

As the door slid open, an eruption of screaming sounded from the children again. "Kill, kill, kill!"

From our position I could see the near lifeless state of the prisoners. They weren't even trying to escape from the container. They looked sleepy-eyed, and I imagined they had been drugged like Kelly. Or maybe they'd been through so much torture they were too weak and hopeless to fight back now.

"Some of them don't look like they can walk," said Blakely worriedly. "How are we supposed to get them all to the hovers?"

I was thinking the same thing, but more importantly, I was watching Kelly as her eyes continued to search the room.

"My dad will find a way. Don't worry," Adrianne assured him confidently, before Cole pulled her away.

Kelly was looking frantically around, and tears began to trickle down her face.

I closed my eyes and called out to her. "*Kelly, stay strong. We're here.*"

Her head snapped up higher. She'd heard me. "*Rain? Where are you?*" Her head turned in either direction, but she wasn't looking towards us.

"*Don't worry about that part. I know they are going to lead you to the pool, but be ready to run with us. The lights are going to go out, and we're coming for you.*"

"*Rain, I could hear you before off and on, but they gave me something to make me sleep. I was so frightened. And then Nata woke me up a few minutes ago, and she said I'm an abomination and that it is her mission to destroy my kind. She said no one would remember me, Rain. Please, hurry.*"

"*Nothing she said matters. Now hang in there. I'm gonna get you out.*"

The children chanted louder now as Nata signaled to Calista and Benjamin. "Get rid of this one first."

She gestured to Kelly, and the children kept shouting. "Kill it! Kill it! Kill it!"

I felt a hand secure my forearm as I began inching closer to the doorway we'd go in through. "Wait," Jabari warned.

"When are they going to cut the lights?" I demanded.

"Forty-five seconds," he said touching his earpiece.

I didn't know what was happening on the other end of that earpiece, but I knew Gallagher needed to hurry up and have Jonah cut the power before they pushed Kelly into the pool. Calista and Benjamin led Kelly to the edge of the pool where a stack of weights was waiting.

Calista turned to the children. "Come forward one at a time. Remember the lesson," she said coldly.

The first child in the row, a boy, stepped forward and took the weight from Benjamin's hand. He clipped it onto the straightjacket that secured Kelly's arms and legs.

"Please, no," Kelly cried out.

"I swear allegiance to Mother, leader of the United Zones of The Authority and as a privileged member of the pure race I vow to purify and protect the UZTA." After he recited the memorized line, the children smiled and applauded him.

Calista patted his head approvingly. He turned and took his place in the row again, and the next child came forward, automatically repeating the pinning of the weights and reciting the same line.

My heart sped up as Jabari grabbed my hand. "Five, four, three, two—"

The next second, the room went black. As I pulled my night goggles on, the applause turned to screaming. Jabari pulled me beside him, and as we raced towards Kelly, I noted Gallagher and his men were already pulling people from the container. Calista was standing as rigid as a board, as was Benjamin, and she was clutching her hands in front of her as if she were praying. Maybe she was.

As we got closer to Kelly, the children's screams were louder. I wondered how they could be afraid of the dark, like most kids might be, yet they'd been trained to torture and were willing to weigh an innocent person down and drown her with a smile and applause. Could they stand a chance at recovery even if we defeated Nata? The question slipped from my mind as Nata's voice boomed through the darkness.

"Droids, restore the emergency lights."

I wondered if emergency lights were in the building, and if Jonah had any control over them. But I couldn't worry about that. I had to get to Kelly. Kelly was looking everywhere around her as we approached. We were almost to her when, unexpectedly, a child rushed forward in a panic, like he was searching for an exit and accidently bumped into Kelly.

As she fell backwards, I pulled my hand from Jabari's, and I sped up. I reached for her as she teetered backwards, but I couldn't stop her in time. I tossed my eye goggles to the side, and I dove towards her, or at least where I thought she'd fallen. It was so dark now; I was going in blind. The water was ice cold, which shouldn't have surprised me, and it felt like it was piercing my skin as I fell to the bottom. I tried to see through the darkness. I barely made out Kelly's form in front of me, and I grabbed onto her and spoke at the same time into her mind. *"It's me, Kelly. I've got you. I'll get you out of here."*

"I can't see. I can't move," she answered.

"I'm here with you."

I reached around her body, pulling her up and off the bottom as my own feet found the hard pool floor. I wrapped my arms around her waist, pulling her completely against me. Once she was secure enough to me, I pushed my feet off the bottom as hard as I could, and we shot upwards. Something pulled me back to the bottom. Realization hit me as the water rushed in my nose and mouth. One of the anchors, which were much heavier than I'd suspected, had pinned my ankle down, and Kelly and I were stuck. I called out in desperation. *"Jabari, I'm stuck."*

"I know. I'm on it." Kelly was instantly lifted off of me. I couldn't see it, but I could feel it. *"How did you get here so fast, Jabari?"*

"I was right behind you the whole time, Rain."

And then he lifted me to the surface, and I gulped in huge breaths of air. He pulled me to the edge, but I only knew it because I felt the side hit my back. It was still dark all around. I could hear voices whispering and knew they belonged to my friends, huddled on the edge of the pool.

"Put these back on, Rain," Marcello said.

I felt the goggles go over my face and once more could see through the darkness. Jabari had his eye goggles on again as well and was effortlessly snapping Kelly from the straightjacket and the weights. As soon as she was free, Marcello pulled her from the water.

Jabari got a strange look on his face and motioned to Blakely. "Cover us up, now."

Blakely crouched down on the side of the pool, concealing us with his image right away.

"What's happening?" I blurted.

Jabari pulled me to his side. The water was above my chin, and my feet could barely touch the bottom. He lifted me higher, and held me close. "Something's wrong."

Before I could ask anything else, the lights in the room flashed back on, and the children quieted down. I lifted the goggles to my forehead so I could see. Jabari twisted his head to peer around the room, still holding me beside him in the water. Blakely was crouched beside the pool and he was concealing us all, me and Jabari just below him in the pool, and Marcello and Kelly, who were right beside him on the edge. Kelly's eyes were huge with fear, mirroring my own, I imagined. But Blakely remained calm, and his eyes, now completely black as they turned darker when he used his image, seemed to stare at no one in particular.

Nata was standing on her throne, an agitated look on her face. "Now that's better. We can proceed with the—" but her sentence stopped short as she looked around the room.

She turned from the container, which was completely empty now, to the pool, where there was no sign of Kelly. Calista was standing rigid beside the pool, as was Bejamin, but none of the prisoners were in sight.

As planned, Gallagher had gotten everyone out of the building already, but now the panic returned to my chest. How were we going to get out of here with Kelly? Blakely's image couldn't move like Zi's. Was there time for Zi to come back for us?

Marcello bent down and handed something to Jabari. He released one hand from me to put the earpiece back in. He and Marcello bent closer to whisper again, and after a few seconds, Jabari pulled me closer. "Get ready to run. Gallagher and Jonah are already outside. But Cole's killing the emergency lights, at least to this room. We'll have to move fast." He lifted me out of the water and I crouched beside Kelly under Blakely's image. Jabari was right on my heels. We huddled close, waiting for the lights to go out again.

"Where are the prisoners?" barked Nata's voice over the silence.

Marcello's forehead wrinkled. "Come on, Cole, you can do it, man," he said urgently.

The lights went out again, and hope filled me anew. But just as soon as they'd gone out, they came right back on. They were flashing.

"What do we do now?" I asked.

Marcello surveyed the room as he pressed a finger to speak into his earpiece. "Where are you Gallagher? How close is Zi?"

Nata was yelling at the Droids to fix the lights. The kids were screaming again in a panic. Calista was still clutching her hands in front of her chest, unable to move.

Marcello shook his head. "Gallagher says he and Zi are racing back to the alley from the hovers. They will provide cover for us once we make it out. He says we need to move now. He thinks Niyol is going to help us, too," he explained to me, Kelly, and Blakely, since we were the only ones without earpieces.

Jabari glanced around. "I don't see Niyol."

Kelly paled and the next moment, she fainted. Marcello caught her before she hit the floor.

I shut my eyes. Why hadn't I thought to contact Niyol yet? "*Niyol, where are you? We need a way out of here.*"

"*I'm coming.*"

"Flashing lights are better cover than none at all," Jabari decided. "We'll need to run. Don't stop."

I grabbed his arm. "No, wait. Niyol says he's here. I don't know—" A ferocious wind burst into the room behind Nata, and all eyes turned toward the sound.

At the same moment, Niyol's voice rang in my head. "*Now, Rain, go!*"

"Let's go!" Jabari ordered. "Marcello, be ready to knock anyone out in our way," he added.

Blakely stood up with us and accepted Kelly's limp body from Marcello. He cradled her, and we ran for the doors, away from the huge funnel cloud twisting its way through the ceremony. Screams were ringing out behind us, and as I glanced back I saw Nata's face in a rage as she watched the funnel move throughout her room.

Her head fell back and she screamed louder than I'd ever heard. "Alarm! Activate the new Combat Droids!"

I came to a stop as my eyes returned to Calista, and I noted the pure fear in her eyes. Even though we'd gotten the prisoners and saved her from having to kill anyone, she still looked terrified. And I got the most bizarre feeling she hadn't told me something important. Jabari and Marcello nudged me forward, and my feet followed after them, but I tilted my head again, straining to see Calista. What if I needed to take her with us now? I had the worst feeling she was in more danger than she'd said.

Jabari pulled me after him and into the hallway, where the emergency lights were flashing on and off over our heads. I yanked my hand away and stopped. "Listen, Jabari."

The group turned back, and Jabari reached for my hand, but I sidestepped him again.

"Don't stop, Rain," he pleaded.

"But Calista. She didn't tell me everything. I know it."

"We can't take her now. And you know it."

"But, we have to. Calista!" I screamed so loud, I couldn't believe it. But I knew I had to save her.

I tilted on my heel as Jabari's voice growled behind me. "Stop, Rain."

Hands with a steel grip picked me up and tossed me harshly over shoulders I knew belonged to Jabari. Tears poured down my face, and huge sobs racked my body as it jostled against his shoulder away from the ceremony.

"Calista," I sobbed. I kicked and struggled to get free from his iron grasp, desperation overcoming me. "Calista!"

"Marcello, help me out," Jabari ordered.

"No," I screamed in vain as warmth trickled through my body, and I recalled the warming effect of Marcello's ability. Unlike Daktari's ability, Marcello's would knock me unconscious. I wouldn't be able to help Calista.

As I slipped away, I pictured her face. And I knew she hadn't told me everything. And I knew I'd failed her.

Chapter 37: Leader

JABARI

Rain's body went completely limp over my shoulder, and relief filled me. She'd given me no choice. I hadn't even had the opportunity to use my mind control ability on her because she'd taken off in the opposite direction. I had to grab her and throw her over my shoulder before she ran right back to the enemy. And as she screamed for Calista and kicked against me, fighting for escape, I knew what had to be done. Having Marcello knock her out was the only thing that had made sense.

I'd known all along that I'd have to protect her from something. And maybe I'd suspected it before, though I hadn't really said it out loud. But now, I was sure, I had to protect Rain from herself.

Sure, she would probably understand eventually that she could have gotten us caught, but she would still feel bad about leaving Calista. Seeing the state Calista was in had been harder on Rain than I thought it would be. But now that I had seen her effect on Rain, I knew I'd done the only thing I could. I had to protect Rain. And as leader of The Freedom Front, I had to protect every person in it.

Her body jostled against my shoulder as we ran, but I couldn't hesitate or stop to wonder if she was hurting. I had to save her.

Marcello pushed the utility room door open, and held it until we'd all made it through. He moved to the exit and pried it ajar and hesitated as artificial light spilled in from the alley. "Gallagher, where are you?" he spoke using his earpiece.

When Gallagher didn't respond, I nudged him forward. "Just keep moving. We can't stay here."

He nodded and we hurried into the alley. The sun had set, but every few feet gigantic streetlights lit up the surrounding area. I pushed the night goggles to my temple and searched for Zi and Gallagher.

"Zi?" Marcello called out.

She appeared a few feet away with Daktari and Gallagher right beside her. Gallagher and Daktari ran towards us, and concern filled their faces.

"What happened to Kelly? And my sister?"

"Kelly fainted, and Rain is asleep. We'll explain later, Daktari," I told him.

"Where's Adrianne?" demanded Gallagher.

"She went with Cole," I said, apprehension filling me. It had been my responsibility to keep her safe.

"You said Cole was killing the backup lights for us. I thought you knew where they were," Marcello added.

"Adrianne told me they were meeting up with you guys again. You didn't hear her?"

"Something must have happened with our connection. We didn't hear her," I told him.

"Didn't Cole kill the lights?" Gallagher demanded.

"Only partially. They started flashing. Niyol came in to distract Nata so we could make it out."

"Then where are they?" Gallagher boomed, fear filling his expression.

He didn't wait for my response. He spoke into his earpiece, his tone frantic. "Adrianne, where are you? We're outside behind the utility door waiting for you."

"We're almost there, Dad," she replied, and this time I could hear her clearly. "We got followed by a Droid and had to lose him. We're coming out now, about twenty feet from you guys, there's a loading dock entrance by that large container."

"Okay, hurry, we're waiting for you with Zi."

We weren't far from the loading dock entrance and the container, but as the alarm continued to sound, I felt a growing sense of dread. We were running out of time, but it was more than that.

I grabbed Zi's shoulder. "Put the image up, now."

She protected us under her image, and a moment later Cole and Adrianne came running out into the alley.

"Hurry. Keep running down the alley, we're under Zi's image," Gallagher spoke into his earpiece.

As they passed the container, an alarm lit up from its door, and before I could comprehend what was happening, the door was lifting up. I hesitated, concerned that there might be more prisoners inside the container, like there had been inside the one in the building.

Marcello's voice echoed my thoughts. "Are there more prisoners?" he asked, worriedly.

But then dozens of Droids, similar to the O3 model, but slightly stockier in build and armed with weapons, were piling out of the container, lifting their arms towards Cole and Adrianne. "Stop or we'll shoot," one of the Droids shouted.

Adrianne threw her arms around Cole, and they disappeared from sight.

"We need to distract the Droids," I called out.

"On it," Gallagher responded.

He stepped to the side of Zi's image and fired a flare gun up and past the loading dock entrance into the side of the building. As smoke fumed from the second story of the building, the Droids moved towards it, and Zi dropped the image so Adrianne and Cole could see us. After the Droids had headed further away from us down the alley, Adrianne and Cole reappeared and sprinted towards us, holding hands.

There was no time for greetings. Zi placed her hands in front of her chest and created a protective image, concealing our group.

"Come on," Gallagher ordered.

"That container," Cole said as we raced. "It had a label on it. It was sent from our zone."

"Now we know what the special assignment is that Zachary got pulled to work on. Armed Droids to replace her human soldiers," Daktari added.

Rain moved over my shoulder, moaning softly. "Calista," she said.

"We're almost out of here, Rain," Daktari said.

She flinched and began kicking again. "Let me down. I have to go back for Calista."

"Marcello, again," I ordered, my voice tight.

He turned as she fought against me and placed his hands on her, and her body went limp over my shoulder once more.

"I knocked her out for ten minutes this time. Sorry, should have done it longer the last time, too," Marcello offered.

Gallagher eyed me curiously, probably wanting to know what we were talking about, but Daktari beat him to the questioning.

"Why did you do that? What was Rain talking about?"

"She tried to go back for Calista, Daktari. She was screaming and about to give our location away. I had to put her to sleep," Marcello explained matter-of-factly.

Doubt flickered across Daktari's face, but he didn't argue. "Rain wouldn't have tried to go back unless she was sure there was no other choice," he said, defending her.

"The only choice we had was to knock her out. If not, Nata would've captured her," I said sharply.

"You better hope Rain has the same story to tell when she wakes up," Daktari shot back.

"Let's just get out of here alive first. Then we can talk, okay?" I said.

"Good plan," Gallagher agreed.

As we came up beside the edge of the building to cross into the hover lot, I looked back over my shoulder. There were rows of armed Droids surrounding the building behind us.

I paused. "Gallagher, she's got an army of Droids."

He turned, surveying it quickly. "Let's get out of here before they start after us."

"I don't think they're after us. They're surrounding the building. Nata must think the threat is still inside. Did you see the way she was watching the funnel cloud move through the room? I wonder if she knows it's her father. I hope Niyol makes it out in time," Blakely remarked.

"If anyone can perform a miracle to save themself, it's that old guy," Gallagher said confidently.

We rushed into the hover parking lot and into the awaiting hovers. Moretti and the rest of our groups were piled inside, along with the freed prisoners. Gallagher grabbed Adrianne's hand and pulled her with him into the other hover. "See you guys in a few minutes," he called over his shoulder.

Blakely set Kelly down on the seat beside him. She stirred as she awakened and tucked her arms around her legs, a frightened look on her face. I imagined she wouldn't even begin to feel relieved until we were far away from this terrifying colorless zone and Nata.

Cole jumped into the driver seat, and Zi expanded her image to hide both hovers as everyone got settled in. Cole flipped the hover lights on so Gallagher would know it was safe to do the same. No one would be able to see our lights as we traveled through the nighttime sky since we'd be protected by Zi's image.

I laid Rain down in the back beside Marcello. "Make sure she doesn't fall off the seat or anything during take off," I instructed.

"No worries, boss," he said, placing a hand on her back to secure her.

I sat down in the front seat as we took off. Once both hovers were in the air, my eyes grew wide. A huge funnel cloud, larger than I'd ever seen, almost like a sandstorm, or what I imagined one would look like, burst out of the front windows of the building, and glass shattered like rain across the street. A great horned owl then emerged from the cloud of dust and took off into the night, away from the building.

The Combat Droids had surrounded the building, to trap whoever had stolen the prisoners, but Niyol had made it out alive, and both hovers were racing away, safely, under Zi's image.

"We did it." Daktari's voice was thick with awe. "Thank the Lord. I only wish Rain were awake to have seen Niyol fly out of those windows."

"You'll have to tell her about. She'll be out for another eight minutes," said Marcello.

"Who made the call to knock her out?" Daktari asked, the awe in his voice replaced with irritation.

"That would be me," I said evenly. I tilted my head towards the back, noting the accusation in his eyes. This was going to be difficult to explain to him, after all, it was his sister. But I had to try.

Chapter 38: Apology

RAIN

I awoke with swollen eyes from crying, and a throbbing headache. There were voices arguing, and I recognized each one of them. Jabari. Daktari. Zi. Marcello. Blakely. Cole.

"But if it wasn't for her stubbornness, you might have left me there," another voice argued. Kelly.

"That's true. But if I hadn't knocked her out, we might all have gotten caught. She was trying to go back for Calista. And as much as I wanted to take Calista, she said it herself. If we took her today, Nata would kill her parents. We had to leave her behind," Marcello replied.

"Listen, Rain knows that. I wasn't there to see it, but why would she risk going back for Calista when she knew we couldn't take her with us today? She wouldn't have done it unless she knew something you didn't," Daktari defended me.

"He's right," added Zi. "You probably misunderstood her in all of the chaos."

"Concentrate on your image, Zi. You've been using it more than usual today," Daktari said, his voice anxious.

"I'm fine, Daktari, like I've been saying for months. I think your touch heals me even when you aren't trying to, and like right now . . . when you're touching me, I feel stronger. Holding the image is easy, I promise. But getting back to Rain, listen, she follows her heart. That's why she's so amazing. I'm sure it was just a misunderstanding, like I said."

"Zi's right. Rain wants to defeat Nata more than the rest of us maybe. When she wakes up, I'm sure she'll explain everything. Why didn't you ask her why she wanted to go back for Calista, Jabari? It sounds like you just had Marcello knock her out without giving her a chance to explain," Daktari said.

"I know it's difficult to believe, Daktari, but I was there, too. Jabari couldn't ask her anything because she started to run from us, and she was screaming. He had no choice but to have Marcello use his ability. She was completely terrified all of a sudden, and maybe she realized something we weren't aware of, but she was about to give us away with all of that screaming. Jabari made the right call," Blakely assured him.

As strange as it was, hearing Blakely take sides with Jabari, I understood. The more my head blared with pain and the more I thought about what I'd done, the worse I felt. Guilt filled me from my throbbing head to my toes.

I'd screwed up.

They were all right about that part. I'd almost gotten us all captured because of my careless actions. But even now, I knew Calista was in more danger or she was keeping something from me, and I couldn't shake the terrible feeling that I'd abandoned her still. If Marcello hadn't knocked me out, I would've ruined everything.

"Well, now we know why Jabari was having those powerful feelings that we needed to protect Rain," Cole said.

"Has the feeling gone away yet?" Daktari asked.

Jabari had hardly said anything in his own defense since I'd awakened to hear them arguing. He sounded strained as he replied. "Just a little. But it's still there. Listen, in the days ahead I'd rather not talk about it too much. I knew what Rain might do. She's never changed. She always tries to help everyone she can. Seeing Calista like that was too much for her. But it's over now, and I made the call. No need to make her feel worse than she already does when she wakes up. She followed her heart like Zi said. It's one of the million reasons I love her."

"Can't say I blame you," Blakely said, a hint of amusement in his tone.

"I'll let that one slide, Blakely. Thanks for going today. If you hadn't protected us by the pool, Nata would have seen us. That was the real rescue today," he said appreciatively.

"Yeah, thanks, Blakely," Kelly said. "And I completely lost it, too. I just fainted. Thanks for getting me out of there. I know we just met, but I've heard about you, Bhavna, Nipa, and Sook in the TFF basement meetings. I'm glad you were there."

"And I have heard about you from Bhavna. You're going to be safe with us at our camp. I heard Gallagher tell Will that he'll move you to his camp as soon as he can so you can be with Maha. He just doesn't want to travel back with too many extra people tonight."

"Yeah, that's what Jabari told me, but I don't mind staying at your camp. I mean, I'd like to make it to Gallagher's before my niece or nephew is born, but Maha isn't supposed to have her baby until late April according to her calculations, and Rain told me Maha is in good hands. She also told me before how great Bhavna is. I'll go wherever it is easiest. I'm just glad to be out of the pure zone and away from Nata."

"Sook is going to love having you there. He heard that you play the violin and wants to add you to his campfire band," he said with a chuckle.

"Sounds nice, but my violin is back in the hideout," she finished.

"Actually . . ." Blakely began.

"We wanted to surprise you," Daktari said. "Rain stashed your violin in here before we left today. You can take it with you to your new temporary home."

"Wow, I can't believe she thought to do that," Kelly said appreciatively.

"You'll love it there," Zi said. "They sleep in camouflage tree houses that Bhavna's dad, Will, designed. So cool."

I figured this was as good a time as any to officially wake up while they weren't talking about what I'd done back in the pure zone.

As I opened my eyes, Marcello reached a hand over to me. "You're back. Let me help you up," he offered.

I surveyed his hand skeptically. "You're not going to knock me out again are you?"

He lowered his eyes sheepishly, but I grabbed his hand anyway. "Just kidding. I know why you did it. Thanks."

He pulled me up, and I noted everyone had turned towards me except Cole, who was piloting the hover, and Zi, who was holding her hands together in front of her.

"Hi guys," I said meekly. "Sorry about what happened back there."

"Don't worry about it," Jabari said quickly.

"What exactly did happen back there?" Daktari asked.

"I panicked. I just got this terrible feeling that Calista hadn't told me something important, and that she was in severe danger. I mean, I still feel like that, but I don't know why. But anyway, I messed up. I tried to go back for her, and I was screaming. I just lost it. I'm so sorry."

"Rain, it's fine. We're all safe now," Marcello said.

Blakely reached over the seat and patted my arm. "Forget about it. It had to be hard to leave Calista. She's your family."

"Yeah, but you guys are my family, too. Everyone one of you. And I almost messed everything up for all of us." I looked at Jabari. "Thanks for doing what needed to be done."

"No worries. Just forget about it."

"I'm sorry I doubted you, Jabari," Daktari offered. Then he looked back at me. "But you know I still wonder why you felt that way about Calista, Rain. I hope she's okay."

"Me too. You think you could fix my headache when we land, Daktari? It's pounding."

"Of course, but why wait? Lean forward, warrior woman," he said with a grin, using his occasional nickname for me.

I did as he instructed and closed my eyes as his hands covered my temple. Within seconds, all traces of my headache were gone, and I felt refreshed.

"Thanks, baby bro."

"No problem. I'll be healing ailments a lot worse than headaches once we land at William's camp. I was halfway done with the prisoners when Gallagher said we had to go back to help you guys."

"We're landing now. So you can get back to work, Daktari," Cole called out.

"You sure Moretti and Gallagher were able to remove any tracking devises from the prisoners?" Jabari asked.

Daktari nodded. "I was with them when they were searched. No one had anything on them. And they had a point; why would Nata have thought to put trackers on the prisoners? She was planning to kill them. She had no idea we were coming. But she had that shield all the way around her. Gallagher and his men verified it. They said Niyol was right. We had zero chance of getting through that thing. She's definitely paranoid."

"That's because her guards turned on her," Marcello said. "Calista told us about it."

"You'll have to tell me the details later. Looks like I have some work to do." He gestured towards Gallagher's hover, which had already landed. Bhavna and her family had lit torches on the ground below and were helping the prisoners out already. Many of them were still injured.

As we piled out, Blakely turned to Jabari. "That really was an epic rescue mission, by the way. Thanks for letting me tag along."

"Tag along? If it weren't for you, we'd have been captured. We owe you one," Jabari said.

"I'll consider it even once you take Nata out of power. And now that I've seen what you can do, I know you will. But if you need my help when you go to Elizabeth Mansion . . ."

"You'd go with us?" Jabari asked, doubt in his voice.

"Of course I would. Border patrol around the camp gets kind of boring. Even with the extra UZTA search parties for Gallagher."

Jabari grinned. "Well then, consider yourself officially recruited for the big mission. Assuming Will doesn't mind us borrowing you again."

"He won't. They can handle keeping everyone safe here."

Kelly grabbed my hand before I stepped away from the hover. "Thanks for coming for me, Rain."

"Thanks for being so strong and hanging in there. I hope you like it here. You'll be safe for now at least, and that's the most important thing."

"I'll be safe. But I'll be worried about you."

"You don't need to. There are enough people worrying about me already," I said with a small grin.

Bhavna happily greeted us and welcomed Kelly with open arms. Someone gave blankets to Kelly, Jabari, and me since our clothes were still damp from being in the pool. Niyol arrived right after us and helped Daktari finish healing the wounded.

Everyone gathered around to say goodbye before we took off. "Nice job tonight saving Kelly, Rain," Gallagher said. "And thanks for keeping Adrianne safe."

He decided not to mention how I'd lost it at the end, for which I was grateful. "She protected Cole, and she was a huge help," I replied.

"Everyone played a part. If it weren't for this kid right here . . ." Moretti patted Jonah proudly, "we'd never have cut the power to the whole building like that."

Jonah blushed. "Yeah, but I screwed up with the emergency backup lights. Didn't see that one coming."

"That's okay, then Cole took them out as best he could," Gallagher said.

"Yeah, but all I did was make them flash," Cole said. "Not very helpful. Thankfully, Niyol saved you guys."

"You were still amazing, Cole," Adrianne said warmly.

"No, you were, Adrianne. You saved us from those armed Droids," Cole returned.

"Speaking of which, I just told Will about the new Combat Droids, but we'll need to spread the word to the other refugee camps. What do you bet she plans to release them to search for you, Gallagher?" Lieutenant Moretti asked.

"I wouldn't be surprised," he agreed. He glanced at Will. "Thanks for taking everyone in. We'll be in touch, and we can try to relocate people into other camps as the need arises. I can guarantee I'm going to have more Authority guards or Droids hunting for me now, which means all the camps need to be more careful. I'm sorry you're in this position, Will."

"I'm happy everyone will have a home here. It's no problem at all."

"Thanks," he said, focusing on Jabari now. "I wanted to talk to you briefly before you go. I think we should move the date up for the attack. Nata is going to retaliate after what happened tonight. I get the feeling we're going to need to move sooner. Plus, as we saw with her shield, she is vulnerable right now. Maybe her paranoia can work in our favor. She's feeling weak and we should take advantage of it. What do you think, Niyol?"

Niyol shook his head, as if silently contemplating, and I wondered what was going on in his mind. After a moment, he shrugged. "I think moving the date up is inevitable," he said vaguely.

A smile curved across Gallagher's face, and he laughed. "Well, that's a pretty specific answer coming from you."

A hint of amusement was clear in Niyol's eyes, but he didn't reply. He stared at me, though, and I wondered if he had any more advice or if he'd just show up in my dreams again with strange messages.

Gallagher patted Jabari's shoulder. "Well, you need to get back before your curfew, kids. And I'll be in touch in the next day or two. We'll talk about moving the date."

With quick farewells exchanged, everyone began boarding the hover. But I wanted to say goodbye to Niyol in private.

I walked to him and hugged him tightly. "Thanks for saving us tonight. We never would have made it out of the pool if you hadn't shown up. And I heard how you busted all the windows out when I was unconscious. I panicked. But I guess you heard that already. I'm worried about Calista."

"You did well tonight."

"Do you think Nata knew it was you in the funnel cloud?"

"She may begin to suspect I'm alive after what just happened, but she won't find me. Don't worry."

"I'm starting to worry a lot about . . . well, everything that's about to happen, I guess. You've said some pretty vague things in my dreams lately."

His expression remained blank. "Have I?"

I sighed. I figured he wasn't about to claim knowledge of my dreams, but sometimes I could swear he was actually talking to me, like it was one of his abilities. "Yeah, you have," I mumbled.

He wiped a stray hair from my forehead and peered into my eyes. "No matter what happens, don't ever doubt yourself, Rainchild, and you'll be fine."

"But will I? I really messed up back there," I said nervously.

"Ever heard that old saying, 'The darkest hour is just before the dawn'?"

I gave him an exasperated look. "Yes, in a vision I had when I was unconscious. You said it."

He smiled, something he rarely did, so I treasured it. When he didn't say anything else I stepped away reluctantly. "Will I be seeing you again? I mean sooner than later?"

"Yeah, we'll see each other again, Rain. Time to go," he said, motioning over my shoulder as Jabari approached.

A moment later, Jabari was leading me towards the hover. "I'm sorry about what I did. I wish there had been another option. And maybe there was," he whispered as we neared the hover.

"Jabari, I understand why you did it." I leaned up on my toes and kissed him lightly. "Thanks for protecting me from myself."

He got the strangest look on his face and sighed. "Come on, dream girl. We've got to beat curfew."

As the hover took off, I closed my eyes, trying not to think about Calista and whatever was happening to her now. Niyol's words played in my head. *The darkest hour is just before the dawn.* And I wondered how close we were to the dawn.

Chapter 39: Breakthrough

RAIN

Along with my worries for Calista and my concern about Niyol's parting words to me, the temperature rose overnight and continued to climb for another two days.

It was only Monday morning, the first week of March, but so much had changed since our trip to the pure zone.

Gallagher was certain Nata would retaliate against the entire country for the rescue of her latest batch of prisoners and for ruining her pure zone ceremony, and we weren't sure what that meant for our zone. Gallagher feared Nata might move the date up for her planned execution of the mixed zones, which was why he'd warned us to be ready to escape at any given moment.

Jabari agreed with him, so we had prepared our families, Takara, and each other. We were ready to take them to our hideout and leave the mixed zone behind if it came to that. I'd promised to signal everyone telepathically, of course, if I got the word first that there was trouble, and Zi said she'd be prepared to use her image to help transport our families to the hideout. But this impromptu evacuation plan was only needed for the next few days or so.

Since all we could do was theorize about an attack on our zone, unless we knew about a specific threat coming our way, Jabari and Gallagher had decided the solution to all of our problems was to move the date of our mission to Elizabeth Mansion up.

So instead of going to New Washington to go after Nata on old Earth Day, in late April, as we'd initially planned, we were leaving in less than a week.

On Saturday, Gallagher, Lieutenant Moretti, and their forces would surface from underground and target the walls of various zones with the tanks, heavy trucks, and even bulldozers they'd confiscated over the past year, beginning with the Indy Mixed Zone. With the help of Landon, Gallagher would send a televised message to every zone across the UZTA right before his attack, asking them to fight with him as he took Nata out of power. And as he was speaking to the masses about joining The Freedom Front, the secret weapon of TFF, me and my friends, plus Blakely, would be sneaking into Elizabeth Mansion and disabling her central Droid operating system so Gallagher would only have to deal with human resistance in each zone, and we'd capture Nata.

There were dozens of details to the plan and countless numbers of people had jobs to do and roles to play in the attack, but my job was to focus on what we, the six original teenagers of The Freedom Front, plus Blakely, would be doing. It should've intimidated me more than it did, but Gallagher felt strongly our plan was solid. Gallagher's idea was that he would be creating a huge distraction and drawing the Combat Droids towards him, while we were entering Elizabeth Mansion. If all went well, we'd power down the Droid army before anyone got hurt.

We'd said the plan aloud so many times in the past forty-eight hours that even though I was experiencing what I assumed was an acceptable amount of nerves and fear, I was still sure it would work. We were ready. Gallagher was ready. The people in hiding across No Man's Land were ready. Niyol had even spoken to me late last night and reassured me we were all ready.

But I couldn't shake the feeling about Calista, and I was still a little bothered about how Nata might retaliate against Gallagher. If something happened to him, we had no resistance. Plus, so many people were hiding with Gallagher and in various refugee camps; I hated to think of the danger they were all in as well.

And even with all of our plans intact, including our plans to steal the remaining fuel cells after work today that we'd need for our final trip out of the zone, my mind kept wandering back to Niyol's warning. *The darkest hour is just before the dawn.* Weren't we living in the darkest hours already? It made me wonder if Niyol was holding some important piece of information back or if he knew something awful that might happen and wouldn't say it. Did it have something to do with Calista? I couldn't figure it out, but in any case, his words were stuck in my head. Even at night the words echoed in my dreams.

I hadn't slept well the last two nights. I'd had bizarre visions of prison cells holding Grandma Julia, Uncle Michael, and Aunt Alyssa, all the while with Calista screaming in the background. In them, I'd yelled at Nata to stop hurting people, but all she would do was laugh in response. I ran down the corridors of the prison blocks in my nightmares, desperate to find Calista, but even though I could hear her constant screams, I could never find her. And always, before the nightmare would end, Niyol would say something vague about me having to finish it or about the darkness before the dawn, and I'd wake up more frustrated and restless than ever.

As I'd promised Calista, I hadn't contacted her using my telepathy, though I'd thought about it at least a dozen times. Instead, I'd used my ability to check in on Grandma Julia, who reported everything was manageable in her house. I had also talked to Francisco to let him know about our latest mission to the pure zone, since Jabari and Michelle wouldn't be allowed to see him for another few weeks. And of course, I'd spoken with Bhavna, who was filling me in on how the new arrivals were settling in, and specifically, how Kelly was doing.

Mom squeezed me closer now, bringing me out of my thoughts. As per our Monday morning routine, we stood outside before sunrise, waiting on the hover transporter to arrive. Unlike the days and weeks before now, today, Daktari, Dad, and I stood under the glow of the street lamp without shivering. Zi was nearby, hugging her own parents as she waited.

Mom kept her arms around my waist. "You know as much as I'm glad it's finally warming up, this time of year tends to bring in bad storms," she remarked, glancing up at the sky as if she could see through the darkness. "Last year, a few homes lost their roofs," she added.

"And they moved the people in those apartments into different ones instead of fixing the roofs," Daktari said with a huff.

"At least they didn't make them stay in housing without roofs. Of course, things have gotten significantly worse since last year. Who knows, they might make us stay in roofless apartments this time around," I pointed out.

"As long as we're together," Mom said, smiling at us.

The three of us, all huddled beside Mom, exchanged happy looks. We were still getting used to the return of her optimism. We had even told her about our early escape plan and that we were going on the mission to New Washington soon. And she hadn't freaked out. She'd said she knew we could do it. I couldn't help but grin.

Daktari shook his head, even as he laughed. "That's the spirit, Mom."

"For real," added Dad, hugging us closer.

"*I'm glad you're back, Mom,*" I said silently.

"*You and Daktari saved me. And your friends,*" she replied.

Dad's eyes widened. "*You've never talked to me with your telepathy before Rain, but I can hear you loud and clear.*"

"*Me too,*" added Daktari. "*I can hear everyone,*" he said, his eyes incredulous.

I didn't know what to say. My ability had never worked like that before. I mean, I could talk to everyone but not at the same time, could I? And they could hear each other? "*How is it possible?*" I asked, concentrating on my telepathy.

"*I don't know, but you know what else is strange? I feel so good all of a sudden, like Daktari's renewed me with energy or something. Like when he heals me,*" Mom said.

Daktari's hand felt warm on my back, too, and then it hit me. *"Daktari, when we're touching. Our powers are stronger when we're touching."*

Comprehension flickered across his face. *"You're right. I can't believe we didn't figure it out sooner. You know, Zi—"*

I knew what he was going to say and I cut him off. *"She's been saying it for months. She said you were healing her when she used her ability, but you were making her stronger because you were touching her while she used her own ability. Only we didn't understand until now."*

"This is amazing, kids," Dad said.

"Hold on, it's about to get better," I replied. Then I focused on Zi. *"Zi, come here quickly. Put your hand on me or Daktari and listen."*

She walked over and despite the curious expression on her face, she did as I asked.

Once her hand was on my back, I spoke to them again. *"Zi, our powers are stronger when we touch. Listen, everyone can hear each other using my telepathy when we're touching."*

"Really?" she asked.

"Yes," my mom said, giddiness in her voice.

Zi's brow shot up. *"Mrs. Hawkins, I can hear you."*

"What about me, Zi?" Dad asked, excitement in his voice, too.

"Yes, I hear you, too, Mr. Hawkins. This is crazy."

"I wonder what happens if I use my ability, too, while we're touching, I mean," Daktari said.

"Well, none of us are wounded," Zi pointed out.

"Doesn't matter, I can see what happens. It worked on Mom a minute ago."

Warmth shot through me from my head to toes, and I felt refreshed and full of energy.

"I could use that sort of medicine every morning, Daktari. I feel stronger. Thanks," Dad said.

"This is amazing. Do you realize how much this will help us when we go to capture Nata?" I asked, so full of hope I was beaming.

"*We have to tell Jabari and the others,*" agreed Daktari.

"*We can experiment later and see what happens when we work together,*" Zi said.

"*I'm so proud of you all,*" Mom said.

"*Me too.*" Dad nodded his head in agreement.

The approaching hover lights interrupted our sidewalk huddle, and we separated. As we boarded the hover, I waved at Mom and Dad. They looked so happy, I wished I could take a photograph and carry it with me. I hadn't seen them like this in years.

Daktari and Zi grabbed my hands as we found seats. I knew why they'd done it. We continued our conversation the entire ride to work. All we had to do was touch and our powers were practically doubled. I was hopeful this was something that would help us fight Nata.

Takara, who relied on her ability to read people, had been telling us for months that us working together was the key to our success. We suspected that maybe she'd been trying to tell us all along. All of the clues came back to me as we talked. Every time I'd spoken to Jabari and he'd been hugging me or touching me, his voice had been so loud and clear. And I remembered when I'd been arrested and talked to him from Metro Prison that I'd noticed how far away he sounded compared to the day before. But I hadn't put it together.

As we landed in front of Agri Plant, thunder rumbled outside in the dark sky.

Daktari stood up. "Guess Mom was right about the storms."

"This time of year," said Zi. "At least we're not freezing for once."

I glanced up at the sky as we exited the hover and climbed the steps into the factory. The air was warm and thunder sounded again, an ominous warning. Niyol's words returned to my mind about the darkest hour, but I was feeling very optimistic for once because of our morning discovery.

I smiled at the sky as if daring it to ruin my mood. The thunder growled again as the first flash of lightening struck in the distance. I walked into the building and got in line to scan my ID tattoo. I decided to tell Jabari the good news. It was too good to save until later.

"*Jabari, can you hear me?*"

He responded with worry in his tone. "*Rain, are you okay?*"

I grinned. "*I'm fine. Listen, Daktari, Zi, and I discovered something pretty amazing a few minutes ago, and I have to tell you…*"

Chapter 40: The Authority

RAIN

"You there, what's your number?" barked an unfriendly, yet recognizable voice from behind me.

My spoon was midway to my mouth, but I paused and set it down as I turned over my shoulder. At least I'd eaten all but a few bites of the broth that was supposed to be some sort of soup for our lunch break at Agri Plant.

Normally, a person should be terrified to see an officer from The Authority hovering behind them demanding their number, so I made myself appear frightened as I answered the officer, who was none other than our friend and ally, Eric.

"One-two-seven-six," I said quickly.

"On your feet. Let's go," he growled.

Doubt and a bit of panic started in my stomach. Was I in trouble again?

"*Eric, are you being serious? Am I in danger?*"

A startled expression swept his face, but washed away a moment later. "*Rain?*"

"*You're taking me away? Is Nata here?*"

"*Just play along. I need to talk to you for a minute, that's all.*"

The O3 Droid in charge of our group started towards me. "You heard the officer. To your feet, One-two-seven-six."

"Move!" Eric ordered.

I flinched, but got to my feet and gave Daktari and Zi a sideways glance as I followed after Eric, away from the O3 Droid and a dozen or more prying and terrified eyes.

"*He says everything is fine, Daktari. He just needs to talk to me for a minute. Tell Zi not to worry,*" I said as Eric reached for my arm and pulled me roughly out of the room beside him.

"*Okay, I will,*" Daktari replied. "*Be careful, still.*"

I knew Eric wasn't going to hurt me, but I was wondering what was so important he'd come to tell me about. It couldn't be good.

The thunder from the storm grumbled, shaking the windows to the factory as he pulled me away from the area of the plant I was familiar with. He turned down a corridor, walking briskly, and then stopped abruptly. My eyes read the words on the door he'd stopped beside: JAN-ITORIAL. He checked the handle of the door and pushed it open, glancing in quickly. Then, I'm sure it was for appearances in the event anyone was looking, he shoved me hard into the room. He shut the door behind him as he flicked on the closest light.

His expression softened. "Sorry about that, Rain. Had to be convincing, you know. In case anyone noticed."

"I understand."

"And wow, I heard you in my head. I wasn't prepared for that. Even though I've heard about your ability, it was hard to believe until it happened to me."

"Sorry. We're even, I guess. You nearly scared me to death. I didn't know if you were here to take me away to Nata."

"You know I wouldn't do that."

"She can make anyone do anything," I pointed out.

"She'll have to kill me before I bring one of you guys to her."

"I wish there were more guards like you. It would make Saturday a lot easier."

"You'd be surprised. But I need to talk to you about something."

"What's going on that's so important you left the prison to find me?" I asked, my voice worried.

"Takara sent me."

I tensed automatically. "What happened, is she all right?"

"She's fine." He held a hand up, reassuringly. "We received new orders from Nata just an hour ago. And Takara heard everyone discussing them around Town Hall and the prison. Nata is pulling all of the remaining human officers out and relocating us within the next ten days."

"What's that mean? We were right? She really is going to try to kill everyone in our zone ahead of her schedule? So we're out of time? Still, we were planning to go Saturday, and Takara knows that."

"You're right. It's awful news about her making us leave because that means she is going to try to kill everyone in this zone sooner than she had planned, but you guys will stop her. Your plan is still good. That's not why Takara sent me here. We found out something else today, and Takara said she wasn't sure she'd see Jabari in time to warn you all. Apparently, Nata stationed some of the new Combat Droids at the hover plant earlier today."

"But why? Is my dad going to be okay? And Michelle? Why would she do that?"

"From what I understand, when all of us human officers are removed, the Combat Droids will join the Droid Dogs in patrolling and policing this zone, and she put the Combat Droids at the hover plant already because she wants to test them out to see how they handle their new role as the police force."

"But she's planning to kill us sooner than later, you just said it. So why would she need to go to all the trouble of testing them out here, and in that case, why even send them here at all? She's planning to shut this place down after she kills us, right? She even had new hover plants built in the Asian Zones, remember?"

"About that. You remember how Gallagher tampered with some of those plants?"

"Yeah, he blew a couple of them up so it would force Nata to use the work force here in our zone a little longer and buy us more time before she could kill us, or at least that'd been his thinking behind it."

"Well, it may or may not be related, but she changed her mind about closing down our hover plants here. She went ahead and had the Asian hover plants completed even after Gallagher messed with them. And she's going to continue using the plants here, but not for hover production . . . For Combat Droid production instead."

"Why does she need so many new Combat Droids?"

"Well, some of us suspect that she'll eventually replace all of her human officers with Droids, and we will become obsolete, but she hasn't told us that yet of course. The only thing she has told us is that she has already been releasing Combat Droids, specially designed to search for Gallagher's facial scan, out into No Man's Land. You guys need to warn him about the extra Droids for sure."

"We will, but I have another question. Who will be her slave labor to keep building the Combat Droids if she plans to kill us in a couple of weeks?"

"It's almost too disturbing to say aloud, so please forgive me . . ." he paused.

"Come on, Eric. Believe me, I can handle it."

"Well, she wants to send in others after she kills everyone here. She'll select people from the other zones who she considers the weakest, or those she wants to punish the most, and slowly but surely she'll work them to death, and then in some sort of evil cycle, she'll keep sending people here as she does her so-called *purification* of The UZTA. Evidently, she wants to use zones like this one, with deplorable living conditions, as sort of a concentration camp. She'll get maximum production out of the people she sends here each time, until she's either done with them or worked them to death. How sick is that? It seems like the larger her pure race grows, the more insane her agenda becomes."

I let his words sink in and took a deep breath. Thunder booming above the factory was the only sound. After a moment, I tilted my head up just an inch. "Don't worry. We'll stop her. We're going this Saturday, and then this whole thing will be behind us. We're getting the last fuel cells today, after—" My voice stopped as I realized why Takara had sent Eric to talk to me, and my heart rate picked up.

Eric paled. "That's why Takara wanted me to warn you," he began.

"We can't steal the fuel cells today because the new Combat Droids are stationed at the hover plant." I finally said the words aloud that were racing through my brain.

"Yeah, and even if you hide under Zi's image, they've stationed the Droids at every door, and Takara says you couldn't open the door without raising suspicions. And since they're armed and still being tested, she is afraid they might fire their weapons without much provocation. There are just too many innocent people, in addition to your team, that could get hurt if one of them were to fire a weapon."

"But what if you were to get us in?"

"We're not permitted to go in during the trial run. I wouldn't even get through the front door without orders. Nata wants to see how the Droids handle the assignment without human officers interfering. I'm sorry, Rain."

"I understand. There's nothing you can do, Eric." I sighed as I searched for a solution, and then I remembered Jabari's mom. "But Michelle is planning to open the door for us later."

"Yeah, Takara wanted me to ask if you could use your telepathy to warn Michelle that you're not coming. By now she will definitely be worried because the Combat Droids are all over the hover plant."

"Sure, no problem, I'll let her know we aren't coming so she doesn't risk trying to let us in. She's probably a nervous wreck if the Droids are already guarding the doors."

"Yeah. I'm sorry to be the bearer of bad news. I know you need the fuel to get to New Washington. Takara is really worried."

"Well, we'll just have to figure out another way to get the fuel cells."

"You think you will?" he asked hopefully.

"Of course we will. Believe me, nothing is going to prevent us from getting out of here on Saturday. I promise."

Eric grinned. "You really are brave going up against her, Rain. I'm sorry I can't do more."

"You've done more than enough. And way more than any other officer in this zone has ever done. And I really owe you because you warned me when Officer Dean was going to kill my mom. I'll never be able to thank you enough for that."

"All I did was point you in his direction. You did the hard part of actually rescuing her. For what it's worth . . . I'm not going to leave with the rest of the human officers as they evacuate us. I've already told the other officers I'll be the last to leave. But even if they order me to go, I'm staying. I'll be here till the end, helping to fight with Gallagher. I'm going to release the prisoners as soon as he starts attacking the wall. And I think some of the other guards, if they are still here when it happens, will help me. And if there are any guards left who are loyal to Nata, well, they'll be the first ones I lock up when the attack begins."

"Thanks, Eric. For everything."

"I'd better get you back to work. And be careful out there. I heard an even bigger storm is predicted for later tonight."

"Of all the things happening right now, the storm is the least of my worries," I said dryly.

Worry covered his face. "I know. I'm sorry. Hey, I'll be in touch with Takara. Maybe I can help you get the fuel cells somehow. We've still got a few days before Saturday."

His voice trailed off, and I patted his arm gently. "We'll find a way. We always do."

"It amazes me how upbeat you can be. You inspire me, all of you do. Thanks for doing what the rest of us couldn't do. You guys are heroes."

"Takes one to know one."

"No, Rain. It doesn't." He shook his head, his expression one of awe, and then turned for the door. "Come on, I'll escort you back to work, and I'll yell at you to focus on your job as I'm leaving. Just so no one suspects I'm on your side."

"Make it convincing," I said with a wink.

He chuckled. "You really are brave."

But even as I shrugged and grinned at him again, my mind was racing, thinking about our latest dilemma. How were we going to get the fuel cells?

Chapter 41: Storm

RAIN

Hours later, I tried to go to sleep as I listened to the storm outside the apartment. My mind went over our meeting. We'd met in TFF's basement again and messaged with our allies, including Landon. He'd confirmed what Eric said. Nata was planning to pull the human officers out of our zone within ten days, and she was hell-bent and determined to find Gallagher with the new Combat Droids, which she had released into No Man's Land. She was also preparing to send people from other zones into ours once she had done away with us. As depressing as the change in her plans should have been, we'd been prepared for it, and we were relieved that we'd already decided to change the date for our trip to New Washington.

But we were all worried about getting the fuel cells in time.

Jabari said we'd figure something out before Saturday, even if we had to break the door open using his strength and sneak in. He figured that was our best bet. Only we weren't sure how we could disable the Combat Droids. We'd discussed trying to sneak Jonah into our zone, but we knew that was a huge risk to ask of him and Gallagher, especially since they were lying low as the extra Combat Droids roamed No Man's Land. Either way, we'd decided to postpone our heist a few days to analyze the situation. Jabari wanted to talk to his mom to see if she could figure out the Combat Droids' new post or any details about their routine during the day.

We'd also spent part of the meeting testing out the discovery we'd made earlier in the day and were amazed at how strong our abilities became when we were physically linked. Even Marcello became more powerful when we touched him, and as long as he was completely focused on the person he wanted to knock unconscious, the rest of us were safe. The result was that the person he knocked out, stayed out even longer than usual. Cole had volunteered to be the guinea pig and had slept soundly for fifteen minutes when we'd helped Marcello. At the end of the meeting, we'd decided to regroup and brainstorm again the following afternoon. We just knew we'd figure out how to get the fuel cells.

When I finally fell asleep, my dreams were turbulent. Niyol was telling me to focus on the light. So I did. I walked down white-carpeted floors in an unfamiliar place, and I could see the light up ahead. It wasn't long before I heard Nata's voice, too.

"You failed me. All you had to do was get rid of them but you couldn't," she said.

"I tried." I recognized the voice of Calista as she pleaded with Nata.

"But you failed me, like all humans do. It's why I have to get rid of them now. And why you are going to help me. This is your final chance to prove your worth or you know what will happen." Her threatening voice terrified me as I cowered in the hallway, hanging on to every word.

"But can't we just teach them a lesson? Why do we have to kill them? They're useful," Calista insisted.

A sharp sound rang out that I instantly recognized. Nata had hit Calista across the face again. I inched closer, watching as Calista tried to stand back up. Her face was red and bruised all over.

Nata grabbed her by her scalp and tugged her head backwards. She peered into Calista's tear-filled eyes. "They're not useful. They're an *abomination*."

"No, we aren't, Nata," I interrupted, unworried about being discovered now. I pushed the door open and made my way into the room.

Nata's head turned as she searched the room around her as though she couldn't see me, even though I was standing right there in plain sight.

"Who are you, mixed breed?" she demanded, her eyes wild with rage.

"My name is Rain, and I'm not a mixed breed. I'm a human girl. Just like you," I said defiantly, stepping closer.

She turned again, trying to locate me, but her eyes wouldn't settle on me. For some odd reason, she had no idea where I was.

"I'm not Nata anymore. You're helping the old man, aren't you?" she demanded angrily. "And he's helping Gallagher Brown. I should've killed them both years ago," she screamed, then grabbed her temple, squeezing it in frustration.

"You murdered Gallagher's wife. You stay away from him," I yelled.

"Where is he? Tell me!"

"I'll never tell you," I replied.

I figured it was as good a time as any to escape. "Run Calista! Quick!"

Calista locked eyes with me. She could see exactly where I was standing, unlike Nata who was spinning in circles, searching for me frantically.

Calista reached for my hand, and I grabbed hold and began pulling her with me. But then she was fading away and I couldn't hold on to her.

As she disappeared, her voice entered my thoughts. "She's coming, Rain. She's coming and—"

The room went pitch black and the only sound I could hear was that of my heart beating against my chest. The temperature in the room dropped, and I could feel Nata's presence.

"Nata, I know you're in here. And I'm not afraid of you anymore. You can't beat the resistance. You just can't."

She screamed from a corner, and then I could see her. She was a little girl again, cowering in the underground shed as her mother beat her with a whip.

"You're an abomination! You'll die, but not until we cleanse you," Clara screamed.

I ran for Nata, and pushed my way in front of the whip as it came down. "Stop hurting her," I pleaded with Clara, who had an empty look in her eyes.

As I watched her, something changed, and right before me, she transformed into the adult version of Nata. Her eyes became red, like fire, as she held the whip above, prepared to strike me.

"Nata, stop. You can't beat The Freedom Front," I said urgently.

"I can, and I will, *Rain*. You're not safe. No one is."

Before she could hit me, her eyes turned to flames, and lightening flashed around us. She disappeared, along with the room, and fresh air breezed across my face. The next moment, I was standing in the thick of the woods.

"Go, Now!" Niyol's voice commanded me.

I knew I had to run, but to where I wasn't sure. Tree branches smacked me in the face as I ran.

Calista's voice returned, echoing all around. "She's coming, Rain!"

Up ahead I saw the light again and knew I had to follow it. I kicked into super speed and was running faster than I ever had. Then the trees parted, and I saw a black-haired girl running away from one of the Combat Droids. Gallagher was chasing after her, but he couldn't stop her. The Droid clamped onto her shoulders, and she was swept up into an awaiting hover and carried away. I never saw her face, but I knew who it was. It had to be her.

"Adrianne!" I yelled after the hover.

I turned around to look for Gallagher, but he was gone, too, and I was alone. Combat Droids burst through the trees, firing their weapons ahead, and I dove to the forest floor for cover. I looked up as they passed and could see the image of Gallagher's face reflecting away from them. They were programmed and hunting for Gallagher, just like Eric had told me.

As they marched away, a new noise greeted me. A familiar noise, grumbling louder as each second passed. And it made me think of a speeding train. I looked around to see why the earth was shaking so violently and why my body was trembling. Maybe I was near train tracks. But instead of a train, I saw a huge funnel cloud unlike any I'd seen in real life. It was a tornado.

As the tornado approached, the wind burned my face, and branches flew all around. The trees were pulled up from their roots and I was swept into the air with them. My body twisted in all directions.

I strained my eyes, and in the very center of the storm I could see the hover plant. The side of the building, where Michelle typically let us in, was ripped off in one strong gust of wind. The Combat Droids that had been inside were yanked from the building and torn to pieces. The fuel cells sat there unprotected, and hope filled me.

Niyol flew out of the plant in the shape of the great horned owl, as Daktari's arm was pulling me out of the storm.

"Go. Now, Rain! It's your chance!" Niyol instructed me.

"Rain, wake-up," Daktari said.

I opened my eyes. My body was drenched in sweat, and Daktari was gripping me by the shoulders. A thrashing sound beat against the roof above us. The storm.

"Are you okay, Rain?"

"Daktari. We have to steal the fuel cells."

"I know."

"No, Daktari. Now. We have to steal them *now*."

"But how? It's storming out there, and it's the middle of the night. I think there's even a tornado out there," he protested.

"The side of the building blew off in the storm, and the Droids guarding the building got swept away in the tornado."

"Are you sure?"

"Well, there's one way to find out, I guess. You can check with me."

I sat up, ignoring the odd expression on Daktari's face. I grabbed his arm and held on tight. He'd see soon enough. I leaned forward and closed my eyes again. *"Niyol, is it time for us to go after the fuel cells?"*

He answered, *"Yes, Rain. Hurry. Now's your chance to get the fuel."* I could see him flying through the storm. Maybe he was the storm. I couldn't be sure if he was causing it or if it had happened naturally.

"In my dream, Gallagher and Adrianne were in danger. Can you warn them?"

"Of course, I will. Now, hurry Rain, the fuel."

I wanted to ask him more. Maybe he could tell me what the rest of my dream was supposed to mean. *"Niyol?"*

But there was no response. And besides, he'd been clear about what we needed to do. We had to get the fuel now, while no one was watching.

I opened my eyes as Daktari stood up. "Believe me now, baby bro?"

He nodded fervently as he bent to pull on his shoes. "Wake Zi up. We'll have to get the others."

Chapter 42: Chance

RAIN

The tornado had left its mark all over our zone. The scent of recently fallen rain encompassed us, and the air felt warm, even in the midnight hour. The tornado might have passed, we couldn't be sure, but the winds were still howling with a force so strong, we clung desperately to one another under Zi's image.

It had been easy to get everyone to agree to the mission. The storm had woken them up already, and Jabari had seen everything since I'd gotten into his dreams again. Before we'd left, Daktari had awoken Dad and told him what we were up to. He'd kissed us goodbye and warned us to be safe. Once outside, Zi had been waiting for us and covered us up with her image. She hadn't woken her parents because she was sure they'd gone back to sleep after the full brunt of the tornado had passed. We went to Marcello and Cole's apartment next, and they, too, had decided to let Marcello's parents sleep, even though they knew about our group and its purpose.

So I guess that's why it surprised me so much that Jabari was jogging down his steps to join us now, with his mom, Michelle, beside him.

She gave me a quick hug as soon as she was under Zi's image. "Are you hanging in there?" she asked, worriedly.

"Yeah, I'm good. Are you going with us?"

"I have to. It will be easier for you. They moved the fuel cells yesterday when they were rearranging to build more Combat Droids. I told Jabari I'm afraid you won't find them without me."

He shook his head, sighing. "I hate to risk her life taking her along, but she insisted."

"You guys risk your lives all the time," she replied. "Now let's get moving before another tornado strikes. I don't think it's done yet," she said, nervously looking at the night sky.

The thunder grumbling not too far off seemed to confirm her words.

"Stay close," Jabari instructed. He grabbed my hand, and we hurried down the sidewalk, Zi at our core, protecting us with her image.

"So what exactly did you see in your dream?" Cole enquired as we crossed another street and turned down Route 12 towards the hover plant.

"I saw the entire back side of the hover plant ripped off by the tornado. Or Niyol. Or maybe both. It felt like he was connected to the storm or maybe even causing it. The Combat Droids that had been there were ripped into pieces and blown away, and the fuel cells were just sitting there, undamaged."

"You sure that it really happened?" asked Marcello.

I spared him a glance, aware of how strange it sounded, but a little defensive. "In my dream, Niyol told me to go, *now*, before it was too late—"

"In your dream," he said worriedly. "Your dreams can be vague," he pointed out.

"That's true, Marcello. I had my doubts, too, but then Rain contacted Niyol when she woke up, and I listened in. Niyol said now was our chance to get the fuel," Daktari explained.

"Yeah, and I experienced the dream with her. The message was loud and clear. This is our chance to get the fuel," Jabari added. After a few more feet he glanced at me. "What about Gallagher? Should we warn him about . . . you know, the Droids?" he finished meekly, his eyes darting to Cole.

Apparently, he didn't think we should alarm Cole by mentioning the fact that Adrianne had been in my dream. I agreed with him whole-heartedly. "Yeah, when I spoke to Niyol, he said he would handle it."

"But we already warned him about the new Combat Droids," Cole pointed out.

"Yeah, but in Rain's dream, there were more, and they were chasing after Gallagher. Maybe they are close to him right now. Either way, he needs to be warned to watch his back."

"I hope they all stay safe," Cole said, anxiously.

I hoped they did, too, and I prayed Adrianne wouldn't really get captured.

"It was crazy, when I held Rain's hand and listened to her talking to Niyol, I could see everything she saw. Niyol was flying as the owl through the storm," Daktari remarked.

Michelle raised a brow. "So it's true. If you touch someone your power is even stronger. Impressive."

"Might have been nice if we'd figured out sooner. Could have come in handy," I said.

"Zi knew all along, on a subconscious level, I suppose. She kept mentioning how much better she felt when I was linked to her while she used her image, but we never put it together," Daktari said.

"Rain figured it out," Zi said, proudly.

The wind howled louder as we crossed another street, and we paused, huddling closer together.

"I just hope we don't get swept away in the storm. I don't think it's finished yet," whispered Zi.

"We're almost there," Jabari said smoothly, motioning us forward.

He led us around the final corner, and the huge manufacturing plant came into our frame. I knew Niyol hadn't led me astray. Windows were blown out along the front of the building, and debris spilled into the streets in front and on either side of the building we could see. The wind tossed large pieces of hovers and Droid parts back and forth along the streets.

Jabari hurried his pace. "Come on, let's get to the back."

My pulse picked up as we passed the wreckage. We had to slow to reroute around large pieces of debris here and there, but then we were staring at the backside of the factory, and Jabari came to an abrupt stop.

He turned to face me, and I couldn't help but smile at him. "I was right."

"It's exactly like your dream," he said, excitedly.

He wasn't exaggerating. The entire side of the hover plant in the back had fallen away as if ripped off in one fell swoop. The Combat Droids and Droid Dogs that were supposed to be stationed there, were nowhere to be seen. The building stood wide open and unprotected, just waiting for us to go in.

"Are you sure it's safe?" Zi asked.

I patted her back. "There's no such thing as safe in this zone, girl. But this is our chance. We need those fuel cells if we're going to go after Nata."

"She's right," Jabari agreed. "Come on, guys," and he took off towards the open wall.

Once inside, Cole turned towards the room we'd gone in so many times before to take fuel.

Michelle motioned him to stop. "They're not over there anymore, remember? Come on," and she took off to the left, away from the route we were familiar with.

It was so dark inside, we couldn't see as well as we would have liked, but the lightening, though eerie, was flashing off and on, illuminating our path. The wind moaned as it swept in through broken windows on the side of the building, sending a chill down my back.

"It's so dark in here, I don't think we need Zi's image," Marcello remarked.

"Leave it up," Jabari cautioned. "Just in case," he added.

Daktari placed his hands on Zi's temple to give her a boost of energy. She sighed after a moment and smiled. "Thank you, Daktari."

"Hang in there," he said comfortingly, holding his hand up to hers, which were placed in front of her chest.

"I'm perfectly fine now. You should hold my hand on every mission we go on . . . the entire time I'm using my image. It makes it so easy."

"Glad we figured it out," Daktari agreed. "I have no problem holding your hand."

Marcello coughed. "Save it for when you're alone, Amigos."

"Come on, kids, we're almost there," Michelle said with a small laugh. "Jabari, do you have that palm light I asked you to bring?" she added.

He retrieved it from his pocket, and Michelle grabbed it and lit it. She led us through a doorway and into another large room, where fuel cells were stacked in rows as far as we could see. Amazingly, the windows of the room hadn't been damaged at all, so everything was in order.

"It's like the entire building was hit except this room," said Cole.

Daktari tilted his head to mine. "I think Niyol really was behind this."

"I agree."

"Let's load up," Jabari ordered.

"Looks like there's power still coming to the wall monitor here," Cole said, standing beside the wall. "I'll alter the inventory log, just in case someone were to notice that this room was untouched from the storm but fuel was missing," Cole decided.

Jabari nodded. "Good thinking."

As Cole hacked into the monitor, Marcello and Daktari each picked up a fuel cell, and Jabari picked up two. We only needed two for the trip, but Jabari said he'd grab the extra for any sort of emergency we might run into. Once we were all set, we turned out of the room, still hiding safely under Zi's image, and headed for the back of the building.

The wind blew hard and rain fell in buckets now, drenching us as we got closer to the opening. Thunder boomed louder as lightening struck all around.

"The storm is picking up again," Michelle shouted warily.

"Too bad we can't wait it out. But we need to get these back to the basement and get home," I called out.

Everyone tilted their heads in agreement with me, and we continued towards the open wall. The building vibrated as thunder broke through the sky. In the corner of my eye, I saw Jabari reaching for me, but for some reason I was moving away from him towards a brilliant light. As comprehension filled me, my mouth fell open. I tried to scream, but couldn't hear it over the explosion.

An electric shock jolted through my limbs, like fire from top to bottom, and as my body flew backwards I saw the lightening bolt in its entirety, and my friends tossed in all directions. My head knocked into something solid.

Time seemed to stop. Or maybe it kept passing. I wasn't sure. The only thing I knew was that I was at peace. There was no sound. There was no color. There was just warmth. A light appeared in the distance, beckoning me closer. I reached for it with my fingertips. But as much as I craved the light and the warmth spilling from it, I remembered my job.

My mission. My purpose. I pictured Jabari's face, but instead of the worried look I had grown used to seeing lately, his face was peaceful, like he was asleep.

I tried to tell him to wake up. But the words wouldn't come, and I wasn't sure if he was really here in this place anyway.

Daktari was crying and praying and shouting at me. "Wake up, Rain!"

But though I hated the tone to his voice and didn't want him to cry, I couldn't make him stop.

Sometime later, I heard Niyol. "Get up and go, Rain."

"But I'm tired, Niyol."

"I know. But you're not done yet," he replied.

"Are you sure I'm not done?"

"Get going, Rainchild. The storm isn't over."

As his voice faded, I heard more voices, and my legs started burning with warmth, intensifying more with each second. And other sounds returned. The wind howling, the rain beating against the walls, though it was growing fainter now, and voices full of hope.

"She's coming back," Zi said.

And then I remembered what had happened. I'd been hit by lightening. I opened my eyes, and Daktari had his hands on my heart, and all of my friends had their hands on Daktari as he healed me.

I glanced around and saw Marcello sitting alone a few feet away, a horrible look on his face. And Jabari, where was he? I looked back at Daktari. He had the most horrified expression I had ever seen, and tears were streaming down his face.

He pulled his hands off of me and turned to the person lying beside me. And then I knew. I snapped my head to the side, where Jabari lay still, the peaceful look on his face, just like I'd pictured in my vision.

Michelle was sobbing, beating lightly against his chest. "Wake up, Jabari," she cried.

"Rain, help me heal him," Daktari begged.

I jumped to my knees and laid my hands on Daktari's arms. I closed my eyes and prayed for a miracle.

Chapter 43: Control

RAIN

With my hands on Daktari as he used his healing powers, I called out to Jabari silently, begging him to wake up. But he didn't respond. The day in the EEG training center he had heard me calling to him while he was unconscious but not now. As each second ticked by, my fear grew.

"Daktari, why isn't it working?" Michelle frantically asked.

I opened my eyes, noting the terror in her expression. "Don't give up," I ordered. I looked around the space. Everyone was linked to Daktari, except Marcello, who was ringing his hands together, watching us with fearful eyes.

"Everyone concentrate your thoughts on Daktari's healing power. We can strengthen him together. And Marcello get over here and help," I screamed.

Marcello's eyes got huge. "But when you were out, I tried to help, and it didn't work. What if I made it worse when I was touching him? What if my ability accidently knocked him out? And he was already struck by lightening when you were, Rain. What if I killed him?"

"Don't talk like that," I snapped.

He stepped back, as his eyes filled with tears. I waved him forward. "Get over here, now, and put your hands on Daktari. Don't concentrate on your ability, Marcello. Concentrate on Daktari's healing power. You can control your ability," I insisted.

"But he might have a point," Zi said desperately. "What if he's having the opposite effect on Daktari's ability? He tried to help a minute ago, and Jabari's heartbeat slowed even more."

"He's hardly got a pulse now," Daktari added.

I couldn't dwell on the despair in their voices. This was not how Jabari was going to die.

"But you *can* control your ability. You control it all the time. You told me that yourself, the day Eric was following me months ago, and you held my hand. Don't you remember?"

Hope returned to his face. "That's true."

"Now, come here, and help us bring Jabari back."

As he knelt down beside us, he reached for Daktari and closed his eyes.

"Now everyone, close your eyes and focus. Daktari, you've got this," I said confidently.

I shut my own eyes, and called to Jabari, knowing they would all hear me since we were linked together, but unconcerned. "*Fight it, Jabari. Come back to me. We're not finished yet. Wake up.*"

I kept talking to him as Daktari's warmth shot through our bodies. I pleaded with him. I ordered him to wake up.

And then, as the thunder seemed a far away dream and the storm had quieted, Michelle began speaking excitedly. "He's moving. It's working!"

"Come on, Jabari," Daktari pleaded.

I stared at Jabari's face, and a rosy tint filled his cheeks. He was back.

Daktari pulled him up to his feet, and we all stood back as Michelle hugged him tightly. "Oh, I was so scared."

Jabari looked around at us, a puzzled look on his face. He walked to me, and grabbed my shoulders. "But I saw you getting struck by lightening," he began.

"You both were struck," Daktari said solemnly. "I didn't know if we were going to get either of you back."

Zi wrapped her arms around Daktari, comforting him. "But you did it, Daktari."

Jabari bent down, kissing my forehead. "I heard your voice in my head. You were yelling at me, dream girl." His voice sounded shaky.

I swallowed as I looked up at him. "I'm sorry for yelling. I can't lose you, you know."

He pulled me closer. "I can't lose you either. For a moment, I thought I had. I saw you get struck and then it was over. Are you okay now?"

"I feel fine. Daktari fixed me. They all did, actually."

"I was only able to fix you both because everyone helped me. We worked together. That's the key, like Takara has been saying for months," Daktari said matter-of-factly.

Michelle wrapped her arms around me and Jabari. "You kids are amazing. Now let's get out of here already."

"Everyone on the ground."

I flinched at the authoritativeness of the man's voice.

Jabari pushed me behind Daktari, and he stepped forward as the human Authority officer shone a light on our small group.

"This might be a good time for the image, Zi," Marcello remarked, his tone casual.

"Cover them, Zi," Jabari ordered.

The guard reached for his waist, and Jabari dove towards him, a lethal look in his eyes. He tackled him and held him down easily with his strength.

I ran over to him. "Why didn't you just use your mind control ability?"

"He looked like he was reaching for his weapon. I didn't have time," Jabari answered darkly.

The guard struggled futilely under Jabari's iron grip. "Let me go. You'll pay for this."

"Stop struggling," Jabari commanded. The man obeyed, and I knew Jabari was using his other ability. "Now tell me, what are you doing here? Are you alone?"

"I'm alone. One of the Combat Droids recorded footage of the side of the building ripping off in the storm. Its video was transferred back to Town Hall, where I was on duty, but the Droid never reported in. It was carried away in the tornado. I decided to survey the damage."

"Go back to Town Hall, and forget everything you've seen here. Except this. Remember, the storm damaged the building and carried some supplies away."

He nodded, completely dazed now. Jabari pulled him to his feet and turned him away from us. Once he was gone, we grabbed the fuel cells we'd need to go on our last mission and traveled under Zi's image back to our basement hideout.

"I can't believe I'm standing in the basement of TFF," Michelle said with a small laugh.

"Let me show you around, Mrs. Ramirez," Marcello offered.

Jabari reappeared the next moment, climbing down the hatch from the gymnasium, where he had stashed the last of the fuel cells for our trip. He crossed the room in two steps, picked me up by the waist, and buried his face in my neck.

My feet dangled off the ground as he squeezed me. After a moment, he finally spoke in a whisper. "I was so scared when I saw you get struck. Don't ever do that again."

"Don't ever get struck by lightening? You either," I returned.

He lowered me down slowly, locking eyes with mine. "I'm so worried about you, Rain."

"You have to stop doing that. If you weren't so focused on me, you might have known something bad was going to happed to yourself. You got struck my lightening, too. And Daktari was really struggling back there. We were so afraid. Don't scare me like that again. This entire night has been scary."

"I know. It all started with that dream." He held my hand and turned to Cole. "There's something you need to know about Rain's dream, Cole. I didn't want to tell you until we were done getting the fuel cells because

I didn't want to worry you. But I think you need to know."

"What is it?" He approached us slowly.

"In Rain's dream, it looked like Gallagher *and* Adrianne were being chased by The Authority. First chance you have tomorrow, hack into The Authority network to see if they're getting closer to finding Gallagher. And Niyol said he'd warn Gallagher for us."

Cole's face paled. "Adrianne's in danger?"

I touched his arm gently. "I don't know. But in my dream a black-haired girl and Gallagher were running from the Combat Droids. Niyol said he would warn them. I'm sure they are being careful."

Cole bit his lip. "Okay, I'll see what I can find out. Thanks."

Jabari pulled my hand, as Michelle and Marcello climbed back down the ladder. He glanced around the room. "Come on, we should get home so we can get a few hours of sleep."

Zi led the way down the tunnel. "I don't know how I'll be able to sleep after tonight," she complained. "My best friend and her fiancé got struck by lightening, and a tornado nearly killed us."

"The tornado actually saved us," I pointed out. "We might not have gotten the fuel cells without it."

Zi laughed in the darkness, and I could almost imagine her rolling her eyes. "There you go being Miss Optimism again, Rain. I swear, does anything get you down anymore?"

"You mean besides getting struck by lightening and getting literally knocked down?" I teased.

"Now she's making jokes. Unbelievable," Daktari said with a groan.

"That's my amiga," Marcello said with a chuckle. "You know, I admit, I lost it back there. But Rain, you gave a great pep talk and made me focus on what I had to do, and it worked. And we really should be celebrating the fact that we used our abilities, linked together for the first time, and it was successful. We're going to be so much stronger when we go after the Big Bad Wolf," he finished.

"I haven't heard you call her that in a while. But you're right, Marcello. Can't believe I'm agreeing with you for once," Zi said.

"To The Freedom Front," Michelle said.

"Conquering the Big Bad Wolf," I added.

Once we were on the street again and huddled under Zi's image, Jabari reached for me. He had a grim expression on his face again, but he didn't say a word. I knew he had another bad feeling, but I refused to ask him about it. The group seemed sort of optimistic for the time being, and I didn't want to ruin it.

He held my hand as we snuck back to our apartments and he kissed me goodbye outside his apartment door. When I made it home, I crawled under the covers and tried to forget the troubled look in his eyes. And I told myself that everything was going to be fine.

Chapter 44: Tension

JABARI

The countdown to the mass murder of our zone was on. Eric had found me earlier in the day to warn me that Nata had already begun pulling the human officers from our zone, and he was one of three who hadn't been reassigned yet. But if everything went according to plan, we would take Nata out of power before she could kill anyone else. So much was riding on the success of our small group of teenagers; the tension was definitely high.

Night had fallen again, encroaching the zone, but the nearest street lamp that had survived the tornado cast just enough light on Rain so I could keep an eye on her from up the block. As I waited for her, my thoughts spun, constantly recycling my worries and the facts.

The storm had disrupted the zone, but only for the day. Throughout the morning and afternoon, the Combat Droids had kept us busy with the clean up of the streets. We figured Rain was correct in her assumption that Niyol had caused the tornado. Sure, a few people had been forced to relocate into other apartments, but over all, the storm had mostly damaged the hover plant, knocked some street lights down, and shattered windows. A handful of people had lost their rooftops, but no one had been physically injured, and we had gotten the fuel we needed. It had to have been Niyol. After we'd cleaned up the glass and debris with the Combat Droids standing over us the entire time, we'd been sent back to work to complete our shifts, so TFF hadn't been able to meet during our regular time.

As I leaned against a brick building in the shadows and watched Rain speaking to Aleela and Takara, my worries returned to her. I felt the constant need to protect her. It was consuming me.

My heart sped up as I thought about the days ahead. As I'd heard about last night, she'd led the group to save me. When they thought they couldn't, and Marcello was having doubts, Rain pulled them back together. So even though I still felt the need to protect her desperately, part of me wondered if I'd overreacted about my feeling and it was just nerves. After all, Niyol had assured me Rain was the key to our success and that she absolutely had to face Nata in Elizabeth Mansion. And even if I couldn't figure out how, exactly, or why she was the key, I was beginning to think maybe I wasn't meant to. Maybe it was as simple as what had happened last night. Rain had known what to do to save me. So I had to hope that she'd trust those same instincts in New Washington and know what to do when the time came. But it was hard to ignore the feeling in my chest. Somehow, I knew I had to keep protecting her because some unknown threat was on the horizon. I could sense it.

As I studied her now, she kissed Aleela lightly on the cheek and hugged her quickly. Aleela clung to her as she pulled away a little, and said something I couldn't hear, but I imagined it went along the lines of *Thank you for helping me . . . again.*

Rain smiled and gave Takara a quick kiss and hug goodbye before turning away and taking off into a light jog down the sidewalk. She hopped over a downed street lamp that no one had been able to budge on the sidewalk, and focused her eyes on me. When she reached me, I took her hand in mine and started walking away from the corner.

"That was really nice of you," I said.

Even though I knew Aleela needed our help, she was one of many people in our zone who did, and we couldn't help them all, but Rain had to be Rain. And I admired her for it. I cared for the fate of others in our zone, and it was the main reason I had taken over what my dad had started with The Freedom Front, but I wasn't like Rain. And I had very pressing concerns, mainly that we'd have to leave the zone ahead of schedule. If my feeling about Rain was off, all the better, but I knew the growing sense of danger I felt was leading up to something. So I had opted to be prepared for everything, including an early escape.

I'd discussed it with Eric earlier when he had found me. He'd agreed to help me get my dad out of prison if we decided to run. I just couldn't leave him behind. I'd messaged Gallagher from our hideout after work, and he'd assured me we could hide in his underground waterfall shelter if we needed to come there. I'd also run the idea past Takara, and she had told me she knew I'd make the right call and to let her know what I decided. Then, I'd managed to meet with each member of TFF at some point throughout the day and night, so they were all prepared. But Rain said she was acting like everything was normal until I gave her the word that we needed to escape, which was why she'd insisted on helping Aleela tonight. But whether or not Rain realized it, she would help people no matter where she was, regardless of the circumstances. She was always a hero. It only made my job of protecting her that much harder.

"I didn't really do anything," Rain said after a moment. "I mean, all I did was point out to Takara that since Kelly's gone, Aleela could help fill her shoes. And then Takara had said that she wouldn't mind the help and she'd make sure Aleela got enough food on her table. Takara's the one who deserves the credit. You and I both know Takara doesn't have that much of a need for extra eyes these days with everything we know about Nata's plan now. And anyway this will all be over with soon enough. I mean, I don't know how fast things will improve after we capture Nata, but maybe once Gallagher is free to help the zones, he can distribute supplies to all of them as the walls come down. Just think, this whole nightmare could be over within the next week."

"And it will be. I'm sure you'll be trying to save everyone still, even after we capture Nata. Twenty zones just like ours are in need of rescuing. So you'll have a lot to do," I said with a grin.

"I hate it. I want to fix it. Or just make it better somehow."

I pulled her hand to my lips and kissed it softly. "I know."

"Oh, did you message Gallagher, by the way? And did Cole find anything out on The Authority network?"

"There you go trying to save everyone again."

Her face lit up with a smile that made me want to smile bigger and forget about our problems. "You're hilarious, Jabari. You saw my dream last night, so I know you're worried about Adrianne too."

"I did see it. And to answer your question, yes, as soon as they let us leave work, we went to the hideout and I checked in with Gallagher. Niyol had spoken to him already, and he stuck an extra detail on Adrianne. And Cole searched the network but hasn't turned up any evidence that The Authority is closing in on Gallagher."

"Good. You know, the dream got me thinking . . . What if Nata tries to go after Adrianne, you know, as a trap. If she were to get Adrianne, Gallagher would turn himself in automatically."

I sighed. "It's a valid concern. I'm sure Gallagher is aware that Nata would do anything to get him. Hopefully, it was just one of your usual chaotic dreams, and Adrianne won't get captured."

Sympathy flickered over her face as she replied. "I'm sorry."

"For what?"

"You know, that you have to see everything in my dreams. I wish I knew how to stop it. You know, there could be a way; I mean, I told Marcello to learn how to control his ability. What if I can control my dream ability? What if I could stop entering your dreams? Can you imagine actually getting a good night's rest again?"

"First of all, I'm not complaining. So please don't try to stop it from happening. You know all of your dreams are not bad. In fact, some of them are very nice," I said, slowing to trace a finger across the top of her hand.

Her face blushed, but she smiled back. "Okay, so maybe I've kissed you a few times in my dreams, but that rarely happens, Jabari. And are you saying you'd rather keep experiencing my nightmares with me just to have an occasional *imaginary* kiss?"

"It doesn't feel imaginary when it's happening. It's totally worth it," I answered without hesitation.

She burst out laughing and pushed my chest lightly with her free hand. "You're terrible."

I picked her up off the ground and ducked into the next alley. I walked a few feet into the alley for some privacy, ignoring her laughter and teasing protests. "Jabari, someone might see us."

"See us what? We aren't breaking any laws, technically. Can't a guy kiss his fiancée?"

She raised a brow. "Technically, you're not allowed to have a fiancée," she pointed out. Then her playful expression faded as her eyes landed on my mouth. "And anyway, you haven't kissed me yet."

My smile faded at the reminder of the law, and a feeling to escape overcame me. I set her feet down, still clinging to her, and pinned her against the brick wall. "I can fix that."

I lowered my mouth to hers and lost myself in the moment. Her hands wound their way around my neck and pulled me closer.

After a few seconds, her words crept into my mind, sending chills down my back. *"Don't stop kissing me."*

"I won't."

Her hands slid from my neck to my throat and down my chest, lingering on my stomach for a moment and finally settling around my waist. My heart slammed against my chest so loudly, I wondered if she could hear it. The urge to pick her up and run out of the zone began to grow stronger and stronger until I had to tell her my doubts about wanting to leave. I broke the kiss, still holding her against the wall. Her eyes blazed back at mine, and her breaths came fast, matching my own.

"What's wrong?" she demanded.

"I didn't want to say it, but this feeling in my chest won't fade like it normally does. I know last night was bad, but after talking with Eric earlier and then Takara, she said to trust my ability, Rain."

She swallowed. "You think we should take our families and go now, don't you?"

"Yeah. I do."

I prepared for her argument, but it never came. She nodded instead. "I trust you. How soon should we go?"

"It's getting worse by the second, Rain." I hesitated and looked up at the pitch-black sky for a moment, like I was expecting something to fly overhead. I shook my head at my own paranoia. Or was it paranoia? It felt real. The danger felt real, and I needed to stop doubting my ability.

She took my hand gently. "I'll use my ability to tell the others. But what should I tell them exactly?"

"Your dad should be getting home from work within the next thirty minutes. Tell everyone to get ready. Contact Zi first. She said she'd help get people into the basement under her image so we don't stand out. She can start now, taking her parents and you and yours. I can get my mom there without the image. Marcello and Cole might want to travel under her image though, too, if there's time. If we start now . . ." my sentence trailed off as an explosion sounded.

"What was that?" Rain's face paled.

"It sounds far away," I began. We raced down the alleyway and peered out into the streets.

"I don't see anything," Rain said.

It exploded again, and my head snapped in another direction.

"Jabari, it sounds like bombs. But how?"

Another one exploded, and I turned. This time, just over the walls I saw what looked like a fireball billowing up in the dark night.

"She's bombing No Man's Land," I blurted.

"She's going after Gallagher. She must be desperate."

I pulled her back into the alley and clenched her hands together in front of mine. Desperation filled my voice and I didn't even try to hide it. "Rain, listen to me. If she's bombing outside the zones, who knows how much time before she decides to target us. We have to go now."

"Maybe that's why you had the feeling. I know this is bad, but how will we get to Gallagher's if she is dropping bombs? And is it really safer there?"

"We just have to get to the hideout with everyone first. As soon as we think it's safe to travel, we'll get out. She can't bomb all night. Let me worry about getting us to Gallagher's. He said we could hide in the storm shelter below the waterfall. It's better than being trapped in here. What if she bombs the school, and we can't get our hover out? We'll never get over the armed walls in here. We have to go now. Takara and everyone knows what to do. Just tell them it's time."

"I know." She leaned back, closing her eyes. "Give me a sec."

"*Takara, Jabari says we have to go now.*" I held onto her as she used her ability, amazed how I could listen to every word.

"*I know, Rainchild. Be careful and keep hope alive.*"

"*But aren't you going? And Aleela? She can bring her mom, too.*"

"*I've already talked to Aleela about the days ahead. She's agreed to help me when Gallagher launches the attack against Nata. There will be a lot of work to be done inside the walls once you dismantle the Droids.*"

"*But what if something happens after we disappear from the zone? Takara, you have to leave now.*"

"*Rain, I'm eighty-three years old. I am needed here. And Aleela wants to do something to help, too. If we leave, we can't help you. In here, we can help. Now go, and be careful.*"

"*You too, Takara.*"

When Rain opened her eyes, there was so much doubt in them.

"She knows what she's doing, Rain. Now contact Zi," I urged her, squeezing her arms lightly.

A bomb exploded in the distance, and she paled.

"Go on, the bombs are far away," I assured her.

She shook her head curtly. "*Zi, where are you? Jabari says it's time to go. And I agree.*"

"*I'm with Daktari. I ran to your apartment when I heard the first bomb. We already talked about it, and we agree. We need to get our families out now.*"

"*I'm coming to you now. I'll help you get everyone to the shelter like we talked about.*"

"*Hurry, Rain. But what about Francisco? Is Eric going to help us?*"

When Rain opened her eyes, I nodded my head. "Yeah, he agreed, but you need to contact him to tell him we need to do it ASAP."

"*Zi, Eric said he'd help us get Francisco out. We're going to contact him now to tell him we're on the way after we get our families to the school.*"

"*Okay, then I'll see you soon.*"

She contacted Eric next. And he replied right away. "*I'll be waiting for you. Once you get inside the prison, have Cole cut the cameras, and have Marcello put my two coworkers to sleep. I'll get Francisco out before they wake up. Or Jabari can tell them to forget what they see or something. Just hurry.*"

Rain took my hand and began to jog out into the street. "We'll all go for your dad, once the rest of our families are safe in the basement. Or do you want to go to the prison first?"

"No, get your family to the hideout first, Rain."

I pulled her to a stop again as the worst fear overcame me. "Wait, Rain. Maybe we should stay together. We can round everyone up together."

"There's not enough time, Jabari. Don't worry. We'll meet up in just a little bit."

She leaned onto her tiptoes and kissed me quickly. "I love you because."

Her breath was sweet across my face. I wanted to make her stay. I didn't want to let go. But she was right. It would be faster if we separated and then met up.

"I love you because, Rain Ramirez."

With a fleeting glance, she spun around and took off in a sprint, and as I took off in my own run, I watched her disappear into the darkness.

Chapter 45: Escape

RAIN

Even if I'd doubted Jabari's ability to focus of late, I knew he was gifted and strongly in tune with his ability, so when he'd told me we needed to go earlier, even before the bombs had started to fall, I'd believed him. I trusted him. And I knew I'd been too hard on him last night when I'd said he had been worrying too much about me. I'd said it because I'd nearly lost him to the lightening, and it had terrified me. But I knew Jabari. And I knew he had a God-given gift to sense danger.

I listened to the bombs as they sporadically fell outside the zones and I wanted to cry. He'd been right again. He'd sensed something horrific, and sure enough the sky had practically opened up the next moment.

As I paced the sidewalk in front of our apartment, my eyes searched frantically for the hover that would bring Dad home from work, and my heart raced. We'd packed a backpack with a few personal belongings, and everyone was ready, except Dad's hover was running a few minutes behind. My mind grew weary of overanalyzing the details. I was starting to worry about Grandma Julia, too, because when I had tried to contact her to tell her we'd come for her, she hadn't responded. Then it dawned on me that I hadn't contacted Niyol since the bombing had begun, and he could help me reach Grandma, I was sure.

"Niyol, are you okay? Niyol, can you hear me?"

"Yes, Rain. I'm fine."

"The bombs are dropping so quickly. Is Gallagher safe? Have you talked to him?"

"Gallagher is fine. People have taken cover in underground shelters. They

are afraid, but they are out of sight."

"Why is she doing this? As retaliation for the pure zone?"

"We have to assume. But Gallagher was prepared for something like this to happen. He warned the people to be ready for an attack. I'm helping where I can. Is it time for you to leave?"

"Umm, yeah. I'm not even going to ask how you knew what we were doing. I guess you know also that we're going to try to make it to Gallagher's camp tonight or by morning. Jabari thinks we need to get out of the zone before we get trapped here."

"That is a wise decision, Rain."

"I haven't been able to reach Grandma Julia. Can you help me?"

"I'll find her and warn her you're coming as soon as you can, okay?"

"Thanks, Niyol."

"Please, stay strong and remember what I told you. I have to go for now."

When he was gone, I paced the steps again. I should have felt better that he was safe and helping people, but I was still a nervous wreck. The bombs falling made me jump again.

Daktari opened the door. "Are you all right?"

"Sure, just jittery. I can't believe we're actually doing this."

He stepped down closer to me and wrapped his arm around me. "Have faith. We'll get through this like we get through everything, sis."

I hugged him back and looked up at my little brother, who towered a head taller than me. "You know, it seems like yesterday you were shorter than me. And now you're a giant, and you're giving me motivational speeches," I said, hoping to lighten my own mood.

"I learned from the best," he said, nodding past my shoulder. "And here comes Dad. We're almost out of here," he finished with a smile.

I wanted to warn him to hold off on the celebration until we'd actually made it over the walls, but he looked so hopeful I couldn't bear to dampen the mood.

Dad ran up the steps and hugged each of us. "Are you okay? I heard the bombing. What's going on? Where's your mom?" he asked frantically.

"Dad, TFF made the decision. It's time to go," I said smoothly.

His eyes darted back and forth between Daktari and me, and he swallowed a lump in his throat. "All right then. Tell me what I need to do to help."

We pulled him back inside the apartment and within two minutes, we were all leaving our apartments behind hidden under the refuge of Zi's ever-changing image. Thankfully, Mom hadn't put up the least bit of an argument. Nor had Zi's parents. With the constant backdrop of bombs exploding in the not-too-far distance, I figured none of them could deny that this was the right thing to do. Outside the walls, they knew we could survive in one of Gallagher's hidden camps. Inside the walls, we were sitting ducks, waiting on Nata to drop a bomb or fill our homes with poisonous gas.

I hated to leave the people in our zone behind, but I knew we'd do our best to save them. Nothing was certain, but out there, we had a better chance of pulling off the unimaginable, of taking Nata out of power once and for all.

And as Daktari pointed out on our huddled trip to TFF's basement, now that Nata had completely lost it and was attacking No Man's Land, whether she realized it or not, she'd given the refugees more reason than ever to join Gallagher and The Freedom Front when Gallagher led the attack against her. I had to agree with him. As much as the sound of the bombs terrified me, it might be the one thing that would bring any doubters out of hiding ready to join the fight. One way or another, Nata had to be brought down.

As we neared the hidden high school storm hatch, Daktari had another thought. "What if other countries find out about the bombing and decide to help too?" he said excitedly. "I mean, she can't possibly expect no one to pick up on the fact that she's bombing her own country, right? How protected is her airspace? She's obviously lost her mind," he added.

"I agree, Daktari. This will help bring her down. She can't keep her secret from the world forever. Not now that she's attacked her own soil so heavily," Zi's dad, Aidan, agreed.

"I can't believe we're actually getting out of here," Li Ming said nervously.

"We are, Mrs. Sanders. It won't be long," Daktari said happily.

He lifted the hatch to the basement, and Zi held the hover in place as we all descended the ladder into the dark tunnel. Once I made it down, I noticed the light streaming from the meeting room and hurried down to see who was already there. Everyone spun around as I entered the room, familiar and unfamiliar faces greeted me.

Cole waved me forward. "Hey Rain. This is my Aunt Trina and Uncle Cesar. I guess you've never met them before."

I walked over to the pair. "Nice to meet you. Marcello looks a lot like you," I added to his mom with a grin.

"Yes, but he gets his attitude from his dad," she teased, pulling me into a hug. She held me back a little. "Thank you for everything you've done so far, Rain. I've heard so much. I'm proud of all of you," she added, greeting Zi and Daktari as they joined us.

"So am I," Michelle added, moving in for a hug.

"Hi Mrs.—" She held up her hand to stop me. "I mean, Michelle," I finished with a small smile.

It was nice to see how hopeful and excited our parents were, and it filled me with a positive feeling. We were going to be all right. Somehow.

Once introductions were quickly finished up, Cole nodded at me. "Jabari is waiting for you guys to join him outside the prison so he can get his dad. He's on the side of the building, so you can meet him there and cover him with Zi's image before you go in. I'm going to take the cameras out in exactly ten minutes, so that should give you enough time to make it there. I'll keep them off for fifteen minutes, but you should be long gone before fifteen minutes have passed. While you're gone, I'll help everyone load into the hover, along with all of the supplies we can fit, so as soon as you return, we're out of here."

"Let's go," Zi instructed, as she started towards the tunnel.

"We need to hurry," I said, starting after Zi, but Marcello waved for me to stop.

"What's up?" I asked.

"You know, they might need me to knock some guards out and Cole could probably use someone with an ability just in case something were to happen here. Why don't you hang back, Rain?"

"We can help, Cole," Michelle said.

Cole chuckled. "I know you guys can, but Marcello has a point. And Rain has got some mad skills when it comes to emergency situations. Marcello's right. Someone should stay here in case we run into any unexpected problems."

I looked up at Daktari. "Is that cool with you? I'd hate it if you needed me and I wasn't there."

"Yeah, it's fine. This should be a quick in and out anyway."

I followed them to the ladder. "Be careful, guys. I'll see you soon."

Once they were gone, I turned to Cole. "Where should I start?"

"You can help the adults to the hover and carry our food supplies and solar lights, and stock it with the remaining fuel cells."

"No problem." I turned to my dad, who was talking to Michelle and Mom. "Want to help me?"

"We'll all help, Rain," Aidan offered.

"Great."

I set to work, transporting the supplies from our room into the main school, up the hatch, and to the hover. Cole cut the cameras to the prison when ten minutes had passed since Daktari had left. And within another five minutes of that, thanks to our teamwork, we had nearly everything loaded and still had room for everyone to squeeze in once they arrived with Francisco.

"Good thing these hovers are built to carry heavy loads," Michelle said, surveying the ample space.

"We should be ready to go now," Cole said, jumping into the front pilot seat. "I just want to get prepped for taking off. It sounds like the bombing is dying down. Before he left, Jabari said he wanted to leave as soon as we got the all clear from Gallagher, and I just messaged with Gallagher a moment ago . . . He thinks we should head out now since his area isn't under attack for the moment." "That's a relief," I said with a sigh.

"Oh and Rain, could you head back downstairs and wait for the others? You can bring the last solar light I left in there up with you when they get here."

"Sure thing," I said, pausing in the doorway to the hover.

Mom reached for my hand and kissed it softly. "Be careful, Rain."

I laughed. "I'm just going downstairs. No worries, Mom."

I climbed down the hatch into the storm shelter and glanced around at the now empty room when a feeling of nostalgia crept over me. This room had been our secret meeting space for so long now. I recalled the first day I'd snuck through the hatch because of Jabari's invitation, and the powerful feeling that had drawn me to him. And here we were about eight months later, and I was engaged to him, and we were about to escape the mixed zone for good.

It felt dangerous but exciting at the same time. I walked over to the table where Cole had always sat to hack into The Authority network and took a seat.

"*Rain, can you hear me?*"

"*Oh good, Bhavna, are you okay? I meant to check on you. Is the bombing near you, too?*" I asked worriedly.

"*The Authority patrol found Sook and—*"

I jumped to my feet. "*Bhavna? Are you there?*"

There was no answer. I called out to her over and over as I paced the small space. The Authority had Sook? This was bad. A feeling of dread swept over me as total comprehension hit me.

If they had Sook, he could lead them to our hideout if they questioned him. We had to leave now. But then another thought occurred to me, and I started towards the tunnel. If they had Sook, he knew about Takara, too, and might tell them about her role in TFF. I had to warn her right away. I had to find her. I knew I could use my running ability to get to her in time. As long as I didn't run into trouble with any of the Combat Droids, I'd be okay.

As my feet hit the pavement, I hesitated a second to glance in either direction for Droids, then took off in a sprint towards Takara's apartment.

I called to her as I ran. *"Takara where are you? The Authority found Sook. You have to go with us."*

When she didn't reply, I called to her again. *"Takara, where are you?"*

"Rain, I'm here."

"They found Sook. You have to join us. He'll lead them to you. He knows your name. He'll tell them everything if Nata questions him."

"Rainchild, he won't tell any of the guards about us. What are the chances that he'll be interrogated by Nata?"

"It isn't a chance I want to take, Takara," I said with a sob as a tear ran down my cheek. *"Please, I can't bear the thought of anything happening to you. Come with us. I'm almost to your apartment. I'll tell Zi where to find us and she can get us safely to the school hideout."*

"Well, let me come out to you, Rain, and we'll talk about it," she agreed.

"Hurry, Takara."

As her street came into sight, my thoughts raced ahead. If Sook was interrogated, he'd have no choice but to give up all of his information about Takara. A memory hit me as I slowed down. The first time Niyol had met Sook at Bhavna's camp, he'd gotten the strangest expression on his face as though he had sensed something. Maybe he had known this whole time that Sook would be captured. Chills ran down my arms at the thought.

"Rain, where are you?"

Bhavna's voice startled me and I tripped over the edge of the sidewalk, falling to the ground just in front of the diner where Takara liked to sit and drink tea sometimes. As I grabbed my knee, I remembered the day I had stormed in there to ask her about Aleela, and I'd nearly gotten us busted by an Authority spy. But this was so much worse than that day. My heart was slamming in my throat. How could I convince Takara to go with us? I had to.

"Rain, where are you?" Bhavna repeated, her voice strained.

"Are you okay? What happened to Sook? You'll need to evacuate your camp, Bhavna."

"Where are you, Rain? It's about Sook; I need to know where you are exactly, right now." Her voice sounded different than it ever had before, but I knew it had to be because of Sook being taken. She was probably scared to death.

"I'm on Route Seven in front of the Seymour Diner. Why would you ask me that?" As soon as I'd said the words, a horrible feeling of paranoia hit me like a truck.

"Wait a second, Bhavna?"

"I'm sorry, Rain. She has a gun to Sook's head," Bhavna sobbed.

"Who has a gun to Sook's head?" But as the words left my mouth, I knew the answer.

Nata.

I got to my feet and turned at the slight noise behind me as bright lights from a hover lit me up in the middle of the empty, dark street. They blinded me and I turned to run. I was halfway spun around when something pricked my neck, stinging on impact.

I swayed, realization filling me. *"Jabari, Nata has—"*

My face hit the pavement.

"Rain? Where are you?" Jabari called.

As I succumbed to the drug racing through my body, I finished my sentence. *". . . me."*

Chapter 46: Gone

JABARI

I crushed Dad into a bear hug and released him quickly. "We have to hurry," I whispered.

He glanced down at his cellmate, who was curled up on the side of the prison cell. "Can Ian come with us? They might hurt him if they want to know what happened to me. He's in pretty bad shape as it is. I hate to leave him behind."

"I have a feeling no one is going to notice in the days ahead. And with the bombing and all of the guards gone except the three of us, they won't want to report to Nata that we lost two prisoners. The Combat Droids haven't taken over the prison yet. Hopefully, they won't be here for long if all goes well with your plan anyway. Go ahead, take him," Eric agreed.

Daktari knelt down and placed his hands on Ian to heal him. I remembered him from the day in the woods behind Rain's grand-mother's house, when he'd been arrested for fleeing from The Authority and trying to protect his wife from being taken to the pure zone. They had married in secret, but his wife had been selected for the pure zone, and because he had tried to escape with her, The Authority had sentenced Ian to life in the prison of Indy Mixed Zone. I wondered if his wife was still alive in the pure zone, and if there would come a time when they would be reunited. I certainly hoped so.

After a moment, he stirred back to awareness and Daktari and Dad pulled him to his feet. "Ian, this is my son," Dad said, introducing me.

Ian looked at me with eyes wide. "You're Jabari?"

"Yeah, good to meet you," I said, shaking his hand.

"I'm Zi, and this is Daktari and Marcello."

"Nice to meet you all," he said.

"Want to get out of here? Destination over the walls, I hear it's nice," Marcello said cheerfully.

Ian smiled, revealing white teeth under his filthy face. "Yes, please."

"Stay close to me so we can get out of here undetected," Zi instructed everyone, bringing her hands to her chest to prepare the image.

Eric stopped Dad and me before we ducked under the image. "Good luck out there. I'll see you when it's all over with."

I grabbed his hand and pulled him into a quick hug. "Thanks for everything, Eric."

He looked from my dad to me with a smile. "It's good to see you with your dad. Now get out of here. Cole said he'd cut the cameras off for fifteen minutes, so by my estimate you've got about nine minutes left. I'll see you soon enough."

As we shuffled down the dark and pungent prison block, I looked into the cells, vowing I would do everything in my power to defeat Nata so the tormented prisoners I was leaving behind could be freed from this terrible place. We snuck past the two other guards who were still unconscious at the front desk, thanks to Marcello, and hurried outside.

Once out on the streets, I had to help my dad along. Sure, Officer Wolfe hadn't beaten him since Rain had taken care of him, and Daktari had used his healing ability on him, but Dad had spent a year in a prison cell, and he didn't have muscle like before. He couldn't walk as fast as us. Neither could Ian. We paused to let them catch their breaths every so often, huddling around Zi.

Dad scanned the streets. "You shouldn't have come for me, Jabari. I don't want to delay you or ruin your chances of getting out alive."

"Did you really think I'd leave without you, Dad? The only reason we never got you before was because we didn't want to leave any evidence or let it point back to us somehow if you were gone. I hated every second that you were locked up in there."

He grabbed my shoulder as emotions flickered across his face. "It was still a risk I'm not sure you should've taken. But thank you. I can't wait to see your mom."

"And she can't wait to see you, Dad. Let's get going again."

I lead the group down the streets, and though I felt a little relieved as my eyes settled on the high school, I mostly felt apprehension. My thoughts returned to Rain. I knew she would be there waiting for us, but I wouldn't feel better until I could see her again with my own eyes.

"We're almost there," Zi said excitedly.

"One step closer to busting out of this depressing walled zone," Daktari added.

"*Jabari, Nata has—*"

I froze as her voice entered my mind and the words registered. Maybe I was imagining it.

"What's wrong?" Daktari asked, looking at me as I held the group up.

My eyes squeezed shut. "*Rain, where are you?*"

Two seconds, maybe three passed, and I heard her again. "*. . . me,*" she said.

"Rain," I called out loud. "Rain!" I repeated.

Horror washed over Zi's face and then Daktari's and everyone's around me. They knew what I was going to say before I could say it. My hand grabbed my heart and my knees gave out. I crashed to the ground. For weeks I'd felt I needed to protect Rain, and now I knew why. She'd only said three words and then disappeared, but I knew what had happened.

Daktari clutched onto my shoulder. "Where is Rain? Tell me."

I looked up at him, choking as I said the words aloud. "I think Nata has her."

His face went white with panic and I closed my eyes. I had heard her. And I called out to her, but she was gone.

I screamed out loud again, "Rain, where are you?"

"We have to keep moving if what you say is true. There are Combat Droids roaming the streets. We're all in danger," Marcello said. He reached for me, but I smacked his hand away.

The ground felt shaky below me. "Rain," I tried again, praying she could hear me and respond and tell me it had been a false alarm.

"We have to keep moving, Jabari," Dad urged me.

I blocked their voices away as nausea rolled through me. I hadn't protected Rain. I tried to look at Daktari, but tears blurred my vision. "Nata has Rain," I repeated. My entire body began to shake. I fell forward, grabbing my temple as I cried.

I felt hands on my shoulder. "Come on, Jabari. We're almost to the school. We have to go before they get us, too. If we don't get out of here, we can't get Rain back." My thoughts began to clear as Daktari's voice registered.

I looked up at him, and he nodded encouragingly. "Do you understand what I'm saying? We have to hurry," he said calmly.

My heartbeat continued to race, but his words made sense. I let Daktari pull me up as I fought off the fear and summoned courage. I coughed, wiping tears away as we took off under Zi's image. "Yeah, we have to hurry," I repeated his words.

We were nearly to the storm hatch when a patch of red caught my eye and I spun towards it. Takara was a few feet away, and her red scarf blew around her neck. She couldn't see us under the image, but she was clearly trying to find us if she was so close to the hideout.

"What's Takara doing out here?" Daktari said before I could.

"Go ahead inside and load up, I'll see if I can convince her to come with us," I instructed, trying to think rationally as I jogged out from under the image.

Takara flinched as I appeared out of thin air, but recovered quickly. "Jabari, it's Rain. She—"

"Nata has her."

Takara's eyes grew wide. "No."

I pulled her close. "Do you know what happened?"

"Rain came for me. She said she wanted me to go with you all. Bhavna had contacted her and said The Authority had captured Sook. Rain was worried Sook would lead Nata to me."

I shook my head. Rain had been trying to save Takara when she'd been taken. Of course, she couldn't have stayed in the basement of TFF. But there was no time to waste.

"We have to go. You're not safe here. Come with us, please."

She shrugged, no fight at all. "Okay."

I led her to the hatch where Daktari appeared waiting with Zi, holding an image over us. I jumped down the dark hole, missing the ladder completely as adrenaline began to pulse through my blood. I reached up for Takara and lifted her down easily.

We hurried down the tunnel and got Takara up the second ladder and into the gymnasium. Daktari raced ahead of us to warn his parents what had happened. My dad shot me looks the entire way but didn't say anything. He had to know I was in too much distress to talk.

When we got to the hover, Grace was sobbing into Isaac's arms. Daktari sat beside them with his hands on Grace, but no amount of healing power would fix her now. As I stood beside the hover door, the misery in Isaac's eyes and the sound of Grace sobbing threatened to undo me. Everyone murmured and scooted closer as Takara, Ian, and my dad climbed into the hover.

Isaac cleared his throat after a second, his voice was scratchy. "Is it true, Jabari? Did Nata get my daughter?"

My stomach bottomed out as he looked at me. I'd promised Isaac I'd protect her, after all. And I'd let him down. I had known she needed to stay with me. I should've insisted she not separate from me earlier.

I clenched my fists, unwilling to lose hope now. I needed it more than I'd ever needed it before. "I'm going to get her back, Isaac."

He nodded as if he believed me, but we both knew he had no choice but to believe me at this point. We had to get Rain back no matter what.

"Come on, Jabari, we need to go while the bombing has died down," Cole called out.

"But where are we going? If Nata has Rain, she might discover Gallagher's camp location, and Bhavna's for that matter. We need to warn them. And we need to know where to go," Zi said frantically. "And how are we going to get Rain?" she added, tears filling her eyes.

I had to make a decision before everyone lost it. And I had to keep them safe, and I had to go after Rain. I pushed the fear and doubt aside and focused on my job.

"First things first, Cole's right. We need to get out of the zone before we're discovered. We'll be safer outside the walls, regardless of what's happening out there. Once we're in the air, Marcello use the Pinkies to contact Gallagher and Will. We'll warn both camps, and Gallagher can meet us at one of his other camps. There are dozens of them that we don't know the locations of, so even if Rain is questioned, she won't know where they are. We'll meet with Gallagher and map out a plan to rescue Rain."

"But shouldn't we just go straight to New Washington?" Marcello wondered.

"Yeah, we need to go right to Rain, don't we?" Daktari asked.

"We *are* going after Rain, and right away. We just need a little help from Gallagher. It's a pit stop along the way. We'll figure this out in the air. Now everyone do your job. We need to get the hover out of here now," I ordered.

Daktari jumped to his feet, and took Zi by the hand. "He's right. Let's get the hover out of here."

Zi concealed the side loading dock door to the old band room, and I opened the school door while Cole guided the hover into the street.

Once Daktari and I had sealed up the door and lock, we hopped into the awaiting hover and took off.

As we flew over the dimly lit streets, I gave one last look at the Indy Mixed Zone. A little while ago, I imagined I'd be leaving the zone for the last time with Rain beside me. And now, she was captured by Nata, awaiting an interrogation and possibly worse. I'd never felt so afraid. But fear had been Nata's most effective strategy against us so far. Somehow I'd figure out how to use that against her.

One way or another, I'd get Rain back.

Chapter 47: Drug

RAIN

My head was throbbing with pain I'd never felt before. I didn't even try to move or open my eyes. It hurt too much.

It took my brain a few seconds to sort out why my head felt like it did, and then it all came back to me. I recognized the stinging on my neck, and realized the strange drug I'd been injected with had knocked me out and had to be the culprit for the splitting pain in my temple and my overwhelming drowsiness. I told myself not to be afraid as I batted my heavy eyelids open and took in my surroundings. It was so bright I couldn't see.

"I'm warning you. You will answer my questions, One-two-seven-six, one way or another, before I get rid of you."

I knew it was Nata even though I couldn't see her past the bright light. She sounded cheerful, as though she was excited about the opportunity to inflict pain on me.

I strained my eyes again and realized my head was tilted backwards, and the brightness was coming from an artificial light directly over me. I tried to move my hands and legs, but they wouldn't budge. I tugged my head forward, and sucked in a sharp breath. Though the room felt as though it was tipping from side to side, like a tossing ship in rough seas, I could see someone. It wasn't Nata.

Calista.

Her eyes were glistening as tears fell from them and ran into the cloth tied around her mouth so she couldn't speak. I tilted my head again to survey my own bindings. Like Calista, I was tied up in a chair, but unlike my cousin, my mouth was free. The last time I'd seen her, she'd been dressed in an exuberant gown, but now, she wore a white prisoner's uniform, and new bruises and cuts blemished her face and arms.

I tried to focus through my blurry vision to scan the room. Even though there wasn't much light, besides the bright light over me and a few small lights here and there, and my head was reeling, I could see that every detail of the room was white, from the walls to the floor, with the exception of one metal table. The ceiling was low. No windows offered an escape or light, and there was a door to my left, sealed, also with no window. Displayed on the table were a variety of objects, some I recognized, such as an assortment of tasers and a burn bar like the one Officer Wolfe had attacked Marcello and me with.

We were clearly in some sort of advanced torture chamber. I noted a single vent in the corner of the ceiling, but I imagined that even if I screamed, no one would hear me. There wasn't a single Droid in the room with us, which made me realize that either Nata wasn't afraid of my abilities or didn't know about them at all, or we were in such a secure place there was no way I'd be able to escape even if I got beyond the door somehow. How would my friends find us? Could they?

"Where are we?" My voice sounded scratchy.

A figured stepped from behind me and crossed in front of my chair. Even in my groggy condition I was sure it was Nata. She was dressed in a business style suit with pants, and every spec of the material was white. As usual, her blonde hair was pulled back tightly away from her face, so I could really see the perfect arch of her eyebrow as she raised it now.

She bent down. "No one can help you. Even if you tell someone with your ability where you are. But that does give me an idea . . ." She paused, standing back up, placing her hand to her chin as she thought.

"We're in Elizabeth Mansion, aren't we? I heard about your transformation of one of the lower levels into your torture chambers."

"Isn't it marvelous?" She held up a hand like she was showcasing the room.

I closed my eyes and focused on my telepathy. *"Jabari, Nata has me and Calista in a room. I don't know where, but it looks like a torture chamber. The ceilings are low. Maybe below ground in her mansion."*

"Rain. Hang in there. We're coming for you." He sounded so far away, but at least he had heard me. If TFF was en route, Calista and I had a chance at surviving.

"Please hurry," I called out to him, but abrupt clapping interrupted my thoughts.

"Pay attention, number one-two-seven-six."

I opened my eyes and she was staring at me darkly, like she knew what I'd been doing. Then a sinister grin curved her mouth upwards. "As I was saying, you haven't even seen it all . . . yet." She focused on Calista now, making me nervous.

"Don't hurt her," I pleaded.

Nata chuckled, and it was such an evil sound my heart slammed in my chest. "Oh, I fear it's too late for that, mixed breed."

"Calista, hang in there," I managed to say, even as my eyes began to droop again.

"You're feeling the drug," Nata remarked. "It makes things seem like they're spinning all around and creates a powerful feeling of drowsiness. I gave you an extra dose just for good measure. It also makes your limbs feel like dead weights and prevents you from fighting or moving much at all. Or so I'm told," she said with a small laugh.

I tried to ignore Nata. I looked over at Calista again. She seemed so hopeless, I just wanted her to come back a little, regardless of how ridiculous I might sound. "Everything's going to be fine, Calista," I said.

If I'd known what allowing her to go to the pure zone would have meant for her, I'd have made her go into hiding months ago. But here she was, because of me. And even though I knew Jabari and TFF were on their way, I also knew from the way Nata was looking at Calista the chances of us surviving were still dim. But did I want Nata to see us so afraid as she tormented us? No.

"Everything's going to be fine?" Nata asked, an icy tone to her voice. "I knew your kind was stupid, but I didn't realize how much. Calista has been a prisoner now for weeks, ever since she failed to prove her worth during the special training I sent her to at my Elizabeth Elite Guard headquarters. She passed the tests, but she didn't quite convince me that she was on my side. So I gave her another chance to prove her worth."

"By locking her in a cell?"

She went on, ignoring me. "I allowed her to leave her prison cell to come to the pure zone ceremony." Her voice cut off as her eyes hardened. "But she failed that, too."

Suddenly it hit me that I'd known all along. At the pure zone ceremony, I'd suspected something terrible was happening to Calista, and I had been right. Calista was already a prisoner when she'd been at the pure zone initiation ceremony. I'd seen it in my dreams.

"It wasn't exactly her fault that Gallagher Brown freed your prisoners," I interjected.

Nata's head snapped in my direction. "So you know about that, do you? Well, let me introduce you to some of my other special prisoners. Gallagher Brown and the old man won't be able to save them," she said threateningly.

The way she emphasized *the old man* with such loathing made me wonder if there was any hope for a woman who hated her own flesh and blood so much. But before I could think about Niyol any longer, the thought of him fled my mind as a cover like a solid curtain of some sort slowly rose and light came out from under it, revealing an entire row of prison cells lining a wall beside us.

The air all but sucked out of my chest. See-through exteriors enclosed each private cell along the wall, and huge pipes opened into the top of each chamber. I suspected they were gas chambers just like the one I'd been in at the EEG training center, designed to kill the prisoners upon activation. And then I recalled how the First Resistance, including Cole's parents, had been murdered in the basement of Elizabeth Mansion and how Cole had barely escaped. I realized I was looking at the same gas chambers, and the last bit of hope drained from my body. I had the terrifying feeling that she planned to murder each of the prisoners, one by one, in front of Calista and me as she tried to get information out of me. And there were so many people I loved trapped within the cells.

Behind the first wall, Uncle Michael stared back at us with desperation in his eyes. Aunt Alyssa was behind the second, sobbing as she gazed at Calista and beat against the wall. Bhavna and Sook were in the next two cells. Sook was curled up on the floor, holding his ribs as if he'd been beaten.

Bhavna placed a hand against the solid wall separating us. *"I'm so sorry, Rain. I couldn't warn you. A camouflage Droid Dog caught Sook along the edge of camp, and I tried to hide but another one got me. They knocked me out before I could run. I think they must have drugged me or something, and when I woke up Nata was there and she wanted to know if I knew a girl named Rain who was helping Gallagher, and I couldn't lie. She used her ability."*

"It's okay, Bhavna."

"But Rain, I didn't tell her about the others. Somehow, she only knows about you, but I don't know why. She thinks you're helping the old man, who I guess is Niyol, and Gallagher. She said something about Calista having to prove herself one more time and made me contact you once she realized I had the ability. She had a gun to Sook's head, Rain."

"Hold on. It's not over yet."

"I just woke up a minute ago. I guess she drugged me again. But I'm calling out to everyone I can. TFF is coming, Rain. Fight her. No matter what happens to me." Her voice hitched as tears began to fall harder.

"Bhavna, it's not over yet."

"But there's a huge pipe above me, and it smells in here. I think she's going

to poison me with gas. I know you'll survive, Rain. Please tell Nipa and my family I love them."

"*It'll be okay.*" I said it, even though I heard the doubt in my own words. Bhavna curled on her side, visibly shaking as she cried.

And finally, Grandma Julia was behind the next wall, sitting still, somberly looking at Calista and me. She stretched her arm out towards us and smiled. She nodded encouragingly, and then clutched her hands together and bowed her head. I could see her mouth moving and instantly knew what she was doing. It stirred a little of the hope I'd thought I'd lost as I watched her pray.

Nata laughed, sending a chill down my spine. I hadn't forgotten her presence, but I'd been tuning her out as I stared at the prison cells. "No one can save you, fool. There's no god who can help you," she shouted towards the cell.

She shook her head dismissively at Grandma and turned back towards me. "As I was saying . . . I want answers before I get back to work. I've got a country to purify. Let's make this quick, shall we? Then you can join one of the other prisoners for one final reunion. I might even let you choose which one you want to die with."

I tried to clear my thoughts through the drowsiness. I needed to stall her somehow. "And here I thought this was going to be a long and drawn out process," I said evenly.

Anger flashed in her eyes. "Of course, I'd love to play with some of my new toys."

When she turned to the table, I looked desperately towards Calista, noting her growing anxiety and hopelessness. "*Calista, can you hear me?*"

She shifted her head ever so slightly.

"*Say something in your mind back to me, cuz.*"

"*I hear you, Rain. You shouldn't have said that to her. Don't provoke her. She'll make it harder on you whatever she has planned.*"

"*I need to keep her busy so the others can find us.*"

"You really think there's a chance? Have you looked around lately? Notice any concrete walls? Notice there aren't a lot of windows in here?"

"Hang on to that sarcasm. I can work with that. We can get through this. You're doing great."

"How so?"

"Just focus on staying alive for me, will you? I'm going to try to get her talking. If we buy some time, the others can find us."

"You really think they'll make it here in time, and past security? I heard Nata say she replaced her human security patrol around the mansion with Combat Droids."

"Don't worry about the details. Have some faith."

"I love you, Rain. No matter what happens in here."

"I love you back, Calista."

Nata turned from the table, holding one of the burn bars, and fixed her eyes on me. "First things first, how did you meet the old man?"

Chapter 48: Spinning

RAIN

Nata approached me, holding the burn bar forward. The tip of it ignited to a flaming red color as she powered it on, stirring up dreadful memories from when Officer Wolfe had tortured me, but even so, I couldn't decide which was more threatening, her weapon or her eyes.

I was so weak from the drug I could hardly move a muscle, and my thoughts were spinning in confusion. How could I resist her power? The last time I had fought her during an interrogation, I hadn't been drugged and I had barely survived. If I fell under her spell, I might tell her too much information, but if I didn't answer her questions, that would be bad for me too. I wasn't sure what her angle was, but I knew it involved pain.

I couldn't avoid her eyes. She studied me as her hand tightened around the weapon. "I said, how did you meet the old man, mixed breed?"

I felt her numbing ability working over my limbs as I lost control and succumbed to her power. The combination of the drug and her ability was too potent. Her blue eyes gazed into mine as she inched closer. And even though I knew the burn bar was getting nearer to my arm by the second, I didn't flinch or try to move away.

"I met him in a dream," I replied, my voice unusually tranquil.

Suspicion or annoyance, I'm not sure which, flashed in her eyes, and my arm was burning and I screamed out in pain. As my flesh melted under the burn bar, it jarred me, and I struggled as much as I could but my limbs didn't seem to budge. The drug had left me immobile.

She finally took the bar off my skin, and I inhaled deep breaths, desperate to feel relief, but the burning still went on even without the bar touching me. I looked at my open wound and then back at her. "But I answered the question, Nata."

She struck my face and my chair fell backwards. My head slammed against the floor, stunning me as pain radiated throughout my body.

Her shoes appeared beside my face and she bent down, clutching my chin tightly. She twisted my face to look up at her. "I prefer more thorough answers, mixed breed. And while we're on the subject, don't call me that name ever again. That girl is dead. Just like you will be soon. *Very* soon, One-two-seven-six."

She released me and stalked briskly to the table. As I surveyed my injuries, I held on to the pain, wondering if it could help me keep fighting and if it could counteract the drug that was keeping me in a sluggish state.

"I have a name, too, Nata, and it is Rain." I put every ounce of energy into my voice.

Steps slammed against the floor as she came back, and my chair was flung upright and she was staring at my face again. "Did the old man tell you about your ability? Is that how you met him?" My feet filled with the potent numbing sensation as it spread up to my torso.

"Niyol didn't tell me about it. I found him in my dreams. I heard his voice before I had ever seen him. And in my dreams he answered me when I spoke to him."

"Your dreams," Nata whispered. Then a cruel smile flashed across her face. "It's a shame really. For you that is. You have no idea how to control your ability. If you had, you wouldn't be here right now. Not that it matters. I was going to kill your zone tomorrow anyway. I still will. But you'll be dead already."

I shook the numbing sensation away and looked at her feet, desperate to avoid her eyes and her power. If Bhavna was right, and Nata didn't know about my friends, I had to keep it that way for as long as possible.

"What do you mean I can't control my ability? Wait . . ."

A strange thought came over me. I couldn't control my dreams and how my ability worked in them. I'd said it to Jabari a little while ago. I didn't know when or how it worked and how I got into his dreams. And I'd wondered if I'd ever gotten into anyone else's dreams.

Nata's eyes met mine. "You've been coming into my dreams for months," she said slowly.

Fear filled me. How much had I told her in my dreams? She rolled the burn bar between her hands lightly. I knew my eyes were deceiving me, because I was seeing double as she paced in front of me. "At first, I didn't think you were real. You made me relive memories of people I'd done away with already."

I recalled the dreams about Clara and Nata's maternal grandmother hurting a baby, saying to kill it. Then I recalled talking to Nata as a little girl and telling her not to hurt anyone. And then I'd dreamt about Nata leading her mother Clara into oncoming traffic. I'd dreamt of her making a car crash with her adopted parents in it, straight into a tree, killing them instantly. I'd seen her trapped in a shed, being starved and beaten, and I'd tried to help her. And at least a dozen times or so, I'd pleaded with Nata to stop hurting people and to change in my dreams. Had she experienced every one of the dreams with me? Could I reason with her now? And would it buy us more time?

I inhaled air, desperate for clarity, and coughed as I leaned forward against the ropes. "I understand about what happened to your mother, Clara," I murmured.

"I killed that woman," she snapped.

"But Nata, I know why you did it. What they did to you was evil. They should have been arrested and locked up. That's why Niyol saved you from the shed. He would've been there sooner, but he was in prison. Clara's mother had him framed. He didn't know about what was happening to you until he got out, and then he came straight for you."

"He was too late to help me. And they were dealt with accordingly," she said hostilely. "Stop distracting me with the past. I've erased my past. You kept coming back to my dreams, mixed breed, but I assumed you weren't real. I thought I was imagining your voice. When it was time for the pure zone candidates to prove their loyalty, something struck me as odd about Calista's behavior. Sure, she promised to get rid of her mixed breed cousins and her aunt in the mixed zone on the date I'd planned, but I wasn't quite convinced. So I tested her again and let her come out of the prison to attend the pure zone initiation ceremony."

"What more do you want her to do? She relocated to the pure zone and taught your lessons."

She narrowed her eyes at me and went on. "Later, after I realized what Gallagher had done, you kept coming into my dreams trying to stop me from hurting people. But I never asked your name." She paused, eyeing me inquisitively. "And then I pulled Calista out of her cell to interrogate her again, and she accidently said the name Rain. Still, I didn't think anything of it right away. But then, last night, before the tornado hit your zone, you came into my dreams again. And this time, you told me your name when I asked." She smiled. "Of course I realized you were real, and that you were one of the *different* mixed breeds. Though I didn't realize you were related to Calista until later. I just assumed you were somewhere out there helping Gallagher. But I'll get to that part in a minute, mixed breed." Her eyes darkened.

I didn't recall her asking my name in the dream, but I did remember her calling me Rain at one point in the chaotic tornado nightmare I'd had. I couldn't believe it, but I'd actually been communicating with Nata in my dreams.

I fought against the fogginess in my head and the fear and stared back at her bravely. "I have an ability like you, Nata. I'm not *different*. And I'm not a mixed breed. That's what Clara and her mother told you, but they were lies."

"Please, save it. You've been saying that sort of thing in my dreams for months now. But you won't be talking much longer, and I'll sleep in peace again."

My heartbeat picked up as the room continued to spin. She really was planning to kill me, and I was running out of time. "So you decided to bring me here? Why not just kill me back in the zone?"

"I was planning to have Calista initiate the gas attack. I will destroy the mixed zones tomorrow. Why not get one more day of labor out of those walking corpses?"

I shuddered as she continued talking. "Then, I'll move the newest prisoners there to take over the hover plants and Combat Droid operation. Slowly but surely, as the pure race grows, I'll rid the world of impurities and erase their names along with their existence . . . *Rain*."

"But you never explained how you figured out I was related to Calista. And why not just wait and have Calista kill me tomorrow, in the zone with everyone else, Nata?" I asked, attempting to sound strong.

Nata shrugged. "I would have, but imagine my surprise when a Droid patrol picked up more refugees earlier this evening, and I decided to interrogate them so I could find out if they knew anything about Gallagher Brown and if they'd heard of a girl named Rain helping his resistance." She paused, shaking her head. "And sure enough, they knew all about you. And they said your cousin Calista was in the pure zone. I should've figured it out sooner, but oh well. We're all here now. So, why not start the festivities early? Calista can prove her loyalty to me once and for all."

"Why do you want to kill people like me so bad? It's because you're afraid of us. We might take you out of power."

"Even with the old man and Gallagher, no one is strong enough, and more importantly, no one is brave enough to stand up against me. I have the power."

"You mean, you threaten people. You make them afraid. You even drug them. Like you've done to me. But that won't work forever."

"I'm not afraid of him or you or any other impurities like you."

"But you have to know that people with abilities like mine and yours are multiracial. That's why you're getting rid of us. You're afraid."

"I'm not afraid. I'm just doing what is right. I'm cleansing the land. You're too weak. You're an abomination."

She jabbed the burn bar into my other arm this time. As I cried out, she kept talking. "You'll die, weakling. You'll never have existed."

I closed my eyes again and called for help, but all I could do was choke out names. "*Jabari, Daktari, Niyol, Zi . . .*"

Nata's voice brought me back as she removed the bar from my arm. "You know, maybe I can find a purpose for you yet. Before Calista has a final chance to prove her worth. I want you to use your telepathy to bring me Gallagher and the old man. If they care about you at all, it will be their downfall. Bring them to me, One-two-seven-six."

"No," protested, keeping my eyes closed.

She tossed the weapon onto the table and grabbed my hair, yanking my head. "Bring them to me or I'll start killing the prisoners." She turned my head so it was angled towards the cells. Grandma was still on her knees praying, and I was glad she wasn't looking at me right now.

"Why don't we start with the old lady who thinks someone can save her?" she said tauntingly. She released me and strode over to the wall and started to reach for a button above Grandma's cell.

"No! I'll do it." I'll bring them here," I cried out.

Nata turned back to me and crossed the room. "Your weakness is why you'll die tonight. And it's why the old man and Gallagher will die, too."

"What are you going to do when you've killed us all, Nata? You try to hide who you are, you think you can create a pure race to look like you, but you're not like them. You're just like us. And when you finally do kill us, you'll be all alone. Forever."

I knew she'd hit me again, and I braced myself for it. Her hand connected with my face, this time bloodying my nose. It throbbed in pain as I bent forward now, dazed. "Shut up, mixed breed. Now bring them to me before I change my mind about the old lady."

I was too drained to fight her anymore, and the room was revolving. I obeyed and called to Niyol. But as soon as I'd said his name in my mind, beeping rang out from behind Nata. The door slid open, and in the custody of two Combat Droids stood Niyol. He had been captured?

He looked at me and silently replied. "*Hello, Rainchild.*"

"Madam President. The building is under attack," one of the Combat Droids reported.

Nata's face twisted into rage. "What?" Before they could respond, she recovered. "One of you, stay here. One of you, activate the newest arrival of Combat Droids, and release them all at once. Order them to leave no one alive."

Chapter 49: Faith

JABARI

Rain was still alive. I repeated it to myself over and over and tried not to think about the passing of time. She'd been in my head not even ten minutes ago. She had only said my name, but it was enough to reassure me.

She was still alive, and I had to believe the words.

I couldn't think about what Nata was doing or what might've happened in the past ten minutes. Niyol had told me I had to get Gallagher to the media room, where he would launch his message to the world to rally support, and I had to get Cole to the control room so he could shut down all of Nata's Droid technology, once and for all.

I'd argued that I needed to go after Rain first, but Niyol had told me I had no choice; the *only* way our mission would be successful was if I followed his orders. His parting words had been, "You have to trust me, Jabari. And have faith it will work out." And then, he'd turned into the funnel cloud.

I did trust him. He'd helped our entire group of refugee fighters, led by Lieutenant Moretti and Gallagher, onto the property, and then he'd gotten my team, which consisted of Gallagher, Adrianne, Cole, Marcello, Daktari, and Zi, *inside* Elizabeth Mansion, which was no small feat.

Everything had happened so fast. From the moment we'd left Indy Mixed Zone behind in our hover, we'd been in touch with Gallagher. He'd already been en route to another one of his refugee camps. Niyol had tipped him off about Sook, so they had decided to evacuate their waterfall camp. Gallagher had given us coordinates to another camp, and we'd met there and dropped our families off before regrouping with Gallagher and Moretti's team. We had also contacted William, who had been desperately searching for Bhavna and Sook, and their camp had decided to evacuate as well. Part of me wondered why Niyol hadn't warned William that Sook and Bhavna were in danger, but part of me wondered if Niyol had even known. His abilities were mysterious, to say the least, but could he be expected to be everywhere and know everything?

As soon as we'd landed at the camp, Gallagher's team was ready to go. He said it was time to go after Nata. Not only did he want to get Rain back, he was worried Nata might interrogate Rain and discover everything. He didn't want any more bombs to fall on No Man's Land, and he'd said it was time to take back our country. Refugees across No Man's Land were in hiding, as Combat Droids continued their hunt for Gallagher, but at least for the time being, the bombing had stopped.

It had taken us forty minutes, from the time we'd left Indy Mixed Zone, to get to Elizabeth Mansion. We'd also stopped to pick Blakely up along the way, and William had looked me dead in the eye and made me swear we'd bring Bhavna and Sook back alive. He had too many people he needed to get safely to other hidden camps, so he'd had to stay behind. Sending Blakely with us had been an easy decision. He knew we needed him to get his daughter back. We'd taken off in three hovers all together, and though we had a lot of soldiers, we'd need every one of them.

But so far it seemed Niyol was the key to our attack. We'd worked together, but we never would have gotten inside Elizabeth Mansion, undetected, if it hadn't been for Niyol.

He'd created an enormous storm with his ability. He'd swept across the exterior security gates in the form of a gigantic funnel cloud and stirred up the winds to a ferocious speed, knocking the Combat Droids patrolling the property to the ground. Meanwhile, Jonah cut the power running along the security gates, and in the midst of the confusion, we'd breached the property. Moretti and his team snuck in and staged themselves, prepared to launch their attack. Blakely had proceeded to cover them with his image, and my team had continued on under Zi's image. We followed Niyol's funnel cloud as he'd instructed us, and while he knocked more Combat Droids into the wind, we'd snuck in the side entrance where they'd been stationed. Niyol assured us the Combat Droids would attribute the security alarm going off to the storm, and that Nata was below ground in secure chambers, where she wouldn't even know about the mysterious storm, and somehow, it had worked.

As I traveled now under Zi's image across the first floor of Elizabeth Mansion, I tried to block the gunfire and explosions out as they assaulted the walls. So many people, including Rain's cousin, Victoria, and Jonah were out there fighting. I imagined Jonah bravely disabling one Combat Droid at a time, while Moretti fought beside him. Shortly after we'd gotten inside, Moretti had launched the attack. The idea was that if Moretti could keep the Combat Droids distracted and draw them all outside, my team could more easily get Gallagher and Cole where they needed to be. We didn't want Jonah to cut the power to the building because Gallagher and Cole needed it functioning in order to complete their tasks, so Moretti had decided to shoot out windows and doors at the onslaught of his attack, so all of the security alarms would be tripped at the same time. And in the midst of the chaos, a small group of us huddled under Zi's image and traveled towards the media room.

I knew more Combat Droids had been released once the attack had begun because Gallagher's earpiece kept him in contact with Moretti, but I focused on getting Gallagher to the media room. Yet, my mind kept returning to Rain. Niyol had said he would stall Nata's plans some-how, until we were able to get to the basement room where she was holding Rain. And while I trusted him and I truly believed Rain was still alive, my faith was being severely tested at the moment. Why hadn't I told Niyol no and insisted to go straight to the room Nata had Rain in? Faith, he'd said. I wasn't sure it was worth the risk. Before we'd arrived in New Washington, Niyol had surveyed the digital maps of the mansion Landon had sent us, and he'd confirmed the location of the media room, the control room, and finally the underground torture chamber we'd heard about. We all knew how Cole's parents, along with the other members of the First Resistance, had been poisoned to death in the gas chambers in that room. I wanted to run straight to it and rescue Rain, but I didn't. I focused on Niyol's orders.

As we turned down yet another white hallway, following the directions Landon had given us, I wanted to scream. For a building I'd seen my whole life through photographs, The White House looked nothing like it had before, now that Nata had transformed it into Elizabeth Mansion. She had renovated the interior and exterior to resemble a military base, and like the pure zone buildings not too far from here, the interior was completely devoid of color, everything white down to the last detail.

Finally I spotted the media room door just ahead, and I picked up the pace. "Come on, guys, we're almost there," I urged them on.

I led them through the doorway into a room full of desks and wondered if this was one of the places Calista had worked before being reassigned to the pure zone. If Landon's intel was correct, Nata's private media room office, where she launched her videos across UZTA, would be right off of the room.

I gestured at the huge white door once I got to it, and Gallagher prepared his gun, just in case anything was waiting on the other side. I used my ability and snapped the doorknob off, and we rushed in with Gallagher in front. A quick survey revealed the room was empty, and the recording equipment was indeed in the office.

Gallagher looked at his daughter. "Ready?"

"Yes, I am." Adrianne glanced at us, her eyes lingering on Cole. "Be careful, guys. I'll see you when this is all over with."

Gallagher patted my shoulder. "We can do this. Be safe." He held up his Pinkie device. "As soon as you give me the signal to record, I'll start talking."

Cole nodded, adjusting the camera so Gallagher was sitting in the right spot. "All you have to do is hit this button, Adrianne. When I give the signal, that is. And we'll be broadcasting to all of the zones. Once you go live, Landon and his team will stream the video to as many countries as he can outside of the UZTA." He hugged Adrianne. "See you soon."

Seeing Gallagher in the chair, prepared to rally the support of the world and every person across the zones, gave me courage. Adrianne waved goodbye and then placed her hands around her dad, where he was poised behind the cameras waiting for our signal, and they disappeared from our sight. Until Cole had deactivated the Combat Droids, Adrianne planned to hide her dad beneath her image so no one might spot them. We quickly exited the room under Zi's image and started towards the control room.

We hardly spoke, but paused every so often to make sure we were following Landon's instructions to the control room, which was two levels below us. We were about to take the door into the stairwell when something exploded beside us and glass from the window shattered in front of me.

I spun around as Zi's image disappeared, and my stomach dropped. Zi had been hit with something and was on the ground, holding her shoulder. Blood was oozing from her wound, and she screamed from the pain.

"Zi, no!" Daktari yelled, even as he fell to the floor beside her.

"A stray bullet hit her from the window," Cole exclaimed.

Daktari grabbed her, shouting for us to back him up with our hands to heal her faster.

I was about to drop with Marcello and Cole as they fell to their knees to help Daktari, when I sensed something, and the hair on my neck stood on end. I wondered if it was Rain, but then I turned, sure there was danger approaching our small group.

As I turned around, my eyes landed on a Combat Droid, and time seemed to slow. As it lifted its weapon towards us to fire, adrenaline sped through my veins, and I dove straight for it. The sounds of the attack outside and my friends just a few feet from me faded away. The only thing I could hear was my heart slamming against my chest as I landed on top of the Droid and smashed it against the floor.

It couldn't get up or we were all dead.

My muscles flexed as I summoned more strength, and before I knew what I was really doing I was ripping the Droid apart, piece by piece. I had to deactivate it before it killed us. I lost myself in my mission, until I finally got to the control on its back and smashed it with my hands. As the red light illuminating its power faded away, I released a heavy sigh. After a couple more deep breaths, I looked up to see everyone staring at me in shock.

Zi offered me her hand. "Um, wow. And thank you for saving our lives, Jabari."

"How is your shoulder?"

Her eyes were still huge. "My shoulder? It's fine."

Daktari shook his head as I stood up. "Jabari, you are *really* strong now," he remarked, his voice in awe.

Marcello patted my back. "Yeah, hombre. That was insane."

"Come on," I beckoned them. "We're almost there. And I need to get to Rain."

As we sped along the hall and down the steps to the lower level, Zi eyed me anxiously, even as she held the image over us. "Rain's strong. She's a survivor. We'll make it, Jabari. I know you wanted to go with Niyol, but he was right. We needed you here. If you hadn't been there a minute ago . . . Well, I know Daktari healed me, but we *never* would've made it past that Combat Droid."

"I'll still feel better about this when I can see Rain with my own eyes. I'm worried she's running out of time."

"No time for worrying," Cole said, pointing ahead excitedly. "We found the control room. Let's shut down the Droids and get Gallagher Brown's face out to the world."

I pushed into the control room, relieved to see it was empty, and watched as Cole got straight to work, typing across the computer keys at an unbelievable speed.

"Message Gallagher. It's time," he said after a minute. A huge grin spread across his face. "Droid Dogs, Combat Droids, O3 Droids, Camouflage Droids, Droid weaponry on the walls, everything Tricky Nicky ever created to attack or police us is officially going down in five . . . four . . . three . . . two . . ."

As Cole counted down, my thoughts went back to Rain. How much time did she have?

Chapter 50: Security Breach

RAIN

"Tie him up over there," Nata shrieked at the remaining Combat Droid.

It obeyed and quickly set up a chair beside mine, securing Niyol to it. Once he was in place, it posted itself beside Nata.

"*What are you doing, Niyol? Can't you use your funnel ability to fight her?*" I asked him silently.

"*The Combat Droid would fire at you and Calista. I'm doing what I need to do,*" he answered me vaguely.

"You must have known *he* was coming here." She glared at Niyol. Even as my head continued to spin from the potent drug, I could sense her sudden increase in rage, and it terrified me. Seeing Niyol in person was clearly making her lose control. I wished I knew what he'd been thinking when he had turned himself in, but it didn't seem as though he was going to explain it to me.

Nata picked up her burn bar again and turned to me. But Calista began moaning loudly and wiggling so violently in her chair, Nata finally acknowledged her.

She pulled the gag from her mouth, and Calista started shouting, "Let them go, Madame President. Hurt me instead," she begged, and tears rolled down her cheeks.

"You know, I don't think I'm going to give you another chance to prove yourself to me. If you can't understand that mixed breeds are an abomination and don't deserve to live, than you're no use to me. Droid, put this one in that gas chamber," she commanded as she pointed to a cell.

"No," I shouted. Even through the haziness overwhelming me, I could still see the scowl on Nata's face as she shook her head at me. The Combat Droid picked up Calista, the chair and all, and carried her to the gas chamber where Sook was crumpled in the corner.

The Droid pressed one of the buttons above the chamber and the see-through wall ascended. Sook didn't even stir as the Droid set Calista inside and exited again, closing the wall behind once more.

Nata spun the burn bar around, taking another step in my direction. "As I was saying . . . You haven't brought me Gallagher yet. Is he the one attacking my mansion?"

She looked at Niyol, and he shook his head. "It's not Gallagher out there," he said.

Nata shrugged. "Even if it's him, my Droids will kill him. No one can defeat them. But let's assume he's not out there. I know you can find him. I heard you were helping him. So bring him to me, mixed breed, so I can end this so-called Freedom Front once and for all. I'll make an example out of him to warn the others. No one will dare to defy me when I get done with him. I'll cleanse this land and purify the United Zones of The Authority. Bring him to me, One-two-seven-six, or I'll make sure the old lady and Calista have a slow and *agonizing* death. You can't beat me. Now get me Gallagher Brown." She pointed the burn bar at me as she yelled.

"I'm trying," I lied.

"Try harder." She pressed the burn bar against my thigh, and it scorched through my pants, melting my skin.

Over my screams, I heard Niyol's voice. "Nata, no! She's just a girl."

She pulled the bar back and I leaned forward trying to breathe through the searing pain still radiating throughout my leg. The room seemed to shift back and forth around me, jumbling my thoughts even more.

"Just a girl? You mean like I was?"

I forced my head up cautiously. There was a lethal tone to her words that magnified my fear for Niyol. What if she killed him?

"I tried to save you. I'm sorry for what they did to you," he said sorrowfully.

"I'm not sorry. I grew stronger. I know what I need to do now. I am not weak." She practically spat the words, like she was accusing Niyol of being weak.

When Niyol didn't defend himself, heat flushed my face. "Only a weak person would attack innocent, defenseless people, Nata," I managed to say between clenched teeth.

She grabbed my hair and bent over my face. "Concentrate on bringing Gallagher to me, mixed breed."

She held on to my hair and tears sprang to my eyes from the pain, but I made myself speak. "Underneath your fake appearance, you're just like me."

"I'm nothing like you. You're an abomination. You never should have been created. You were a mistake." She spoke smoothly and emotionlessly, as though reciting memorized lines that had been drilled into her mind over and over.

My heart ached for the child she had been. I knew they'd made her believe every one of those heinous words.

"I know they told you that," I said with a whimper.

I closed my eyes as the pain became excruciating. "*But it's not true. You were just a beautiful, innocent little girl, and they made you the way you are. But it's not too late, Nata. You can change. You can be free from this anguish.*" I said it into her mind, desperate to calm her down.

"*There's no freedom from what they did.*" She replied calmly in my mind, and her grip on my head lightened just a fraction. I wondered if she was considering my words.

"*There is freedom. You just have to believe. You are loved and you were created for a reason, Nata.*"

She stood up abruptly, releasing me, and I could see that I had lost her. "Don't talk to me about my creation. There's no such thing as God.

There's no such thing as love. Those are imaginary things weak people like you invent to comfort themselves. But I don't need comforting. I'm stronger than the rest of you."

I was drained, and feeling weaker by the minute, but I summoned courage from deep inside. "You're like us."

"I'll never be like you. Your kind will die off. One way or another, I'll see to it."

As her eyes focused on mine now I could see that she meant every word. She wasn't going to change her mind about us. Niyol had turned himself in, and I had assumed it was to distract Nata while TFF got Cole to the control room, as we'd originally planned before I'd been taken, but where were they? And was Niyol going to help me? Jabari was nowhere in sight. I needed to fight through the power of the drug and try to focus on survival.

"Even if I get Gallagher Brown here, he will stop you," I said confidently, hoping to keep her distracted before she hurt anyone again as I desperately tried to come up with a plan.

"You really believe that he has a chance to defeat me?" she asked, her numbing working its way over my body so I had to tell the truth.

"Yes," I said easily.

"How? He's one man with a small military force. He doesn't stand a chance against my Combat Droids. Even if he's outside right now, my Droids will defeat him. If he'd tried to rescue those prisoners at the pure zone a moment later, the Droids would've stopped him. He escaped before I had even released them. And do you think because he found one mixed kid with an ability to do telepathy he can win? You'll be dead before long anyway. What makes you think he can defeat my Combat Droids?" she asked, a sudden curiosity in her expression.

The numbing was trickling through my body and I had to answer truthfully. "My friends are out there, helping him, too. And like me, they're gifted."

Nata's features darkened. "Where are your friends?"

Niyol spoke up. "You didn't think Gallagher Brown was behind The Freedom Front all by himself, did you, Nata? Even you have known since you were a child that there were others like you. You knew about me . . . And I've only ever grown stronger. Like Rain's friends. You could've become stronger, too. If only you'd use your abilities to do good. It's not too late for you, Nata," he finished.

She strode to him and grabbed his chin, gazing into his eyes. "I am powerful enough. Now tell me, who is behind The Freedom Front? And who is helping Gallagher Brown?"

"Don't you remember? Your ability doesn't work on me. It never has."

Nata slapped her father and shrieked. "Why didn't I kill you years ago? Today, that changes," she vowed. "You should have stayed in hiding, old man. You've never been of any use to me. Combat Droid, put him in one of the chambers."

As the Combat Droid began to move Niyol, Nata placed a hand on either side of my face and pressed hard. "Look at me and tell me . . . Who is behind The Freedom Front? And where is Gallagher Brown?"

A ringing noise erupted from the Combat Droid and it crashed to the floor. As Nata released my face, Niyol spiraled towards the door, disappearing in a funnel. "*Someone needs my help. Finish it, Rainchild,*" he spoke into my mind as he broke through the door, leaving it lying on the floor in his wake.

The Combat Droid was motionless at Nata's feet, and she drove her foot into its side. "Get up!"

I stared at the Droid, and hope filled my chest. Cole must have shut the Droids down from the control room. A TV monitor I hadn't noticed before illuminated on the wall, and a voice I knew called our attention.

"Hello citizens of the UZTA. I'm Gallagher Brown. The time has come to take back our country. Tonight we'll end Elizabeth Nicks's reign of terror. Maybe you're not fully aware of her terror. But as the screen changes now, you can see footage from the twenty mixed zones across the UZTA. As you can see, people have been beaten, starved, worked to death, and suffering under this regime. All of the zones have suffered, not just the mixed zones. And pure zones have been developed as Nicks tries to create a human race that pleases her. But we won't sit back any longer. The Freedom Front has penetrated Elizabeth Mansion and deactivated *all* of the Droids across the UZTA."

My bleary eyes shifted from the screen to Nata's face as it blanched. His words were terrifying her.

"Now is our chance. Join me, to fight. Help us remove the control buttons on the back of each Droid to make sure that no one, Nicks or any other person, can ever reactivate them. Secure any resistors who are still fighting for her. Band together. Free your prisons. The Freedom Front will be working in the days ahead to bring peace to the country. We'll tear down the walls that divide us. We can do this, one step at a time. We can't undo what she has already done, we can't bring back the lives of so many she has killed, but hear this . . . Today, Elizabeth Nicks is finished. She can't hurt us anymore." The camera faded into scenes of torture and abuse I was all too familiar with, and I prayed it would have its intended effect and rally the support of people everywhere.

As the images moved, Nata's face contorted and turned bright red. "He'll pay for this." She picked something up from the table and pressed a button screaming into the microphone. "Combat Droids, send a unit to my media office now and secure Gallagher Brown."

Evidently, she really couldn't believe that her security could be breached. Or maybe she was just so self-assured of her power, she was simply in denial. She waited for a response, but nothing happened. After a moment, she fixed her eyes on me. "What is happening?"

I was still dizzy, and I was afraid, but I held on to the hope Gallagher had just given me. "The Freedom Front deactivated the Droids," I whispered.

She stood up a little taller and picked something up off the table. I figured it was a taser, but wasn't quite sure. "The old man left you," she said grimly. "But before I kill you, you'll tell me who shut down the Droids and you'll watch the rest of those numbers die."

Satisfaction crept over her expression as she pointed at the gas chambers. My eyes shifted from the weapon in her palm to the chambers. As I was staring at my friends, each confined to a cell, her hand came out of nowhere, and hard metal slammed into my mouth. My chair tilted backwards, and my face hit the floor. Nausea rolled through me, and blood poured from my mouth.

I closed my eyes, "*Jabari, she drugged me and I can't fight her. Where are you?*"

"*We're here, Rain.*"

I pried my heavy lids open, and across the floor, just inside the door, I saw a set of feet. There he stood. As he spotted me, his mouth fell open.

Somewhere in the room, an alarm sounded. "Commence extermination" blared through speakers. Nata had activated the gas chambers.

Chapter 51: Shatter

RAIN

"Rain!"

He called to me, and I fought off the vertigo. In the background, I heard harrowing screams from the gas chambers as the poison engulfed them. My chair tilted and I was set upright again. Jabari started for my bindings, his face frantic.

"Breakdown the walls first or they'll die, Jabari," I shouted at him, and I had no idea where the energy was coming from. I could taste the blood in my mouth, my arms and leg were burning, my head was throbbing, and the room felt as though it were whirling back and forth, but I just knew he needed to free everyone first, before the toxic gas killed them.

With a reluctant glance, he pivoted away and vaulted towards the first wall he reached, instantly shattering glass across the floor.

As he ran inside after Grandma Julia, my eyes settled on my friends who had surrounded Nata in the corner. Marcello stood in front, with Daktari, Zi, and Cole on his toes, and I understood what they were attempting. They'd hold on to Marcello to make him stronger as he used his ability. Marcello lunged for her, and my chest rose as I held my breath. If he could knock her out, this would all be over.

She dodged to the side, twisting away, and before any of them could stop her, she had a knife to Zi's throat. "Back away from me or she's dead."

Marcello halted, and Daktari and Cole froze on either side of him.

"Who shut down my Droids?" Nata asked, staring at Daktari.

"Cole," Dakatari said automatically, and I knew she was working her power on him.

"Who is Cole?" she demanded, searching their eyes.

My head fell forward as the dizziness overcame me. "*Don't look her in the eyes*," I called to Daktari silently.

"I am," Cole responded to her in a calm voice.

"*Don't look her in the eyes*," I said to Cole.

I urged my head up again as Jabari jumped out of the smoky chamber, setting Grandma Julia down somewhere behind me. He started towards Nata, but Aunt Alyssa appeared the next moment, hitting the chamber wall desperately as she screamed for help.

"*Get her out of there, Jabari*," I begged him.

As he threw his body against the next chamber wall, and it broke into a million pieces, Nata's eyes widened, but she held the knife firmly to Zi.

Marcello edged closer. "Stay back. Sit down on the ground," she commanded.

Instantly he fell down.

Jabari emerged with Aunt Alyssa in his arms and set her down beside Grandma. With a fleeting glance at the gas chambers still full of prisoners pleading for their lives, he stepped closer to Nata. "Let her go," he ordered, his voice low.

Could his ability work on her? My chest tightened as he stepped towards Nata, continuing to talk to her. "Let her go," he repeated.

She released Zi, and a blank stare washed over her face. His ability was really working. He took another step towards her. "Now, on the ground," he said calmly.

I felt more hope rise.

Nata sat down, and I sighed, the desire to fight slipping away as I imagined our victory. Despite Niyol's warnings in my dreams, Jabari would save us.

"How do you shut the gas chambers off?" Jabari asked her.

"They can't shut off once you activate them. They shut down after everyone is dead," she said, peacefully.

Fear returned full on, and I recalled the chamber from the EEG headquarters. It, too, was programmed to release all of the gas before it could be shut down. Calista, Sook, Bhavna, and Uncle Michael were still trapped inside the gas chambers. "Get them out, Jabari." Even as I shouted, a hand rapped against the wall. Jabari tilted towards the sound instinctively.

Bhavna screamed, her face pressed to the wall. "Help me!"

Nata jumped up and grabbed Cole, "You're coming with me," she said, and wasting no time, focused on Marcello, Zi, and Daktari. "Stay back."

As Jabari turned back towards Nata, torn between going after the prisoners trapped inside the chamber and helping Cole, Gallagher stormed into the room aiming a gun at Nata's head. I was relieved that Adrianne wasn't with him. Nata couldn't use Adrianne against him. But I realized she wouldn't give up control so easily.

Though Gallagher's gun was trained on her, she didn't even flinch. I strained my eyes through the wooziness, noting her grip around Cole's neck tighten. "Come any closer, *Gallagher Brown*, and I'll kill him."

Bhavna's hand beat against the wall again, and I couldn't take it. "*Jabari, save them*," I called again. And he lunged at the chamber wall containing Bhavna, breaking through it.

"*Keep going. Get them all*," I called to him. They were running out of time. One by one, Jabari smashed the walls down and raced in and out of each chamber. While Nata held her knife to Cole's throat across the room, Gallagher took another step towards her.

"Stay back," she ordered. She pulled Cole to the table and retrieved another weapon.

"Don't look her in the eye, Gallagher," Zi cried out.

I turned back towards Jabari. I'd sent him in to save my loved ones, but he was the only one who could stop Nata. He set Sook on the floor nearby and jumped back into the chamber. Calista was the last one in there. He'd gotten everyone else out, and they were all coughing where he'd dropped them on the floor. But at least they were breathing, and the remaining gas was tapering out through the holes I could barely see, which Jabari had apparently punched out in the opposite walls of each chamber he had entered.

My weary head bobbed here and there, as I searched, praying to see Jabari leap through the gas with Calista in his arms.

Gallagher shook his head at Nata. "The entire building is under my control. *All* of your Droids are down. You have no power. It's over. As we speak, my people are removing the Droid power chips just to be sure you can't activate them again. And they are talking with allies outside of the country. More help is on the way. It's really over, Nata. Put the knife down and let him go."

She shook her head and a cruel smile lit up her expression. "I always have power." Before I could warn him she was using her ability again, she ordered him to obey her. "Aim your weapon at *Rain*."

Gallagher tilted the gun towards me automatically. She had used my name instead of my number so he would obey, and it had worked. Jabari jumped from the floor where he'd just set Calista and stepped between Gallagher and me. "No, Gall—"

Jabari's body spasmed violently. With horrified eyes I watched him fall, and saw the taser in Nata's outstretched hand.

"Jabari," I moaned.

Nata turned to Zi and Marcello. "Sit down." And they obeyed.

Nata shifted to Marcello. "Pick him up," she commanded. As Marcello moved for Jabari, she turned back to Gallagher. "Keep the gun aimed at Rain."

Gallagher's face remained blank, and his hand remained stretched towards me.

"*Don't listen to her, Gallagher*," I pleaded with him, but he couldn't hear me. His eyes were emotionless.

Nata yanked Cole backwards, keeping the blade pressed against his neck as she reached towards another button on the wall behind her. The wall ascended, revealing an even larger gas chamber. "Everyone inside the chamber, or I'll have Gallagher shoot Rain."

Marcello held Jabari over his shoulder, but his eyes began to clear, and I knew he was fighting off Nata's power. Daktari's and Zi's faces shifted to doubt, as well, and I could see they, too, were fighting against it, but they were struggling.

I summoned all of my strength. "Don't listen to her," I yelled.

"Get into the chamber now," she ordered Zi. "And you two take all of them into it also," she instructed them, gesturing towards the small group of prisoners Jabari had freed.

She shifted to Gallagher again. "Press the gun to Rain's temple," she ordered.

I felt the metal press against my head, and I called to him. *"Gallagher, fight Nata off. Don't listen to her."*

But the gun remained on my head. In my peripheral vision, I noted the prisoners, most choking still, too weak to fight back, as Marcello and Daktari numbly obeyed Nata's orders and transferred them into the new gas chamber.

"Niyol where are you?"

But he didn't respond, and then his words came back to me. For months in my dreams he'd said to *finish it*. I had the sinking feeling it meant that he wasn't going to save me this time. It was up to me to get us all out of here. But how? My head was splitting, my whole body ached, and the room around me was whirling.

Once everyone was in the chamber, Nata placed a hand on Gallagher, peering into his eyes. "Put the gun on the table."

Not only had she used her mind control on my friends, she'd played on their fears and made them think she was going to have Gallagher shoot me just to get them into the chamber. And she'd knocked Jabari unconscious because she knew he was able to fight her with his own ability. But even I knew she wouldn't have Gallagher shoot me. That would be way too easy of a death for her to give me.

"Don't do it," I yelled. "Keep the gun, Gallagher, aim it at Nata."

"Don't do it, Gallagher," Cole managed to say.

Nata pressed the blade into his neck, cutting it slightly, and Cole quit struggling.

Gallagher glided to the table and set the gun down. Nata smirked. "I knew I'd capture you eventually, Gallagher. Where's *The Freedom Front* now? Walk into the chamber."

I cried out loud to them all. "Snap out of it. Fight her. Get out of the chamber!" But like so many who had died because of her ability, my friends might, too.

She focused on them all again, keeping her hand and weapon firm against Cole's throat. "Stay right where you are," she spoke to the entire chamber.

She lifted a hand to press the button, and as the see-through exterior closed, I called out desperately to my spellbound friends. "Fight back!"

Chapter 52: Number 1276

RAIN

Gas began to pour into the chamber, and my pulse shot out of control. Nata tugged Cole towards the door, and I fell forward, focusing on my ability. *"Wake up, Jabari. You can break the wall."*

He didn't respond, and I tried over and over. *"Wake up, Jabari."*

I called to all of them. *"Marcello, snap out of it! Wake Jabari up!"* But still there was no response, and their forms were fading away in the hazy chamber.

How did Niyol expect me to finish anything? No one was responding to my telepathy, and I was nearly paralyzed in the chair, so I couldn't run. There wasn't a rat or spider problem in the basement of Elizabeth Mansion, or wildlife for that matter, so I couldn't call out for animals to come to my aid. What could I do?

I sat back up and screamed aloud. "Wake up, Jabari! She's going to reactivate the Droids!"

Nata's retreating form paused in the door. "Yes, I am. Cole is going to reactivate them for me, but I almost forgot . . . I have a parting gift for you, One-two-seven-six."

She hastened to the wall, just beside the gas chamber containing my loved ones, and pressed a clear button. The white paneling slid up, revealing a cage I never would've known was there, and slowly a very malnourished and terrifying German shepherd stepped out. He looked like he had been beaten and tormented and trained to fight or tear things apart. He focused on me now, growling and baring his teeth.

"Dog, stay," Nata ordered.

Everything Niyol had said now made sense. All of my friends were incapacitated, and I was tied up. Nata was about to charge off and reactivate the Droids. But I could stop her. Even though I couldn't move my limbs. Even from this chair. She had no clue about my ability to control animals.

She shrugged as she held the knife to Cole. "Dog hasn't eaten for a while. I'm sure you won't mind the company. He's one of my more entertaining methods of interrogating. Sometimes I get bored."

He began to foam at the mouth, growling louder from where he stood awaiting Nata's next command. She went on. "I was going to let you watch the others die before I got rid of you, but really, I have a country to run. Once my Droids are working again, and let's be clear, no one will stand in my way of reaching the control room from here, and I have plenty more Droids that Gallagher doesn't know about. And even if they were to stop me, they couldn't resist my power. No one can. Shortly, this whole thing will be like a bad dream." She paused, grinning. "Oh, I guess you won't be having those anymore. And I won't be dealing with your obsessive dialogue. Pity. Some of my memories I didn't mind reliving."

Now was my chance, and I called to the German shepherd. "*Don't kill anyone when she tells you to. Grab Nata by the throat, hold her down, and don't let her go.*"

She turned to the poor animal beside her and spoke a single word. "Kill."

Before Nata could understand what was happening, the animal lunged for her. Cole knocked her arms away and ducked as the German shepherd dove over his head, straight for Nata's throat. She fell to the floor, and he held her down, obeying my commands.

Cole ran to the gas chamber and beat against it. "Wake Jabari up!"

I saw motion from within, but wasn't sure who it was through the smoke. And I wasn't sure how much time they had left.

I tried one more desperate plea to Jabari. *"Wake up, Jabari, open the chamber door or you'll all die!"*

"Rain?" he answered me, and my spirits soared.

"Yes, open the door, now, lift it up from the bottom. Use your strength. Now!"

The door slowly began to rise, and I held my breath as Jabari came into my line of sight. He lifted the wall all the way up, and as his eyes met mine, Daktari, Zi, and Marcello staggered out around him, each of them leading someone with them. Cole rushed to their aid. One by one they emerged, most of them still dazed, all of them coughing, some of them worse than others. A few people had already lost consciousness, and Daktari rushed to the most critical cases to heal them first.

They hovered far away from Nata, staring at her with horrified eyes even though the German shepherd wasn't letting her move a muscle. Gallagher rubbed his eyes and started towards Nata, then halted.

Jabari came out next, quickly surveyed Nata pinned down by the German shepherd, and looked at me knowingly. He placed a hand on Gallagher's shoulder. "Everyone stay away from her," he said, glancing around the room.

He ran over to me, kneeling to rip my binds away. I collapsed against him as they came off, wincing from the pain, my limbs still heavy.

"Daktari," he said roughly.

"No, wait," I murmured.

Concern etched across his face. "She tortured you," he whispered. "Daktari needs to heal you."

"I know. But first, I have to finish it," I said, gesturing towards Nata.

"You've been through too much. I'll do it, Rain," he said assuredly.

"No. I have to do this."

As understanding came into Jabari's eyes, I called to the German shepherd, who still had Nata helplessly pinned by the throat. *"Keep holding her down,"* I spoke to him silently.

"Turn me around to face her, Jabari. Hold me steady."

With gentle hands, he picked me up. My legs buckled, but he didn't let me fall. He turned me to face Nata and held me firmly against him, making sure I was steady. Gallagher, Daktari, Zi, Marcello, and Cole circled around us, as I faced the German shepherd. I was sure Grandma, Calista, Bhavna, and everyone else were watching from a few feet away, and I wanted to keep it that way. Any one of us could fall victim to Nata's powerful eyes if she were to look at us, and the further away they stayed, the safer I felt.

"Keep your distance from her, and no one look at her," I warned them.

Those gathered around me nodded their heads, and I focused on the German shepherd. His growl was low as he kept his mouth clamped over Nata's throat. With one command I could order him to kill her, and this would all be over with. But I couldn't. I knew what I had to do.

Jabari's grip on my arms tightened as I swayed, and I closed my eyes. "I need you to grab her by the foot and drag her into the chamber as fast as you can."

I could feel the tension behind me as soon as I'd spoken the commands. I'd said it aloud so they would know what I was doing. The German shepherd obeyed right away, and as soon as he released Nata's throat, he sank his teeth around her ankle and pulled her directly into the gas chamber.

She started screaming at us. "No-good mixed breeds. I'll kill you all!"

I reached for Daktari. "Hold me up while Jabari closes the chamber door." I glanced at Jabari. "Close it as soon as I get the German shepherd out, and do not look at her."

He nodded as I leaned in to Daktari, and he stepped away. He perched beside the door, ready to pull it down, and I called to the German shepherd.

"Leave her behind and run out to me," I commanded.

The German shepherd trotted to my side, and as Nata jumped to her feet, Jabari slammed the gas chamber wall closed in front of her.

Her hands rapped against the see-through wall. "You'll all die for this!"

I looked at the German shepherd. "Curl up against the wall. We'll take good care of you, soon."

As he curled up to lie down against the wall, Jabari turned back to me, holding up his hand for me to join him. "Help me, Daktari," I whispered.

He carried me to the wall beside Jabari, and everyone followed. As Jabari held me up, I eyed the button above the chamber that would activate the gas. "Don't look at her," I reminded them.

Nata tapped her hand against the wall, directly in front of my face. "You can't win, mixed breed. You're going to die today."

I still feared her words, even though I knew she was on the other side of the wall. My friends reached their arms towards Jabari and me, so we were all connected, unified in what I was about to do.

Niyol had said for months that it had to be me. I'd never know how his premonitions and abilities worked, but sure enough, they had. I was key to finishing the fight against Nata, he'd said. And though now I understood that he had meant I would have to use my ability to control animals after all of my friends had fallen to Nata's power, part of me understood that it was more than that. Maybe because of the way I had unknowingly communicated with Nata all this time, I was linked to her downfall in a way even I couldn't understand or explain. And as I stared at the button, her screams in the background, belittling my friends and me, I knew I was the one. I couldn't let her walk out of here. She'd proven today that she didn't want to let us live in peace. She'd always hunt us and try to hurt people like me. It was me and had always been me who had to kill Nata. Niyol had been right all along.

I had to push the button and finish it.

"You're a worthless abomination. You're useless," she spat.

I didn't look at her; I knew she might use her spell on me. I lifted my weary arm up and was inches from the button when she beat the glass in front of me again.

"Please don't look at her, Rain," Zi said from behind.

I told myself not to look, but Nata's face was now right in front of mine and she was calling to me. "Rain, please, Rain, you can't do this. You're not a killer, are you? Just look at me, Rain," she said pleadingly.

My eyes roamed to hers and for a moment I saw the little Nata, the one I'd seen in my dreams, so innocent and afraid.

My hand fell to my side, and as I hesitated, her eyes darkened. "Open this door you filthy mixed breed. You can't kill me. You're just a number, One-two-seven-six. You're too weak."

A tingling sensation started in my feet and worked its way up through my body. Her words ran through my mind, telling me to open the door, but somehow I could hear Niyol's words louder than hers, telling me to finish it. Now I was stronger than her ability. Maybe it was because everyone was linked to me, maybe it was because Niyol was somehow helping me, but I felt stronger than I'd ever been. I fought against the tingling, and it faded away.

I raised my hand again, just beside the button. "I'm not weak. I'm strong enough to do what has to be done. May you find peace, Nata."

Her eyes filled with terror as I raised my arm and pressed the button. "Commence extermination" rang across the room, and toxic gas began pouring in.

Hands stroked my back and arms, "Don't watch, Rain. Just don't look," Jabari urged.

I shook my head. "I have to."

Nata sank to her knees, her eyes focused on mine. "You're a no good abomination!" she shrieked.

And then the fumes enveloped her and she disappeared.

I didn't budge. My eyes searched the foggy gas-filled chamber as everyone gathered in closer. "Heal her, Daktari," I heard Jabari instruct, and I didn't protest. Daktari placed his hands on my back and my throat, and I closed my eyes. Warmth spread throughout my beaten and drugged body, and all of my pain faded away. It happened so quickly, all of my injuries from the burn marks to my bleeding mouth healed. I knew without looking that everyone had linked themselves to Daktari as he healed me. Like Takara had always told us, they'd worked together.

Once I was healed, I still didn't move. I stared into the gas-filled chamber and I waited. As I leaned against the wall, the group remained close, as though they were afraid to leave me on my own. As the gas kept pouring into the chamber, I heard some of them weeping. I imagined they cried tears of sadness for all we'd been through and tears of relief for the end of Elizabeth Nicks's reign of terror. I wanted to cry, too.

But no matter how I tried, the tears wouldn't fall.

Maybe I was more like her than I'd realized. Maybe I was a killer. I only knew that I'd done the only thing that would free the zones. If Nata had managed to escape, she would have found a way to regain her control over us.

In the corner of my eye, I saw Jabari wipe away a tear. Still, I couldn't cry.

It took eight minutes and thirty seconds, I would be told later. In eight minutes and thirty seconds, the leader of the United Zones of The Authority had lost her life.

And I, Rain Hawkins, number one-two-seven-six, had taken it.

Chapter 53: Muted

RAIN

An hour later, I was standing inside the Oval Office of what was once the White House of the United States of America.

Although it looked nothing like it once had. Nata had converted it, along with every other room in the former White House, to match the rest of the all-white military style building. I imagined that it wouldn't be called Elizabeth Mansion for long. And eventually, the building might be restored to its former grandeur.

Emotions were high, and voices celebrated around me, but they seemed muted. It was happening so fast. I couldn't quite convince myself it was over. Maybe if I really believed it was over, the tears I needed to cry would fall.

But it *was* over. And the tears still wouldn't fall.

I had killed Nata. She was really dead. I'd stayed beside the gas chamber until the end, even until Lieutenant Moretti had shown up and sent one of his men into the chamber to check Nata's body for a pulse.

"She's dead," Officer Samuels had confirmed, and then Gallagher had patted my back and told me I'd saved everyone.

I had immediately corrected him.

I had fought alongside The Freedom Front, and I didn't want anyone giving me that much credit. We were a team, period. Even right after it had happened, we'd set to work, helping Daktari to treat every wound of each victim on the property. Miraculously, no one had died in the battle against the Combat Droids while we'd been below with Nata. Though many had been injured. Blakely, Sook, and Bhavna had joined us, too. We'd placed our hands on Daktari as he treated each victim, finding his healing worked even faster when we were linked to him. I'd seen Niyol from a distance, but I'd been told he was busy securing the property and helping Jonah, and Lieutenant Moretti and his men, track down and disable the remainder of Nata's Combat Droids that she hadn't released.

After we'd helped Daktari, Gallagher had brought us with him to the office, where he had temporarily set up his communications with our ally from Indy Mixed Zone, Officer Eric, and all of the refugee camps. He'd contacted his camps to tell everyone in them, including our parents, the good news and that we were okay. Then, Eric had helped connect Gallagher with people in various zones across the country, including other Elizabeth Guard officers, who, like him, had joined the efforts to remove the chips from Combat Droids, Droid Dogs, and O3 Droids as soon as Cole had powered them down. According to everyone Gallagher had spoken with so far, as soon as the people had heard Gallagher's message, they'd taken to the streets where they found the motionless Droids and had banded together, removing Droid chips long into the night. Gallagher had promised reinforcements to begin the dismantling of the walls and to deliver supplies, but he was still organizing the details.

The energy in the room, even though it was nearing two a.m., was brimming as everyone listened to the outpouring of positive reports from across the country. Everyone was there with us: Grandma Julia, Uncle Michael, Aunt Alyssa, Calista, Bhavna, Sook, Blakely, Adrianne, and the rest of us, the original teenagers of The Freedom Front. Gallagher had said we should stick close to him because so much would be happening and so very fast, he felt better with us by his side. Landon's cyber leak had gotten Gallagher's message out to the world. Calista agreed to help us meet Landon in person in the days ahead, and we couldn't wait to thank him for all of his help. Gallagher had already received word that international aid was on the way.

Jabari hadn't gone more than two feet from me since we'd left the basement chamber, and as he eyed me now, he abandoned his conversation with Blakely. He reached for me, lifting me just off the ground as he held me tightly against him.

He set me back down and wiped a long curly lock of hair out of my face. "Niyol was right," he started, keeping his arms around my waist. "You were the key to bringing her down. We couldn't resist her power. But you did."

In the moments after Nata's death, Jabari had said so much. He told me about rescuing his dad from Metro Prison and everything that had happened until they'd gotten Cole to the control room and then finally gotten to me. He'd been terrified of losing me. He said it had been the biggest test of his faith, but that he'd followed Niyol's orders. Still, as he looked at me now, I could sense his lingering anxiety. He bent down and kissed me, and I imagined his apprehensions and fear fading away.

He grinned at me after a moment. "You're amazing. All by yourself, you stood up to her."

I smirked. "Technically, I was tied up in a chair. There was no standing involved."

"Very funny. Come on, admit it, you were incredible. Even after she drugged you and tortured you, you kept fighting. You even fought her at the end and resisted her ability when she looked you in the eyes."

When I didn't say anything, he went on. "And you controlled the dog. Nata was so sure of herself; she never thought to ask you if you had other abilities. Her ego helped destroy her."

"I know. Even up until the final moments, she didn't believe Gallagher, Niyol, or anyone could take her out of power," I agreed.

Jabari kissed the top of my head. "You're a warrior, dream girl. You saved us. Admit it," he said, looking at me with a huge smile that melted me down.

I finally smiled back. "Fine, I'm a hero. But I couldn't have done it without Angel," I said, bending down to stroke the top of the German shepherd's head.

"Is that the name you decided on? Is Angel a suitable name for a guy?" he asked with a chuckle.

"It ends up, he is a *she*, and anyway, she was our guardian angel for sure. And she seems amenable to the name. I could let someone else take care of her now, since she's been locked in a cage for who knows how long, and I'm sure any place to live would be better than this. But I think she's already growing attached to me."

Jabari patted Angel's head. "I don't blame you, Angel. I'm attached to her, too." Angel welcomed the pat from Jabari, and I smiled once more.

"Again, I can't take all of the credit. Sergeant Jacks gave me a can of stew they had in their hover supplies to feed to her. It'll have to work until I find more suitable dog food. But I guess since I fed her, she's officially attached to me."

Gallagher set his military radio he'd been using down on the desk and walked over to me, Adrianne tucked under his arm. "Rain. I have to hug you again. I know you don't want to admit it, but none of us would've made it out of there if you hadn't controlled the German shepherd with your ability and then gotten through to Jabari. Thank you," he said, tears filling up his eyes as he reached to hug me.

I wanted to cry, too, but still, they wouldn't fall.

Adrianne hugged me next. "Yeah, and I would've lost my dad and you guys, Rain. He left me upstairs when he went looking for you because he didn't want Nata to hurt me."

I hugged her quickly, tilting my head towards Gallagher. "Well, if you hadn't gotten everyone here in the first place to shut the Droids down we wouldn't even be having this conversation," I reminded him.

"Everyone worked together," Gallagher agreed. "Lieutenant Moretti and his team, you guys . . . But Niyol really came through for us all. He got us inside the mansion, and then he saved Adrianne. I left her upstairs, where she was supposed to be hiding under her image." He spared her a glance. "But she thought she heard something and that someone might be in trouble, and when she investigated, she came face to face with a Combat Droid that had mysteriously reactivated. But Niyol showed up just in time to shield her and take down the Droid. I heard he was everywhere he needed to be, actually . . . just in the nick of time," Gallagher finished.

"Where is he anyway?" asked Zi.

"Still helping my men," Gallagher replied. He tilted towards the others. "Hey, gather around, will you?"

Once the entire room was listening, he continued. "Listen, guys. There are only a few hours left before sunrise, and tomorrow means a lot of work for us. This is just the beginning. We have to help the zones, there are walls to come down, the pure zone kids will need so much help, there are hungry people, sick people, injured people from the bombing out in No Man's Land, refugees in No Man's Land who need help, UZTA prisoners we captured, like the EEG officers who are still loyal to Nata, that we will need to transport to secure prisons . . . to name just a few things that need attention," Gallagher hesitated, seemingly exhausted from the list of to-dos, but then his face brightened. "I can't wait to get to work."

Everyone laughed. "Gallagher Brown for president," Cole called.

"I second that," Bhavna agreed.

Blakely beamed. "No one will run against you, Gallagher."

"I doubt we'd even have to vote," Calista remarked.

"The people are going to need you now more than ever, Senator Brown," Grandma Julia said.

Gallagher flushed. "Mrs. Taylor, please call me Gallagher. Even though we've never met until today, I feel like I know you after all of these months working with your grandkids and their friends. I've heard a lot about you."

"Well, then by all means, call me Grandma Julia, like the rest of them do, young man. And I still say the kids are onto something. You'd make a fine president. You might need to abandon your mountain man look first, but you've got my vote."

"Thanks, Grandma Julia," he replied with a chuckle. "Really I don't want to run for president. But I'm going to help rebuild our country, and I won't leave it unprotected. There will be free elections again, and I'll work until it's the way it should be, even if it takes a lifetime. I'll need help. And you guys, the original Freedom Front, I'm really going to need your help. And I'm telling you right now it won't be easy. Will you help me?" Gallagher searched our expressions. Jabari looked down at me, and something prompted me to reach for his hand. And as I took it, I reached out for the hands of TFF. They knew what to do, and the next moment Jabari, Daktari, Zi, Cole, Marcello, and me, the original members of TFF, formed a chain, our hands linked together.

"*What do you think, guys? Are we ready for retirement?*" I asked them silently. Smiles broke out and I knew they'd heard me.

Marcello responded first. "*Can't get rid of me that easily.*"

"*And someone needs to keep an eye on Marcello,*" Zi added.

"*And someone needs to keep an eye on you keeping an eye on Marcello,*" Daktari said, a mischievous expression intact.

Cole spoke up next. "*And you guys are my family. So whatever you do, count me in.*"

"*We've been given these gifts for a reason. Someone needs to help the survivors in the unknown days ahead. It might as well be a group of teenagers from Indy Mixed Zone,*" Jabari added.

"*Cole said it. You guys are my family now. If Gallagher thinks we can help, let's do it. As long as we're together,*" I said.

Jabari smiled at Gallagher as we let go of our hands.

"So," Gallagher began, "you guys want to help rebuild America?"

"We wouldn't miss it for anything," Jabari assured him.

"And you can count us in, too," Blakely added. "Unless Sook plans to launch his dance career right away."

Sook grinned. "I see myself as more of a party and event planner, but first I want to help you guys. *Then*, we'll have the biggest party you've ever seen."

"Sooook," Bhavna cooed playfully, a knowing look on her face.

He shrugged, his expression sheepish. "Okay, so we might need to have a few dance parties here and there, along the way, you know . . . before we finish fixing the entire country." His eyes met mine. "I know I said it earlier, but I'm sorry I got captured and helped lead Nata to you, Rain."

Bhavna's face sobered as well. "Yeah, we're both sorry. But Jabari's right, you know. You sure saved us, Rain. And look what happened. She's gone. And I know Nipa and Dylan will want to help Gallagher, too, however he needs us. And you know since I mentioned the other gifted teenagers I found outside of the country, I've been thinking. I bet we will find others in America, like us, in the days ahead."

I was sure she was right. There had to be more people like us who had special abilities, and I prayed they would use their gifts for good, unlike Nata. But that would be something we'd have to keep watch for, and right now, all I could think about was closing my eyes.

Calista took my hand. "There's so much to be done. I want to help rehabilitate the children I helped Nata brainwash. No matter how long it takes."

"It will take some time," Gallagher agreed. "I'm counting on you all."

"Yes, we're going to help you. All of us are. But we're going to need a couple hours of sleep first," Marcello interjected, and the room erupted in laughter.

"I agree with Marcello for once," Daktari said.

Gallagher thanked us again and started organizing sleep arrangements. "Girls can sleep on this side of the office. Guys over on that side.

Oh and my men tell me they found showers with real hot water for whoever wants one."

"Hot water? Real showers with hot water? And we're sleeping in the Oval Office?" Daktari asked excitedly. "Are you sure you don't want to run for president, Gallagher? I'll be eighteen in two years, and you've got my vote."

Adrianne and Cole passed out blankets, and I laid mine down beside Grandma Julia, leaving space for Angel to sleep beside me, too. She curled up where I told her she could rest. I glanced up at the doorway as Niyol and Jonah stepped into the room. I was vaguely aware of Jonah joining the other guys, but my eyes were locked on Niyol. As he stood, staring at me, my heart sped up. And I realized why my tears hadn't fallen yet.

They couldn't fall until he told me it was okay to cry.

I had to hear from him that I'd made the right decision. I stepped over to him slowly.

"I hear you saved Adrianne," I started. "You always know who needs rescuing."

"I trusted my instincts. Just like you did. You did it, Rainchild. You finished it."

He wrapped his arms around me, and I rested my head against his chest, listening to his steady heartbeat.

Finally, I choked out the words that had been eating me up. "I killed your daughter, and you're hugging me."

A lone tear escaped and ran down my face. I was glad I'd done it, but I hated having to do it all the same. Why had I been chosen for it?

"No, Rainchild. You didn't kill my daughter."

He held me back, and I looked up into his eyes, confused. "The truth is, my daughter died a long time ago. You killed the evil person who replaced her. And you did it to save us."

As another tear glided down my cheek, my hands pressed into his arms. "You mean, you don't hate me? It's okay that I was the one to do it?"

"I could never hate you. I told you before; I knew it had to be you. You were chosen. You're a gift from above, like your name means, and you were destined to save your friends. But not only them . . . I can't wait for you to see how many lives you've helped free in the days ahead. Nata walked in the darkness, but you're led by the light within you, Rain. Keep shining your light. Let it guide you. And you'll always be okay."

I laid my head on his chest, and as he patted my back, the tears that had been threatening to pour for the past few hours erupted, finally falling. As I let them go, some of the heaviness lifted off my heart.

Chapter 54: Names

July 2051, Indianapolis, the United States of America

JABARI

As the hover sped away at pulse speed, I watched Rain take in our surroundings. No matter how many times we'd traveled by hover after the fall of Nata, it never got old to just see with our own eyes how quickly things had changed for the better. And it felt so good to see how far Rain had come. She sat perched beside me in clean clothes, denim shorts and a red, white, and blue tank top, with her brown hair falling in ringlets down her back. She looked healthy and refreshed, no longer suffering from malnourishment. Like the rest of us, she was healing, but I knew she had a ways to go.

I noted the relief in her eyes as she glanced at a family sitting across from us chatting away happily about a recent visit with their grandparents. For the first time in years, people were allowed to go wherever they wanted, and every single wall across the former UZTA had come down. It was an exhilarating feeling.

It had been nearly five months since Nata's reign had ended. In the weeks that followed, the United States of America was reinstated. There were still so many details being worked out and issues being addressed, but slowly but surely the country was coming together, and the help was not only from within our own borders.

As soon as Gallagher Brown's Elizabeth Mansion address had gotten out, the world had responded. Landon's team had streamed the message, along with the footage Calista had dared to prepare while working in Elizabeth Mansion, and they came to our aid. Once the automated Droid weapons that had secured the border to UZTA were inoperable, they'd moved in. Relief organizations from the United Kingdom, Canada, Europe, Mexico, Australia, New Zealand, and South America, to name a few, arrived to help.

During her rise to power, Nata had deceived the world into trusting her as well, and by the time other nations realized what had happened, it'd been too late for them to save us. It turns out a few had tried to penetrate our borders, but every mission had been unsuccessful against her Droid protected borders. Even though other countries had demanded answers, Nata had continued to send out fake propaganda videos, hoping they'd buy it. Some of them had. And the ones who hadn't weren't sure how to take her out of power.

Two countries, Mexico and Canada, had been alerted in the days right before we attacked Elizabeth Mansion by some of their own multiracial gifted teens. Just like Bhavna had said, she'd contacted them, and they'd tried to warn their governments. But until the proof was out, it was a difficult story to believe. How could a nation once so powerful succumb to the power and control of one person? Some countries said they believed we'd supported her because, after all, she'd gotten the country out of debt and continued to export hovers, including the popular Liz Hovercraft XT, even in the days right before her fall. They hadn't known her success had come at the price of slave labor. Most people said they knew something was wrong, but hadn't known how to help. But none of that mattered now.

So much had already happened during "The USA Restoration," the term agreed upon by the survivors. As Chief Defender of The USA Restoration, Lieutenant Moretti was in charge of everything from helping to reestablish police forces around the country to reopening and reestablishing all of the military branches that formerly comprised the United States Armed Forces, which was an enormous undertaking. He joked that when his mission was finally accomplished, he planned to go back to training with his old Navy SEAL team, if he wasn't ready for retirement by then. Gallagher was given the title of Chief Operator of The USA Restoration. One of the first things to change was the use of Droid technology. Moretti had collected every Droid Dog, Camouflage Droid Dog, O3 Droid, Combat Droid, and Droid weapon and had them disassembled. He wanted humans, and humans alone, to protect our nation until a safer way, at least a more dependable method, to use Droid technology could be developed.

People from every single one of the former zones had come forward, ready to take part in The USA Restoration. Things might never be exactly how they were before, but the people were unified in trying to restore our country and our freedom. The horror of Elizabeth Nicks, or Nata, would never be forgotten. We'd never forget what she had done, but we, as a people, were forging ahead. Together.

It would take years. The mess of trying to sort out housing alone was an obstacle in itself, but Gallagher had the best team of people helping him to figure it out. So many people had been relocated and taken from their homes. Some of the people didn't even want to return to their old homes. Many people had perished under Nata's regime and *couldn't* return to their old homes. The various relief organizations were still working alongside our people to provide temporary housing across the nation, even constructing new housing in some areas. Regardless of the difficulties we were facing, the important part was that people had a place to sleep and food to eat, and everyone had jobs to do. The core members of The Freedom Front, along with our families, had decided to stay close together during The Restoration.

Rain and her family had returned to their home in Zionsville when the occupants had decided to return to their old home. When we had realized that a few houses in Rain's old neighborhood were empty, as the former occupants had returned to their old housing and no one wanted to live in them, Gallagher had arranged for all of our families to relocate to the neighborhood. It was nice having our parents and families living so close together, especially since we were traveling a lot to help Gallagher's team resolve issues around the country. Our parents themselves had become leaders in the community, helping with their own sets of skills wherever they were needed.

Though Moretti had gotten rid of the Droid technology, at least for now, hovers were being used to transport people wherever they wanted to go. Plus, cars were on the road again, though not like the cars we had known before New Segregation. Nata had figured out how to use green energy but hadn't allowed us any of its advantages. She'd only used it to control the factories we'd worked in and to regulate the power to our housing during our captivity. Meanwhile, the rest of the world had gone ahead and developed clean energy cars, using her technology. Our allies had sent us batches of the newest and most advanced cars, built for the road. So while it was nice to see hovers actually transporting people to places other than slave factories, it was also nice to see something close to the cars we'd known growing up, driving around about the cities again. It brought a sense of normalcy to our ever-changing world. The roads were open for travel, and the walls had all come down.

My eyes settled on the little girl sitting with the family across from us now, and she got the most excited look on her face and started tapping her father's leg eagerly. "Dad, Mom, you guys, it's *them*."

I could feel Rain's hand heat up in mine as she looked down. It still embarrassed her when people acted so thrilled to meet us. Everyone knew who we were. Gallagher had been sure to recognize our achievements and give us credit for forming The Freedom Front in the first place, right after he'd taken command of The Restoration. The little girl couldn't contain her delight, and now her entire family was smiling at us.

"You're Jabari and Rain, aren't you? Part of The Freedom Front?" the little girl asked, her eyes full of awe.

Rain cleared her throat, clearly uncomfortable, and I had to chuckle. "Yes, we are. Rain's a little shy. She doesn't realize how big of a hero she really is. I keep trying to tell her."

"Oh, but you are a hero, Rain. My cousin was locked up in a prison cell because of Tricky Nicky. You saved him. And my neighbor, and my teacher, and well, just about everyone I know has been rescued because of what you did," she exclaimed.

I shook Rain's hand lightly. "You hear that, hero?"

She flushed, looking at me with the slightest bit of irritation. She was struggling with her feelings after everything that had happened. But then she looked at the little girl and smiled.

"I think *hero* is a strong word. The Freedom Front was never one person. Everyone worked together to fight for our freedom. And everyone will have to keep working together in the days ahead to secure our freedom. I hope you'll always look out for each other and help us." As Rain finished talking she dazed off a little, turning to look out the window.

The little girl bobbed her head. "I will. I even have one of—"

I shook my head back and forth, and fortunately, she stopped her sentence short. I winked at the little girl and put my finger to my lips before Rain could notice anything, and she grinned, understanding. It was, after all, a surprise, and if I was going to pull it off, I had to get Rain to the ceremony before anyone told her my secret.

As Rain turned back to them, the little girl beamed at her. "Well, Rain, you'll always be my hero. So thank you. You too, Jabari."

Her parent's nodded, agreeing, and her mother wiped a tear away. They looked at each other somberly and then back at us. "Thank you for what you did. We thought there was no hope. You saved us, just like our daughter said. We'll always hold a special place in our hearts for TFF, and especially TFFG," the father said.

Rain seemed to have lost the ability to speak again as emotions overcame her. "Thank you, sir. We really appreciate the support," I assured him.

As the Hover slowed to moderate speed, and we approached our destination, I thought about our new role in the restored United States of America. The Freedom Front had become an official government agency with various divisions playing roles in its job to help defend the country from "special" threats. Not only had it become an official agency, it had become a household name. After all, so many people had been part of The Freedom Front and helped take Nata out of power. Refugees in hiding had fought alongside Gallagher and Moretti in the months they'd stolen supplies and hidden people from Nata's Droid Dogs and Combat Droids. And people within the walls of each zone had fought with TFF when Gallagher's message had rallied them. And Gallagher hadn't been kidding when he'd asked for our support back in the Oval Office. He had given our group the title TFFG, which stood for The Freedom Front Guardians, and we had a huge responsibility.

The members of TFFG were Rain, Cole, Daktari, Zi, Marcello, and me, and also included Jonah, Adrianne, Bhavna, Sook, Nipa, Dylan, Blakely, Takara, and even my dad. We were to be guardians, in the sense that we were always on the lookout for any threats to our nation's safety. Landon and Calista had joined us, too, and even Kelly and Aleela had asked to be assigned to help us. Rain's loyal companion, the German shepherd, Angel, went with us wherever we went, and everyone called her the guardian angel of TFFG. Our team was deployed to assist Gallagher or Moretti with special missions and to assist wherever we were needed, from rehabilitating EEG officers to talking to victims still struggling with the emotional aftermath of Nata. People felt encouraged when they met us and heard our story. It helped them heal in a way. We also searched for others like us, because we knew they were out there. And we spent a lot of time helping Calista, who had asked to help with rehabilitating the pure zone kids. They were finally beginning to understand we weren't their enemy, but for some of them, the brainwashing instilled by Nata had been so effective, it would take a long time to heal them. Basically, we were wherever Gallagher wanted us to be. He said he didn't want the nation to ever forget our role in securing their freedom, and he wanted us to have a hand in every step of The Restoration.

Gallagher had opened a central office for TFFG to meet just outside the greater Indianapolis area, in Zionsville, not too far from our neighborhood. Rain had insisted we needed to meet in a scenic area. She refused to work in a paved city, surrounded by concrete alone, and Gallagher had delivered. Our office building was a small but fortified three-story structure hidden in the cloak of woods, with a landing pad on top of the building for hovers, for travel back and forth to our various destinations and assignments. We had two more locations besides the one in Zionsville, including one in Washington, DC, and another at Fort Freedom, one of the newly established army bases on the east coast.

We were the youngest government employees, some of the members weren't quite eighteen, but we were, according to Gallagher, the most important people on his team. When we weren't traveling or on assignment, we also completed our education under the tutorial of a staff of professors, including, of course, Takara, who'd insisted on resuming her role as our teacher.

If I had known a year ago how fast our lives would change after the walls went down, I'd have had more faith. For the first time in my life, I had no doubts about my purpose or how I was intended to use my gifts. We were stronger than ever before. Each member of TFFG had a job, and we were closer than ever.

As the hover landed, I scanned the other occupants, noting the energetic and joyful expressions on their faces. There was hope in their eyes. We'd suffered, some of us more than others, but we'd survived. And it bonded us together. There was only one person that still worried me, but I knew she just needed some more time.

Rain looked up at me now as I led her off of the grounded hover and into the bustling streets. "I can't believe this is happening." She pivoted, slowing surveying the city. "And I can't believe we are actually here again. Look at this place," she said, her eyes wide with amazement.

Our hover had landed in the midst of the former Indy Mixed Zone. Today was the Fourth of July, the Independence Day of the United States of America, and there were happy people everywhere we looked. So much had happened in our old zone. We'd only been back once and that had been to witness the demolition of the old projects we'd lived in. Gallagher had preserved only a small area of the former zone, including some housing and the factories and prison and turned it into a memorial and museum so that no one would forget the victims of the UZTA. The rest of the zone had been demolished and though many buildings were still under construction, so much progress had been made preparing for this day. Most of the former zone now resembled a city park, bustling with trees, flowers, and greenery everywhere. Gallagher's idea had been that each of the former zones would keep a portion of the zone as sort of a memorial and museum, and that they'd be surrounded by beautiful landscaping since Nata had prohibited us from having that for so long. As I took it all in, my hopes rose again. It was beautiful.

I pulled her hand, hoping to catch up with the others before the ceremony began since they'd left ahead of us. "You're right. I never thought this place could look so pretty. Hearing about the progress was one thing. Seeing it is entirely different. It feels a little surreal, right?"

"Yeah, I keep looking over my shoulder, half expecting one of the old TV screens to shoot up from the sidewalk and Nata to tell us this was just a dream." Her eyes worried as she glanced up at me. "But she's not lurking in the shadows. She's really gone. I guess I'm finally starting to accept that I killed her. I mean, because I had to, right?"

I halted and turned her to look at me. "Yes, you had to. Look around you. Do you see Droid Dogs perched on every corner? Scared, hungry people being worked to death? Tell me what you see when you look at them."

She paused, scanning the streets, and a slow smile formed on her lips. "I see people who look well fed, not wasting away to skeletons. They don't have holes in their clothes and shoes . . ."

Two police officers, dressed in navy-blue uniforms, waved at us as they passed. "Happy Fourth, Jabari and Rain," one of them called over his shoulder.

"Happy Fourth," I replied cheerfully, before looking down at Rain.

Her jaw had dropped open a little as she gazed at the retreating officers. As she tilted towards me again, her mouth curved into a grin. "I see human police officers from the Indianapolis department, *not* the Elizabeth Guard, patrolling the streets. I see families and friends carrying miniature American flags in their hands and dressed in red, white, and blue. I hear patriotic songs coming from the speakers on the streets. There are street vendors with popcorn and cotton candy for the celebration. Children are talking about the fireworks display they'll get to see after sunset. I hear laughter . . . I see happiness and hope in their faces. I see trees and flowers, and it's just beautiful."

"Exactly. You helped do that, Rain."

I kissed her lightly, and she lingered, holding on to me tightly and kissing me more. Whatever was going on around us and no matter how she was dealing with her emotions about killing Nata, the feeling between us never changed or lessened. She was like the air, and I needed more. And I knew I was the same to her.

Still, I had to get her to the ceremony in time. I broke the kiss.

She raised a brow and smiled. "Tired of my kisses so soon?"

I brushed my mouth to hers quickly and grinned back. "I'll never tire of you or your kisses. Why do you think I've been after you to marry me so much? We're both eighteen now. And I know you're hoping to wait until everything feels back to normal here in the USA, but no matter how you feel about what happened or what's happening, you and I won't change."

"I know. I'm just scared that you'll wake up one of these days and realize you're married to a killer. I don't want *you* to regret anything."

"I will never regret you, Rain Hawkins."

I shook her shoulders gently. And I kissed her again. "You know . . . it hit me the other day how well we compliment each other. When the walls were still up, every time I started to have doubts, you held me together. And I've always tried to do the same for you. I've messed up. Nata still managed to capture you, and you'll never forget what she did to you. But I'll always do my best to hold you together and help you through whatever is bothering you. And even though Nata is gone, we'll always have the memories. We'll have these tattoos to remind us of what happened. Sometimes it will be harder than others, and you'll have nightmares, and I'll see them, too. And I'll comfort you as best I can. The things we've been through, well . . . they won't ever really go away, but you and me? Rain and Jabari? We'll be okay. We're the only thing that makes sense and feels right. I need you, Rain. But I'll give you as much time as you need before you say *I do*. I just don't want you to hesitate because you think I would regret anything. I love everything about you. And I love everything you've ever done. I'm always going to love you."

She wiped a tear away. "Now you've got me all emotional and crying. I'm sorry I delayed the wedding date so much. I know I did what I had to do with Nata, but I was afraid the repercussions of what I did might hurt you in a way. But I can see now that you're right. Regardless of everything else, we will be okay. I don't want to hold us back anymore. Why don't you kiss me again, and we'll talk about the date," she teased, leaning up on her toes.

I got lost in her kisses and felt so hopeful that she'd really marry me. "Hey we're going to continue this conversation later, you hear me? But you're distracting me from my job. And I've got to get you to the ceremony in time or Gallagher will kill me."

She laughed as we took off in a fast walk. "I can't have the leader of The Freedom Front Guardians upsetting the Chief Operator of The USA Restoration."

"I think we might have him convinced to run for president when the elections are held next year."

"That would be amazing. I can't believe this is really happening," she said, looking around again as I pulled her ahead through the maze of people.

Though there was happiness in her eyes, a part of her would always grieve for what she'd had to do. She was haunted by the fact that she'd killed Nata, even though she knew I would have done it for her, and that we all had stood beside her while she'd pressed the button to the gas chamber. For weeks she'd relived the experience over and over in her nightmares. She didn't mention it much, but I was still experiencing her dreams along with her, night after night. In her dreams, I felt her emotions, teetering back and forth between guilt and being justified about what she'd done. Her dreams faded between images of the faces of those she'd killed, starting with the man who'd tormented Maha in prison, Officer Darryl, switching to Officer Wolfe, and finally to Nata. She'd taken three lives during our captivity, and each incident had taken a piece of Rain that she'd never get back. And though I knew she'd never fully recover, I was hoping and praying that she'd be able to cope with it and that with more time passing, the nightmares would subside. It killed me to see her tormented at night, though she smiled and acted fine during the day. But today, especially, I was hoping that she'd realize how many people were grateful for what she had done. I hoped that today she would truly believe it, and maybe even let some of the pain go.

Finally, the stage came into my frame and I started to jog. A huge American flag soared to the side of the stage for all to see. The crowd of people parted for us, cheering after us. "It's Jabari and Rain!"

By the time I pulled her onto the stage beside the rest of our friends and family, she got swept away in their greetings. Daktari, Grace, and Isaac embraced Rain first, and I imagined them chatting about how far they'd come since those early morning hugs they'd shared while waiting for the hovers to transport them to the factories. All of our families were there. And everyone who had ever helped TFF was there, from Lieutenant Moretti to Officer Eric to Chef Yoshi. Maha and Anthony had finally been allowed to get married, and had done so the day after Nata's death, thanks to Gallagher finding a pastor in one of his refugee camps. They walked over to Rain with their three-month-old baby girl, Isabel, who Rain had already met and become the godmother of, shortly after her birth.

Gallagher pulled me into a bear hug. I nodded approvingly at him. "I'm still loving the new look, Gallagher. But do you miss the beard? You had that thing for a while."

He chuckled as his hand shot up to his chin, running over the smooth skin. "Amal really likes this clean-shaven look," he began with a sly grin.

"So, the rumors are true?" I teased. Everyone knew that Amal, who Rain had rescued from the burning book fires in our zone, and Gallagher had developed a close friendship, but neither Gallagher nor Amal had admitted that there was more to it. Still, we knew, and we were just glad to see them happy.

"People don't care about us. Everyone wants to know when a certain wedding is though." He hesitated looking over towards Rain. His expression sobered. "How's she doing, by the way?"

"She was dragging her feet to come back here. But I got her here," I said solemnly.

"I know this is hard on her. Don't worry. She'll come out of this eventually."

"He's right. She will." The voice beside us had me turning. Niyol stood staring at us and reached for my hand. I turned from Gallagher and into his hug. Niyol had chosen to remain an anonymous contributor to TFF, but if anything, he was more active now than ever, and routinely joined us for meetings and assignments. Of course, he'd accepted the invitation to be here today, which made me so happy. Rain would feel better after seeing him. She always did.

"Her nightmares are constant," I said.

"She had the hardest part. Killing Nata. But she'll be all right. You'll see."

"I know. I have faith. I might have struggled with it before, but not now."

Niyol smiled, which was so rare I had to smile back. "I'm proud of you, Jabari."

Rain approached him now and folded herself in his arms, and he spoke with her in whispers, comforting her like he always did. She wiped a tear away and grinned up at him as Gallagher called our attention to place our hands over our hearts for the Pledge of Allegiance.

Today, Gallagher addressed the victims of Nata and the UZTA. He spoke of how we were one people of one nation, how regardless of our cultural backgrounds and outward differences, together we were prismatic, like a rainbow, and he'd defend us against any threats of segregation. Despite what Nata had tried to instill in us, we were all humans, and all of us mattered. He promised to finish building the monuments in each of the former locations of the zones across the country as a memorial to those who'd fallen. He thanked Rain's dad, Isaac, whose new job as Executive Architect for The Restoration had included the building of the memorial we would see today, in addition to the rest going across the country. He thanked TFF and everyone who had fought with them, including the founding members, honoring my dad, Takara, and the man, Tony, who'd helped my dad initially before his wife had turned my dad in. Gallagher thanked TFFG and said he was honored about the work we were already doing to serve our country. Around the monument, as a tribute to the original date of Earth Day that TFF had planned to go after Nata, he'd planted trees in our honor, promising that plants and trees would be planted in each of the former mixed zones as a symbol of new life.

The curtain dropped, revealing the towering monument. It had the name, not the number, of every person on it who had lost their life to The Authority. Rain's hand shook in mine as she stared up at it. Niyol grabbed her other hand, Takara took his, and everyone in TFF followed suit, joining hands for the moment of silence.

After a moment, Rain spoke into our minds as we were still linked together. "*I can see it now. I know I had no choice but to kill Nata. When I look at all of the names inscribed across the monument, I realize I can stop hating myself for the three lives I took. It was war. And now she can't hurt more people. And I don't want to keep hurting because of what I did. We did it together. The Freedom Front ended her regime so no more names have to be written on that memorial. Thank you for asking me to join TFF, Jabari.*"

"*Thank you for having the courage to finish it, Rain,*" I answered, squeezing her hand.

As everyone silently responded to Rain, Gallagher called us to attention.

"And now the moment you've all been waiting for," he said with a grin.

Rain looked around in confusion as we dropped hands and the crowd cheered. "Wasn't that the moment? When he revealed the monument?" she asked nervously as we all smiled at her.

"There's just one more thing," I said.

Gallagher nodded at me, giving me the cue, and I stepped forward in front of the microphone. "Hello, fellow citizens of the United States of America," I paused as they called out cheering in response.

"I know you've heard of The Freedom Front and also The Freedom Front Guardians. You probably heard about the final stand against Nata, who you knew as Elizabeth Nicks. TFF was forced into a gas chamber, and we almost didn't make it out alive. But as you've probably heard, one member of TFF came through for us." I glanced at Rain, whose face was bright red, and they went wild cheering.

"As many of you have heard, while we were living here, in what was the Indy Mixed Zone, I made a bracelet out of thread for Rain. Each color on the bracelet stands for something meaningful. The blue symbolizes the rain and the sky, just like Rain they are gifts from above. The red represents her fire within and passion for life. The pink symbolizes her beauty and our love, and the black signifies her power. The bracelet reminds me of all the qualities that I love about her, but also that those qualities are what got her through the fight against Nata. Rain doesn't think she's a hero and doesn't like the title. But join me now in showing your appreciation for what she did in the final moments against Elizabeth Nicks."

I pulled back the cuff of my long-sleeve shirt and raised my arm into the air, revealing a bracelet like the one I'd made for Rain. And as planned, on my cue, TFFG and everyone on the stage and in the crowd, every single one of the hundreds of people gathered there, did the same, revealing the matching bracelet they all wore to honor Rain. Gallagher had made them and distributed them to anyone who wanted one. And keeping it a secret from Rain had been the hardest part.

As I held my arm high in the air, I felt the air around me buzzing with excitement and emotion. The little girl from the hover ride was in front with her family, proudly holding her arm high, revealing her bracelet. Rain's eyes were huge as she took it all in, and tears streamed down her cheeks. After a moment, Takara pulled her into a hug, and the crowd erupted in applause.

As they chanted the words I knew might upset her, but I knew she needed to hear, I joined them. "He-ro! He-ro! He-ro!"

As they kept cheering, I strode over to her cautiously. She gave me a hostile look. "Did you have to do that?"

I laughed. "It wasn't me. It was Gallagher's idea. I just helped make it happen."

She looked out at the crowd. "They all have a bracelet like mine?"

"Well, just the bracelet, not the ring," I said, picking up her wrist and admiring the ring attached to her woven bracelet. "Which reminds me, we need to get you a real ring."

She grinned. "But I like this one."

"You know . . . you're going to have to raise your standards again now that the world is getting back to normal. You're a hero, Rain Hawkins. Now about that last name . . . Do you want to change it? Or, just like the ring, do you like it the way it is?" I teased, leaning closer to her lips.

"Let's change it, Jabari. Like I was trying to say back there before the ceremony. We can talk about the date but—"

I put my finger over her lips. "No, don't say *but* anything. I'm willing to wait however long it takes, like I said."

She laughed. "No, Jabari, I was going to say, *but* we don't have to talk about anything if you'd like. You can pick the date. I see that now. I've got to let go of the bad stuff. Even if we'll never really forget what happened, we don't have to dwell on it. I want to live my life. And I want to start a new one with you."

"Are you saying what I think you're saying?"

She laughed. "Yes. I'm ready when you are. Let's get married already."

I paused to make sure she could see how big my smile was. "How's tomorrow work for you?"

But before she could reply, I kissed her and kissed her again. The applause and chanting erupted even louder. The people cheered, "T-F-F-G! T-F-F-G!"

And I kissed the woman I'd love for the rest of my existence.

Chapter 55: Wildflowers

August 2051, Zionsville, Indiana, USA

RAIN

Months ago I'd dreamt of our wedding day. I'd been walking through a field with Jabari, holding hands, admiring the flowers dotting the landscape. He'd worn a black tuxedo, and I a long sleek wedding gown, and I'd known we were going to our wedding. Even though that dream had ended in a drastically different setting, as I replayed the memory in my mind and stared at my reflection in the mirror in front of me, I grinned.

Nata would not appear to ruin my wedding day like she had in my dream, and for once, I felt at peace with my role in her demise. And peace, it turned out, looked pretty good on me.

Zi stared, wide-eyed, and couldn't stop grinning. "Seriously, girl, you look like you're stepping off the cover of a magazine. Not like some girl who almost died of malnourishment at the hands of an evil dictator in the mixed zone."

"Oh, Zi, you're awful," cooed Grandma Julia. "But you're right. She looks divine."

Grandma pinned another curl up, putting a couple of tiny wildflowers in it she had picked from the woods. They'd been working on my hair for just a little while, arranging the curls half up, leaving the rest down, and pinning a few white wildflowers here and there. I'd argued against it at first, insisting that they not fuss over me. But now that I was looking at the end result, I couldn't stop smiling.

"You guys did that. I'm sorry I argued with you."

Calista beamed. "I'm so happy you like it, cuz, and you look amazing. Jabari's going to faint when he sees you," she said, artfully applying another flower.

"Yes, he is," added Victoria with a fervent nod.

"Because he likes it or because he's having second thoughts?" I asked, my heart picking up.

Mom put one hand on either of my shoulders and gazed at me tenderly through the mirror we faced. "Because he won't be able to believe that a woman so stunning and so amazing is going to be his wife. You are breathtaking, Rain. And I'm so proud of you." She let go of me to dab at her eyes as tears fell.

"No, no, no," I protested. "No crying before the wedding," I threatened, smiling at my mother.

I turned to hug her despite her protest. "Don't you mess up your dress, Rain."

"Don't you make me start crying already," I returned.

She grinned. "If I haven't said it enough . . . Thank you for saving me and getting me through the darkest times, Rain. I never would have dreamt seeing this day was possible. But you never gave up."

"I just said not to make me cry, Mom." My voice shook a little now.

"I love you, honey,"

"I love you, too, Mom."

"Oh, now I'm crying," complained Grandma Julia.

"I knew this was going to happen, ladies," Zi said matter-of-factly. "Here, take a tissue, Grandma Julia, and here's one for you, Mrs. Hawkins."

She handed them the tissues and then turned back to the girls, who were all gathered behind me, dressed in champagne-colored dresses. I had more bridesmaids than I needed, but Zi had insisted on organizing the wedding and had wanted it to be as lavish as it could be for a "wedding in the woods," as she called it. Victoria, Zi, Calista, Adrianne,

Bhavna, Nipa, and Aleela were the official bridesmaids, and Kelly wore a gown like them, too, but she would be providing the violin music as I walked down the aisle. They looked so radiant and happy; it warmed my heart.

Zi placed a delicate hand on her hip. "Now, we've got four minutes before Sook cues the music. Kelly is in place. Everyone knows what to do. Now focus on your job. I don't want Calista making eyes at Marcello and getting distracted by his flirtatious glances." She pointed at Calista playfully.

"Yeah, save it for the dance floor. I heard you two were officially an item now, and I want to talk to that young man about a few things," Grandma Julia teased.

"He makes me so happy," Calista gushed.

Zi snapped her fingers. "That's exactly what I'm talking about. No getting distracted, girl. Pull yourself together. And you, too, Adrianne. I'm watching you, honey. I heard about you and Cole," she said, lifting an eyebrow at her.

"I still can't believe Dad finally gave his consent for Cole to take me out," Adrianne remarked excitedly.

"Well, he did help bring down one of the world's most evil dictators ever," Victoria pointed out, ignoring Zi's warning look.

"True, true," Mom agreed, warmly.

Zi clapped her hands. "Come on, ladies, pay attention to me. We need to line up in front of Rain and get going. Remember everyone, follow the path we created through Grandma Julia's yard and into the woods, and don't let your dresses drag across the ground." She waved a finger towards Mom and Grandma. "Daktari should be here any second to take you two to your seats."

"Speaking of Daktari, don't you go getting distracted either," Aleela interjected.

Zi had to laugh. "Yes, he's so handsome, sometimes I just can't believe he's mine," she said dreamily. Then her brow furrowed together, "Hey, Aleela, you're messing with me. Not funny," she said, jabbing her finger at her. "Now come on, get moving, we've got a wedding to pull off," she urged them, smiling all the while.

Calista shook her head. "That's right, listen to Zi. We need to stick to the schedule. Oh, and Rain, I can't wait for you to see the decorations. Zi organized it all."

Daktari pushed open the door to the room, and his eyes got huge. "Wow, sis, you look like one of those wedding brides from the movies. And I should know . . . Ever since we got power back, Zi's been having one movie night after another."

"It's true," she nodded. "I didn't realize how much I missed real entertainment."

"I imagine Sook will really entertain us after the wedding," Daktari said with a laugh. Then he looked back at me. "You look perfect, Rain. I hope this is the best day ever. You deserve it."

"Thanks, baby bro. You're looking good in that black tuxedo, your-self. They've been working hard to make me look like this."

"You would look beautiful no matter what. I'll even let the baby bro thing slide since it's your wedding day," he added with a wink.

Zi gestured towards the door. "Focus, people, the wedding is about to begin."

Mom laughed as they ushered her out. With one fleeting glance she blew a kiss to me. "I love you, baby."

"I love you, too."

A minute later, Bhavna reappeared at the door. "Ready? Zi told me to make sure you got to the aisle, where your dad is waiting to walk you, since I'm the last bridesmaid in the procession. And she told me to hurry. And I'm not going to be the one to disobey her. You know, I think she should consider wedding planning as a career. I mean, if she weren't part of one of the most important government agencies of this century. She's bossy like Nipa," Bhavna said as she giggled.

"Just don't let her hear you calling her bossy."

Bhavna curled her arm through mine, leading me out of Grandma's house. I saw the path. Zi had lit it up with tea lights on either side, leading from Grandma's house all the way into the woods.

As we started on our way, Bhavna smiled up at me. "So are you ready to marry that hot guy waiting for you in the woods? Jabari, I mean? You know Blakely is out there, too, and he'd love to marry you. Of course, you could really get any guy you wanted. And now that you're famous, I mean *any* guy."

"Troublemaker," I teased.

"I'm serious, Rain, you're an international celebrity now. Do you have any idea how many important people are waiting in the woods to see you marry Jabari? There's a group of officers from The USA Restoration, Gallagher Brown, Niyol, Chef Yoshi, Takara . . . Oh, and a group of Navy SEALs are with Lieutenant Moretti and all of his men. And I'm just throwing it out there, but some of those guys are really good-looking, Rain, and you could take your pick from them, too," she said playfully.

"You trying to calm my nerves by distracting me?"

"Yes, is it working?"

I slowed my pace and gave her an amused look. "I'm not nervous."

"Of course you are. How could you not be nervous? You're getting married for crying out loud. I'm never going to get married, at least not for another decade, so this is huge. You should be nervous. Oh crap, Zi would kill me if she heard me. Don't tell her I said any of that. I'm supposed to be getting you to your dad. I had one job. I can hear her now," she finished with a sigh.

"I know it may seem strange to everyone watching. I mean, since we are young. We're only eighteen years old. But I've never been so sure of anything in my life, Bhavna. Jabari said it best a few months back.

No one will ever understand what we've been through together in the mixed zone. And we were old enough to go to battle to save our country, and I think we're old enough to get married. Besides, my dad would've done something to stop this wedding if it weren't meant to be, trust me. Jabari Ramirez is the guy for me. And I'm going to marry him in a few minutes," I said happily.

Bhavna squeezed me in a light hug, careful not to mess up my dress. "I was just testing you, Rain. I know you two are meant to marry. And today is the day. I lost a bet to Blakely, that's all. This was part of the loss . . . I had to make sure this was what you really want."

"Remind me to deal with him later," I said, amusement in my voice.

The clearing where we'd met Grandma Julia in the months leading up to our freedom and where I'd spent my youth playing among the birds, trees, and flowers, was just in front of us. A flower-covered trellis archway signaled the entrance where I would walk through, down the aisle. Dad stood waiting for me just on this side of the trellis. He looked so strong and handsome in his suit, and so happy, I felt tears welling up as I recalled the years of labor, malnourishment, and abuse he'd endured. But he had gotten through.

Bhavna left me with him to proceed ahead down the aisle. I could hear Kelly's violin standing out above the rest of the musicians.

I tucked my hand through Dad's arm, and he regarded me tenderly. "Rain, those days I told you to keep the fire alive? I was saying it more for myself than for you and Daktari. You see, I was having a hard time holding on to that fire. But seeing you and your brother, not only hold on to it, but use it to free our country, fills me with a joy I'll never be able to explain. And that young man waiting at the end of the aisle for you is the one for you. I can see that."

"Thanks Dad. You helped me keep the fire alive, you know. I love you." I pulled him down towards me so I could kiss his cheek. As he stood back up, he wiped a tear away.

"Not you, too," I said, my voice thick with emotion.

He let out a deep laugh that had heads turning our way as we perched at the entrance to the archway. "Now, remember, Rain," he said in a whisper. "I approve of Jabari. But like I told him, if he ever does anything to hurt you, I'll kick his butt. I don't care how much super strength he has. I worked in that hover plant for over five years. This is genuine muscle under this jacket."

"It's not just your muscle that makes you so strong. You have strength unlike most people. Mom never would have made it to the other side without you getting her through it. And now that she's helping restore the old Zionsville Library and reading to the kids again for story time, she's so happy. You saved her, Dad. And now I have my mom back. Thank you."

"What happened to my babies? You're both so strong, brave, and mature."

"It's time, Dad," I said, motioning towards the aisle that the bride's maids had just cleared out of.

We crossed through the archway and I held my breath as I looked around. Zi had decorated the lawn with white chairs, lanterns, party lights, and medleys of flowers. Over to the far left, she'd lined up picnic tables and covered them with white table cloths, roses, and dishes prepared for our meal. She'd even created a makeshift dance floor, where I imagined Sook would lead the celebration. The tables awaiting our after-wedding dinner made me think of the dream I had months ago when Nata had stormed out of a funnel cloud and into the woods where we'd all been feasting together. But today, she wouldn't do that.

I smiled as I turned back to the guests. There were so many I couldn't count them. With a glance, I noted that Takara and Niyol were there, Jabari's parents, Gallagher, Amal, Chef Yoshi, and lots of people from their former camp. Bhavna's family and others from their old camp were there. Lieutenant Moretti and his men, Maha, Anthony, and baby Isabel, Eric, Landon . . . just about everyone who had ever helped TFF was there, including all of our families. To the side, I saw Kelly and a small group of musicians. Even Angel sat perched beside Grandma's feet. To the right, the guys were lined up and looked amazing in their black tuxedos. There was Daktari, Cole, Marcello, Blakely, Dylan, Sook, and Jonah. The girls were to the left, and just above the entire bridal party Zi was casting the image of a rainbow into the sky.

I met her eyes from a distance and silently called to her. "*It's beautiful, Zi. Everything.*"

"*Anything for you, girl. You are so special.*"

As we took another step, Jabari, more striking than ever in his tuxedo, edged his way out into the aisle so I could see him. As he smiled at me, I returned it, grinning from ear to ear. "*I love you, Jabari Ramirez,*" I said silently.

"*I love you, Rain Hawkins. You're the most stunning bride that's ever been a bride. You're not having doubts, are you? Because I had some of Moretti's Navy SEALs assigned for security. They're barricading a mile radius around us just in case you try to run. I know how fast you are. You are the fastest person alive as far as I know. I had to take precautions.*"

I couldn't help the small laugh. "*You're kidding, right?*"

"*Maybe,*" he teased. "*So are you having doubts?*"

"*Never,*" I said.

As we approached, Jabari turned to my dad, held his gaze for a moment, then looked back at me.

"You're stunning," he managed to say after a moment, taking me in from head to toe.

The pastor welcomed everyone to the ceremony and opened with a prayer. He asked who was giving the bride away, and my dad placed my hand in Jabari's. As the ceremony went on, I was so focused on Jabari's face I hardly noticed Francisco carrying a pillow towards me, or the two rings resting on it I'd never seen. Embarrassment washed over my face.

Though we'd talked about it a few times, I'd forgotten about the rings, and I guess I'd just assumed I'd be wearing the fabric one Jabari had made me forever ago.

Francisco smiled as he offered us the rings. I looked at Jabari and he grinned. "Surprise. They were my great grandparents' rings, family heirlooms. Mom and Dad hid them in our old house and went back for them after the walls fell," he explained.

"But—"

Francisco stopped my protest with the shake of his head. "No one could wear these rings but the two of you. Michelle and I agreed, these rings need to be worn, and what better couple to have them than you and Jabari." He leaned in to kiss my cheek and stood back.

"Thank you," I whispered.

I tilted over my shoulders towards Michelle. "They are perfect."

She dabbed a tear from her eye. "Perfect for you two."

I quickly admired the intricate design of my white gold wedding band and then placed my hands in Jabari's again, and stared into his dark brown eyes.

The pastor continued talking and saying the vows I'd only heard in storybooks and movies from before my relocation to the mixed zone, but I hardly heard the words. I heard the silent messages Jabari was sending me, and I heard only him. I managed to say *I do* in all the right places, but it felt like a dream.

When at last the pastor came to a close and was saying the words I was waiting for, my heart threatened to drum out every sound around. Jabari inched closer before the pastor was finished with the sentence, "You may now kiss the bride." And as his lips met mine the woods around rang with applause and cheering.

After a moment, Jabari leaned back and beamed. "Everyone, I present to you the girl who I wasn't sure was real at first. The girl who literally ran into my dreams, my wife, Rain Ramirez."

Around us, I heard Sook calling for music and dancing. People cheered even louder. But I couldn't really hear them. Jabari grabbed my face and leaned down again, his eyes so joyful.

I spoke to him silently. "*I'm so happy you found me, Jabari.*"

He kissed me again and as he did he silently replied, "*Thanks for being real.*"

Ten Months Later

June 2052, Zionsville, USA

I was running through the woods. My feet ran faster and faster. They propelled off of moss-covered logs and vaulted me over streams of water. The scent of wild honeysuckle growing in sun-lit clearings warmed my heart even more. Sweat trickled down my back, but I welcomed the heat. I welcomed the burn through my limbs. I felt alive. And it felt amazing.

"*Meet me at the clearing*," I called silently.

My feet raced on, and I tossed a look behind me. "Keep up, Angel, You can do it."

At last my destination came into view, and I sped up, pushing myself to the last minute. Finally, I leapt over a tree limb and landed on the side of the bank. The sound of gurgling water made me grin, and I bent down to scoop some up into my hands and splash it on my face.

My faithful German shepherd arrived a few seconds later and spared me a small glance that I interpreted as *You run too fast*, and she gulped water from the stream. Then the red cardinal I'd called flew into the trees and landed just beside me where I knelt down by the water. Angel's ears shot up in curiosity, and I chuckled.

"No, leave the cardinal alone, Angel. He's just saying hi."

It tweeted in response. I spoke to it silently, "*Come a little closer, friend.*"

It approached me cautiously, and I grinned in triumph. "You know, a while back, I was chasing birds like you down the streets of the mixed zone. But no wonder you didn't want to linger there. It's so much prettier here in the woods."

I thought about the days of New Segregation and sighed. Jabari was right, the further we got away from them, the easier it got, though we'd never forget them. I wasn't having nightmares much anymore, just sometimes, and now that Jabari and I were married and had our own home, he was always there to comfort me when I woke up.

With the genius handy work and design of Bhavna's dad, William, and the money we'd saved up working for TFFG, we'd made it happen. Grandma Julia had helped, too. She'd given us a small parcel of her wooded property behind her home. William had designed and helped build the small, two-story, tree-house-style home, situated in the tree-tops. He'd even made sure to make it blend into the trees, like the tree houses at his former camp had, so we could really remain off the map, which was nice. We didn't need a lot of space, and it was perfect. Not only did it have voice-activation in some of the rooms, which he'd pro-grammed with the same voice, Harmony, from my old room, it had the best bathtub with *hot* water. After living with only cold water for so long, having hot water was my favorite part of the home, plus it was under the scenic refuge of the trees. It was my dream home with my dream guy.

The only thing I could possibly say concerned me lately was that my powers were growing, and I wondered what it meant. But when Niyol had visited me the last time, he'd promised me it was perfectly normal. And that since I was actively using my gifts doing good work with TFFG, my powers, along with those of my friends, might continue to grow.

The bird chirped again and Angel let out a low moan. She probably wanted to chase the bird off into the woods. I tilted my head towards the cardinal. "Thanks for coming to see me. Care to stop by my grand-ma's patio before you go home? She's sitting out there this time of day, and it always brightens her day to see a cardinal."

The bird chirped again and flew away. I knew it would do as I asked, and Grandma would tell me about it later. Now that my abilities had strengthened, I controlled animals more easily, I ran faster than ever, and my telepathy was clearer. Before, when I had spoken to Niyol with my telepathy, I could sometimes visualize what he was doing, but now, it happened no matter who I contacted telepathically. I could actually see where they were and see what they saw, no matter how far away they were.

As I stood up, I noted footsteps snapping twigs as they approached, and heavy panting. The next moment, Jabari scooped me up by the waist and lifted me into the air so I was facing down at him. Angel tilted her head up to give us a bored look; then curled up beside the stream.

Jabari had a comical expression, and sweat poured down his handsome face. "You know, you may be the fastest human alive, and I mean that. You are faster now than you were before, but I am still the *strongest* human. And I'm getting stronger." He laughed as he held me over his head. "Now what was that all about? You trying to kill me, my beautiful wife?"

I burst out laughing as he set my feet on the ground so I could lean against him. "I always said you were an old man. I just want to keep you in shape, husband."

"Old man? In shape? One, I'm only three months older than you. And two, have you looked at my muscles lately?" He stepped back and pulled up his t-shirt, making my stomach flip. "These are called ab muscles, Rain," he teased.

"I know what they are," I said with a grin, tracing my hand over his chest and smiling up at him. "So, you are strong and muscular, I admit. But technically, you did have three months on me and—"

"Rain Ramirez, will you please," he said playfully as he swept my feet out from under me, and cradled my fall.

He perched on his elbows on the grass beside me so he could look at me. I saw his eyes change and knew he'd kiss me. His mouth met mine, and I returned each kiss, so grateful we were together and the nightmares were behind me.

"I love you because you're old—I mean mature," I teased.

"I love you because you're impossible—not to love," he returned, kissing my neck now.

"I love you because you're strong."

"I love you because you're beautiful."

"I love you because any lingering pain goes away when you're near," I whispered as his lips brushed mine again.

He tilted his head back and swallowed. "I fell in love with you the first time you ran into my dreams, Rain. I love you because we were meant for each other and nothing feels right if you aren't with me."

"Even though I run you to the point of death sometimes?"

"Just one more thing I'll tell our grandkids about . . . how dedicated to my health their grandmother is." He paused, twirling my bracelet around my wrist, as I'd done so many times it had become a habit. "I love you because I have to, there's no other choice."

"We should write this stuff down, you know. Those supposed grandkids you love to speak of might need to now about what a smooth talker you were."

"We've gone over this before," he said, kissing me quickly, before sitting up and pulling me into his lap.

He wrapped his arms around me and nuzzled my neck. The crickets began their nightly chorus around us as the sun began to set. Nothing about the darkness of the woods scared me. Here, listening to the nighttime noises of the woods, with Jabari's arms around me, I was right where I needed to be.

"What have we gone over?"

"The story we'll tell our kids and grandkids." He traced a finger over my ankle tattoo.

My voice sobered a little. "Oh, you mean about our tattoos and what happened to us."

"Sure, we'll tell them about that one day, but that's not the story I'm talking about."

He kissed my cheek and gently pulled my hair off of my face.

"Well, then what story are you referring to?"

"You know the one. We talked about it the night I proposed. When we were behind the walls. But now we're free, and I think here, with the crickets singing their tune, is as good a spot as any to go over the story we'll tell them, *Mrs. Ramirez.*"

"Do proceed, Mr. Ramirez. Oh, wait, I remember now . . . Once upon a time, a girl chasing a bird ran into my dreams . . ." I began.

"Correction, once upon a time, the most beautiful girl on Earth ran into my dreams . . ."

"Details details," I murmured. "You do tell a good story."

He shifted me in his lap so I could see his face and bent down, tilting my chin up, kissing me once more.

When he paused, he smiled. "This is just the beginning of our story, Rainchild."

Peace settled over me. I wrapped my arms around his neck and pulled him closer. "I know it is."

And to the growing chorus of nighttime crickets under a free sky, with trees, not walls, enclosing us, I kissed the only guy who'd ever have control of my heart.

In Between

A poem in honor of Rain and Jabari, by Sarah Elle Emm

You hold me
as though walls aren't tumbling,
the world isn't spinning,
like I'm a puzzle piece
fallen into place.
It's safe here.
My breathing finds a steady rhythm.
You've battles to fight.
My share await me, too.
Still I stay here,
my head on your chest.
This in-between gets me through.

Meanings Behind the Names

Rain: Blessings from above
Jabari: Fearless, Brave
Zi: Graceful, Beautiful
Daktari: Healer
Marcello: Young warrior
Cole: Victorious people
Calista: Most beautiful
Takara: Treasure
Niyol: Wind
Nata: Speaker
Bhavna: Meditation, Thinking
Sook: Light, Clear
Nipa: One who watches over
Dylan: Lord of the sea
Blakely: Dark meadow
Gallagher: Eagle helper
Adrianne: Rich, Dark
Victoria: Victory
Francisco: Free one
Michelle: Gift from God
Jonah: Dove (Old Testament prophet)
Aleela: She cries
Amal: Hope
Dominic: Belonging to God
Isaac: He will laugh
Grace: Graceful

Kelly: Brave warrior

(Grandma) Julia: Youthful

Maha: Beautiful eyes

Anthony: Praiseworthy

Isabel: Consecrated to God

Zachary: God remembered

Yoshi: Good, Respectful

Li Ming: Pretty, Bright

William: Determined guardian

Anshula: Sun

Eric: Brave ruler

HARMONY RUN SERIES

PRISMATIC
Brilliantly colored; iridescent

OPALESCENT
Exhibiting a milky iridescence like that of an opal

CHATOYANT
Having a changeable luster; twinkling

NACREOUS
Exhibiting lustrous or rainbow-like colors

Acknowledgments

Once upon a time, I dozed off in a loveseat, had a dream about Rain Hawkins and her friends from The Freedom Front, and the *Harmony Run Series* was born. I rushed to my notebook and outlined *Prismatic*, and within a few days, I was telling Rain's story. I wasn't sure if I'd find a publisher, but I didn't care. I just had to write this story. In 2011, I finally found the right publisher. So first and foremost, thank you to the staff of Winter Goose Publishing for reading and loving *Prismatic*, and for making the *Harmony Run Series* come to life. Thanks to Jessica Kristie for stunning cover design, again and again, and for being so supportive of my writing process. To the Editor-in-Chief of WGP, James Logan Koukis, thank you for your amazing editing talents and for your consistent enthusiasm.

Thank you to Dan and Brooke Brand of Brand Photodesign for the wonderful author photographs. You make me look good.

I want to thank my husband, Charles Mereday, for nodding at all of the right times when I am venting (I know you're listening), for constantly reassuring me it's okay to dream big, for believing in me, and most importantly, for giving the world's best hugs. I am so glad the younger me moved to an island with the younger you.

Thanks to Jacquelyn, my mother, my rock, my therapist, and my friend, for putting up with me and helping me. I realize no one could possibly know how much you put up with, so I'll offer up my humble apologies and thanks in the back of this book, in hopes it will ease your suffering. Thanks for always being available to talk, for your guidance, your prayers, and your encouragement. Thanks for being the first set of eyes on my messy manuscripts and for helping me to polish them.

Thank you for letting me hide in your basement and for watching my children when I just need to relax and regroup. Seriously, I love you so much, I can't tell you. I know I'll always be your favorite middle child.

To my father, Dr. Mark Standring, thank you for teaching me about heroes, classic rock, for making me watch every action and war movie known to man, for making me conquer fear from age five in the Ohio River currents all the way to college when you motivated me to keep my travel plans to Italy in spite of anti-American protests. You've always inspired me to go on adventures and to go after my dreams. Thanks for always being there. I love you, Dad.

I don't know what I'd do without my friend, the world's best sister, Coleen Standring. Thank you for another year of amazing motivational speeches and cheers, for making the trip from Boston to see me when I can't leave town, for sending Lego to Audrey and Sabrina, for teaching Audrey how to ride a bicycle without training wheels, and thanks for always having my back. You constantly amaze me with your multitask-ing skills, your intelligence, your loving nature, and your ability to make it look so easy. If it weren't for you and Sam, I wouldn't know how to write about siblings looking after each other like Rain and Daktari do. I love you, big sis!

To the coolest guy on Earth, Samuel C. Standring, my "baby bro." Thanks for being the best little brother ever. Your loving, charismatic, fun, energetic personality has inspired so many moments in the *Harmony Run Series*. Thanks for listening to me whenever I need to talk, thanks for encouraging me, and thanks for being my friend. You are a super dad, business operator, and all around talented man (but you'll always be my baby brother). I love you, Sammy C!

I want to thank my Grandma Phyllis for being the most loving per-son, for having the warmest, gentlest voice, and for always speaking with kindness. You have the biggest heart ever, and I love you so much. Thanks for reading my books.

To Muriel, my fabulous mother-in-law, thank you for always reading what I write. Thanks for being so positive and encouraging and for sharing my work. I love you.

To my other in-laws . . . Yen, the best brother-in-law ever, thank you for reading my books when I know young-adult fiction isn't your typical genre. It means so much. To my amazing sister-in-law, Mollie, I just want to say thank you AGAIN for pointing me in the right direction to get my first women's fiction novel published.

I also have to give a shout out to my awesome Aunt Sharon. Thanks for reading the *Harmony Run Series* and for passing down Grandma's book of poetry. It was the best gift.

How could I end an acknowledgments page without saying thank you to my gorgeous friend Sonja Andersen? Nothing will ever change the love I have for you, my friend . . . not time, not our busy lives, and not even that huge ocean between us. Now tell that handsome man of yours to bring you to America. I miss you and love you.

I have to say a special thank you to my daughters, Audrey and Sabrina, for being my biggest fans. Whether you're pretending to be characters from the *Harmony Run Series* with special abilities or just telling me what's on your minds, you two always make me smile. I am so blessed to be your mother.

To all of the readers of the *Harmony Run Series*, thank you for your kind notes, for leaving me reviews, and for sharing this series. I appreciate you so much.

I'll always be thankful for the love and support of my Grandpa Doc, the kindest soul I've ever known, who passed earlier this year. I still cry regularly over his passing, but I know he's in Heaven. I'll continue to be grateful to him for teaching me to set big goals, for inspiring me to learn foreign languages and to travel, and for all of the laughter he brought to so many lives. I miss getting your e-mails and text messages, Abuelo. And I miss your smiling face.

Finally, to my daughters, Audrey and Sabrina, my nieces Kiley and Chloe, my nephews, Lane and Coale, and to all of my cousins, relatives, and friends making this world a beautiful place, I love you. May God bless you as you bless the world around you. Here's to harmony!

With love,
Sarah Elle Emm

About the Author

A native of Evansville, Indiana, and graduate of The University of Evansville, Sarah Elle Emm has traveled extensively, including living in Germany, England, Mexico, and the U.S. Virgin Islands. Her love for travel and experiencing different cultures has shaped her writing, and helped develop the *Harmony Run Series* with intricate levels of humanity and emotional connection. Sarah currently resides in Naples, Florida, with her chef husband and their two daughters.

CPSIA information can be obtained at www.ICGtesting.com
Printed in the USA
BVOW08s1854061015

421243BV00004B/146/P